top of off

Jason Roche

This book is a work of fiction. Names, characters, businesses, places, events and incidents are either products of the author's imagination or are used in a fictitious manner. Any resemblance to actual events or locales or persons, living or dead, is entirely coincidental.

ISBN:

DEDICATION

For my inspirational daughters,

Emily & Anna

One minute apart

Chapter » 1

Dropped

The laws of physics dictate that should an object, such as a ball, take an errant direction, then the causal forces that created the eventual effect are explicable, understood and even expected. There is normally an overt rationale - the red light blinking in the darkness - that makes every reaction intelligible; rewind the tape to see how it happened … ah, there it is, now I understand. She did that thing which meant the ball went that way and then he, ah yes, easy, thanks.

Sometimes not.

The distraction of something as simple as stepping into an annoyingly deep puddle, bemiring a neatly polished school approved shoe, would mean Enid missed that moment which had come to define her father. Walking to the shop on a functional excursion for stationary, a haircut or something else you could live without but choose to attribute worth in getting done, too old for arm in arm and glancing up barely long enough to show she was road aware but missing the magnetised puddle. The spray would collaterally damage her dad's shoe but his attention had been drawn elsewhere then quickly back to Enid, a benevolent, pained mouth moue, then back to the function of functioning. A couple, backs to them both, laughing, flailing their arms in octopoid directions, an unidentified item juggled in retreat.

"What happened?" bruited Enid's inability to miss anything in life, no matter how shallow, prying open the abidingly closed jar.

"That puddle happened. Your mum's going to—"

"I'll clean when we get home. Who were they?"

"Nobodies of any consequence; let's get home."

Then she knew. Not quite Cape Canaveral lift-off moment but one familiar enough to know what it meant. Those mocking tentacles, somewhere between patriotic chagrin and recognition of a deed so well publicised, it was almost inexorable. His expression dull though, not bothered by this … this … injustice. His shell, deflecting bullets all day long until one day it would creak, crack and bust into the same sand surrounding it, but for now, the brave face for his daughter, setting the parenting precedent for how to rise above, lift the chin but fail to soar. No more convincing than the cleanliness of the puddle's contents.

Nothing spoken on the drive home, the blur of grey-brown shops and terraced houses interspersed on the high street and surrounds, their blinkered train tracks towards home, a cleaned shoe and Dad shutting himself away in his study for the rest of day. No more games and giggles, the ubiquitous ball flying passed Mum-accompanied screams of 'No balls in the house!' and moderately prices breakables.

Drawing the three stumps in the sand now washed away, the only trace the dug out bowler's crease, defiantly repelling the tide, each around and over the wicket bent and straight leg delivery digging heel and toes to scrounge an accidental sand castle, holding firm. Since that day, that tournament, a memory early enough for Enid to know something had changed but without the unfortunate worldly-wise awareness to pick through the bones.

Chapter » 2

Direct Hit

That quiet of a school corridor before the intra-lesson hysteria. Motionless lockers, intersected by the trophy cabinet, the shrine flush of late, the school with a rich history despite what the board termed a 'transitionary period' of acclimatising to the introduction of female students.

The inevitable descent, the corridors filling like water, charcoal and gold uniforms egging up the volume to a practiced crescendo, the relief of a completed class tempered ever so slightly by the impending follow-on learning, fact, admonishing, adulation or tedium. Corin was always out of the classroom first, hop-skipping to escape whatever confinement was imposed even if her allocated desk was back right, weaving, hips undulating through the sedated masses to hit the door finish line first and maximise that moment of freedom. On this day though, she was second, a monster truck chap filling the doorway in what was likely an overdone lunch hunched dash to the little boys' room, his width nipping in to give away the clench. This might or might not have irritated Corin to the point that what happened next was completely avoidable had she been out of the classroom first.

Corkridge Castle School for Boys (and girls) long held an unwritten rule that sport captains had freedom of the city, or at least license to get away with most below the murder category. By excelling on various fields of dreams there was an innate respect that splattered forth and not the other way, a slow-mo strut down the corridor not often without applause, bashful glances and metaphoric back slaps (touching said sporting captain was a hazard not synonymous with that occupation and something to be avoided at all costs). Corin did not get that vaporous memo and, if she had, she would likely have crumpled it up, taken aim and fired it somewhere specific: a window, a bin, a toilet. Corin tended to pick things up rather swiftly, case in point the javelin, having never thrown one she managed to break the regional record with her first throw. Her sister and her had become famous for their throwing, legendary even, a gathering of parents, teachers and sports enthusiasts congregating whenever a throw was involved: javelin, ball-throw, discus, even shot-put.

Those girls could throw.

Which made what happened next predictable in its unpredictability but unprecedented at Corkridge School for Boys (and girls). Cricket Captain Chad de la Ampelas, allrounder and County Captain, materialised from a sheltered vestibule, entourage in full slipstream, at the precise palpitation Corin stole past the large lad gunning for the loo door. Onlookers would vouch that Chad floundered backwards but the voulu social media reality became Corin slammed into Chad and went sailing down hightailing butt alley corridor for her accidental troubles. Either way Chad wasn't impressed and the buzz of break sandwiched between history and physics became a stand and stare, galleries of parochial peanuts pointing phones planted in protective just in cases.

"You watch where you're going little girl. You might get hurt next time," rebuffed Chad, dusting off the imaginary sparkle dust she might have deposited on his person and trying not to act winded.

"Sorry," blurted Corin, more in shock than generally contrite, then coming to her true senses. "I might be but it's probably not my fault," glancing towards the now stationary boys' toilet door and trying not to imagine what was going down behind trap three.

"It's never your fault, is it? Just like it wasn't your dad's," taking his eyes off her likely permanently and continuing down the corridor, the gangsta rap re-establishing itself and the 'there's nothing more to see here' embedding now that Sir Chad had dealt the inveterate blow.

No one would dare respond to that. Would they? Corin watched as Chad melted into the melee of heads some distance off down the corridor, a few superfans giving her the 'don't mess with the bull' look or an accompanying 'she's the daughter' comment and cross-eyed pencil case fumble. Corin felt nothing for a moment then another moment then not a raging fire that builds in the belly and rises but a hot forehead and itch under her jaw and behind her ears. She glanced around, the trophy cabinet to her left, the glass slightly ajar ... it was logical and poetic to most but to Corin it was just opportunist. The bright shiny cricket ball, brand-new, the white seam crusty hard in prominence, white ants in two uniform rows marching in perpetuity. The Dukes logo, shimmering in the fluorescent corridor lights, calling to her, the taboo of never meddling in the cabinet so far away, a caterwauling from three streets away.

That cold hardness of the ball in her hand, familiar yet alien, almost painful on the bottom of her fingers, pressing unnaturally so that the seam began to pull the blood capillaries towards the surface of her skin. Then the fleeting glances of the bobbing aureate mass of Chad's head hair, appearing only momentarily then disappearing again behind the rabble, a dimly lit buoy distress flashing further out to sea than the horizon. And the corridor's ceiling: low with lights inconsiderately jutting down, school chandeliers that could absolutely not be harmed. But that head needed harming and if Corin had stopped for five more seconds to consider the chances of this happening, she would have recoiled and gone back to class, less than a metre afforded for the aperture of the trajected arc and the distance increasing with every sashay. That's the double-edged sword of instinct: it happens as planned to those either with low risk tolerance or a belief that they can pull off the impossible, the implausible, the downright brazenly stupid fantastic retaliation.

The whip of the arm happened at an irregular angle, somewhere between an overthrow and a side throw. The ball would power off a red-haired girl's curls, nicking her spongy head and accelerating as Chad's head disappeared then appeared four times in succession from release to proximity incursion. One of Chad's minions would shout "Chad! Look out!" just at that perfect moment when the inimical Adam's apple rubicund missile would skim the last obstructive light and begin the ever so slightest downward arch, patrons and followers alike parting in disloyal self-preservation, still fumbling for portrait video capture whilst trussing backpacks, books and laptops. Turning to tolerate the commotion, the cherry would tan Chad on the right leaning frontal lobe of his temple, shooting straight up to the ceiling as Chad instantly flinched, tucking his mirific chin onto his chest in appalled distress. The power of the throw combined with the angle of cranial connection would result in a triple ricochet of some force: ceiling ... floor ... then back up into

Chad's face as he cowered, the yelp of a dislocated piece of tooth palpable by those already seated in class. The seam would embroider a tyre track across Chad's head and the ball would come to rest against the girls' toilet door, made unsteady by the ensconced triangle of tooth, a three-wheeled car missing a tyre coming to a wonky stop. Chad's donated tooth was whiter than the polished seam, preserved from the countless maintenance shines, now a significant yet not insurmountable challenge for his award-winning private dentist. The head teacher would appear at this inopportune moment, as would Enid, eyes wide at her sister's redundant podium.

This girl could throw.

Chapter » 3

Dismissal

There's something oppressive - prison like - about the principal's office: no escape route jotted in big red arrows out of a secret passage or a window too small to fit through. On those days no sun peeks through the window either, just outside grey enveloping the window, holding back the adjournment, preventing the nostril exhale, the slow closed eyelids and unfastened fingers.

Even for parents.

Principal Daniels was affable enough, a permasmile surrounded by consistently large features, bones and body, the only blemish a dyed moustache redacted in the abnormally large space between the lower curves of his nostrils and a puffy upper lip.

No sign of an awkward silence, Daniels looking involved yet with enough feigned sorrow not to betray his tee off time in thirty minutes. Mr and Mrs Hanratty sitting alongside each other yet miles off aligned, Bronwyn jaw clenching lasers to Daniels to alter his stance and Duane, mesmerised by an inanimate glass engraved list of sporting achievements, the upright rectangle moving backwards and forwards against his pinkie, the trance shattered by a diagonally spat glower from his wife.

"This is really her first offence," continued Bronwyn. "Granted, not quite model student … yet, but no real serious black marks to speak of … until now."

"Well, that's not strictly correct, is it Mrs Hanratty?"

"That was just a serious misunderstanding: girls being girls and getting used to being around a lot of boys I suppose. Plus it was Enid who resolved all that."

"Yes indeed," lingered Daniels. "But we are not expelling Enid; we are expelling Corin."

The 'e' word shunted Duane into the slipstream of the conversation then a sufficient silence to the rescue, lollygagging him back to staring at the glass list …

Regional County Champions 2017-2021: Corkridge Castle School for Boys

Divisional Cricket Cup 2014-2021: Corkridge Castle School for Boys

National Rugby Finals 2019: Corkridge Castle School for Boys

Swimming Nationals 2020: Corkridge Castle School for Boys

Tennis Federation 2020: South East & Nationals School Champions

International Summers Cup for School Cricket XI 2021

South East Regionals Cricket Winners 2021: Corkridge Castle School for Boys

South East & Nationals School Champions, Digners Cup 2018: Corkridge Castle School for Boys

South East & Nationals School Champions, Digners Cup 2019: Corkridge Castle School for Boys

South East & Nationals School Champions, Digners Cup

2020: Corkridge Castle School for Boys
South East & Nationals School Champions, Digners Cup
2021: Corkridge Castle School for Boys

Digners Cup: a prominence not afforded to the other achievements. And there were more, the sprinkle on engraved glass littering all the way down to the final millimetre, intruding to spill onto the desk if enquired after, noted Duane, his own feats in the Digners Cup long since forgotten.

"We really just don't want to split the girls up either," Bronwyn implored, gripping her wrist then alternating hands.

"Mrs Hanratty, the boy in question required an HIA from our sporting medical team and might be out of the cricket team for a week. His parents have resisted supplying the dental bill in exchange for the expulsion. It is, I'm afraid, what we call a done deal, signed on the dotted line, board approved. I'm really sorry for you both and for Corin but there simply is no going back from here."

Chapter >> 4

Partnership

The catharsis staring at a ceiling. Profound answers. Solutions, suggestions, dripping down on faces, sticky treacle soup for the soul. Head aside head, facing opposite directions, both with inactive toes kicking a curtain or knocking over a jar of collected shells, Enid and Corin stared, beams up, the room solemn; the deed done, the fact checked, the horse dead in a ditch.

"I'm not going to let you face this alone," said Enid, lifting her knees to hug.

"Mum was livid," replied Corin. "I could tell because the repetition of being admonished got louder and with more life ruining ramifications."

"And Dad?"

"A church mouse would have asked him to turn the volume up. The longest car ride home since Green Book."

"Think I saw Mum crying."

Corin whipped her head to the side, headbutting Enid's ear.

"Sorry," shifted Enid, protecting her stinging ear. "We just always tell each other the truth, right? Not matter how hurtful."

"You're right, I'm sorry. I'm just shocked - normally it's a slight triage then back to backing us up but this felt different; final somehow. Like my final strike with her."

"With Dad, feels like the final strike was a while back. Do you know the story, the full story?"

"Follows us everywhere; impossible to avoid."

"But has he ever spoken to you about it; what actually happened?"

"I just figured he got tired; tired of us, being with us. He was such fun. Maybe we lost interest before him."

"There's more to this than the barrage spouted out on social media."

"Can't argue with a video. Full coverage. Thank the Lord!"

"What about Patty?"

"He's not playing. Think he pretended to join a club at uni but really after Dad checked out, so did he."

"I miss the games in the back garden: one-hand one-bounce, Bizmarck included as a fielder, catching out the tree, hit the fence post you're out, windows miss an innings—"

"Caught behind into the flowerpot, Dad batting left-handed, making everything fun."

"I'm leaving CC. Too."

"No. You're set there. This will just make the coals I'm yet to get dragged over even hotter. Plus, it won't be good for you. I'm off to Shaky High, where dreams go to die."

"At least we'll be at a school where they don't pretend to welcome girls. We'll get them to rename it Shackleton School for Girls ... and boys."

Corin couldn't resist giving Enid an affectionate punch on the meaty part of her shoulder, the obvious delight at having her sister at the same school tempered by the barefaced loss of opportunity and scuppering a good start. Enid had always led, been the sensible, measured one, able to either diffuse a situation or turn it to be beneficial for all those standing staring at their toes. Corkridge Castle had initially been difficult for all the intake girls, but Enid had adapted more quickly and better than most, unconsciously figuring out that boys don't really like to be shown up by anybody, especially girls in the minority. So she'd been content to blend into the background, winning teachers over and avoiding the alphas to the extent that no one really knew who she was or what she stood for; not that any would have wanted to show an interest outside their own kernel of self-importance anyway.

Enid slowly turned her head from Corin and back to the ceiling past a picture buried on Corin's corkboard of the two of them both going for a lofted tennis ball, their dad's releasing fingertips cupping the air in anticipation, the glee on the young girls' faces material, smiles stretching in staunch endeavour to pip a sibling to the punch. From the angle of Mum's photograph, it is a safe bet to have assumed Corin would pouch the ruffled, beach-darkened tennis ball, but alas, Enid's memory interjects, replacing the physical evidence with a somatic manifestation - her left non-catching hand tingling between the two of them on the bed - of the post snap mortem. An instinctual angle where the dominant hand and the sibling are betrayed by that spontaneous decision that her dad knew you couldn't coach, the twisting of the wrist and inviting cup served together as the only real outcome. Young enough for tears but old enough to catch.

Enid caught the ball.

CHAPTER » 5

DECLARATION

Allowance for coincidence is fate's way of ensuring that itches get scratched or, more poetically, demons eradicated or, more positively affirmative, destinies fulfilled. And sometimes fulfilling said destiny is more about the nicks, cuts, bruises and tears along the way than the destination of everything flicking from loud to mute upon arrival. But as is human existence, sometimes coincidences are engineered: a motorist passing a cyclist with enough proximity venom that there is a possible dual outcome, neither of which would likely displease the rancorous driver. So when Corin arranged to meet Enid on her last official day of school right near where the 1st XI were netting, one might argue that there was no coincidence but, in fact, it was genuine – Corin had no conception there was a net practice underway and that route of Corkridge walkout seemed the most picturesque, past the old oak tree and 1st team cricket field that sloped down towards a roving burn where both the girls often like to skim the right-shaped stones, Corin's record of twelve bounces on the water not easily toppled.

Chad, not easily mistakable or avoidable, was batting and

managed to loft an extra cover drive out of the net and inches away from Corin's head, shortly after congregating with Enid. What the girls had failed to notice moments before was Chad's signal to his left-arm finger spinner to toss one up, his chin strap jutting in the girls' direction to signify game on. Initially both girls jumped, startled, then Corin instinctually picked up the ball, strutting over to Chad and the rest of the boys' team, for Call of Cricket Duty round two: the corridor becomes the net! At about ten paces Enid stepped in front of her, stemming her strut and placing her hand out to instruct her younger sister to hand the ball over. Corin's indignation could only be surpassed by what Enid was about to undertake.

Remember ... those girls could throw.

Without so much as a hint of any retaliatory prosecution, Enid would swivel to espouse her sister's one-girl-until-now plight and fling the ball back in Chad's direction. And the ball would propel, just as Corin's had but from a significantly further distance, almost catching Chad unawares but once bitten afforded him the split second to secure his bat in both hands and swat the intrusive missile over the pavilion and into the farmer's neighbouring rapeseed field.

"Middled that," he shouted, approaching the girls, his cricket posse following all in whites, his trailing bridal veil. The approaching entourage gained in menace, the odd spiked kick of turf or swing of a bat to engender hostile agenda. The pointed arrowhead of Chad arrived, his pronated heels tucked-in walk, piercing through the sisters' cloak of solidarity, using his height, weight and width advantage to enter into the unwelcoming space that most people protect as their own, a few inches from the tips of their noses.

"Thought we might have learnt a little lesson ladies, flinging balls and all," Chad began, his Australian upbringing filtering through to betray his private school twang, the accent merging 'balls and all' into a lone word.

"Thought you might have learnt a little lesson Chadmeister to not put a part of you in the way that might be damaged indefinitely," retorted Corin.

"No damage done," said Chad bearing a blindingly unnatural white their way, the death light at the end of the tunnel with nothing on this shine.

"Picked up a bit of whitening toothpaste along the way?"

"Actually, my guy uses diamonds; these are actual diamonds to rebuild my tooth, so I should thank you really as I now have your full family tree's wealth in my mouth," with a few supportive sniggers from the middle order.

"If you lick your lips really solidly - like you would on a teacher in class - you'll taste what really comes out of your mouth."

"What are you little girls actually doing here? You're not allowed to be here. You're out remember. And as for you," gesturing dismissively at Enid. "Who are you again? Are you two related? Wait, chaps, lob a ball at each of them to test out ..."

The minions all seemingly sprung upon instruction at once, a multi-volley of cricket balls in various states of net usage hurled, the first few easily caught - Enid channelling the beach catch to protect her sister - then a horde of ricochets off the chests, shoulders and faces of both, Enid lasting a few seconds longer than Corin before shelling.

"Whoop, there it is - like father like daughter. Genetic predisposition."

Enid's bones creaked, and not from the balls being hurled her way. Something else stirred; something she thought she felt when the passers-by juggled in front of her dad but now something undeniable: the legacy was betraying not only a good man but someone she knew had done more for the game than most. The creaking bones turned into bile bubbling into a light quickfire sweat into raged calm, Enid stepping forward to counter Chad's now sweat-laden beaming down on her. Her eyes locked onto his, the equivalent of seizing someone's face with your hands and pointing your beings together, not tolerating any glance to a passing distraction, no matter how appealing.

"Are you guys actually the 1st XI; the best Corkridge has to offer?"

"Not only Corkridge, love; we're the best in the region, district, county and across all schools. In fact last year we played in a tournament where we beat the best Indian and Aussie school teams to win the Summers Cup. Put simply, there is not another team out there able to, or inclined to beat us. When you're this good, it's disingenuous to call us a 1st XI; we're more like the BEST XI."

"Wow that's impressive. You playing Digners this year?"

"Does a dog lick itself if it can?"

"I'm not sure that's the right metaphor but, hey, that's assumed to be an affirmative."

"Digners is still the pinnacle in England and Digners without Corkridge is like the Oscars without a special needs winning performance."

"Wow, again, not sure comparing your team to the highly inappropriate R word is the best association but we're getting to the point - slowly - that we're going to see you on the pitch."

Chimps all slapping each other in haphazard unison erupted, some laughter so forced the only remaining act would be to kick legs into the air while rolling on the floor.

"We're going to play … girls? This team? Mostly the same players who took Corkridge to four straight titles? This is beyond ridiculous."

"Shackleton has a team," Corin piped in. "Why shouldn't girls play?"

"We'll play you and we'll beat you," said Enid defiantly.

"Wait. Girls aren't even allowed to play Digners. Plus you're staying."

"I'm joining my sister."

A slight pause from Chad then an eyebrow twitch, a cartoon villain not surprising anyone then retracting into public-school-rap-battle etiquette.

"This is priceless - really - but this sort of bravado is going to end badly for you. Seeing as we're sparring though - me with a semi-automatic rifle and you with a toy rubber knife - it might as well be worthwhile. We don't really get much out of hammering a school that doesn't play cricket so you're going to need to sweeten the deal to make this little baby seal clubbing grudge match happen."

Corin's instinct was to blurt "Anything, name it!" but Enid, sensing this, placed a reassuring hand on her sister's wrist, her expression expectant without being complacent.

"I want the ball. I know he has it. From that fateful day we all hung our heads in shame because of your old man."

"Done," said Enid.

Chapter » 6

Cross Seam

The walk home, along the stream across the rickety bridge and through an unused field was more hurried than usual, more anxious, with Corin shadowing Enid, the latter allowing the obvious doubt to filter out of her face now that the train had departed the Chad station. As Corin quickened her pace to interrogate so Enid reciprocated, the roles somewhat reversed: Enid's impetuousness getting them both into trouble this time. And their dad.

With the hazardous lumps of untendered earth coming to an end at Corin's feet, she grabbed Enid by the arms, a tug-o-war halting traffic light stop, Enid's one leg hurtling towards home, willing to reach the sanctity of her room but Corin held tight.

"How could you involve Dad?" asked Corin. "After everything—"

"I didn't involve Dad," responded Enid, making the 'involve' more accentuated that it needed to be. "You were there. He involved Dad."

"But you agreed to this … this … I don't even know what to call it: slaughter, humiliation … and now all that for us and

Dad. We haven't even played cricket since Dad stopped ... caring."

"He didn't stop caring. It just likely all got too much. A constant reminder. And maybe he didn't want that for us ... longer term."

"Well, he has it now. Right in his face. Playing the best cricket team in existence with two girls and a school who think cricket is how you fix your neck! The easiest is just to get the ball and have done with it."

"Is that what Dad taught us: to throw in the towel at the first sign of adversity?"

"He did; threw it pretty hard after the drop."

"That's different. Nobody comes back from that level of public scrutiny. Not in this country. You're a hero for a decade then a zero for the rest of your life based on one act. No one ever mentioned his hundred or wickets earlier in the game. The public never forgive the soundbites, the headlines, the GIFs."

"God Enid this is so bad. I'm already in so much trouble for the ball throwing and now this raises the profile rather than letting me just slink into obscurity at Shaky High."

"Us ... let's do this: let's not tell Dad for now and get the old kit out, try it out at the nets. If we can still play and transfer that sparkling beach form, we'll know we have a shot. Everything Dad taught us: the most individual team sport. One person can change a game."

"Yeah but the others have to be able to hold a bat; or bowl without looking like they're lobbing a grenade to the moon. And field. And think. Dad always said the game was more cerebral than any of the others. And catch."

"And throw."

"At least they know we can do that. There will be caution on the cheeky singles if we actually get to play this madness."

"I'm not sure Chad nudging one to a fine southern belle in the covers will change any intent. Those robots are programmed to dominate, to attack, to be aggressive."

There was nothing left to do but hug, the two sisters sealing the pact through face to shoulder pressure. No tears though just resolve because crying is for girls.

Chapter » 7

The Toss

Starting a school mid term is never easy. Students notice you're new but without acknowledging, stolen glances in class and an unwillingness to engage, part teenage cool reserve, part uncertainty. Shackleton was marginally different in that it felt asleep, dispelling both Corin and Enid's preconceived trepidation that it would be the Wild West meets slasher horror film, more sedated Stepford than reprobate teenage sanctuary, keeping disobedient bodies warm until juvenile prison or actual prison. The life and times of a Comprehensive's failing teacher standards and facilities surrounded students without shame: packed classrooms, broken water fountains that would never be repaired, a canteen harbouring crimes against biological humanity.

Enid and Corin were able to stick together for the first month, placed into the top class and able to recall all the content from Corkridge lessons some years back, perhaps the tonic to mobilise the Shaky cricket unit prior to the season's official start. Yet the cricket promise, the commitment, the self-implosion remained largely unspoken of since the day Enid blew up her scholarship opportunity and even more colour drained from her mum's eyes then failed to step off the ledge, her stubborn resolve likely the only thing stronger than a wasted future. But she was a good student - no, a great one - and was worldly-wise enough to know that the shifting socioeconomics of the country would allow university entry from any downtrodden angle. For all Corkridge's blatant patronising of female students, Shackleton possessed a self-inflicted bias: the girls wore too much make-up and spent time gossiping and getting off with boys, more interested in TikTok fads, slayin' and inane celebrity events than anything real, anything relevant, anything important. And the boys wandered around breaking things, unable to function cerebrally away from the collective - in fact at all in some cases - primordial, battering forearms wherever they'd been gingerly repelled and only able to deal with the one lone reactive item requiring attention at that moment, planned foresight rarer than a functioning toilet. The disregard for authority was palpable yet unthreatening, the lack of endeavour lumping the lack of intent to a faraway galaxy, occupied in the crowded space with YouTube, cousins who dealt weed and smashing up abandoned houses.

Home time became welcome time though, for the girls anyway, escape from the unknowns and the underwhelming now-knowns, enjoyable respite coupled with no real homework focus and a mastering of each subject some years back, so an unlikely coast period. Idle hands are fate's playthings.

The large bag of logs in the garage had spilled and Bronwyn's glaring instruction was that someone should clean it up. Corin was the first to lob a swollen chunk of apple wood across the garage and into the 1m cubed white sack, Enid initially chipping in by holding the sides open then flinging in unison once the critical mass of the base had been established. There began an array of launches: underarm, through the legs, behind the back, bit of spin on, slower ball, back of the hand, left hand, no hands ... each one finding the mark, not a drop of kindling spillage in sight, the metaphoric opposite of the impending cricket match's spilt milk. There were two game changing moments: one where Corin first bowled the wooden block using the full arch of her boomeranged arm across her eye - a transitory pirate's patch to obscure double-eyes vision and two, nearing the end, both girls discovered an old cricket pad beneath the rubble. Channelling Goonies, Enid dusted off the old, protective flap, the 'Alan Lamb' drooped across by the lifeless Slazenger flap.

"Dad's old U14A pads," marvelled Corin, lost in a memory of sorts, the Velcro flimsy, worn and almost worthless.

"I remember putting these on and charging to the wicket in the back garden," said Enid.

"And Dad bringing this kit to Patty's practice sessions so we could play in the nets during his matches."

"You made me wear the even older ones - the leather buckles are probably buried somewhere in here too - always got your way."

"Think I just loved the sound of the Velcro. Back then they came up to my eyeballs."

"You'd bat, I'd bowl. Until either one of us stropped off crying or we had no more balls left."

"I only remember the latter."

"Most you belted into the trees. Poor Dad looked for hours. Felt like he really saw something in you. And we didn't even really know he was off playing for his country in those days - just seemed like he was away every now and again and on the telly."

"I remember him standing with you at the other end showing you stuff: always pushing his right hip forward and landing on his front toes, his fingers going splayed like a peacock's tail—"

"Leg spin. Clear as a bell. I bowled a ball and cocked my wrist - almost accidentally - and Dad's eyes lit up. He shot over and made me do it again. Landed near your toes and you missed it."

"'It's tuning away from the right-hander' he'd yell. I remember. 'Get your foot across, to the pitch so the turn doesn't get you caught in the slips'."

"Balancing the parental seesaw."

"But he spent extra time once you started that. He wanted me to cope with it but that was his real golden goose."

"He'd say it was the most difficult art form and that no one, in over a hundred years of cricket, had truly mastered it. Leg spinners were the *Poets of Cricket*, he'd say. So I was focussing on rhyming couplets while you were trying to kill everyone every time you had the ball in your hand."

"'It's okay to be wild, when you open the bowling. If the batsman feels uncomfortable and doesn't want to face another ball from you then that's a good thing, so it's okay to be unpredictable, a bit crazy even'."

"That about sums up your childhood," Enid coyly lobbing the final brick over her shoulder to cherry on top the pile, the debris below the logs a mess Mum wouldn't derive great mojo from.

"Let's go, let's do it. The kit is all there. We can match together discarded bits of old kit," said Enid, inspired, breathing fitfully but with ready tears forming. "You always loved dressing up in unmatching colours."

"I've an even better plan," responded Corin. "See all this mess you've made. Whoever goes out more … cleans up."

Enid's jump to Done response was curtailed by the leaning tower of logs coming tumbling down around them, irregular Lego and vast physical effort put flat on its back, dead wooden soldiers lifeless but for the small puffs of wood dust surrounding each, misty headstones of sorts.

"That little challenge just got a tad bigger."

Chapter >> 8

Off Season

Possibly the only thing sweeter than beating your sister at something she claims to be better than you at, is beating a common enemy bully boy who claims he's better than everyone. A runway ahead stretching further than the eyes could focus, but a start: the old-fashioned propeller starter jumping to reach the blade.

The first ball would get lost. Flung so far beyond the net, sailing over the top bar, an unsurprising Boeing taking off, Corin blinking incredulous then immediately nonchalant after a run-up that spanned three pitch lengths, more hufflepuffing than even Hermione could muster and a wide of the crease no-ball. This was harder than it looked on TV and going to be harder than when all the sinews, all the fibres, all the muscle memory worked in perfect unison, the hiatus now regretted and scorned in equal measure. Enid would hardly notice the ball sailing almost twenty metres above her head, padded up after an eternity of retraining the brain to put the straps on the outside, unable to resist the jibe "Perhaps the next one will land," dragging Corin out from behind the insouciant mask she'd been perfecting over the last few years and firmly back to incredulous, sprinkled now with an indignation Enid knew might be to her detriment.

Ball number two, Corin charging back in, an upright bull kicking knees up above ankles, more anxious anticipation than rhythmical repetition, lengthening the run-up approach by even more this time to acquire maximum speed, her ability to jump off her front leg and pivot to the side somewhat hindered. This one, swinging wildly into the side net with significantly more force than the first, clanging against the upright pole and ricocheting towards Enid at an unnatural angle, clean bowling her.

"That counts," spat Corin, getting off the ground and dusting imaginary humiliation particles from her person.

"Oh yeah, sure," responded Enid, muffled behind her ill-fitting helmet. "Like it counts if I wander up and whack the stationary ball for four."

"Go on then. Fill you boots."

Enid's strut towards the ball, now completely void of spinning on the spot, the slight dent from the pole sitting atop, a proud indented cherry on the cherry, had purpose, and with the same tense surety of Corin's run-up, she swung, a golfer severely out of nick, fresh airing and spinning back around to face the lonely wicket, no real fear in the wickets' or the ball's eyes. Neither blinking, inanimate in stubborn defiance, either ends of the cricketing objectives.

"Let's start again," would be Enid's sensible war cry, re-tightening the pads and adjusting the bat's flaking grip.

"Let's not," Corin's response. "I feel like I'm getting the hang of this again. Plus I'm up: one wicket for zero runs."

"Okay, if that's the way it's going to be then we go with the facts: two wides and two no-balls so four runs for no wickets."

Corin, returning to her mark at the Outer Hebrides, swinging her arms around in large circles, whipping it at the end, the ultimate gesture towards settled muscle warmth.

Then the charge, once again, frenetic but with the seam straight and pointing upwards this time, and enough fatigue to slow down the approach's pace to something resembling rhythm, the clickety-clack of trainers on Astroturf sounding more drum solo than orchestral warm-up. This time, in addition, hitting the crease with less of a forward leap and more vertical, whipping the arm through lower and with more of a back arch, sending the ball down towards Enid, hitting the turf just in front of her and going straight on to the vicinity of the middle stump. And Enid, suddenly unconsciously getter her elbow up and body fully behind the ball, defending the ball under her flank, a back defensive shot trickling back towards the bowler, the bat rejuvenated from slumber, middle located.

"Mhmf," Enid would tut, mouth turned down, head cocked to the side, now twirling the bat in her hands, readying for something a bit extra.

"Mhmf," Corin would tut back, retrieving the ball, inspecting it all over and wiggling her shoulder, less overt defiance and more belief than before. "If you put the ball in the right place," she'd recall her dad saying. "With your pace and natural swing and seam, it'll do the rest on its own."

The next ball would dance. More street dance than ballroom, jagging back in off a slightly short length and cutting Enid in half, crumpling around the imaginary path of the ball like a fallen spider, the back net copping the whoosh of the delivery's upward trajectory.

Praise where praise is due but with a less obvious excuse slipped in to linger between comedic effect and impending comeback. "Good ball but might have hit a little twig I forgot to dust away," Enid's back to Corin approaching in triumph, the comment hunching the shoulders by an amount a microbiologist would struggle to spot. When Corin turned to return to her mark, Enid would too, squinting down at the imaginary twig and sweeping it away with her shoe, finishing off the exit at the edge of the net with the bat, Corin blissfully unaware. Then in again and this ball Enid's to own: too full and too wide, fostering a sumptuous cover driver: the princess of cricket strokes. The sound of the middle of the bat would reverberate around the desolated nets. Echoing through corridors.

They could play; they remembered, muscle memory and a doting father enough to sporadically drag each back into the groove, the clouds forming to darken proceedings and start the debate of heading home for tea. But neither would, hours later, sprinting, swinging and wading through the heavy rain, kit wet, hair bedraggled and smiles reinstated.

Enid could bat again and Corin could bowl again but each would need not only to hone further back into the groove but adopt the other discipline to further strengthen their game. Plus Enid could bowl and Corin could bat, most certainly and most unequivocally respectively. Oh, and that small matter of finding nine other willing and most important of all able-bodied cricketers to buy into the obscure cause, play for their lives and somehow ... somehow ... miraculously ... win.

Chapter >> 9

Coaching Manual

The girls had managed to secure a pre-season meeting with the head of sports at Shaky and arrived early outside his office, a small building tucked away from the main school, alongside an abandoned warehouse and storage location with broken windows. As the girls were early, they decided to go down the lane and past the football fields to where the cricket field supposedly resided. They approached with some excitement yet with the sufficient temperate cynicism that had kept them alive and functioning and surviving in the teenage jungle this many years.

The first assault not only on the senses but on the physical space surrounding a person - the vaporous safety net - would be a charging aggravated cow, the blurry white and black of the hide a film reel spinning towards the girls. Corin, an instant bullfighter, would step to the side and shove Enid in the opposite direction, two waves parting around an angry rock. With a perception of the danger having abated, the girls rose above the high grass stalks in unison, two onlookers, eyes goggled at something as cataclysmic as an alien ship landing or the sun exploding.

What lay before them had no semblance of an actual cricket field but for a rickety old-fashioned scoreboard with some unsightly graffiti and misspelled profanity, and a pavilion with a balcony that had fallen to the ground, now at a forty-five-degree angle across the building, a relevant do not enter red stripe, scarring the face of the structure. There was no boundary to speak of other than where the shade of untendered grass changed shape and hue, darkening beyond the boundary with a richer activity of insect. The pitch itself, likely oppressed somewhere towards the middle section of the wild field, would be marked by the torn seat of an old roller floating above the inflorescences at one end, pointing the opposite direction. Both sightscreens lay flat, grass and weeds invading through the slats, knitting the rotting wood to the tacky ground. The girls picked out the tip of one lone mutinous stump, tippy-toeing in last gasp insubordination at the opposite end to the roller, the bail groove black and mouldy. Cows and the odd sheep would break the monotony, moving in languid arcs, solidarity luxuriating in the fallen field, an abundance of between meal subsistence and bulbous brown country flies to tail swat for short-lived respite, boomeranging back to a moist snout or creamy eye. As though the scene couldn't get any more disheartening, the final nail gesture of a cow's orientation confusion mounting another cow would rip the last shred of hope from the girls' collective soul.

This wasn't a project.
This was futile.

The walk back to the coach's office was solemn. When the girls arrived, the door was slightly ajar and from the depths of the murky interior the girls could make out the holey soles of two shoes, one placed neatly on top of the other, dissecting high-rises of stacked papers and folders. As one they knuckle knocked, the double team tap on wood startling the shoes, air-running in fright to slice through two of the piles, a split leg karate chop kick. A little man appeared from the desk's horizon, raising his eyebrows at the intruders while grabbing stray pages.

"Mr Yapa?" Enid enquired, nudging the door. "We have a meeting scheduled?"

"What to meet about?" said Mr Yapa, now underneath the desk.

"We're here to talk about sport," chimed Corin. "Cricket specifically."

A pause. A figuring out pause but perhaps something else. Corin's pronunciation of 'cricket', a soothing, resonating assurance then back to reality.

"But you're girls? Aren't you?"

Corin's expectorated look reached Enid, exchanging the angry baton for the calm version.

"Well, yes we are girls," replied Enid. "But we play cricket ... well, we want to play cricket for the school."

"There is no cricket at this school ... no longer. No funds."

"So there has never been a Shaky cricket team ... ever?" piped Corin, her frustration in check but aerated.

"We had cricket when I first start here but no one wanted to play, so the budget allocated elsewhere ... football, most likely."

"You're the head of sport here though, so shouldn't you know where it gets allocated?" Corin continued interrogating.

"Girls. We don't get anything for anything sport related. Any funds that come this way go to new academic temporary teaching posts or repairs. School building repairs. Not sport."

"So, what do you do all day?" asked Enid. "In here, with all these papers?"

"I rest. And I find ways to avoid the sporting grants being fully shut down. Without me, no back up teachers when illness strikes; without me, no flushing toilets; without me, no working lights. All these papers: some form of reallocation of school funding."

"Well, we want to join the cricket team!" Corin realised she had shouted.

"Not possible. Sorry girls but we cannot simply change things here. It doesn't work like that. Forms will need to be filled and panels will have to agree. Everything government constrained. But biggest issue ... girls cannot play cricket. Against the rules of the school and the league. Not my decision."

With his body language's final delivery of the word, he stepped forward, ushering the girls out of his office, bumping the desk with his thigh. The highest stack of remaining yellow and brown folders, perching on the front left corner stapling the desk to the floor, would wave and then collapse, splattering across the length of the desk like a Vegas dealer laying out a full deck of cards. As the final folder came to rest before the end of the desk, the unwitting pen and pencil holder was shunted to one side, clipping an old, faded trophy which in turn perfectly found the sweet spot of Mr Yapa's coffee cup, the words 'Coach This' spinning to blue-blur and off the table. Predominantly instinct and perhaps luck, but Corin would stick a hand out and catch the plummeting coffee cup by the handle, salvaging the stale contents, avoiding an unwanted clean-up and, judging by the relief behind Mr Yapa's eyes, preserve something that actually meant something to him. With the handle spinning like a flicked wingnut, the chances of grabbing the cup flush on the handle were low to say the least, the freak occurrence quickly dispelled by Corin's gentle return placement of the cup in the one remaining spot on the desk not covered by clutter.

Chapter » 10

Watchwoman

English was a rare subject where Enid and Corin were allowed to sit together, their general respect for authority not backed higher than the perceived disdain for an easy syllabus in other subjects. Miss Hazard allowed them complete free reign as she welcomed their contributions yet didn't want to always make them the focus of the lesson, what with plenty other students in more dire need of that helping hand towards the basics such as punctuation, full sentences and grammar. Every now and again though, she would let her veneer down, when swept up in the complex elucidation of the grace bestowed upon Shakespeare's Lear or Wordsworth's Daisy - her unstinting teaching skills more out of place at Shaky than the sisters responding with all the correct interpretations. Miss Hazard's manner was one third laissez-faire, one third bookish nerd and the final third this potential of unbridled excitement that, although welcomed by the sisters, put her at risk of the lethally inept blend of ridicule and disinterest. She glided like a dancer across the classroom but with sufficient clutzy disdain and misunderstood poise to fuel the inane mimicry.

The exchange would be sufficiently cryptic to pique the girls' interest yet maintain the required level of arm's length from an insider betraying the institution. Miss Hazard, an active doodler, couldn't resist the subtlest inclusion of a seamed cricket ball on the inside of the folded note, placed on the side of Enid's desk. The girls knew better than to look at one another, Enid casually yawning out a paw to place her wrist over the note and slide it back in towards her side, Corin's pursed mouth and twitching nostrils the only visible giveaway. Enid relocated the note to her lap and opened it, staring directly forward as Mizzard distracted the class with a cavalier admonishing of a student unable to disassociate the innuendo in semicolon.

'Meeting in the hall this evening - will include the chair of the board of governors, a woman named Abigail Arendse. Good time to table the inclusion of girls in the sports teams ... if that is your game.' Then the ball, no smiley face, no making the instruction flippant. Enid tilted the note Corin's way, who was able to speed read it while "a butt with a semi!" was extricated from the classroom.

"Not much time," Enid would proclaim. "To put something cohesive together."

"Keys in the hand and windmill in," responded Corin. "This is kind of our only chance; that or disguise on the cricket field!"

"Adjust your box loads and you'll fit right in! That's all they do, all game."

"This is our only chance. If we use this as the excuse for Chad and the box-adjusting bureau, it will just be perceived as bailing out."

"Plus, it'll put a bit of fear in him ... the lengths we're willing to go. To make this game happen."

The hall was sparsely populated when the girls crept up on the occasion, heading towards the low murmur. The obligatory audience gallery was laid out in front of the straight-desk panel, two torpid attendees – a resting janitor and another person in the wrong venue – dotted in opposite corners. Abigail Arendse, omnipotent, dominant and essentially bored, sat dissecting the school board representatives, her blood-red power suit a traffic light between the grey-brown dullness of the suits bordering her splayed elbows.

As the wrapping-up commotion ensued, papers unnecessarily gathered and brows metaphorically wiped in relief at the apprehended escape, Enid and Corin burst through the door, not quite gun toting but with enough intent to force Ms Arendse's attention away from the glass of wine only moments away, garnering reciprocated frowns.

"Ladies and gentlemen," Enid proclaimed reaching metal rimmed table. "If you would allow my sister and I to make one more proposal for your consideration. We will be quicker than any of your preceding topics, so if you would forgive the intrusion and allow us this one lone proposal to improve the gender balance and female representation in sport at Shackleton, that would be beyond appreciated."

Ms Arendse was the first to drop her briefcase, more in protest to the increasing tuts and headshakes from those around her than the endeavouring young ladies before her.

She was listening.

"We would like to challenge the ruling both at school and league level of boys-only sports teams," continued Corin. "We feel that teams should be represented by any gender as long as the representation is merit based. This will not be a quota system, just the opportunity for girls to play more sport at Shackleton and be part of the development and success of these extra-curricular activities."

"Starting with cricket," Enid persevered, pretty darn convinced the word dusted an ephemeral twinkle across Ms Arendse's eyeball. "The actual beautiful game."

Chapter » 11

Overpitched

"It's gone viral."

"What's gone viral?"

"Your little launch on Chad, pre-expulsion ..."

"Thanks."

"Sorry ... just situational context; no reminder intended. The angle is golden. Behind his head. Your throw heading directly towards the camera. Makes you want to duck out the way. Then another cut to in front of his face – someone else's phone."

"Must've been the Cinema Society if they used multiple sources. Don't remember a drone hovering though."

"Chad's expression change is priceless. Like as it hits he gets this swollen cabbage shock, his face contorting far beyond his manicured, practiced expression."

"Let's see it ..."

"Here it is ... up to over a million views ... and counting."

"Gawd. Any names?"

"Only the schools ... at this stage."

"We need to control this. 'Control the narrative' as they might say in a political interview."

"Or at least influence it. Get it working in our favour."

Both girls knew, looking at one another, an eye-ball high five, back of the hand, up-top and fist bump all in one glance. Neither would scrabble for the phone, content to breathe in the marketing campaign, absorb the potential this could bring to the non-existent Shaky High cricket team. After the tour of the field and Mr Yapa's reluctance there was a retracted conjecture that, despite the best efforts of both girls on the field against the strength of opposition undulating in fits of unplayable deliveries and cogent willow, the diamond in the rough nestling in the worn Shaky corridors would (at best) produce a boy or two able to hold a bat for more than seven seconds without falling over to stop a ball with both knees. There was no AB De Villiers flunking maths and history, biding his time to reveal himself as a fully proficient, competent and coordinated being, mastering the technicalities of a sport technically multifarious and impossible to master.

They had to go wider, deeper, outward looking, scouring the high plains of Sussex to trawl up one or two of nine who understood their cause and loved the game for what it truly represented ...

Justice.

External recruitment commencement.

Corin placed the phone back in Enid's hand who began composing the message. Her conviction was certain, never backspacing or requiring caps to shout the message, just a subliminal message for anyone in a similar boat; anyone riding through choppy waters while the neighbouring cruise liners batter through icebergs, making waves so killer, they can't be surfed, only serving to topple small boats. The message had to resonate, had to touch something deep rooted in perceived insecurities and lifelong struggles but it also had to appeal to vanity, to belief in wanting to win; a bunch of bullied losers, eyes swollen from crying and peering through industrial-strength glasses weren't going to pull off the match-winning cricket heist of the season.

'Ever wanted to play cricket like a girl? Ever wanted to show the ones that call themselves the best what it feels like to be on the receiving end? Want to understand what became of the ball throwing girl not only taking on da man but the establishment too? Come join Shaky High's brand-new co-ed cricket XI ... now recruiting ... all shapes, sizes, genders and dispositions. Only one attitude accepted though.'

Enid posted and breathed out and then in again suddenly as though the last hint of air was about to disappear. She handed Corin the phone who peered through her eyebrows at her sister, smiling a maniacal smile and then baring her teeth.

"He's going to see that ... Chad and his cronies."

"Counting on it."

Chapter 12

Digging In

No trumpets blowing, strutting down the Shaky school corridor, nodding from side to side in slow motion; no whoop-whoops, clapping, back slapping adulation, smiling faces cheering the girls forward, social media warriors taking on the man. No nothing. Just another tedious day, the excitement of the buzz generated by the clip spill now no more than a fleeting memory. The girls would gently inquire with most kids oblivious, blinking back in dumb confusion, the understanding of a cricket ball striking a bullyboy in the head about as comprehensible as calculus.

It seemed a shame to waste the opportunity to recruit talent, so the girls enquired with Mr Yapa about the prospect of recruiting people into the Shaky team from outside the school - all hypothetically of course as the current status quo remained. Stereotypically reluctant at first, Mr Yapa did mention that a few years ago the basketball team has drafted in a brother of one of the players, won a rare game then suffered a barrage of complaints from teachers, parents and school organisations which ultimately came to nothing: the result stood but lil'Jimmy Smit wasn't allowed to play the next match. The girls took encouragement though, almost as though the school had made the decision to appease the reaction rather than it being a hard and fast enforceable rule.

Meanwhile, despite the obstacles, the girls attempted to improve their skill levels through a series of drills they'd recalled from their dad. They wanted to improve sufficiently back to past levels of proficiency before approaching him for help; plus they knew they'd both have to face the elephant dominating the width, breadth and height of the room square on - both within themselves and with their father - before any further action. And this act scared them more than taking Chad and his chums on, uncertain how to approach and what big pappa's reaction might be. They'd called Patty at university who'd advised to leave it alone with Dad and that some things were better left untouched, unsaid and unaddressed; that although the family mantra had always been candidly smack each barrier head-on, this was bigger, more serious and affecting so caution should be exercised. It was something none of the children understood or really wanted to understand, the hurt suffered by their father so personal that laying it bare would create a potentially unsalvageable wound. And not in the humiliation sense either - that was too superficial for the Hanrattys - but at a level of having no control of the legacy, an unintentional mistake overshadowing a lifetime of conscious kindness and success.

They needed to solve some other issues too; that or it would appear done before it started. There was the girls' acceptance into mixed teams, the facilities, Yapa himself. There was also the small matter of the opposition, growing stronger by the day, the results against men's club sides appearing too easy for the precocious youths. Corin had given up tracking those results whereas Enid had developed a spreadsheet to begin tracking and correlating modes of dismissal, venue, conditions to deconstruct which parts of their opposition posed the biggest threats. She'd made copious notes and whenever she came to a conclusion, the next match would dispel the hypothesis. Was Chad susceptible to left-arm over pace? He was until a 'magnificently paced' hundred, pushed up the order to open the batting against two lefty openers. Was Chad's opening bowler, Charlie 'Chuck' Hastings' stock delivery – the short rising ball directed at the pharyngeal region – his only real wicket taking delivery? Not until he took four for twelve, pitching it right up and moving it both ways. Looking at the stats, he was undoubtedly their key strike bowler.

She'd also started building profiles on each of the players, a dossier of sorts, her hyper-organised approach to most problems in life serving well to categorise and break down elements of play, technique, psychology and weaknesses to exploit. Even physical attributes, wherever possible to glean, painted a picture; for example, the right-arm finger spinner, Danny Hallow-Jensen, slightly on the portly side and unable to field in the deep for his perceived lack of pace. Danny's reputation was that he came on early if the quicks had taken early wickets, which they invariably did, and wrapped up the tail through skiddy, straight bowling. Corin suggested that this was likely a double bluff, a first change spinner following on from the destructively quick openers thought to assert the calibre on show and rip the guts out of the exposed lower order, the ball expected to turn around corners. But it didn't. And with each of the slightly inepter batting tail playing for the turn, they'd play down the wrong line and get bowled by straight bowling, Enid confirming that over 70% of his wickets were bowled. Chad's team had not faced many conundrums, yet the girls were not naïve enough to believe they didn't have other strong strings to the team's bow: an arsenal of cricket pedigree more likely to explode through the vault door than pick the lock. Which is why this team – if it ever happened – had to be true, thinking locksmiths; the only hope was out thinking and strategising this team rather than toe-to-toeing a boatload of privately coached, to the cricket pavilion born, buff Williams, all conquering the hapless, eyeless Harolds.

There was also a potential psychological element to exploit, boys being numbskull boys and all that. Danny's sister, Rebecca, was dating Charlie and according to her best friend from junior school, who'd ended up at Shaky, the triangular dynamics were impacting the team dynamic. Danny and Rebecca had never been the best of sibling-buddies either, the constant tension allowing Rebecca free reign to wind Danny up with tales of Charlie's amazingness. The buzz back was that Chad captain smashed any burgeoning issues affecting the team, a quashing more potent than his pull shot, having already dealt with each boy, threatening team dropping and extra laps for Danny if they couldn't figure out how to work together for the good of the team.

"Plenty of good cricketers in the wings," had been the exhausted quote. "Corkridge Cricket is about more than two squabbling little bitches who should be more bros-before," demoting the pair from loading the clay pigeon trap until "Pull" was yelled from the Corkridge Shooting Club.

Chapter » 13

Taking Guard

Hope began to dwindle, that is, until one of Chad's teammates inadvertently sparked interest. The gone in sixty seconds media sensation that is a funny video gone viral on social media was exactly that ... gone and replaced by a cute cat or middle-aged survivor of a tragedy. Even Enid's call to arms fell on deaf ears, the attention span of connecting the girl-power stand against oppression and joining a cricket team too far removed for your average teenage keyboard warrior. Plus, those with noses buried in an iPhone were unlikely to be the hidden gem recruits the Hanratty girls were seeking to unearth in this increasingly unlikely quest to preserve what they believed to be their father's dignity.

When James Smith-Franklin, a middle order brute of a hitter by all accounts, began tagging Shaky and Corkridge in an effort to stand up for his man crush pal Chad, the responses and attention became more focussed, such that fabricated details on cricket trials began to be circulated with genuine enquiries. James's folly, as Chad would later point out, was not only playing the fee-paying school dominance card but the male queen of clubs too, posting old fashioned pictures of women cleaning, cooking or batting eyelids to a 'home from work' male, juxtaposed against snaps of his team winning, complete with human pyramids, more bro-hugs than a Zach Efron film and whoop-whoop triumphalism that went so far beyond the boundaries of celebration, it looked more obscenely like celebrating just because that's what a generation of young males were programmed to do now that the threat of world war had all but subsided.

The response comments from most girls were cynical and combative yet non-committal, but when James laid down the challenge that his Corkridge team could thrash any he / she / they losers out there, a defiance crept in that would shape not only apathy but make Enid's comments more than palatable, forsooth fully fathomed. People from all over began requesting to be part of a team that would #takeontheman and, the more the enquiries flooded in, the more James and increasingly some of the other teammates laughed off the suggestion than anyone, including a ragtag assembly of social media nerds, could stave off anything the #CorkridgeCricketLegends had in their locker.

The groundswell was pleasing to the girls but also bewilderingly daunting: this grudge match was becoming progressively more real which meant they'd actually have to assemble a team, and what if all the blustery gusto was just rhetoric and no one actually had the resolve to get inside a right-arm around the wicket neck-bouncer and hook it for six? Logistics aside it was getting nasty too, a wider community of #nogirlsincricket drawing on the nation's fear and loathing of equality. Enid and Corin would have to get involved but with social media accelerating from zero to a hundred in quick virulent succession, they decided to let this play a while to hopefully weed out the statement makers from the sleeve rollers.

Chad posted too, a rare excursion, but one enough to get

the girls' attention. It was a picture of their father, his face contorted and the dull red of a cricket ball spilling out of his cupped hands with the caption ...

The losers' ball I'll be allowing my dog to fetch after the match

#matchtrophy

#betsabet

#pathetic

The girls couldn't help noticing the losers as plural, shoving the plastic bag over their collective head, the Hanratty family now all painted with the same brush and further illustrating the benefit of an award-winning, highly remunerated English department to convey the most delicate of gut punches from across the villages.

Chapter » 14

Spell

Yapa was none too pleased. His slumber had been interrupted - invaded even - by a slew of emails from prospective students, sports enthusiasts and, most suitably, cricketers. The Shaky admissions board was also in a spin, what with the previous days' influx of applications, taking the count of five over last term to a number bigger than the secretary and bursar's email was able to handle, the antiquated mailbox size limit dangling precariously between two noughties Windows releases.

He was wholly unaware of the social media showdown, yet had only one double-trouble venue where this could reside, eschewing approaching the Hanratty girls for fear of admitting what he'd been up to in the background. The cows no longer existed on the cricket pitch, relocated to their designated spot on the hill sloping up at (well, it had to be, didn't it?) cow corner. He reappropriated some of the maintenance budget as a one-off payment to a local farmer with an industrial size hybrid between field plougher and mower, clearing all debris prior to the blitz and letting the cash-in-hand grizzled old farmer loose on the entire space, removing the vast majority of foliage that hid the wonders beneath. The result though, as anticipated, was far from the final solution, the outfield's grass a mangled concoction of weeds and earth rather than the billiard table of ryegrass and fescue that would be required to make this function. It was a start though and a start meant some form of optimism which, admitting to, might just sway too much sanguine attention his way, not only upsetting his languor but accelerating his schedule which he wished to keep fluid, and by fluid he meant able to pull out of and deny at any point.

The requests had to be actioned and logged though and there was no way Yapa wanted more paperwork. The day after the girls almost destroyed his office, he'd binned a few towers worth of residual pulp, his shredder shredding the cobwebs to shed nothingness communications dating back to those days he couldn't even remember what the school was like. In addition, he'd gone all Indiana Jones and armed himself with a Robert Dyas torch he'd been dying to use at home and a multi-zapping bug spray to venture into the depths of the abandoned sports store warehouse. The venture had tested his resolve and fear of anything with more than seven legs able to crawl into small intimate spaces, the ecosystem of crawlies more operative than anything on the pitch pre-mow. Right towards the back right corner, through nooks, crannies and overhanging webs the likes of which Yapa would never want to speak of again, he found the stash of cricket kit: a smorgasbord of Duncan Fearnley bats, balls broken in half, beautiful old wooden wickets, plastic cones, gloves that had been eaten into Fagin-style, pads with thick powder lines of dust in the grooves and not a thigh pad or helmet in sight. Ah, the good old days he marvelled, before a dead spider dropped down the back of his collar, agape from being hunched over, the crumpled arachnid slippy-sliding down the draining sweat, Yapa's knees up above eye level in instant protest.

What he was really looking for though, he found: a bulbous cricket bag with a worn, water-damaged picture of a lion holding a sword, surrounded by lotus petals and a blue and yellow circle. Untouched from where he left it, his wife unable to accommodate the space request in the loft or garage all those years back of cleansing clean-out. Dragging the bag from the warehouse was no picnic and equally treacherous, Yapa's blend of frustration at not being able to lift a bag he'd lugged around the world and not acclimatising to the new species that began appearing out of shattered paradise curiosity at ten-thirty, one-thirty and twelve o'clock in his periphery plus the odd tickle over the toes, a fleeing bug or eleven taking shelter as he dragged the case to light, salvation and freedom.

All this for nothing, he kept telling himself.

Waste of your 'close-to-retirement' energy he admonished.

These kids never follow through on anything he told himself.

Chapter » 15

Line Up

It was an ambush of sorts; ill-advised but attempted anyway, Patty the reluctant yet involved accomplice, complicit more out of curiosity than expectation of outcome. Patty had emailed Duane to request some old pictures of him playing school sport as a fake university project with an illogical personal element. Enid and Corin knew their father Duane, not the most tech savvy of paternal folk on the market, would enlist some help to trawl through the erratic photo repositories, interspersed between a confusing acronym-heavy array of folders, clouds, OneDrives, Dropboxes and old iMac hard drives. The request was for a chronological example of each year so there were no cutting corners to provide whichever samples first stumbled upon, the girls in the starting blocks ready with a premeditated arrangement of memories that would unashamedly drag Duane back to those happier times when cricket was a gift shared with the kids rather than a chill your bone reminder of over-reported events.

The pictures were all action, all smiles and all family, Bronwyn's reluctance to get directly involved more than adequately replaced by her amazing eye and finger-to-moment reaction speed with souped-up digital camera in hand to fossilise that iconic commemoration. From the spray of a wet beach tennis ball whipping past the outside edge, a Ferris wheel of splayed droplets, to ducking inside a garden lifter past the face, either from that extra slight-anger induced effort ball at not getting the batter out or nudging a lawn undulation, Bronwyn never failed to dig past the blurred trenches of daily tedium into the specific uniqueness of a particular trice, innings, ball or holiday.

When the girls had begun compiling, Enid had noticed not only a dearth of pictures post Ashes but, for the scant few that remained, a hollow melancholy in Duane's eyes, as though the effervescent green had sunken into a lost grey. The smile sometimes remained but the oomph behind it was gone, the energy and excitement at just playing the game an unwavering reminder of being careless about what you wish for, an Icarus of sorts, the hallowed sun nirvana burning past the delivered ball fingertips to render cricket the double-edged sword. No enjoyment without pain. No success without failure.

Cold outside, the patio awash with sprinkled intrusive drops of rain, Duane's face, momentarily propped up by the barrage of situational recollections, sunk even further when almost through.

"So, I just zip these up and send onto Pat?" he asked the girls, rising from the kitchen table to will the new swathe of rain clouds away.

"We'll take care of that Dad," replied Corin. "Easy enough." Enid went to talk then thought better of it, her father's square shoulders the physical barrier. Enid looked at Corin then took a breath ...

Before the plunge.

"Dad, we're playing cricket again," she began.

Duane's shoulders tightened, his inner trap muscles fluttering. His head dropped slightly, making his neck taut as the tree stopped shaking in the backyard.

"We want you to coach us … and help put together a team."

This was that moment there was no more running away from it, ripping the plaster off and hoping there was enough skin, bone and sinew left to function, to bowl, to bat, to live.

"Girls," Duane began turning around slowly, more in reluctance than deliberation. "I am so happy you're playing again, but … I can't get involved. There is just too much … stuff."

"We know what happened Dad," blinked Corin. "And we don't care, well … care about that … the drop or what the media says. We just want you to be a part of this …"

"And maybe tell us what actually happened …" chimed Enid.

"Feels like a while ago now, a lifetime ago. I've tried to move on from that, leave it behind."

"You left your Test, ODI and T20 batting averages all above 50 and bowling mid-20s … that's a record to be proud of … one small moment easily forgotten against that pedigree."

"It's not though. My legacy is defined by that one fumble … what transpired before meant nothing to the vast populace … and I'm okay with that really. I've dealt with how that could taint everything that preceded it, fair or foul, but I don't want to reappear and embrace the sport that created such strife. This is the first time we've spoken about this."

The Ashes were tied at two a piece, England having heroically dragged back a 2-0 deficit to level the series in Australia 2-2, entirely down to Duane Hanratty's courage with ball and bat, scoring three hundreds and taking thirteen wickets in the 3rd and 4th Tests. Apart from the obvious statistics of scoring runs and taking wickets, it was the manner of the willow swinging in a negatively charged environment and the tactics employed with ball in hand. The Aussies, acutely aware that a drawn 3rd Test would mean the Poms were unable to win the Ashes, had bowled wide of leg and put the field deep to strangle runs. Duane's approach, in after another early collapse, had simply been to clear the boundary, exchanging sixes for singles, twos, threes to the outfield or fours, picking shots from deep within the wagon wheel repertoire and initially receiving a barrage of abuse from the traditional safety-first commentary team. But as the runs piled on and the deficit reduced, he'd successfully carried the tail and fallen with the number 11 bat, before consciously bowling a too-full length on a hunch that the Aussies were weak against the yorker and susceptible to late swing. Carted around the park initially, the ploy then worked with England batting well the following innings and dragging one back prior to the 4th Test, which in itself was a spin on the heels' abandonment of the 3rd Test tactics in the most modern illustration of adapting to circumstances until the South Africans learnt how to drive a sandpapered ball.

What happened next would go down in cricket folklore. And not exclusively because of the single culminating moment but the situation that led to it: the game had been a see-saw affair with both sides momentarily up then on the back foot again before the drop of sweat hit the turf. A low scoring game with wickets at regular intervals, Duane had, once again displayed heroics, nursing a hamstring injury when an Aussie fielder recklessly careered into him while batting, being refused a runner and batting with the majority of the tail. He'd bowled through the pain and done a decent enough job to pry out the only two batsmen able to take the game away from England. Known as one of the best fielders in the side, Duane normally fielded cover point which connoted the usual jack-in-the-box stops and required a Deadeye Dick arm for run outs. His hands were safer than a pedestrian crossing during that match, the entire cricketing world either baying from the SCG stands or glued to the TV, neutrals even breathless at the tension, ratcheted up four or six notches every ball.

Late afternoon on the 5th day with the series tied at 2-2, The Australian 4th innings total was at 110-9, chasing a measly 111, but with a competent number 11 bat and the number 4 still at the crease, it looked like Oz would sneak it once again at the death. The lights had been switched on despite no significant deterioration in light and protests from the England captain, many of the bulbs lit at different illumination strengths. In the lead-up England's keeper had dropped three catches, a sprained thumb and early career nerves the primary culprits. This likely featured in Duane's decision to take matters into his own hands, unconsciously at least the moment it mattered most. So with a single to win and the number 4 on strike, an effort ball from a tiring England attack got big on the batsman during a pull and the ball went sailing into the heavens, seemingly lost forever in the gossamer clouds between the batsman and Duane at cover point. The keeper, keen to make amends, called for it, rushing over towards Duane, arms and gloves coming at him like an uncoordinated mugger. Duane had shown him the palm, vociferously over-calling and claiming it as his to take, setting himself as the ball, spinning and angry reached the apex at some grotesque height, the late afternoon's gusts pushing and stopping the inimical red dot on the way up, ricocheting back towards the earth, shunted from side to side on the way down. His eyes were locked, the dot getting bigger on the descent, speeding up and zigzagging in the flurries but this was something Duane had dealt with his whole career: part of the job. The keeper had not heeded the instruction, diving across Duane who had to adjust at the final second to get his hands above the lone glove being shoved in his face. It looked like it was going to stick, the Barmy Army already celebrating once they saw Duane under the final catch.

The scene that ensued would be replayed on just about every sporting documentary since, England failing to wrestle the Ashes from Australian soil, Duane and the keeper bereft in a distorted puddle on the floor, the hysteria of the taken single from the Aussie players seeing batsmen raised aloft on shoulders and teammates hugging on the pitch.

The ball lay motionless next to Duane, his eyes blinking to refocus, the word out, ragged red leather marble glinting in the stadium lights, the new definition of Duane Hanratty as a player, person and human being.

The same ball Chad wanted as a trophy.

Duane never played cricket again, the story and the drama too tantalising for the press, everything before forgotten and the iconic meme repeated ad nauseum until welded into the nation's psyche.

"I don't believe in excuses - you take your medicine for your actions on and off the field, but this felt different somehow or maybe just talking about it now to you both makes it feel different after the fact. I've taken a million catches and dropped a fair few too, but I always felt the same for either scenario. As though when I dropped a catch, I was subconsciously aware that I'd incorrectly judged or positioned something: my feet, my hand position, the angle of a dive, the steadiness of the grass underfoot. Every catch I've ever taken has just felt right and, honestly girls, this just felt right. Everything was in place. It was going to drop into my hands."

The girls looked at each other, tear line warpaint back of the hand smudged in regular swipes.

"But it didn't and that was what made me question all certainty I'd had about everything up until that point. I'd been wrong."

Chapter » 16

Coin Toss

There would be a vote and it would be tight but the trickle of information that arrived via Miss Hazard was that girls in the sports team were a go. The council had agreed to trial the idea of mixed teams only in the South East with certain sports such as rugby off limits. The buzz was that Ms Arendse, so impressed by Shaky's intent to gender neutralise sport, had single-handedly not only championed the inclusion of girls but ensured the Digners Cup would become the flagship for this change. This meant additional funding for the Cup, an overhaul of the knockout structure and improvement of the publicity surrounding the tournament with the inclusion of streamed televised matches and allocation for digital technology across certain venues. With the incredible standard served up as part of Digners each year, the belief amongst the traditionally highest achieving teams was that there was little or no chance of girls of this age (or any age) being able to cope or compete at this level of cricket. And, of course, who turns away additional cash to grow the sport of cricket and put these elite cricket athletes, specimens and talents in the world's shop window to be snapped up by future county, IPL, Big Bash, PSL, CPL and MSL deals? Nobody and specifically not Daniels, who saw this merely as woke posturing to ensure girls got to bat eleven and not bowl in some substandard school XIs, likely destined to get as close to the knockouts as a person with a nut allergen wandering around the Corkridge locker rooms after nets.

This had also fuelled the Corkridge 1st XI's belief that the bet was now firmly on with the structure updated into four regional pools of six teams each, the draw to happen two weeks prior to the season commencing. There would be a points system with the winner of each pool playing in a knockout semi-final then final, rumours abounding that the final would be played and televised from the home of cricket, Marylebone CC's finest ... Lord's. A rule was introduced which stated that the winner of each pool could select any of the other teams in another pool which had failed to qualify as a warm-up match prior to the semis, Chad's opportunity to crush the bet with his prize of the most iconic ball in the history of cricket so real he could taste the residual sun cream and sweat left on the ball. A minor digression en route to a fifth title on the bounce for the Corky Boys best ever XI!

There was supplementary complexity for schools like Shaky too: those without a track record in Digners. They had to qualify for the pools or the tournament risked serious injury and embarrassment with a mismatch of abilities, red blurs of flung balls and swung willow more dangerous than anyone who'd never played the game could imagine. Of the six teams in each pool, five qualified automatically through recent involvement, historic records and general cricketing pedigree while the new additions would have to scrap it out for the final spot. At this stage there were many high achieving sports schools across the South East with Kent, Sussex, Middlesex, Hampshire and Essex having an embarrassment of riches littered across the abundance of cricket facilities as part of the area's number one pastime, but there was uncertainty about how many schools would apply to be part of the feeder tournament and also some ambiguity about the criteria for qualification including, but not limited to, the coach's credentials, facilities, rule awareness, ability to field a team on a regular basis and ongoing commitment to the schedule.

The corner of Miss Hazard's mouth turned down and her eyes windscreen wiped a clear film of molten lachrymose as she told the Hanratty girls that they could play. She didn't need to reach out a reassuring palm on the shoulder to say congratulations … her adulation sat proud on her face, the burning glare back enough to tell her that when she became the team's maiden fan armed with cucumber sandwich and foldable chair, there would not only be some fight in these warriors, but something a bit extra.

Something a bit spectacular.

Now it meant something.

Chapter >> 17

Opening Stand

"Too old fashioned," said Corin.

"Agreed," responded Enid. "That's the play."

"We don't have to build the entire approach around this, do we?"

"We do … and we don't. The other elements will be just as key, just as important but this will be the Brigadier Block slow poison at the top of the innings. It will be the first pawn move that absolutely has to work, even if only to give us some breathing room, so a cornerstone absolutely."

"Mad Chad would have never seen anything as blatant as this: if it works, the frustration etched on his plucked brow will be worth the admission of getting walloped on the field of dreams alone."

"We're the wallopers remember. And besides, we need to use Chad's walloping against him."

"Rain, wind and godly power all belting against a wall only for the wall to stand firm, resolute … standing up to tyranny Ukraine style!"

"Precisely! It's going to take a special type of individual though, as this will be a significant mental test. If it works and Chuck's frustration peaks, they'll likely turn to bullying tactics so this mystery chap or chick will have to not only have the defensive technique of a wall but the mental fortitude of the Great Wall … the one in China for instance or that property down the bottom of the road."

This section of the spreadsheet remained hazardously sparce, the cursor blinking back at the girls' lit faces, the laptop flipped open at an unnatural angle, both lying on their tummies with their feet in the air. The tab was named 'Batspeople' the girls unable to live with the modernised Aussie 'crack' of 'Batters' and felt factually incoherent listing it only for men when the certainty was the team would be comprised of both genders. A lone column numbered 1 through 12 was accompanied only by the cells aside 1 labelled 'Opener: Not Out'.

"One of us will probably have to open with our wall," said Corin.

"Perhaps, but more likely we'll be adapting ourselves to the rest of the ragtags as opposed to each of them slotting in around us. Who knows? Who knows what we're going to get … if bloody anything!"

"This chap - let's call him or her Stone - he or she will need to have the reaction times of a polecat. I heard they clocked Chuck at the ninety-mph mark at an indoor practice session."

"Jeez. Did they check for no-balls? Indoor though, always quicker."

"Bat left the net after that in tears."

"New level propaganda this, but we'll need to start some of our own. As Dad used to say, some teams have already lost the game when they step onto the pitch, based solely on the perceived reputation."

"I remember that too - said when he opened U14A, some crazy reputation quickie smacked his fellow opener in the face, opening up his chin, pre-helmet days, and the rest of the team wilted, blissfully unaware that they were only a few balls away from double-bouncers as this guy had no engine."

Enid typed in 'reaction time' and captured 'mental fortitude' too.

"Where do we find our cornerstone? Good defensive techniques, increasingly rare, don't appear in cricket teams anymore. If you're under a one hundred strike rate you're dropped down to the 4ths."

"Swashbuckling, express yourself, swing at anything cricket all the rage."

"This is what we'll be up against: in your face, blast-you-out-the-park cricket. Not seen many headlines like 'Corkridge dig in to win match' or 'Corkridge grind out win'."

"Yeah, words like 'obliterate' ... 'decimate' ... 'annihilate'."

"Lots of 'ate'ing ... more like hating."

"Maybe mating ... I've seen how square leg glances at Chad's overly tight cricket whites."

"Speaking of overly tight ... pity we couldn't get a kid who is a huge fan of Strictly or something."

"I'm even more lost than usual: where are we and what's a crappy, overdone, overtired, lost-its-gloss-a-long-time-ago-if-it-really-ever-had-any-in-the-first-place TV show got to do with cricket?"

"Footwork."

"How much work?"

"That's it!"

Enid jumped off the bed and spun around in crazed unbottled ferment. She grabbed Corin by the shoulders without shaking, only squeezing with the full length of her fingers so there was no reeling back, sharp-pain ouch, just an anticipatory disquiet as Corin let her sister run this course to some form of detonated conclusion.

"Openers need a cast iron defensive set up and technique; we both know this. And what makes for this? Footwork. And who has the best footwork?"

"Dancers," said Corin giving slightly in to the realisation that

Enid was onto something, but with enough circumspection to not fully pander to the revelatory premise. Her eyes asked for more.

“If the footwork is there, then the batting technique will follow. Easier than the other way around: getting a slugger from a baseball team to learn to step and transfer weight into the trajectory of the oncoming ball is a higher mountain to climb. It’s back and forward, nothing more. There will be no scoring shots remember, just a good old fashioned defensive masterclass, protecting the stumps at all costs with little or no regard for safety or well-being.”

“That might scupper your plan, no? Aren’t dancers - especially male ones - meant to be ... well ... on the slightly more ... erm, ‘delicate’ side?”

“Oh Corin, ye of little faith and stereotyping sister! We’re better than this! Aren’t we?”

“Well yes, we should never judge a book and give everyone an equal chance and all that; it’s just that I haven’t met any ... male dancers ... in my time. Just seen the overtly camp stereotypes they churn out on US sitcoms I suppose.”

“He has to be able to move, that’s all, the feet first. If we can get the feet moving before the brain, we have the bedrock.”

Then Corin’s eyes gave the ghost away, widening in belief. She grabbed Enid back, missing the shoulder mark and hitting her elbows, Enid’s bottom lip pressing up in suspicious discontent not enough to counter the counter.

“There’s a dance school in the village ...”

Enid’s bottom lip wavered as Corin drew out the divulgence, the magician’s code unable to hold a torch, candle or even lit match to her.

“... run by our very own Miss Hazard.”

Chapter » 18

Weight Transfer

The sisters, not quite sure why, went in disguise. Corin was talked off the dying hair ledge and opted for a henna rinse which would – according to the earthy Etsy packaging – wash off within days. Much to her consternation and Enid's amusement, Corin's thick melty blond curlicues went that awkward shade between ginger and auburn depending on the light at the time. So, a hat accessorised the disguise ensemble with only a tartan Tam O' Shanter hat available, making her look like a Scottish-heritage rugby supporter from England at Murrayfield.

Enid would follow suit but not at the same level of caricature, more concerned with deceiving Miss Hazard than challenging Clouseau, although not to hoodwink their teacher but rather as passive observers of the dancers. Enid wore a grey-green puffer jacket and unremarkable shades with her hair left uncharacteristically down. Her hair had always hung in a dead straight line, the end of a paintbrush, even the same dark golden colour, much to the attention of anyone who got to see the mass in all its glory, the resulting shy away from attention to tie it back in the tightest of ponies and get on with whatever more-important-than-hair job was normally on display at home, school or on the sports field.

The dance studio's setting and vicarious attention was just about perfect for the recruitment escapade. Milling parents, more concerned with deriving a bang-for-buck in striving towards the Sadler's Wells dream than engaging with fellow parental competition, jostled effectively to establish a plaster barrier at the viewing edge, while Miss Hazard took the pupils through the warm-up routine. Enid and Corin were able to position slightly back to the left corner where some raised steps gave them a birds' eye view of proceedings. The school was popularly girls of about the same age as the sisters with a smattering of younger girls, focussed to the point of mesmerisation, despite Miss Hazard's efforts to make it an expression of enjoyment rather than oppressive instruction. That was what the parents were there for - both during lessons and mainly in the car ride home. During lulls in activity, parents would approach Miss Hazard with new instructions, her ever-accommodating demeanour dissipating as the tide of overtures broke onto her furrowed shore, more intent to let the dancers express and twirl and smile and work together.

"Are we wrong to assume this has to be a boy? There aren't many," whispered Corin, her hat feeling wonkier than it appeared.

"It's a stats thing, not a girl-boy thing," Enid responded, from in between her two curtain clumps of hair, framing her bespectacled face like two books in an open bookshelf.

"I can only see a few males ... and they don't look as steady on their feet as some of these girls. My gawd, did you see the ice princess with the purple leotard … thought she might actually be floating."

"There's a certain level of base capability that has to be there from a cricket perspective. Not saying these girls couldn't pick it up in due course but we don't have due course and unless there is that foundation of understanding of the game – Mum or Dad at minimum chucking balls to their kids – then the mountain is too high to climb. And unfortunately this sport is statistically a boys' sport – there will be a higher proportion of boys who started playing the game at a young age."

"Risk of no one having held a cricket bat at any stage, irrespective of blue or pink nursey."

"Indeed. But that's irresponsible parenting as far as we're concerned. It's a parent's duty to ensure their kids can at least catch a ball."

"Dad just took it to another level I suppose."

"Think he just loved us loving the game."

"The games. All the variety made it some much fun … the intrigue, the competition, the unknown end result …"

"Hurling balls at each other – Patty as the biggest target!"

"Celebrating those fake hundreds too, such—"

An almighty hush interrupted the girls nostalgic whispering, the sea of dancers parting to avoid the majesty about to unfold, a proud mother, arms folded in chronic smugness, anticipating her boy's entrance, stage right. A series of outlandish flick-flacks followed, an Adonis of a male specimen emerging, whipping head-and-arms, criss-crossing glistening legs to use the full length of the floor and come to an immediate halt inches from the skirting mirror, a slight glance at himself to admire a posture that no one there was really able not to admire.

"Did he just wink at himself in the mirror?" Enid not quite sure what had just happened.

“Swoon. We’ve found our opener,” Corin ready to depart, red hair banishment wash number five on the cards.

“Not sure. His body moves like a tornado but let’s watch his feet.”

Captain Dance Fantastic would then proceed into a volley of flurried steps, whipping his hips around in perfect unison with his fringe, the two synced ice skaters guaranteeing the gold. The dance exposition required no additional participants, the feet as quick as the jaw taut. His eyes even twinkled, tropical sea green and Corin found herself unconsciously scooping clumps of hair under the tartan barrier: orange (that day … it had to be didn’t it!?) under red, a fox’s tail disappearing behind a gaudy painted sunset. Enid couldn’t help believing she’d spotting the slightest toe on toe fumble, as though he could’ve gone even faster in his revolutions, a spinning top hindered by an imbalanced chip in the wood. She wondered though, whether his flawless demeanour and arrant approach to fuelling the alpha fire, a literal wee-wee line of petrol onto the intrusive flames, was a bit too Chadesque; a bit too entitled and a bit too little greater good. She forced herself to shelve her prejudice and watch his moves intently, seeking something that could tell her whether he could actually open the batting, keep out the barrage from Chuck Hastings but all she could come back to was maybe he was a bit more flash, middle order. They were after the grunt, the unglamourous, the unheralded, block brigade at the top of the order. At minimum, just to piss both Chuck and Chad royally off!

Without emitting a drop of sweat or even a glow of exertion, Patrick Swayze 2022 but taller and better looking, pirouetted past a small boy staring at the floor, his glasses teetering on the edge of a pudge nose that looked like a deformed plum. As the chosen feet danced through, Enid noticed a shining light just in front of the boy grab his attention, cat like in the sudden dominance of his convergence, the glasses slipping effortlessly away from the plum and onto his face, locked into place and ready for action. Enid nudged Corin and with the nudge the light moved, the two looking at one another in realisation that Corin's phone was reflecting the alluring mottled shimmer.

Enid nudged Corin again. And again. So the light danced, further away from the boy, out of reach almost, a few metres away now, his legs unfolding from beneath him to reveal tap dancing shoes, aberrantly dull and worn, the white flanks a dark grey. Then a parent - perhaps the boy's - walking into the path of the screen's reflection, the line's ideology extinguished and the boy's attention returning to the floor. So a butt nudge, hard this time, on the polished wooden seat, Enid WWE force level slamming Corin across the bench to re-establish the beam, an East German guard spotting an errant dash for freedom. Corin, momentarily irritated at being shifted involuntarily with so little warning, now had the light and the responsibility.

Then something. From everyone's angle an inhuman launch from seated, twirling in the air, feet poised in sublime symmetry, to land with a gasp-inducing thud in front of the light and heel-toe-heel-toe tap announce some real shit was about to go down.

His tapping began, the rhythm of his feet, shifting between legs to a plethora of heel toe clackety-clacks, in beautiful arrangement and with enough delicate dexterity to get nowhere near offending the ears, the dilapidated shoes betraying their station by creating an almost orchestral sound. And all of this peripheral; seamless against the main quest of stomping out the light, his tap dancing a waltzed tangoed salsad rhumba of smorgasbord magic to hunt down and toy with the inferior teasing light. Corin would have her work cut out too, moving in a direction that posed enough of a challenge to keep the boy interested and able to show his wares, on display now as many parents began to clap and even the man of the moment moments ago stood in semi admiration of what was being murdered on the dance floor. At the end of the routine, having scoured all reaches of the dance studio, even tippytoeing up a flight of stairs to change the undulating topography, the boy would end with a flourish, the final stomp killing the glow, Corin's hand barrier the just reward.

He looked up and nodded in thanks, his glasses drenched in sweat but firmly where he left them at the start of the chasing the sun sequence, an acknowledgement that with the right creative incentive, anything - even shattering the monotony of another dance lesson - could be possible. Miss Hazard stood crying, the beauty of the display and randomness of its inception all just too close to what she hoped to accomplish every week.

His name was Jacob and his small, kind looking mother would beam a smile across the floor to replace the light he was rummaging for, further illuminated by his reciprocal smile back at her, each wonky tooth an endearing RE: pictogram. The exertion required mopping up, the dancers that followed becoming amateur ice-skaters on a rink of polished maple wood, arms windmilling back from the sweat sheened surface. Jacob's mother, effortless from the back of the group, shorter than the rest of the towering, hovering helicopter parents, would launch a crumpled dry towel into the air, arcing towards an unexpectant Jacob.

And, ah yes, the best thing of all ... he caught the towel. As though he'd done countless times, soft hands to cushion the receipt, unnecessary on coarse cotton but oh so God damn necessary when stopping a red leather Dukes Crown Prince cricket ball from touching the ground.

Chapter » 19

Chinaman

Knocks at the door invariably occur when you least want them to, the range from wispy tickle of the wood's entrance barrier à la old-neighbourly village leaflet drop-off to side of the fist my next delivery depends on your speedy approach to retrieve package DPD driver. His code that only they knew, but really didn't want to know, but couldn't escape once you knew of it. The neighbourhood's favourite pest and no-friends fan boy to the Hanratty girls, embracing every opportunity to interact and show his mighty worth, the ubiquitous knock pause slap pause knockety-knock-knock, long pause tapping fingers making Enid wish she wasn't the family's lame duck collector.

"It's your boyfriend," rings out from Corin's room. "Again," clearly taking advantage of Enid's marginally softer spot for Wei Ping Tan and by marginally we're talking she'd lose patience a millisecond later than Corin on occasion, up to the eyeballs with the hard-trying shenanigans. Plus, Enid knew Corin had endured other homework interruption escapades while she'd been at piano, a volley of "He's probably more in love with you really," falling pithily off

Corin's feathered back, the duration of her nonplussed yet revulsed look enough to push Enid from her studies and approach the front door. Undeterred and determined to the last, the secret knock Wei Ping Tan had developed to let the girls know he was visiting was in essence a double-edged sword in that he felt this was a key screw in their bonded Lakeview Avenue woodwork yet, like pointing the umbrella towards the sideways rain, it was possible to prep, counter and shun the trifling pestering.

This visit, though, would be different, his appearance - fully garbed in immaculate, brand-new, ill-fitting cricket whites, the red NB logo on the shirt and trousers shining in the Spring sunshine, Enid genuinely taken aback, stumbling backwards allowing Wei Ping to enter the household and further He-Man his proud attire through Castle Grayskull's foreboding entrance. Puffing his mighty little chest out, two sweat wristbands giving the game away, he'd nod in proclamatory "Whadaya think?" of this, the final masterstroke to rescue his damsels in distress, his black undies illuminating through the whiteness of the trousers.

Enid was speechless for a moment, opening her mouth with a cutting, witty retort then quickly deciding against encouraging this behaviour in any way, shape or lack of form. Without another viable option she belts a pleaded cry for Corin, holding the 'ooooor' and 'iiiiii' long enough to SOS her sister, who might not have been able to rescue her but could go a long way to sharing the shameful burden, his little round face beaming with macho pride.

"I understand you girls are putting a team of cricket player together," he said, casually flicking an imaginary underarm rounders delivery.

"Cricketers," corrected Enid, catching the invisible ball in her gut, as Corin appeared in the hall then attempted to backpedal away, the heels of her socks betraying the intent, her backside planting onto the wooden floorboards.

"I play from your team. Wherever you need me. Throwing, catching, wicketing, whacking, coaching, making drinks."

"Do you know how to clean a changing room loo and warm the seats for the team?" asked Corin, now unable to hold a modicum of patience any longer, the comment not deterring his chin-jutting heroics at all, the wind tunnel blowing his cape still at full throttle.

"Wei Ping," began Enid, breathing out a little like a talent judge poised to provide a reality-check cheque. "Have you ever played cricket before?"

"It's been my life ever since I found out you were putting a team together."

"Cricket is a game that is, erm, in-built at a very young age."

"Your bà was a gun cricket player, wasn't he? He taught you, so you could teach me. All I want to do is help."

After all the nagging, the little brotheresque persecution, the hiding in the woods to get away from him, both Corin and Enid felt the same wash of sympathetic compassion at the same moment. Without needing to glance over at one another, his dogmatic pursual never dented, never in doubt, a kind of venerated loyalty, his outsider status winning something deep in the girls' souls.

"Okay, let's, um, how about you just help out a bit?" Enid suggested.

We Ping took a breath - his first real form of acceptance - fighting a multitude of new urges to oversell the epicness of his contribution.

"You'll need to practice hard - on your own - to understand the nuts and bolts of the game. So when you help out, you are informed and, um, useful," Corin tempered with a distraction technique for their top historic groupie.

"I will watch every YouTube video on cricket and helping cricket players," Wei Ping beamed. "You will never regret employing the services of Captain Cricket - he will support making you the best cricket players. When do we start?"

Chapter >> 20

Transfer

Daniels, hadn't looked up in an age, forced indifference as his hand scuttled the mouse cursor around a non-existent calendar entry, blank email or the faces of his golfing buddies on the desktop.

"Just a minute, gentlemen," he uttered, pursing his lips to concentrate. "All good things."

"Of course Sir, as long as you need," said Chuck, receiving an admonishing glare from Chad, having taken the lead and spoken out of turn. Uncharacteristically, Chad decided to jump the gun, forcing Daniels to actually pay some attention.

"Sir we need another spin option for the team," puffed Chad from the breadth of his chest. "And we've found one," causing Danny's cheeks to crimson, that hint of blood in the water only noticeable by those close to him.

"Now hold on, gents … it feels like we've been through this already. Do not in God's name tell me you want to put a leggie in our team. Setting a field for a leg spinner involves placing fielders behind the boundary rope, remember!" Everyone except Danny chuckled, a polite chortle of sorts with a harder climb ahead, Chad front and centre with Danny and Chuck his winged lieutenants and James in the corner of the office, the bouncer preventing anyone entering … or leaving.

"Sir," continued Chad. "It's a left-armer … and not so much about embracing leg spin but rather bringing a level of unorthodox to the team."

"Oh my actual Lord Chadley!" riposted Daniels, then shifting to indemnify. "Gents … perhaps you feel I sit in this office doing bugger-all all day, but that is simply not the case. I speak to the ECB chair almost every month; we play golf together - he hooks way too often to be a consistent threat to my handicap by the way. He always says the same thing - one which I wholeheartedly agree with - there is no place for leg spin in the game. All these bloody Asian countries with their wrist spinners, looking like they've stuck their fingers in an electric socket. Answer this for me - why have we not seen a leg spinner in the England Test side in forever?"

As rehearsed, the boys all respond in unison, "Because you can't set a field in the crowd, Sir," the congruence applaudable.

"Hallow-Jensen is our man for this task, our man for this statement too. I mean, he's … you're not going to take many wickets, right, but you're going to plug up an end to allow the big quicks to do the damage the other end … right!?"

"Yes, Sir," said Danny, looking further into his swollen lap.

"His economy is below three Sir, so the team is functioning as planned," interjected Chad.

"Then why fix something that just isn't broken; not even dented and without minor scratches? Are you boys actually concerned about playing those girls? That were here?"

The G word rings out, James stiffening his posture and Chuck clearing his throat.

"No Sir. Even if they field a team, they've got more chance of making the England men's team than the play-offs."

"If we put out a leg spinner, we're saying the longer format has a longer-term role for these types, a future. Remember Warnie was a once in a generation bowler - pre DRS - who took more wickets with his attitude than his ability to spin the ball with his wrist. If he played now, his tally would be lower: 20% of his wickets were LBW - that's even more than he bowled. The pressure he created through psychologically imposing himself on the opposition - now, that's a lesson to take into cricket, but controlling the uncontrollable: getting a ball to land where you want it to when delivered from the side of a hand is just plain folly gentlemen. All your coaches attest to this same mantra: if a batsman doesn't need to score runs, a leg spinner is redundant."

"Isn't the game about scoring runs though Sir?" James chimed from the back, the room floored but likely more accepting of this as a face-value statement rather than challenging the principal's authority.

Daniels took a moment to reset ... regather ... reload.

"No Corkridge team during my tenure is going to pin the hopes of the highest performing cricket team in the land, on some freak defying all the physics and tradition of our wonderful sport."

"I suppose this is not the most opportune moment to inform you that he is from Africa, Sir."

Daniels stoked his temples, the frustration now spilling into 'day ruining' territory.

"We've done a lot for a lot of communities, both within England and worldwide. We've funded more farm schools in rural locations than any other school and even offered that bursary - which, granted didn't work out, but the intent was there. We cannot hand out financial assistance unless perhaps, this player is a good enough bat. All of your financial assistance is not well known by anyone other than your parents, is it? We cannot have this 'allowance' common knowledge."

"He bats. Shaky are pulling out the stops to recruit him

too. He might be that good."

Daniels took a real moment, even if the cinder in his eyes belted "They can have him." When he eventually spoke it was more considered, more purposeful, the evil Bond villain channelled like never before. "So we'd be depriving the girls' team. Even if he sits on the bench, in the 2nd XI or you never bowl him, he'd be unable to turn out for Shaky if we bursaried up. That's what you're telling me?"

Chad nodded, followed by James and then Danny. Chuck kept still for a moment then followed suit, his enduring obedience in silence holding true like an industrial strength padlock.

"It also might be time to make a few calls on another … erm, related matter. There's a loophole forming in the Cup where tournament organisers are considering participation from outside the school. Time to put that one through the covers, even if it won't make a difference. Just in case …"

"Just in case."

"Just in case."

"Just in case."

"Just in case."

"Just on the off chance, there's a ringer banging about we've never heard of."

"Any team with a girl in it will lose."

"Plain and obvious and simple and soon to be apparent for the nation."

"Just in case."

"Any genetics with dropping skills at that cataclysmic level is bound to be easy fodder for our boss-level team … gun bats and bowlers aplenty."

"Just in case."

Chapter » 21

Outside Off

The Shaky cricket trials had been advertised on the school bulletin board as a starting point to tap into the local talent. The turn-out was not woeful, aided in part by Miss Hazard's instruction to most of her fellow teachers to issue this as a punishment over the past few weeks for unruly students, adumbrations of ball skills registered for any classroom missile violations. Some arrived, signed the attendance sheet and departed, the migration of backpacks over the shoulder contracting to become a series of horizonal dots along the parallel path's border.

A sudden commotion preceded Enid's nth attempt to instigate the discourse, Jacob crumpled in a crying heap clutching his temple, the discarded tennis ball bullet nestled in the grass beside him, coated in one spot by a small, powdered sheen of foundation. Yapa, face ... butter - even the spreadable, softer version - rock solid taut in his mouth, unaltered and unaccountable. The girls might have expected it though, having bigged up Jacob's footwork to the point where Yapa was bound to test what he called "reactionary hand-eye coordination" although it might have simply been to shut down what looked like a Twenty Twenties' take on Footloose, the third and least wanted in the franchise. Whatever the intention, the outcome seemed to have a constructive upshot: Jacob's sniper rifle fall not only sent Wei Ping scuttling to attention in the correct supportive posture ("For today ... you're a ball retriever ... let's play fetch!") but dragged the emerging dance troupe from splayed fingers into shoulders back attention. Yapa began ...

"If you want to learn cricket, stay. If you want to be play for something, stay. Otherwise, go."

Bamn! Even Enid shifted nervously at the blatant simplicity of the call to arms. Yapa looked towards Enid to continue, so Corin jumped in ...

"This is not about building Shaky's non-existent school spirit, but it could be - this could be how we change the way things happen around here. Yes, this is about pride and about taking it to da man but unfortunately this is also a technical game that requires specific skills, commitment and avoiding dying at the hands of a hard leather ball and solid chunk of willow. We have to be brutal today - there are only eleven people in a team with a few backups for injuries so if you get a tap on the shoulder, you may return home. We don't have the luxury of a kiddie training camp for anyone with the coordination skills of a marmoset."

The group shifted uneasily, looking across for a first bolter, Enid's glare perfectly backing up her sister's words.

"We need honesty here," continued Enid. "Everyone start by raising their hands, both arms please."

Reluctantly, the full group emerged held up at gunpoint by Enid's request. The split was about even on the gender front, with the female trialists a blend of resolute determination and curiosity, the boys somewhere between disinterested and not wanting to be outdone by any girls.

"Lower one arm if you've never played an actual game of cricket - doesn't have to be hardball but must have been a match not orchestrated by your parents in the back garden."

Even Yapa flinched as all but two went down.

"Now put the other arm down if you've never played any cricket, held a bat, bowled a ball, taken a catch.

The honesty was remarkably sobering as about three quarters of the group stood arms at sides, shoulders sloped in chagrin. Corin, Enid and Yapa looked anxiously at one another as the intent was to split the group equally.

"Okay, that's fine," said Enid whipping on an imaginary fireman's helmet to rescue the situation. "Stay as you are and those with arms up, come stand behind me. Of the reminder, raise your hands if you've ever been bullied or told you're useless and want to find a way to prove the doubters wrong."

A madcap re-hold up Mexican wave this time, all participants' arms back up. An enviable synchronicity. Something to work with? Maybe if it wasn't rent-a-crowd, Corin thoughts deafening to nobody around her. Shoulder tapping some down-and-out versus digging a disappointment hole without any bodies to throw in it … classic Enid, always empowering the lame ducks, waddling home with her in servitude. It had to be down to her to be bad cop, to shatter some dreams or else they'd be fielding the equivalent of the entire cast of the ridiculous WWF or E or whatever was flavour of the month into a little old eleven-strong cricket team. Why did everything … always … have to be so bloody inclusive with Enid!?

"If a cricket ball hits you," renewed Corin. "You'll likely die on the spot. With all your family and the friends you might have watching. But not before you violently convulse, going into some hybrid of epilepsy and anaphylaxis … frothing at the mouth … shaking … bleeding … swelling … dogs' eyebrows scything off … cats falling on their back from trees—"

A few arms went down slowly, mainly deterred by Corin's conviction and confusing closing side-effects. When you didn't understand something, why mess with it? And, let's be faithfully ingenuous … no one really understood cricket. At this stage that is. Enid, ever the optimist, chucking a visual lasso around Corin to curtail her 'death to all cricketers' speech putting sport in the same category as bomb disposal. The Hurt Locker indeed, sweat dripping from either attire, padded to the absolute maximum in protective obduracy.

The wind ceased. For a moment. Only a moment. Then, as if reminding everyone that life's harsh reality stood still for no man or woman for that matter, an interrupting sheet of thick rain planed across the field, an architect's extension of a party wall moving at pace and purchasing some semi-legal space, drenching the makeshift coaching unit, the 'cricketers' learning jazz hands from Jacob and the Disney line-up of downtrodden losers - the arms almost all down now, prisoners executed in one fell swoop by the British weather.

Yapa, ever the pragmatist, decided to shut down the Tom Brady Superbowl speeches and act decisively, manhandling the applicants into uniform spaces, along the line. He looked across at the girls who both embraced the momentum and did the same, Enid taking the supposed batters and Corin the bowlers from the group that had claimed to play, Yapa the remainder in front.

"Simple game of catch," launched Yapa, revealing a heavy blue bucket of worn cricket balls, now sloshing in an inch or so of water. "If you drop three in a row you go home; if you catch three you go stand at side of football post. Understand?"

There was no farting around here as the threat of full exclusion became conspicuous, most getting into crouch position, fingers splayed towards the launcher. Some unsure what to do, mimicked but with varying levels of efficacy, fingers distorted in rap battle commencement pose, backsides so far out it was actual adorning objectified eye candy in a rap battle, some even with palms shut to restrict any slappy palm contact. Corin went for a bat to hit the catches and Enid just shook her head in fear of injury and the consequent lawsuit. Yapa just started throwing, lobbing underarm as all hell broke loose, carnage of the most extreme ilk: cartwheels, slapping balls away like bees, catching balls in shirts, evading faces diving into hips, clutched balls contemplated with wonder, ball palmed up into the face, bullseye pings between the eyes, broken fingernails, screaming, clutching at misjudged trajectories, meeting the ball on the volley – footballing skills in abundance, one kid even trying to catch the ball with his teeth – an oversized mouth almost realising its destiny, and the list goes on …

A rustling, uncontrollable chuckle would bring proceedings to a halt, ironically thankfully so after the scene on display, the adjoining woods that verged the field drawing everyone's attention as the balls came to rest, scattered shrapnel from a battle's flagrant defeat. Corin and Enid knew exactly as two boys charged in the opposite direction into the density of the trees, waving an iPhone in triumph without any intention of hiding the hilarity or inauspiciousness of what would happen next. Chuck and James likely from the size of them, having remained charily hidden for the duration of the stuttering session, malevolence and an even bigger sense of superior contentment bellowing forth accompanied by the "whoop-whoops" and "looooosers" when heading for the nearest upload opportunity.

The combination of the intrusion, the rain, the catching exercise gone horribly wrong and the general dejection of reality left about ten kids at the football post, mostly willing and unable. Corin, Enid and Yapa gathered in a huddle.

"We have to maintain standards," whispered Corin. "Otherwise we're setting up to fail."

"Agreed," said Enid. "Better to have no team than a laughingstock team, although likely that horse has already bolted. We'll be social media sensations shortly no doubt."

"Again," tutted Corin. "Cricket ball motif with me the rest of my life it seems."

"And Dad's," choked Enid bringing Corin's flippant quip back to sobering reality.

"We look for specifics we can work with," said Yapa sensing the girls slipping into hurt territory and providing a rare sense of buoyant momentum. "We can work on rare, unique skills ... and positive clever mindset. Attitude very important always in any sport. Look for awareness of how ball bounces and how to adapt body, hands and head for approaching ball. These the best we have so we aim for those able to solve problem under pressure. Thinker over doer."

His resolve strengthened the girls' so they left the huddle with the mental equivalent of a "1-2-3 let's go!"

Ten bats were laid out on the moist grass in various states of disrepair, an eclectic amalgamation of Yapa's nineties residue stash, Patty's childhood kit and an excursion to a Sevenoaks charity shop after an opportune spot of the lesser spotted SS Jumbo, lazily propping up the wall in the display window.

"Each of you please pick up a bat," instructed Enid. "Completely naturally: hold the bat in whatever way feels comfortable; don't try and guess what the correct way should be."

An inauspicious start with Jacob, first out the gates, tippytoe fluttering feet towards the gladiatorial row of ordnances, twirling once en route to retrieve the willowed extension, holding it exultantly the wrong way up, thick end clutched and handle dangling far away from his person. With enough attention mustered, he winked at the girls and cavalierly flipped the bat the correct way, intending to cogently catch it and take a symbolic swing, only to fumble and drop the wood onto his precious toes. An aberrantly tall girl would follow, likely way above six foot even in flat, worn

Converse trainers - maybe a whopping size 10 or even 11 - sauntering up to the remaining line of bats and reaching down to Lilliput, aiming to secure the biggest club, only to not quite make it: a bat all the way on the ground was just out of reach for such a limb-laden creature and the exertion would result in her having to take the knee to retrieve, but not before overbalancing and stumbling sideways. She too would hold the wrong end initially but settle on it as a suspicious counter to Jacob's twirl bluff epic fail, still wincing in protest at his throbbing foot. The third-in bronze medallist would provide some hope, placing both palms facing the grass on the middle of the handle, his eyes lighting up when the lift looked and felt natural. With the bat tossing treatment a poor substitute for what should have been taking place with the balls, he decided to switch hands mid-air, right over left then vice versa without a hint of fumble, each grip looking increasingly comfortable. The coaching/selection trio all took encouraging note. The remainder that followed all looked safe middle of the road in that they'd likely batted before but without any significant comfort, prowess or efficiency. One participant, a tiny girl with a tussled Parisian fringed bob, considerately waited for all compatriots to be armed before approaching the line to discover no remaining bats. A blue plastic bat nestled at Yapa's feet and he instinctually flicked it at her, her reaction to catch the bat awkward yet secure.

"Take your stance," yelled Corin. "Some missiles be flying! You just swing or hit whatever feels right, but give yourselves some space first," with the previous events on display a key indicator that proximity was a potentially fatal construct in this workout. Each of the designated three flingers knew that anything wide was an additional danger, a hook, pull or cut likely to find an adjacent member, the ensuant Health & Safety breach liable to shut down the Shaky Cricket team before the coin toss. So, the throws - strictly underarm to start – were flush in line, watching for transfer of weight, alignment and lever freedom. Jacob's feet were abashedly targeted, testing his ability to move them in the correct direction – unfortunately with his recent 'near-fatal' injury he spent the majority of the time sliding his feet any which way except towards the ball, a time-lapse running on the spot comedy display. Wei Ping, largely forgotten for a period, inched his way forward from the outer boundary region not only to establish some relevance but even Wei Ping could clock that not too many balls were bound to fly his way for retrieval. That is until Audrey Tautou's doppelgänger melted one, plastic bat and all, twenty feet over his head, after a forceful cupping sling from Yapa at her head. She insisted on being called Larry – short for Lauren – the only daughter among five brothers, her dad the owner of a golf driving range.

Corin and Lauren in the middle order. Daring to dream. Sorry, Corin and Larry … not quite the same ring as a catchy middle order such as Worrell, Weekes and Walcott. Besides, catchy was not really order of the day as Wei Ping went off in search of the ball, his dumpy legs passing one another as consecutively fast as possible to serve a purpose. He'd have caught it if he was in the right place he felt, pumping his arms, but that ball is quite hard after all, grabbing it and flinging it back to the rabble with all his strength, only to propel it about a third of the distance. Nice height on it though, as he once again tore after it, this time in the opposite direction and back towards the action.

The tall drink of Amazonian lady water did not connect one ball, the swipe and intent using the full range of motion from her all-elbows approach. Yapa, undeterred, kept peppering her, a frantic swatting away a storm of flies around her person ensuing. The bronze medallist to the bats, initially the most encouraging boy at the party, would in a sense lose interest and become more intent on retrieving the balls and returning them to Enid, first left-handed then right, then both at once. A medium sized non-descript boy, when passing the tall girl, obviously couldn't resist, the exchange something like ...

"What's the weather like up there, Slim?"

"Never heard that one before."

"Maybe you didn't hear me, up there with all the pigeons cooing."

"Now that I genuinely haven't heard."

"No retort. Short joke back at me? I'm squint you know and dyslexic."

"No point is there. Two wrongs and all that."

"Think I like your style, even if it is all acquired from Jacamo!"

"Ohp, there it is!"

"Sorry, couldn't resist. There's likely more where that came from."

"Sure there is."

"Like don't bump your head on the sun. Or the moon."

"Not biting."

"Or Pluto."

"Nope."

"Not even a dwarf planet comeback? It was set up so beautifully."

"Planes not so good; concerts amazing."

"You're quite a functional specimen, aren't you? Facts over sarcastic spice? I'll have you insult me before the day is out, just watch Ichabod Crane."

"Who?"

"Just be careful swinging that thing near me - for all your lengthy power potential, I might be the unlucky recipient if you decide to unleash."

"Not really the unleashing type. When does anger ever solve anything?"

"Can't be a good feeling being denied access to a parking

lot due to height restrictions? Or only letting your folks buy cars with sunroofs?"

"People only say things like that when they're hunting for a reaction, or someone has hurt them sufficiently to warrant meanness."

"I'm Noel."

"Daughtry. It means high bank."

"No way."

"My parents are both below five foot six. Who knew."

"Mine means a Christmas carol and I was born in June. Parents: more madness than any method. Nice to make your acquaintance HB. I'd reach up to shake your hand but probably couldn't reach."

The collapse into Yapa's office resembled a knot of people falling through a door giving way, bust for eavesdropping in a harmless US sitcom, except for the exhaustion etched on the sisters' faces, marked territory that might be difficult to return from. To amplify the emotional scars, their shoes were soaked, fingers bleeding, cheeks muddy and shirts unlikely to receive 'high praise' from Mum come washing cycle.

Yapa waddled up to the board, casually rubbed off some of the exercises that had been somewhere between in vain and in pain, then flipped the board around. Without turning his back on the board, he slowly edged backwards towards his desk chair, Corin collapsed along the adjacent wall and Enid draining the last hospitable drops from her trite water bottle. As it stood, the girls had no real aspirations for any of the applicants, the summit of Chad Mountain just too gallingly high with the adumbrative humiliation of "Catch It If You Can" about to hit a small screen near you!

Yapa just sat staring at the board, arms folded across his stomach, fingers clasped and tapping in alternate hand unison. The girls, supposedly used to his retracted demeanour, now reached boiling point where his complete inability to even support their frustration was, well … frustrating as hell! Was he blind or was it because this didn't really matter to him, nothing on the line for him if truth be told. Enid felt herself hold back the tears, not a current just a dejected trickle but enough to scrunch the towel in her hand and load the arm trigger for launch into the ring, Rocky's bloody corpse for once not getting up at the eight count. Corin, noticing this, took a weird shot at feigning support only to realise that her muscles had abandoned her in her sister's minute of need, unable to stand up from the exhaustion of coaxing actual cricketers out of keen, clutzy outcasts. Yapa just stared at the board.

"We're going home now Mr Yapa," said Enid moving into polite disassociation. "Thank you for your help today. When the dust has settled, I'm sure we'll look back with a fond 'tried hard' and 'no cigar' type mantra."

"Three more in the team," said Yapa, his laser focus at the board unwavering even in the midst of a mutiny.

"Is there a little tree you have somewhere, to grow cricketers?" asked Corin. "We have a money tree in our garden, or so Mum always says do we think there is."

"Six. Ten. Eleven. Today. Six to do a bit more and Ten some alterations."

The girls were now forced to look at the board, the whiteboard markers still faint but with Enid's dominant scribbles circumvented by Yapa's edits when they were last listing the possibilities.

"And opener … perhaps. Not sure on your dancing sugar plum but we try. Most important positions still open but we move towards six who can play if you two get back into the groove."

The girls, eyes clingfilmed over from the unholy concoction of wind, dust, rain, exertion and futility, at first did not register, the board some way away in the murky office, no spotlight to support a drumroll. But Yapa's circles unmistakeable, annotated before the trials and uncannily sanguine even if a bit embryonic …

6: Lauren Vangellis

10: Noel Pothas

11: Daughtry Turner

"These are the three you earmarked," said Corin, almost incredulous.

"We have no keeper – Larry, with reaction time from dodging and catching golf balls bats at 6. Noel, ambidextrous – a big surprise for opposition team. Tall girl – too many fast twitch fibres not to make ball fly through the air fast if incentivised right way. Plus, she calm."

Enid, not fully convinced, held her eyes on Yapa, still not a hint of self-congratulations anywhere in the room.

"Still much to do," said Yapa, his credentials raised somewhat even though the girls both felt the only hope – if any at all – lay with the three recruits.

Chapter » 22

Opposition

"It just doesn't seem ... necessary," a rare pipe up from Rufus, from somewhere behind the two double seater sofas.

The prefects room felt more rammed than normal when the Corkridge 1st XI gathered for a team briefing, the orderly green leather sofas shotgunned to death by the regular starters, the supporting cast members often relegated right out of the room. A fire crackled in the corner, carefully constructed under strict duress by one or many of the new boys in Chad's boarding house, Lombard. There was sometimes a rotation to the other houses but invariably, prior to a significant match or tournament, Lombard was the abode and Chad wasn't one to accept any lowly hospitality in his house, the stream of coffees, teas and toasted sandwiches complete and shut out for the soirée.

The outburst saw Chad almost choke on his pâté, pickle and cheese toasted sarnie, spitting the hazardous chunk clean across the room and into the fire, triggering a thwarting crackle before engulfing the layered morsel into the green-glowing flames. Even when expressing appal, his aim was awfully accurate, a Robin Hood who not only shattered William Tell's apple but kept all the loot for himself.

"Necessary!" he said rising. "Necessary? I'd like to know what your version of necessary is Roofy?"

"Well ..." said Rufus, gingerly approaching centre stage through the red sea parting of teammates eager to stay out of the firing line should any collateral damage be forthcoming. "We're a cricket team, right? And a good one? So why do we need to humiliate opposition we probably won't even get to play and, if we did, they wouldn't hold a candle to us?"

"That's precisely the reason," Chad wound up, compellingly grabbing a cricket bat to help 'support' the point. "What's 'necessary' is that we should not have to be breathing the same air as these amateurs; these little girls should not be allowed to even think about being in the same hemisphere as the Corkridge XI."

"You made the bet."

"I want the ball, don't I? And our little trailer shot from the woods by Jimmy and the Chuckster - well done boys, sterling effort by the way, the footage is magnificently hilarious - is the same as the ball."

"I don't follow."

"Deterrents in this woke world by blabbing: talk is overdone and cheap and everyone's desperate to take a chunk out of our institutions until there'll either be none left or we'll be so marginalised, that mediocrity will reign supreme. We have to 'show' deterrence so that little ventures like the Sisters Grimm thinking they can take us on NEVER happen again: not here or any other boys' school in the country."

"Yeah but let's show through our cricket?"

"Why waste any time actually playing these bitches? The deterrent happens before! They don't even enter our sacred house: the cricket pitch."

A cacophony of macho nods rippled throughout the common room, the beginnings of moustaches pushed towards the nostrils in downturned mouth accord. If there was a dissenting voice in the room, it was hidden behind clammy, musk-scented, glassy eyes and libertarian conservativism. Rufus was never a mainstay in the team so, as much as representing the Corkridge squad carried a weighty kudos, bowling twenty-three overs and three batting innings last season materialised as a sacrifice worth exploring. And not really because he felt like being the anarchist in the group or to be heard or stand up for a cause he was ambivalent about, but more because the video was so far removed from cricket, Rufus felt it worth as least allowing the defence lawyer in him to make an opening statement. The video was clearly hilarious, the final edit trickling past CK-wetting stage - especially when one fielder dived out of the way and the ball hit the girl behind him flush on the tip of her nose - but, in Rufus's mind it didn't relate to Corkridge's opposition. It was just a funny video that would likely do the rounds.

"Chad, you're the boss, and you know what's best for the team. I've said my piece, I just think we don't 'need' to be associated with that ... shitshow."

"That video is going out and it's going out today. When I get the ball - the Duane Hanratty shitshow ball - that's going out too. Until this whole exercise is not about beating a silly girls' team but rather eradicating them ALL from the board so we can get back to winning Digners again without distraction and signing some big ass contracts, first for England then, schedule permitting, at the IPL."

Orchestrating an on-cue move, Chuck spat an olive pip up into the air, the arc looping over the heads of the boys in front of him, just past Rufus's shoulder. Chad, twisting the bat to reverse hit the expelled object, swung and swung with intent, skimming Rufus's shoulder and jaw but also following through to smash the pip square in the middle of the bat, the clank of the fireplace's pitcher mitt ringing in the air and generating colossal applause, Rufus left to rue getting in Chad's way.

Chapter » 23

No-Ball

The ball had always been a necessary reminder; a form of reality check - albeit hidden in the back section of the cabinet for some time now - to bring Duane back from his own non-existent, self-imposed lofty heights. It had been well covered by the media how he came to be in possession of the scarily iconic dropped ball, the Aussies retrieving the ball after the fateful match to have it encased in a square glass tomb with the words "Thanks, Mate!" engraved in yellow lettering, presented to Duane at an awards evening. Duane, in the beginnings of checking out from public life, had accepted the token with the prevailing decorum and humility which had characterised not only much of his cricketing career, but his life. Later, at the afterparty in a show of solidarity, one of his teammates had launched the glass square, shattering it to the raucous applause of both teams. Undeterred, the resourceful Aussies had retrieved the ball, fashioned a Sharpie substitute for the inscription on the ball with the same sentiment … "Thanks, Mate!" marked in aggressive thick black lines across the ball, unwanted scar tissue on an unsuspecting organ. Not content at that, the Aussies had taken the ball on their celebratory Ashes tour with them, treating it like royalty and keeping it in pride of place on the bus tour, at the dignitary functions and on talk shows.

The ball had then appeared at the MCG and Australian Sport Museum, on display until the travelling party departed for England to defend the Ashes, the word "Ooops" in the shrinesque display juxtaposing the ball's defacing "Thanks, Mate!" inscription. That Ashes had almost gone exactly according to plan for the Aussies - their tails now up at having nicked the home Ashes and new talented youngsters emerging - hammering England 4-0, the only saving grace of a 5-0 whitewash, the Headingly weather intervening when England were so heavily on the ropes, the ring might have actually broken apart with one more fatal punch. Duane's career had ended after the previous Ashes, along with many of his teammates, but when coaxed out of hibernation to receive a Wisden award for best bowling and batting average against Australia in the modern era (easily forgotten by Joe Public and Joe Media), the presentation had been hijacked by the current Aussie captain, who'd been kind enough the bring the ball and present it back to Duane to overshadow the diminutive Wisden plaque. Duane, exhausted by now from the constant association, hadn't the energy to do anything grandiose like whip it into the press rabble, so had meekly pocketed the "Thanks, Mate!" ball into his suit jacket, rueing letting Bronwyn persuade him to accept the accolade in the first place. The press, more eager to mould something out of something as tedious as solid authentic cricket statistics, had captured the pocketing of the ball on camera, the evening news gleeful to run with the caption "Duane Hanratty pockets ball ... for once. Thanks, Mate!" hoping beyond reason that the non-cricket following could crack the commentator's association of catching with pocketing. They did, of course, in this instance.

Duane's study was an amalgamated, orderly mess of existing business ventures, current consultative employment and those hobbies that might or might not be looked at once standing up quickly from the sofa became a chore. The cabinet, much to Bronwyn's annoyance, had acquired layers of additional clutter throughout the years, not least the girls' early cricket trophies - thick plastic to the core even at junior county level - along with Patty's achievements, some photo frames, a beautiful bible from Duane's sister / Patty's Godmother and a baby photo of Duane that could have easily been mistaken for the Gerber baby.

The ball, not through harmful or regretful intent but rather the sought after distance between painful memories, had been relegated an inch or so a year until now it gloomily resided at the furthest back point, resting against the cabinet's backboard. Bronwyn had been on Duane from immediately after the Wisden presentation at Lord's to just get rid of it, cleanse the soul and move on. Duane, in some sort of faux masochistic way liked to gaze upon the ball - a generation X version of self-harm, the cuts decorating his eyeballs - it kept him real, grounded and grateful he told himself; just depressed Bronwyn countered. Now, though, it was out of sight if not out of mind. Bronwyn had, in fact, binned it once some time ago only for Duane to retrieve it from the study's woven, waste paper bin, hold it up curiously - like a suspicious Snow White if she ever had the prophylactic sense - wondering how such a small, innocuous, dull, roseate orb could cause so much suffering, uncertainty and disillusionment.

When Corin burst into the study there might or might not have been a dash of unconscious inquisition, if only to check whether the darn thing existed. The Hanratty family was not at all prone to secrecy or the 'what's mine is mine' mantra of most families, a caring, sharing ethos pervading the house yet, if discovered, it would have been a hard sell to justify what exactly Corin was doing in her dad's study. So the semi-fabrication shouted up the stairs if "Anyone had any Blu Tack?" met with a reassuring "Check Dad's study," from all-knowing mum Bronwyn, gave Corin the snoop license, setting off alarm bells in Enid's head.

"Bust!" whispered Enid, stealing into the study.

"You must have then," Corin's eyes widening in realisation.

"I have not; nothing of the sort. I don't accept defeat as easily as some it seems."

"It is not that at all; I just want to make sure it still exists. Did you even understand its significance - its real significance - up until now? All those years it was on the shelf; pride of place."

"Not really, it was just ... a thing ... that somehow was important yet toxic to Dad ... and Mum. Who notices anything when you're a kid?"

"Well where is it now then?"

The two gazed up towards the cabinet in unison, their heads turning like the air condition shutter of their Volvo. They gathered in a huddle as Mum shouted "You find it?" to which Corin responded "Almost" as Dad returned into the neighbouring kitchen from the garden, apparent from the fridge door opening.

"What does it admit if we find the darn thing?" whispered Enid. "That we've lost the match before we've even played it."

"Jeez, shoot me for just wanting to see it, touch it, understand it ... a bit better. It's not there. If we happen to lose, what then ... would you give it to Chad?"

"I would. I'd have to. I've committed with my word."

"And Dad? The impact? Chad's not going to take it out for a little net session and forget ... that thing is going to be held up like Simba on the rock when he gets his greasy paws on it, but there won't just be couplets of badly drawn animals below; it will be the world cheering his Simba-ball!"

"Which is exactly why we can't let it happen."

"What about a replica? We make one that looks like Dad's?"

"What's the point … if we reveal the real ball, we've not honoured the challenge; if we don't, no one's the wiser."

"Maybe it dies down then we reveal."

"And just reinvigorate the whole story. Dad dragged through the mud all over again … just what he felt like from his daughters."

"Maybe we should tell him? Get him on board?"

"We tried that: no fly zone."

Duane's footsteps clattered towards the study, a functional gait completing or starting a menial task as opposed to a hurried suspicion, Enid and Corin's hunched shoulders pointing towards each another in consummate guilt. The rattle of the hallway's drawer - keys the orchestral accompanying violin to the drawer's trombone - soothing … reassuring … steps back into the kitchen brief respite … but for how long?

"I don't think it is even there anymore," Corin susurrated, instinctually programmed to defy her sister - years of perfecting - Enid grasping at air to stop her departure from the huddle. Enid momentarily gave up, questioning whether she actually wanted it found, leaving Corin's hands to scout about the usual shelf, until … an expression change that told Enid enough. The grasp of a cricket ball, so familiar yet foreign in this case, Corin surreptitiously pulling her hand from the back of the shelf, slowly skimming the tops of all the frames and trophies as though nudging one too compellingly would result in her hand exploding.

The reveal shocked Enid, stumbling backwards as she gazed upon the haunting entity, still a few steps away as Corin approached, arm increasingly outstretched, Chernobyl's reactive core oozing graphite onto her culpable palm. Her hand shielded a third of the words yet she dared not rotate the ball, the scrawled words equally dirty and precariously erasable in their presence. Enid shook her head, not wanting it any nearer, mouthing (an inaudible) “Put it back!” (scream) as Corin stopped, frozen, channelling Frodo in curious suspicion now. The ball felt heavy, cumbersome, compelling some sort of raucous launch up up up and away from this place, this sanctity, this team, this family, this planet.

Why could such a malevolent force be allowed to coexist with Dad’s kindness, his endeavour, his skills, his devotion, dedication and generosity?

All this ... was about this! Corin’s hand opened, parlously balancing the long-in-the-tooth, dull orb with almost 90 overs of hidden skulduggery, its first move an intimidating dummy to fall, wobbling towards the thumb region, Enid innately leaning to take a two-handed catch. Then still, an awkward angle on Corin’s wavering palm - a hat worn at the Queen’s Platinum Jubilee - pinned on the side, flouting gravity, enjoying its time out of the shadows, ready to play the final act.

Enid, ever aware of another’s germs, even if years before, took over, strutting two steps to retrieve the ball from Corin’s mitt, the filth of Duane’s teammates’ gob and baying flaming galah Aussies obliging her to pluck it between middle finger and thumb, hustle towards the cabinet and drop it from whence it came, her two exposed fingertips anxiously waiting for a dollop of hand sanitiser from Dad’s desktop.

The ball’s sudden absence lifted a veil of darkness from the room, light permitted back into each of the girls’ pupils, twinkles and effervescent colour contours reinstated after the ephemeral banishment. Corin breathed out while Enid showered her hand in sanitiser then hurried towards the bathroom for another contrivance to remove whatever that ball had left on her.

Chapter >> 24

Wheels

Mr Yapa's string pulling off the back of the increasing hype of the upcoming tournament and the so-called allocated funds for developmental, inclusive sports such as cricket began to bear fruit; perhaps not big golden apples and juicy swollen summer watermelons but a few wonky pears and lesser-known damsons, pocked and bird-pecked but encouragingly present. His first procurement was an ageing bowling machine, to which Yapa had fastened a high handrail step ladder with an admix of tape, elastic cables and seatbelt webbing. Corin climbed the ladder with a blend of caution and forced optimism, the jarring creak and complementary sway to the side jolting her into widened stance, splayed arms, surfer babe.

Jacob vacillated at the other end of the cricket net, fully padded up with ill-fitting helmet, undeterred by what he deemed "Running Man's Sub Zero garb" attempting to find his slight of foot and light step even when weighed down by two foreign pads, a thigh pad (on the outside), chunky gloves and a helmet squeezing his face so tightly shut, his glasses pushed beyond his nose and likely out of focus. Jacob refused to stand still, which boded well Enid kept telling herself and she went through the basics of footwork to get his body positioned correctly as the ball approached, abetting contact directly beneath the eyes, bat and pad hugging bedfellows ... no gap and no follow-through. The ball had to just drop below him, she explained, his foot marginally on the inside of the delivery with the angle of the bat letting the bowler know that this fortress was impenetrable, body in position so early (as a result of the footwork) you could pour a cup of tea and eat a cucumber sandwich between planting the foot and playing the defensive shot. In theory. Jacob seemed to be getting it as Corin fired up the bad boy at the bowler's end, a splutter of smoke getting the wheels turning.

At Corin's end the two large spinning wheels appeared misaligned, the right slightly raised and the left at an irregular angle, pointing towards the grass rather than impeccably horizontal. A shrug towards Yapa, who might or might not have taken a step back out of any danger zones, as Corin tested the speed dial on each wheel, independent ranges from zero to one hundred. The wheels blurred in angry rotation, only on twenty yet still feeling like they might take off. The makeshift ladder shook as Yapa passed Corin a bucket of balls and Enid removed herself from the net giving Corin the thumbs up. Jacob took guard on leg stump, so Corin motioned him left only to see him take a gigantic step and expose all three stumps. Corin didn't instruct further, probably feeling Jacob was safer closer to completely out of the way, the noise of the spinning so deafening she feared any gesticulations would be a tick-tock back and forth across the stumps.

Corin retrieved the guinea pig ball from the bucket, a uniformly cratered hockey ball designed for these old-fashioned bowling machines, and placed it vigilantly at the entry point of the gap between the two spinning wheels. She felt the ball sucked into the vortex then plop a couple of metres in front to the right, nowhere near reaching Jacob's purposeful backlift. Jacob raised his palms as though this was interfering with his actual cricket masterclass, so Corin tried again just as Enid approached, the second ball spinning in an arc and connecting Enid on the shoulder. The blow hurt more than she made out, programmed not to even rub it or wince, classic resolve against an intimidating bowling attack, yet the distinctive plastic density and point of contact on the ACJ stung a little more indignantly than Enid had anticipated (anticipation a moot point with this relic firing out missiles indiscriminately, the girls wondering whether the windows on the far side of the flanking warehouse were in danger).

Corin decided the only remedy was to amp up the speeds but maintain the right wheel as slower to counter the wobble and the misalignment, her A* in physics sure to come in handy here. With Enid now safely behind the structure, Corin let rip with the third which did reach the warehouse window and went cascading through, shattering a cracked pane. Yapa looked nonplussed as Corin took a breath and foraged forward, now altering the dials in a haphazard manner that betrayed any physics lesson in the last couple years. The fourth was a bullet, slamming directly into Jacob's previously injured foot, failing to twitch flinch but then dropping like a crumpled sack of grain losing its resting place against a wall. Tears might have been forthcoming in any other situation but, with two girls in attendance, Jacob's machoism made a cameo and he stood up, took guard and raised his bat, defiant even if now actually shitting bricks for what might happen next.

The fifth ball flew - straight as the fourth but Corin felt even quicker - pitching at a sumptuous length and bowling Jacob middle peg despite what looked like a good stride and straight bat. Enid nodded in felicitation, Jacob aware he'd done the right thing ... sort of, as officially he'd still have been out. But he'd been listening and he had moved his feet. The sixth through ninth flew in contrasting directions, decorating the side of the net, the back net and a host of points short on the pitch, the most encouraging the eighth: a bouncer where Jacob was able to sway out of the way, despite an unwonted inswing shape, following his face in measured retreat. The tenth was an actual yorker and Jacob slid his feet out of the way and dug it out to rapturous applause even though everyone knew no one bowled yorkers anymore.

Yapa wanted the machine moved closer, the girls protesting for Jacob's young life, a blindfold a likelier innovation.

Chapter >> 25

Accumulation

You wouldn't directly call it looking up and down but there was simply no other way to put how the Corkridge XI welcomed the newest recruit, a sceptical, even irregular "Welcome to the team." Onka was an irregular shape to look at too, his lankiness imbalanced by comparatively shorter arms and a high waist that made him look like he'd pulled his trousers too high. Earlier that morning, Daniels had welcomed the mother to the South East even though to Onka's Mom, the South East was the Transkei! Onka had watched Daniels walk her to her car as they departed, a disquieted expression on her face, papers in hand: undoubtedly the 50% bursary that Daniels had offered as they were gearing to leave South Africa. Onka himself felt uneasy about a bursary: bursaries were for people in financial need and they certainly were not; would an academic scholarship (albeit a significantly lesser percentage) have been more becoming of his fortes?

Chad strode through the team, the peasant masses making way for the king, shoulders back, smile fastened on, hand extended like a lance to welcome this … this … unorthodox looking, playing and everything else in-between foreigner. Onka watched Chad approach, instinctively holding back his hand, the last few years in a Covid ravaged nation not permitting that level of skin-on-skin familiarity. His elbow twitched outward, getting ready to substitute at a moment's notice.

"Chad," said Chad. "The captain," his arm still outstretched, the brevity of the introduction – he'd learnt in debate club – more punchy, impactful and indelible.

"Onkarabile ... but my friends call me Onka. Saves on the correcting. In my culture we use elbows."

"And what culture is that?" said Chad, undeterred and keeping his palm ready to be landed upon.

"The culture of containing the spread of Covid," generating a few chuckles, likely Rufus at the back.

Chad, realising this might be folly and a stand-off not worth losing, disembarked, opting to slap Onka three times on the back of the shoulder.

"Must be bizarre ... being here, now."

"I've been to the UK a few times; just not permanently."

"You're a batter first and foremost and Chinaman second?"

Onka considered this loaded statement, the echo of the indoor gym's structure encapsulating the 'd' longer than anticipated. He looked around the room, quite dishevelled for what seemed such an organised school: fencing gear strewn in the corners, masks littered like some Japanese samurai death scene; nets rolled up chaotically resting atop one another, an oversized Jenga that wouldn't topple; more discarded cricket bats and accessories than Onka had ever seen, quality kit surplus to requirements.

"Haven't heard it called Chinaman for a while, perhaps just some of my older teammates' dads. Do you know where the term originated?"

A shuffle went around the group, all looking at one

another in consternation, unable to field the South African's trivia. Chad would know surely, as the group huddled into safety, fanning in.

"The origin of our great game centres on England and Australia, quite frankly. All the greats come from one of these two cricketing nations, so anything from Asia probably doesn't make the grade if you know what I mean," Chad's deflection allowing the back feathers of his team's arrow pointing at Onka to fan back out.

"In 1933 at Old Trafford, the West Indies had a left-arm wrist spinner from Trinidad named Ellis 'Puss' Achong," Onka sermoned, the story's character's nickname generating a puerile snigger from some of the team, Chad's look admonishing for even acknowledging. "The papers said he was the first Chinese man to play cricket even though he wasn't fully Chinese. The association between something the cricketing world had never seen, and their fear of the unknown - the unorthodox - made the association between the 'heathen Chinese' and innovation in cricket before it was celebrated as innovation. Different just had to be attributed to something 'else', in this case racial heritage."

"That Test probably meant nothing; easily forgotten against the great bodyline series of the era."

"That's the one where Jardine - the father of bodyline - got some of his own medicine, peppered by Martindale and Constantine, yet still put 140 on the board."

Needing to quickly shift the point of attack and supposed outwitting of the colony's native heritage descendants, Chad swung the verbals, not willing to concede just yet.

"The West Indies had a patch yes, but they're a spent force now. Bit like your big pin-up: what's happened to AB De Villiers?"

"He's still playing; retired from International though."

"Now like all South Africans you're going to tell me what a great player he was; what an innovator; the greatest?"

"His record can speak for itself across all formats."

"Didn't he make the record one-day score against the washed-out Windies; wearing pink on a track that had become a batter's paradise?"

"Everyone remembers that; I liked the 125 he made against the Aussies at St. George's in 2018 when all others were tumbling around him; he made batting look easy, clipping fours off his hips from outside the off. And facing a sandpapered ball."

Menace descended on the hall, a snowy veil of lines crossed, coating what had now become red and blue corners: team of many versus the resolution of one newcomer, his demeanour not threatened but sealed in conviction of belief. Chad creaked his neck, this side then that, lips more pursed than normal, his villainous roar either doused or about to pop from fester into blistering action.

"Everyone was altering the state of cricket balls; everyone knows that."

"Doesn't make it right. Plus, slight difference between some sugary saliva and DIY on the field of play."

"They've served their time; their records speak for themselves: Smith and Warner," Chad's Aussie twang now more apparent.

"There should be no grey area on these types of infringements: either you play in the spirit of the game, or you don't. You wonder how different their records would have been if they hadn't cheated."

"Okay, let's talk about cheating … Hansie Cronje …"

"… didn't actually do as much wrong as everyone claimed. He declared an innings when cricket needed it but never compromised performance. He was stringing the bookies along making them believe he was throwing games or influencing players but, unlike Warne and Waugh, his transgressions were exposed for the world to see. But he did hurt a lot of us … while still maintaining the highest win percentage of the era."

"Sandpapergate was just that: a load of overblown hoo-ha."

"Cracking series though: Proteas against an Aussie side that hated losing so much they'd revert to underhand tactics like that; and still the Proteas won."

"No one remembers that do they?"

"Precisely."

"Smith and Warner are going to go down as two of the greats of the game."

"That's the tragedy. Compounded with Smith's wander over to off stump hitting everything on leg and being dropped or reprieved at key moments legacy."

"They're T20 world champions ... as we stand."

"Shouldn't have been allowed back in the game. Time will tell how history judges those two."

"As winners."

"Sometimes winning isn't worth selling your soul or your integrity."

"You have an answer for everything, don't you?"

"Just stuff I feel strongly about, that's all."

Onka got the bus home, his first full day at Corkridge under the belt - a taster day of sorts, his familiarity with the bus schedule already embedded. He didn't recognise any of the bus riders wearing Corkridge unforms, a swathe of bloated cars impregnated with blonde bespectacled mummies jostling for pole parking position at the day houses. He'd worn his old South African school uniform, the only smart attire he'd packed in a hurried exit north and not yet at the point of the 'event' of wincing at the school's shop prices, especially when converting from Rands to Pounds! The bursary didn't cover uniforms and accessories - a form of cross-subsidisation he noted from his economics lessons, the margin on a one hundred quid striped blazer enough to cover a few pitch covers. He wanted to get back to playing cricket - his addiction - perhaps that would make it all worthwhile but, despite missing his friends back home and the wholesome salt of the earth nature he associated with all South Africans, he knew he'd be having an introspective discussion with his mother shortly. "Drugs pay the bills ... wherever we are," she'd told him as he opened his phone to trawl Twitter for the latest cricket stories.

The first that popped up, chewing through his measly starter data package, had done the rounds with more likes and RTs than he'd seen in a while; plus it was top of his recommendations which intrusively meant it had to be about cricket. The footage, obscured every now and again by trees, showed what appeared to be a calamitous fielding session, human targets fleeing from balls bound for them, the hashtags ShakyXI, ShakyTrials and FieldersOptional accompanying the Tweet. It was difficult not to find the video funny, a cricket ball assault Warner Bros Cartoon style, segments in slow motion when the balls struck, changing expressions accompanied by the score from Platoon. As a counter, someone had tagged Chad being struck in the corridor and Onka instantly recognised his captain-to-be.

The walk from the bus stop to the pharmaceutical company's service accommodation was short, convenient even, along an attractive line of post-Victorian terraced houses, not a wall or guard in sight, sash windows on display for even the most limited criminal to contemplate. Onka knew his mother would be home as she was settling into remote working, an ironic circumstance thought Onka, traveling all the way to the United Kingdom from the southern tip of Africa only to work from home some of the time.

When he entered and dropped his backpack his mother knew instantly, but the parental push towards perceived 'right paths' and excellence had to kick in, even though she knew her son oh too well. And, without admitting it, she'd felt it too.

"Mom, it's ... um, just not right for me. But I know the sacrifices you've made to get us here ... and the bursary."

"My son," said Onka's mother, reaching upwards to take his face in her hands. "I have always backed your judgement: you above all others in my life, know what is best ... for you. And whatever you want to do ... I'll support. Even if it means ditching that snooty place. But understand what you're giving up ... longer term."

"There's a school called Shackleton - it's not, erm ... the same as Corkridge."

"Not many schools are."

"This school - Shaky they call it," averting his eyes from his mother's fleetingly. "They're putting together a cricket team."

Chapter >> 26

Tandem

"You two are going to be joined at the hip from now on," Enid exclaimed, quite matter of fact for such a prescriptive fiat.

"What, me and the big fella?" Noel, from beneath Daughtry's shade.

Yapa and Wei Ping set up apparatus in the background, an isolated corner alongside the cricket pitch, behind the clubhouse to the right and close enough to the stream to hear it gurgle. A disused Tennis wall, that most almost failed to notice during the clean-up, had been rectified to past glory with a line of tennis rackets laid out perpendicular to the wall. Yapa surreptitiously reviewed a piece of paper, shoved it back in his pocket then instructed Wei Ping who, now even more confused, continued to pull the heavy high jump mat towards the bars.

"Might be easier the other way around," Corin, mucking in to secure one side of the bars.

"Feels like we're celebrity guinea pigs," Noel, scrunching his nose in derisory excitement. "Can't we get back to my head attached to her hip?"

"Daughtry, you're going that way," Enid motioning towards the now assembled high-jump mat. "And Noel you're with me this way."

"This might hurt," Daughtry, as they separated in east west directions.

"Can't be more painful than the trials," Noel, march-skipped behind Enid.

Within earshot of both, Yapa set the scene: "You, must use both hands to play cricket and you, must get your limbs twitching; faster. Ambidextrous ability and long limbs. Both for speed; one for confusion; other including height. Clear?"

"As the birds in the rafters after a visit from HB."

The bluffers guide to cricket had preceded this soirée including Larry who had to dash to help out at the golf range, a protraction of development as far as Yapa was concerned. All three seemed keen and had the basics of the game and general coordination down pat enough to warrant moving into more obscure, natural skills enhancement territory. Corin was yet to be convinced, an acrophobe peering over the edge of a building.

Daughtry's first high jump attempt was set at a whopping two metres, intentionally so as Yapa was aware she had pole-vaulted in the past. There was no fear of the height for her, just the mechanics of how to approach, the lanky limbs all needing to work together in the approach and then the bit Yapa was most interested in ... the snap: arm, leg, hand, shoulder twitch muscles to move in unison quicker than Daughtry had ever experienced. He was trying to bend her into whipping limb speed, getting those levers to fire in quick succession around a suspended bar. The first few jumps were not half bad, a head butt of the bar or two and an increasing acceptance the height might never be cleared aside. The approach, movement and beginning of the snap all equally encouraging.

Noel, at the other end facing the Tennis wall with Enid,

knew he needed to snap out of joker-boy, charming charmless disassociation mode and flaunt some boss-level knacks. His task was to keep the ball going, hitting it against the wall and back to himself but interchanging racquets on the floor, alternating hands. Wei Ping marvelled at how equidistant his racquet placement was, which went unnoticed by Enid. Wherever the ball went, Noel would need to pick up the closest racquet, but ensure his hands always alternated to hit the ball above the net line, chalked on the wall. Once Noel took up the mantle, his first attempt went to double figures which he seemed mighty impressed with, glancing over at Daughtry to see if she was watching.

She wasn't, more intent on clearing the bar as the possibility grew.

Enid wanted Noel to get to 100 consecutive transposing, above-the-line shots, struggling to resist scoffing in the face of a stretch challenge. That afternoon felt markedly warmer, as summer's impending encounters approached, a nervous disposition clambering upon the Hanratty girls with each sunrise and set. Just as darkness descended, Daughtry, her body bruised from the intent, gave out a victorious holler, Noel peering fleetingly across the beetle-humming dark field on 98, only to ping one over the wall. It was too dark to continue and Noel collapsed in dejection, knowing he was two strokes from glory as the revelries emanated from the grey shadows, the jumping up and down on the PVC mat perhaps even involving Yapa. It was nice to hear Daughtry laugh, a deep, guttural titter from high up in the darkness.

Enid, holding onto the missing two glance, resisted congratulating Noel, knowing he'd want to make up for it sooner or later, if only to impress his fellow quick. A torch shone to illuminate the scene …

Wei Ping was always prepared.

Chapter » 27

Conditions

"We have problem. Problems," rattled Yapa, holding up a printed email. "We have to qualify before the season - or we cannot play. Qualification will not be easy: badly organised, old blind umpires, wet pitches, bad grounds, unknown opposition."

"How many qualification games?" Enid asked, leaning forward to straighten something on Yapa's desk.

"All knockout. Lose one: gone. Sixteen teams vying for final spot in four pools with pool draw mandatory two weeks before start of season. If no completion of qualification matches - down to the four new teams to arrange - forfeit. Not yet clear how the sixteen will become four - how the group broken up - but have to be complete in one month."

The sturdiness of the reality that the season started in six weeks was the slap across denial's face that was probably necessary. Acceleration of plans now became the order of the day and corners sliced to smithereens as, two of the next four weekends required two winning matches on April pitches after a thunderous March.

"So, we don't even know who we're meant to play yet, but

we have to play them?" Corin asked, slumping back in the chair.

"These challenges not uncommon," Yapa retorted, matter-of-factly. "In school sports, deadlines often set without proper consideration of lead-up. We need to make sure everything works in our favour: force games, structures, venues without waiting for confirmation. Bureaucracy will take too long."

"We don't even have a full team yet," Enid, ripping the elephant out of the corner and into the centre of the room.

"Will have to just field eleven humans; continue building the team while playing matches. You two will have to win games on your own."

The two girls looked at one another, a now familiar reaction to most things cricket, life, consternation and peril. They could do this … just one innings or spell as surely the opposition couldn't be that good.

"Much interest in Digners because of funding, broadcast, so many teams want to make it: qualify and play. There will be good players. Lots of boys' schools want to secure funding for future years."

"Well, if we're going to do this thing we've got to … beat the best to play the best."

"Then lose," responded Corin flippantly, instantly regretting deflating the modicum of mojo left dangling from the elephant's trunk.

Yapa wasn't done: "Qualification criteria assess coach credentials, facilities, pitch condition, rule understanding, team participation, player availability and more."

"Poifect," Corin spat.

Just then there was a knock at the door, a welcome (if atypical) distraction from any more of Yapa's dénouements. Enid instinctively hopped and opened the door. It was raining outside, now even more unwanted moisture than before … a lanky boy who didn't seem too accustomed to the rain or favouring his face being damp in any way, nodded a polite if slightly impatient greeting Enid's way, desperate to get out of the downpour. He wore casual summer clothes: a dark green t-shirt and kaki orange-beige shorts, all sodden right through, stuck to his skin like fly paper.

"Sorry to interrupt," he said stepping through the entrance, bringing his accompanying wetness like a cloak behind him, wiping his face with his palm and looking as though he needed to shake the film of water on his hair but considerately opting to stay still in fear of soaking the girl who'd opened the door. "The headmaster said I could find you here - Mr Yapa? Today is meant to be my induction day at Shackleton but I think meeting you might just be it. I'm Onkarabile."

God has answered our prayers. Well, a few of them anyway.

Chapter >> 28

Deflection

The coach had drilled them hard that day, the pre-season fitness routines, likely a nudge from Daniels given the impending season and added significance of the expanded competition, interest and pride at stake. The Corkridge XI had previously never fallen foul of Mr Miller - the Human Kinetics (fancy name for PE) head and Conditioning Coach - mainly because they hadn't needed to, blitzing most opposition in front of them without nicking a sweat. Yet sweating they were today, despite the initial filthy glances - Chad included - when charged to belt out more burpees. Half-way (hopefully) through the session while Danny and James threw up in the rose bushes, Chad had diplomatically played the old 'we function best with a bat and a ball' card as opposed to military style rugby training that many had been involved with but accepted more readily in rugby season. Mr Miller, not in any mood for pushback, had ordered Danny to sit on Chad's back during the plank as a result, the waft of Danny's sick breath and extra few pounds he'd acquired over Easter enough to push Chad closer to the flopping down brink, a nose in the grass almost unfathomable, as he defiantly glowered up at Miller's dense pink cantaloupe calves.

Mr Miller was notorious for never cracking a smile, not even a smirk bar that one isolated incident during gym vault practice when a kid hit the front of the trampette at full pelt, careering chest first into the wooden horse, shattering the apparatus, leaving his bunny ear legs sticking out from the middle and his glasses over by the rings. Even then, though, onlookers said it was a mild nostril flare at best, yet Chad was convinced Miller was smirking as his elbows shook beneath Danny's encumbrance, brittle attempts to transfer the tension by making contact with the ground admonished by Miller who took to kicking Danny's suspended feet. Chad could feel his forehead blood boiling as Miller finally relented and allowed them all a ninety second water break.

At the water fountain, the Corkridge cricket team were done, breathing like upset soap stars, red blotchy faced, crusted lips all clambering for the one dribbly fountain, a dog-eat-dog zombie apocalypse to secure hydration. Chad, normally corroborating chatty tuition come rain, shine or apocalypse, hadn't the energy to even muster any form of rebellion, his arms limply by his sides, Danny steering well clear even at the risk of missing the fountain. Chuck, traditionally one of the fittest in the group, sat with his back against the small brick wall at the outer edge of the quad, without the energy to perch on top. It was inevitable and it would be James, frantic to liquidate his parched, burning insides, who dipped his head into Pissing Pete's stream, the nymph-inspired, fish-holding statue in the middle of the quad providing brief - if dangerous - respite. A teacher wandering by would surely dish out a detention or ten but when compared with actual death, James felt this was a worthwhile risk.

"Time's up," belted Miller's tune from the field of tortured dreams. "Almost half-way! Let's get trotting around the field once again to get the blood back to normal lactic pump levels."

At the end Chad, Chuck, James, Danny and Rufus trudged back to their boarding houses, dragging the lids of their feet, a beleaguered Boyband exiting stage left to no rapturous applause.

"The black Saffa's gone," piped Chad eventually. "To Shaky."

The other four, if they'd have had the energy to reel back in shock-horror, would have, but they didn't, a dissenting grunt about as much as each could muster.

"No great loss," Chad continued, finding untapped vigour in admonishment. "He wouldn't have bowled for us, but he will be part of the opposition now - no matter how pathetic they are - so we'll have to treat him as such."

"I saw some videos of him on Insta," began Rufus, wiping the al dente sweat from his temple. "From a while ago but he defected from a rival school: Michaelhouse to Hilton or something, and they hated him for it; he'd committed the cardinal sin of playing for the enemy. But he looked a tidy bowler, giving nothing away, even—"

"Wait!" interrupted Chad, stopping the group in its tracks with the foisting eureka moment. He looked at each in turn, then his glare came to rest on Rufus.

"You've given me a splendid idea Roofy ... and you're going to be the one to execute it."

Chapter » 29

Lofted Drive

Once Miss Hazard got wind of the qualification criteria, she set about gathering momentum across the school, delving into the empty coffers of school spirit to build enough solidarity, momentum and hype to get Shaky over the line, whatever the ask. She pommelled from all sides, championing the cause to prove the left-field assessments including school spirit, facilities, understanding of the game and readiness to host matches. This meant the spotlight would be more like a strobe, starting with support (read: removal of detention allocations and test resitting to prevent year failure) to clean up and improve the cricket facilities and shining all the way to taster (read: bluffer) courses after lessons on the rules, basics and fundamentals of cricket, her own brand of representing the quirks and subtleties of the game unmistakable.

The kudos grew, Miss Hazard's energy and conviction contagious enough to sway even the most cynical of Shaky's underachieving finest. There had been no chat of captaincy or vice-captaincy, but by design the school simply associated the leadership of the cricket team with Enid and the supporting wingwoman role with Corin. Having often been viewed as a single entity, it was welcomed to have the perceptions fitting into more defined roles, and the notoriety became irrefutable even if a bit misunderstood. The Hanratty girls had become mythical creatures, 'masters' of a game few royally understood, a game that appeared technical, brutal and … dare anyone admit this … fun!

As Shackleton's official colours were yellow and brown, Miss Hazard ran a poll to establish new colours for the cricket team, the end result ordaining purple, sage and magenta. The clubhouse became a spotless kaleidoscope of the three designated colours, and the pride of the upgrade even blushed the toilets sparkly like a five-star hotel. The clubhouse's balcony – previously a treacherous health and safety disaster, unable to cope if a pigeon's stray feather settled there – got some love and structural attention from a student's father in the building trade, a spare afternoon for the greater good becoming endemic. This was the improvement montage Shaky so desperately required, now the cricket team had to emulate the progress.

T-shirts were printed, inscribed with "Shaky Cricket XI … sockin' it to da man" to honour Enid's first practice and call to arms. The garments failed to fall foul of the 'cool kids' who brought their mode including tying a knot above the belly button, drawing various rude appendages around the word 'man' and wearing it over their blazers. As Miss Hazard stated, "If it flies, let it go," to some quizzical glares from the most rigid teaching faculty members. A cheerleading group formed from the drama students, a mischievous mix of genders bringing a version of pompomless street dance, that defied the tired popping, locking and breaking, conducting a creeper-weed explosion of limbed emotion that it was difficult to argue didn't perfectly embody Shakey's new inward self-awareness. It was likely a clash of styles and cultures when pitted against the deep hum of a boys' school anthemic, elbow-locking, primal chanting.

None of this happened overnight but the speed with which Shaky's version of solidarity was attained was impressive. The anarchist rebels who were so mainly for the sake of, remained so, even staging a mini protest while the clubhouse was being decorated, chaining themselves to the balcony, arguing than conformity of any institution - in particular a recreational sport which 'embraced Colonial evils' - was blindly following in a one-way maze. The decorators, too lethargic to point out the irony of fighting non-conformity with non-conformity plus the maze analogy confusion where the mere essence of a maze is multiple-choice, instead took to a physical protest of their own, accidentally-on-purpose shoving a chanter over the edge of the balcony to hang out there indefinitely. Despite the other protesters' best efforts, no one could pull the dangling ze/zir up, a few errant splatters of purple, sage and magenta paint going accidentally-on-purpose astray over the edge of the balcony until the spectacle was complete: "If you support the Shaky Cricket team, raise your arm and scream Ahhhhhhh!"

Chapter >> 30

Next Pair

Rebecca was a good golfer. Her parents, attempting to steer her away from the social elements that blighted many a teenager's prospects, had encouraged smacking plastic balls into an Amazon-bought home golf net while Danny bowled finger spin between Belvita snacks. Rebecca's relationship with Charlie Hastings had been more of a cover - a visibility cloak - than a relationship where anything actually happened.

Between the two Hallow-Jensen siblings - with only ten months separation - there had been a contrary allocation of genetics between angular and curved ... round to the naked, less discerning eye. Rebecca's angles had accentuated as her teens progressed as did the curvature (translation: roundness) of Danny's features. Her jawline, pointed upturned nose and diamond-shaped eyes along with linear body proportions gave her too much "Are you a model" surplus attention, as Rebecca neither wanted to model or have little boy flappers wanting her to be their model. She'd spotted Chuck at one of the rare excursions to watch Danny's team play, a lack of crowds at these events there never was, and he seemed like the tall, confident, almost-alpha type who might be a foil to shun the advancing masses, yet busy and driven enough not to want to hold hands at the latest Marvel disaster.

The beginning of the relationship was perfect for Rebecca: her air cover established with 'Chabecca' the clunky collective for them as an 'item' and Chuck with cricket commitments aplenty, honing her golf skills while keeping tabs on her Charlie through her brother. And Chuck did have a feared reputation around the schools in the region too: a rumour had floated that Rebecca was asked out by a rival cricketer from her co-ed school. As the unfortunate timing between Rebecca's refusal permeating in Chuck's direction and a school match between her school and Corkridge, the puppy-keen opening bat received what onlookers described as a ferocious onslaught of quick bowling, everything short and mostly around the wicket. One such delivery rose to decimate the potential suitor's helmet grill, forage through towards his nose and break it in the process. While he wept blood on the pitch, Chuck inscribed the word 'Chabecca' with the edge of his spike, creating grooves for the smelted blood to flow down, mythical fantasy trailer style. The boy was caried off on a stretcher and would wear two racoon-black eyes for months as punishment for sniffing in Chuck's girlfriend's direction, his broken nose healing faster than his and his team's pride after Chuck tore through the rest, taking five wickets and leaving a delible mark to aim at on the pitch.

During Rebecca's fine-tuning of her draws and fades at the golf range, she befriended the owner's daughter who worked there with her brothers ... Lauren was her name, but she insisted on being called Larry. Rebecca's first encounter with Larry had been curious: with her number one wood out and already making some pinging, crisp-sounding connections, Rebecca really got hold of one, whipping her hips through the ball and unleashing a full-blooded swing that felt and sounded ideal, the rubber tee quivering to a standstill and the pink Titleist making for the outer realms of the driving range, past the 250m mark. Suddenly out of nowhere a girl with what looked like short hair appeared from nowhere and the ball struck her on the head, a gathering of boys aligned next to her appearing to have pushed her into the flight of the ball. There were no other punters that day, so Rebecca had sprinted over to make sure whoever had stumbled into the ball's path was … alive.

When she arrived at the scene there was a clump of boys admiring the girl's egg on her forehead – a swollen slushy badge of honour it seemed – and the girl herself, eyes a grey-green shine, small statured with a messy fringed bob, hysterical herself. Rebecca, looking around for medical attention in the form of parental help, would instinctively push the boys aside and stare over the girl, her scruffy hair perfectly framing the bulge, parenthesis on either side of an Asterix of dark blue (*). The girl's hysteria presented as laughter and Rebecca would come to know that this was a game – much to their father's distaste – of avoiding the drives but leaving it as long as possible, a skim, glance or graze being awarded extra points. That day Larry had made the schoolgirl error of taking her eye off her older brothers, permitting an opportunist shove into Rebecca's golf ball's trajectory … cue mirth, felicitations and merriment.

Since then, Rebecca had spent more time with Larry at the driving range, a bond forming as the egg subsided and the personalities emerged. Rebecca marvelled at Larry's cavalier attitude and toughness, never shying away from any brotherly challenge and making gay abandon look like something underplayed by anyone risking just about everything, all the damn time. It made Rebecca question many a life's motive, in particular, stringing Charlie along while she discovered who she was, so when she mentioned taking a small break, all hell would break loose, largely manifesting in Chuck's precipitous inability to bowl. Initially merely what Chad termed "Not ideal conditions for the quicks and not his best spell" and not particularly concerned, what with the fast bowler reserves at his disposal, when he couldn't land the ball anywhere of accurate note three matches on the bounce, Chad's early bowling changes became ... observable. Chuck at full pelt was a key part of the Corky XI puzzle and, his swollen eyes and wet pillow threw up a conundrum that Chad would employ Danny to fix. Almost out of character, this break hit Chuck harder than the golf ball struck Larry, and his inability to shake this for the sake of the cricket team spelled drastic action as the season approached. Chad instructed Danny to sort his sister out while he went about sorting Chuck out, whose action not only lost that fluid rhythmical approach of all good fast bowlers, but reawakened a forgotten bad habit which had almost landed Corky in hot water some seasons ago: Chuck's bent elbow on select deliveries. Much of Chuck's early pace had come from apprehensions that he threw the ball, his elbow going past the fifteen-degree allowance, resulting in video evidence of matches being heavily scrutinised by the ECB and Chuck forced to lessen the fulcrum. The Corkridge cricket academy directors had removed Chuck from the system while he underwent extensive recalibration and training, to emerge faster and closely on the borderline of the fifteen degrees legal versus illegal deliveries. When the new assessment happened though, Corky's academy had supplied extracts of match and indoor training footage, so Chuck was deemed a legal bowler for all school, club and junior county tournaments. Most observers felt though – in particular the 'bloodbath spell' – that Chuck was throwing to generate more pace and lift.

Chuck, likely not having had much rejection in his life, moped around the boarding house, refusing to shave, smile, lift his eyelids or his knuckles from the ground. He took to texting Rebecca incessantly, a detailed description daily at minimum, about how she was the girl for him, bestowing her virtues on her (and Larry as the two found jollity from reading them aloud and miming her princess traits for an audience of one) when in fact Rebecca felt she wasn't the girl for anyone, the ownership intimation of a male's 'girl for me' rhetoric nauseating to the point of actual stomach acid popping above the trachea when fake-hurling. The communications pushed Rebecca further from ending the small break, instead widening the distance to the point of establishing permanence. She loved Larry's reaction to it all too: a clear form of entertainment but with enough sympathy and forbearance to know that this was an actual human being's feeling, so being heartlessly cavalier in response would be cruel. Also Larry didn't prescribe anything concerning Rebecca - she never told her how to act, what to do or how to treat Chuck - there was no ulterior motive but there was an entertainment quotient that would be sacrificed if Rebecca fronted up and told Chuck it was time to stick a fork in 'Chabecca'.

Chapter » 31

Rain Delay

Wei Ping, increasing his worth with every ball shined and phone call made, was instrumental in making sure the qualification matches happened. It got complicated as the Digners format was still under debate, the ECB, county junior bodies and school sports administrators all wanting different formats emphasised, some wanting a more substantial return to Test structures to recure the national game, others intent on embracing even shorter than the shortest format, and further others wanting to reinvigorate what was believed to be flagging before England won the World Cup: One Day or 50 overs. Some small factions even wanted to embrace the village cricket leagues with playing to time, time-based declarations and overs from a certain point touted until sanity prevailed with the poor confused spectator held as fodder to keep it simple, stupid.

With negotiating not normally associated as one of Wei Ping's core character peculiarities, he astutely picked the format where Shaky would likely have the best chance, both from winning and getting completed standpoints. Not only did he orchestrate that the other three in Shaky's 'group' were comparatively weaker teams (cobbling together through a whole day on the phone to agree structures, venues and formats) but he also managed to guarantee that the two T20 qualification matches would take place on the same day. There were two snags: one that this was the final weekend to complete the qualification rounds with the previous washed out (only minor showers forecast today), and two, that it had to be far away from the now sparkling Shaky Cricket pitch as one of the opposition teams had no ability to travel so, Wei Ping sorted a cricket venue behind a distant relative's Chinese Takeaway near the school. Wei Ping had caught a train after school to check the venue out and, although the girls were dubiously prudent about Wei Ping's increasing cricket knowledge - specifically pitch conditions - they trusted his intentions and, after all, how bad could bad be? Wei Ping had asked his cousin's uncle twice removed to pop down to the ground with his mower the day before so at worst, the ground would look shorn and ready for play.

Well ...

It was a sight and the lump that formed in Enid's throat coagulated in Corin's when she threw a ball down hard on the pitch and it didn't bounce ... at all. With the Chinese restaurant's presence, the field was sort of a ghost shape, the establishment clearly having been built without planning permission, approved by a council desperate to flog off semi-used amenities. A good straight bat six might end up through a window and served with the chicken chow mein! Undeterred, the owners had set up outdoor stalls to sell snack Chinese take-away pots, the margins eye-wateringly opportunist for a captive audience that likely didn't have spectator parents to bring the cucumber sandwiches.

With Jacob yet to formally transfer to Shackleton, it meant that five places had to be filled to join Enid, Corin, Onka,

Daughtry, Noel and Larry, the luxury of a twelfth man too much to even contemplate. The trialists group - some consistently unequivocal in their cricketing self-belief - had largely boycotted when the sisters and Yapa came calling, touting pride and exclusionary discrimination despite the wave of positive sentiment sweeping through Shaky as a result of Miss Hazard's tireless campaign. One girl did relent, however, but forgot her glasses so would play the entire match blind with a prescription somewhere between 5 and 7. The four remaining places in the team were predominantly Shaky kids who were always picked last during PE, the stragglers who'd never really played cricket yet wanted to be part of the patriotic madness and help (help!) however they could even if it meant putting a foot between a travelling ball and that strange thick rope than surrounded what appeared to be a circle with a dent containing a Chinese restaurant. Those girls had misrepresented on the bus when explaining the shape of a cricket field!

The kit adopted was ... sundry, both of the assortment adjective and Australian extras noun. Despite a concerted push from Miss Hazard, the official kit supplier was nowhere near ready. So, without any matching kit, the eleven - including some of the incumbents you might assume to know better - came in all styles, cuts, colours, shades and expressions: two of the new enlistees wore superhero shirts, Corin convinced that Batman was a better fielder than Spidey; one wore denim shorts and another a gilet. Other accessories included a beanie (Noel), a crop-top, jeggings, a base layer (Daughtry), flip-flops (Larry), a bright red McEnroe headband, hockey shin guards, weights gloves, a Man City football shirt and a slogan t-shirt with WTAF emblazoned across the chest. Indeed.

So if the day began with a voyage of misguided, haphazard, increasingly pessimistic discovery, the news that greeted the first Shackleton XI in over two decades was, well ...

encouraging. The fourth team of the group - scheduled to play Shaky in what was hyped as the first semi, forfeited, meaning Shaky progressed straight to the final, as long as the other game could maintain attention long enough to complete, the dandelions outside the boundary already all blown to smithereens.

After hurrying up to wait true cricket style, even if the pontification was more headless newbie official / coach than a structured, unnecessary hour-and-a-half obligatory warm-up, the first semi did eventually get underway even if both sides were so full of MSG there were select cricketers glowing radioactive as the toss-winning opening batting pair slumbered out to take guard. The first ball almost saw the demise of the day's credentials as the ball failed to reach the batsman, embedding into the pitch, freakily finding the only remaining tuft of untended grass, causing differing brands of consternation from both teams. Once the tuft had been flattened, play resumed and thankfully the ball made it to the bat, even if keeping lower than a lawnmower's blade and bouncing six times en route to the keeper who promptly misfielded and allowed the first run - a bye - jotted down by Wei Ping, who had accepted the scoring duties with aplomb, whipping out his iPad with cricket app downloaded and tons of YouTube instructional videos absorbed. As per the rules, there was another scorer alongside, the table, now with only hot and sour soup and spring rolls outstanding, a pressing station for doodles in an old scorebook that was actually full, the most recent date captured 1983.

As the game progressed with what seemed like more appeals than the litigious United States of America - one appeal even after a four was mowed over cow corner - Corin checked out, deeming this a forgone conclusion, fork protruding, won and home before Dad ordered the curry. Enid, however, was more guarded, especially with the introduction of a number 3 bat from the side chasing, the first innings wrapped up for a double figure score. His technique looked clumsy - cumbersome even - but he seemed to be unwilling to go out despite a half-decent medium pacer perhaps moving the ball away and a variable pitch that threw up skidders and bouncers in succession. He somehow found a way to stay in and then sound judgement when to score, seeing the chasing team to victory with an over to spare, a full 39 overs complete in the day thus far, a minor miracle at the start of the day.

The break was longer than normal as some dark grey clouds teetered in the distance, the opposition in the final claiming exhaustion as rationale to push the match to another day, the not out bat Enid was wary of the only desperado keen to play more cricket. After much cajoling, the toss happened and the opposition, patently wanting a breather away from fielding, chose to bat and set a target as the sky became increasingly dark. Noel and Daughtry opened the bowling, a nifty left right-hander bowling combo with Corin happy to be first change for the greater good. The pitch did little to support what looked like good pace through the air, even if Noel wasn't swinging anything and Daughtry kept scuppering her heightened reach by collapsing her front knee. The errant nature of the opening spell saw extras as the likely top-scorer and, with the odd wicket to keep Shaky's buoyancy teetering, Enid deciding to hold Onka and herself back as long as possible with wrist spin likely redundant on this track, especially if overpitching as both leggies had correctly erred towards all throughout their junior years. From over eight an issue developed: four down with the clutzy keeno blocking up Corin's end and a hotstepper turning all of Onka's deliveries into full tosses, established an obdurate yet free flowing stand that threatened to make the chase problematic. With Noel and Daughtry bowled right through, having used up their four overs maximum each, Enid had to keep some of Corin's spell back until the death, a left and right hand tandem of leg spinners - despite being mouth-watering to the enthusiast - proving high risk against this opposition, with flight dying before reaching the stumps and flatter getting no bounce and certainly no turn. The partnership grew, taking the opposition's score - much to the surprise and merriment of the onlooking team members - to a respectable 100 with three overs left to bowl. Larry even had a trundle, tired of holding the squatting keeping pose, which ended badly as the support fielders in the team lost interest on the boundary and started picking baby daisies rather than stopping edges. Corin, visibly raging at the state of affairs finally broke the partnership and wrapped up most of the tail for a neat Nelson's 111. Bouncy, smiley, clutzy fellow remained not out, peppy gas still pestilentially in the tank as Shaky sped off to pad up, the first drops of rain speckling the shoulders of the players.

Word from the dugout - if you could stretch to call the now decimated Chinese box graveyard a dugout - was that if ten overs couldn't be bowled the match was forfeited, Wei Ping's officious Googling unable to bend the more entrenched regulations. Enid instructed Larry to pad up - she was opening the batting - and supplemented something like "Those pads had better be on before I finish this sentence," Larry's response a saluted aye-aye as Corin was already having throwdowns. The umpires, doddering as a kind description with teeth longer than attention spans, eventually made their way out into the middle, wincing upwards at the increasingly heavy rain spatters, followed closely by the two opening bats. The fielding side, sensing a way out of this with some shelter in the Chinese restaurant promising, were even more lethargic, Corin having taken guard before the first field placing was gingerly instructed. When the opening bowler had measured his mark for what felt like a dozen occasions, the second innings kicked off and what happened next would go down in qualification cricket and Hanratty family folklore … alas for Corin.

A full toss above waist high appeared, red, rosy, swollen and appetising before Corin's eyes, the umpire not wavering and Corin, in that split-second, not gauging that the ump hadn't signalled an above waist high full toss no-ball. Corin swung to beat the weather, kick the game off with a juicy maximum and chase down this score early, skying the ball directly over the bowler's head. A chasing fielder, suddenly energised, tore from deep extra cover, a moth drawn to the flaming red ball. Not many people even noticed this, but the ball grazed the television aerial on top of the Chinese restaurant, hitting the horizonal extensions in a flurried pin-ball effect, then popping up just outside the fielder's reach. What happened next made the situation even more bizarre yet distracted from the invisible aerial deflection sufficiently to make it plausible: the hurtling fielder couldn't brake in time so just kept running, the ball striking his foot, flicking upwards across to cow corner where the fielder, chilling there, plucked it out of the air and claimed the catch. The umpires, after a brief consultation, give it as out and Corin was forced to depart after one delivery. Onka was in next and managed to observe actual flames coming from Corin's nostrils so, ever the pro, knew to leave her alone, nodding and heading past her towards the crease, ready to get on with the job while the opposition continued celebrating.

Onka needed to suss the wicket out and did so before receiving a pea shooter along the ground to bowl him, the force of the impact barely enough to dislodge the bails. He kind of apologised to Enid who, not unkindly, ignored him as she strode to the crease to join Larry, daring not to think how few batters remained, their tail rivalling a ring-tailed lemur's! Cricket was a funny old unforgiving sport where a freak occurrence, a good ball and a misjudged shot or two could destroy the batting chase and, having not yet reached double figures, Shaky were in tangible danger of being skittled out for an embarrassing total and never even getting to bowl a ball in anger in the Digners Cup. Larry, blissfully unaware of the direness of the cricketing situation with two of the rarefied recognised batters back in the hut, swung at just about anything, her small stature a fizzing ball of vim even when only making contact with the air surrounding the ball. A few edges here and there at least meant the score climbed, with Enid finding the twos and threes to a lacklustre fielding unit. A scary moment took place in the sixth over when still grinning double not out chap whipped one in from cover point: a direct hit with Larry some way out of her ground. The umpire's potential three figure innings and failing eyesight claimed the fielder was in his line of sight, thus he couldn't give it out, Larry unperturbed, weaving and bobbing in anticipation for the next delivery, body language un-obliviously 'in by a mile'.

Enid then held much of the strike which was a blessing as Larry's cavalier luck was bound to run out, the fielding side sensing they might have a shot, so concentrating efforts and making bowling changes that made actual sense. The rain began sheeting down, waves coming through drenching the players as Wei Ping yelled on "Ten overs minimum to complete the match," Enid nodding knowing that she had probably one over left to smash 20 runs. There was no way this game could get to ten overs, so she had to deal in boundaries in the eighth over and get to 112. The first three balls went for fours leaving eight from the last three, the coaches motioning them all to come off. Enid, going for a six, miscued and found a fielder, refusing the single as the words "Last over; you must come off!" rang from the sideline. The next ball she also failed to middle but found a gap between mid-wicket and square leg, scampering through the driving rain, their kit completely drenched and shoes sloshing as they turned for the fourth run but, realising this was a guaranteed run out, left Larry with an urgent ball to face and five runs to win. As the bowler begrudgingly strode in, Larry came walking down the track, really from necessity as the rain made it impossible to see the bowler or where the ball was coming from ... Enid heard a bat on ball connection of sorts as the ball went flying over the keeper's head, looking like a one bounce four, only for the other ageing umpire to squint into the distance, removing his glasses, signal a six then hobble for cover followed by the protesting fielders and two bemused batters.

As they all huddled under the overhang of the restaurant, a debate ensued, Yapa getting more demonstrative with each contravention put to him. Ably supported by Wei Ping, arguing that the signal had been made and recorded in the scorebook, the game was won by Shackleton, hence no need to complete the designated ten overs minimum. There was a muted celebration by the victors, few – including the Hanrattys – fist pumping a treacherously precarious nudging over the line.

The bus ride home was sombre, the unyielding rain a persisting reminder of the earlier events. Some might argue that the tone should have been relief – an embracing of the fortune (and misfortune) bestowed upon the team having (likely) qualified for Digners – but instead a reality crept in that to beat good teams there would need to be a seismic shift in ... something. The plucky underdog story wouldn't wash when playing a team that actually knew how to play cricket. The sisters sat side by side, staring ahead as the calm bus driver navigated the increasingly nocent conditions outside. Neither fiddled with a loose strand of cotton; no nervous energy, just a spent consciousness that even personnel improvements would do little to change the outcomes. The cynical seed growing in Enid was that, even with the utmost planning and tactics for specific individuals, there would always be the conditions to contend with and, more importantly, the high probability that the best laid plans couldn't be executed as intended; and even if they could, improved opposition had their own tricks and adaptations to counter.

Corin took her sister's hand, sensing something was draining - the see-saw tipping her way, instinctively realising it was her turn to push off the ground. Corin didn't have the answers either but, having restored some sanity after her first ball royal duck rock bottom, it felt like the experience had to make them all stronger, mentally at least, but something was missing from the team. She couldn't help thinking of her father, and the magnitude of what he'd gone through compared to sneaking a tight game in front of an intrusive Chinese restaurant against a team that would probably never play a game of cricket again. She shuddered, a whole cricket team fielding on her grave: if winning felt this low against that team, how would losing the Ashes against the Aussies in the final play of the game feel? She felt a tear dribble down her cheek and quickly wiped it away with the back of her hand but not before Enid spotted her.

"Dad?" asked Enid.

Corin nodded. "Playing a match … it became a bit more real: his endeavour … and his pain."

Enid squeezed back, strengthening her resolve. "He hid it from us so well, but it feels like this is our remedy; our light; for him."

Chapter » 32

Draw

"The draw is being televised, live on Sky Sports."
"No way!"
"Way."
"Digners??"
"First time; the media interest is hyped."
"Which channel?"
"Sky Mix I think."
"That's not really Sky Sports, is it?"
"It's on TV!"
"Probably, like two in the morning, on a Tuesday."
"On Saturday before the England Test; part of a school sports segment they're running."
"Who do you think we'll get?"

Two weeks out from the start of the season, schools all across the South East gathered in living rooms, common rooms, in front of laptops, phones and even with neighbours, friends and acquaintances for those without Sky. Corkridge permitted special dispensation to miss some of Saturday school, gathering to witness the draw, Chad insisting the new boys laid out the chairs in a Wi-Fi crescent formation, condensing down to one central belvedere in front of the screen for the captain. He wasn't happy with some of the precursory clean-up efforts, so assigned additional recruits to the room prep efforts until the army had scrubbed, wiped, shined, polished, scraped, moved and washed every inch of the common room, even using linseed oil on some of the wooden furniture to make the experience even more 'crickety'.

Wei Ping invited the team around to his house, the order, snacks and cricketyness no less than Corkridge, his mother beyond delighted that this represented actual evidence that he had friends and was part of something bigger than the Game of Thrones online fan club. There were even girls coming! Bixia might be smiling on her some time down that path, who knows. She didn't know much about cricket but knew for certain than her son's involvement with a live TV event was something to be cherished, embraced and supported: her mix of homemade snacks and M&S picnic food to cover all bases in case anyone had allergies, was fussy or just fancied variety. By Bixia her son had friends! When Yapa was the first to arrive - a grown man of Sri Lankan descent - it threw her whims of an extended litter of little Wei Pings, until his polite demeanour and announcement incarnating role of school coach greeted and put her instantly at ease, offering him a chicken-and-sweetcorn sandwich filler with crackers before he'd had time to remove his shoes.

When Chad walked into the prefects' room - the first to inspect - the linseed smell greeted him and he sucked it all in, this feelgood precursor to his team's name up in light for the nation to bathe in; he wondered whether the captain's name would been read out as he had circled in yellow, green and blue highlighters on the application form. Even the sight of a small mousy boy still scrubbing the hearth couldn't indent his spirit, but that also failed to lessen the verve with which he kicked the boy out. This was Man time; Corkridge 1st XI time; Digners Draw: their Cup; their draw.

Enid and Corin arrived next, cordially handing on the homemade chocolate brownies they'd prepared, Wei Ping's mum gleefully accepting while ushering them both in, spouting "No need, no need," in case of an attempted escape. Miss Hazard pulled up in her brown Skoda and was also welcomed into the home with no let up of enthusiasm, a drink of something colourful placed in her hand. The lounge had been laid out as the epicentre of the event, garden chairs, old sofas, study chairs, utility stools and dining room chairs placed in orderly formation, the correct channel already playing what looked like Gaelic football.

The senior members of the defending champions filtered in, met with cupped sideways-fives, often authenticated with a little chest-on-chest bump action, with one significant absentee. Chad had been forced to make an executive decision based on the team's disposition, not only in the eyes of the adoring school and wider public, but the team itself: having Chuck around at the moment was just plain bad business as he remained more cut up than kirigami's finest, the Rebecca saga far from 'spanked through the covers' sorted. James had picked up much of the emotional slack left trailing like Just Married tin cans so, when he arrived, Chad held him a little closer, a little tighter, to express his gratitude. James, thinking nothing of it, kicked one of the chairs closer to the screen, fake-belched and manhandled a few of the team in preparation for the draw, now drawing mouth-wateringly closer.

»

Onka, Jacob, Daughtry and Noel followed with Larry last through the gate, having brought her friend Rebecca, introduced to the team mainstays, coach, Wei Ping and his mother, now in full-blown delirium of fussing animation.

»

Chuck made a snap decision to attend the draw in the common room with the rest of the team despite Chad's instruction to the contrary. Adding to his increasingly homeless chic, he came wrapped in a blanket, his musky solace in this cruel world, followed in close succession by his almost unbearable BO and patchy stubble. Chad, rolling his eyes to allow James to settle Chuck at the back before another bout of crying, couldn't wait for the transfer he'd spoken to Daniels about to come to fruition: Corkridge had bought the legendary Neethaniel brothers, a left and right set of opening bowlers, feared in the north of England and jettisoned down with an assurance of not having to get above 30% in any of the entrance exams. Chad twitched his head sideways, so Danny sprayed the cloth with the screen cleaner and wiped the screen's surface again, rendering the presenter's teeth glare back in brilliant contrast, appearing whiter than anything else in the studio.

»

By contrast Wei Ping's television screen was dull: no HD; not even 4K and ... not even flat, those old-fashioned sets with the back elongated and jutting out like a big fat bum, the brown wood-effect panel on the left old enough to be super-trendy. Onka, approaching the set, surveyed it like an alien craft, unsure whether to push a button and risk destruction, call for help from NASA or use the voice command he was used to, but scanning the room for a voice activated remote proved fruitless. He swung his requesting smile to Wei Ping who nodded back that they were on the right channel.

»

Daniels was not blind to the filth being served up by Chuck, elbow now more crooked than a witch's nose, flinging more errant deliveries than the world pre-DPD, so he'd shown Chad a little black ops folder of new recruits from the depths of his locked filing cabinet, the words 'Northern schoolboys bust for steroids' dropping out as part of a cut-out newspaper article. Daniels had hoped Chad would think him trendily retro still keeping old newspaper clippings; sometimes cool needs to be shown rather than acted. The Gaelic football credits ended, thank God Chad thought, as he shooed Danny away, shooshed everyone down and took his pride of place.

»

Daughtry kept bumping her head on a fake chandelier, the splashback connecting her again on the follow-through, Noel cackling at every opportunity when HB's height got in the way of her normal functioning as a human being. Every time Daughtry's head took a swing at the imposing light fixture, Wei Ping's mum would gesture and revert to speaking

Chinese, the message somewhere between profuse apology and irritation at Wei Ping's dad for not replacing with a sunken ceiling design, the touch of modernness likely to ruin the room's genuinely retro charm, with thick brown, red and yellow patterned carpet, pink tissue box covers and lace table coverings watching from just about everywhere. To cap it off, Noel asked for a phone snap of Wei Ping's mum and Daughtry, fascinated by the accentuated height differential and purposefully cutting off Daughtry's head from the top of the picture.

»

Chad couldn't help but feel distracted, fidgeting uncharacteristically, his legs and crotch composition unable to settle on a viewing pose. Pictures of the brothers had done nothing to dispel the rumourmongering: they looked like flying squirrels with yellow demonic eyes and bad skin, layers of dorks decorating pocked lizard-scale craters along their cheeks and chins. Scary to look at, let's just hope equally scary to face thought Chad, catching a glance of himself in the reflection of the flat screen TV as the adverts faded to black, his GQ-cover features enough to counter any ugly journeymen brought in to plug the festering hole of a delicate, torn up, loved-up soul. Was that a slight blemish above his left nostril? Nah, must have been a clean swipe that wasn't rubbed over properly on the set. Standards. Digners in a few years' time was toast. This era reigns hard, hammering opposition of any size, shape, gender or ability … for breakfast.

»

"Good morning sports fans! Welcome to our special edition of the South East's premier school cricket competition: the draw for the Digners Cup, a tournament steeped in the rich history of the area's public schools, now proudly appearing on Sky Sports as part of our grass roots development of the game in conjunction with the government, ECB and school sports councils of Kent and Sussex. With me, my esteemed co-host Clodagh, welcome to the draw."

"Thanks Ramsay, delighted to be here on what promises to be the start of a ground-breaking swathe of interest, support and attention for schools cricket in the region, the first time both boys and girls will be permitted to compete against one another in fully integrated teams across the schools that have qualified."

"Clodagh, for those new to this, let's educate the viewers on the structure and format of the competition this year: Digners Cup for beginners!"

"Indeed, Ramsay. We find ourselves two weeks away from the first match of the season as part of Digners ...

Not a twitched neck muscle in Wei Ping's abode, heads army-rigid, facing straight ahead, too troubled by the certainty of the modest epoch, willing Clodagh to crack on and move towards the large fake blue helmet - open side facing the studio ceiling - that likely contained the names of the teams.

High fives all round the common room, the slap of palm on palm normally so reassuring for a captain rallying the troops but, on this occasion, uncommonly sedate, even circumspect, his blinkered face also not employing any neck twitch muscles at this stage of proceedings.

»

... with four regional pools comprising six teams each. All teams in each pool play each other, so five games in total, the venue decided between the schools based on conditions, other commitments and pitch availability. Once the pool matches are complete, the top team from each pool play the knockouts starting with the semi-finals."

"Anywhere special, Clodagh?"

"Yes indeed. Although confirmation pending on the semis, the final has been confirmed to take place at the home of cricket: the Marylebone Cricket Club ... Lord's."

"With tickets available to purchase through Sky Store or using the Sky Sports app. Keep an eye out for free giveaways and whole class attendance excursions, compliments of Sky Sports as we approach the final."

»

If the two weeks wasn't enough, the mention of Lord's just made this real; so real Corin tasted her previous evening's meal at the back of her throat and the area behind Enid's ears cooled with sweat as her ears heated up.

»

"Lord's baby!" were the cries. "We're going to be playing at Lord's! Whoooo0 ... that is now my house and nobody comes disrespecting me in my house! Corky's own Lord's ... home ground advantage!"

»

"There's a quirk, isn't there Clodagh?"

"Yes, Ramsay, there is: the winner of each pool will be able to select a 'lucky loser' to play against as a warm-up game, before the knockouts."

"So, a few of those legendary school rivalries we always hear about will get the opportunity to slug it out on the pitch?"

"Shall we proceed with the draw?"

»

Wei Ping's mum, still running on excitement fumes, knew this was the moment to slink into the background, stopping short of offering snacks to all the guests for the umpteenth time.

»

A few brave backslaps dragged Chad from his stupor, one from James's huge gorilla paw. "That's how we get you your ball Bruv: if we're not in the same pool, we choose those loser bitches for the warm-up."

"Of course," snapped Chad, shrugging off James's clamped, heated hand. "What planet have you been on to not know this? Corkridge 1st XI don't live under rocks, mate; and we don't say Bruv either," Chad resuming listening out for his name in pole position.

»

The school names in the first two pools were largely unknown to the Shaky spectators, only Rebecca occasionally nodding when the printed paper was turned towards the camera. Corky, in contrast, booed and jeered most of Pool A and Pool B, artfully named after some legends of the game's forename initials, Sky's bid to make the pools more emblematically recognisable. Pool A was "WG" after the grandfather of cricket WG Grace, whose beard was once almost as wide as his bat and Pool B named "VVS" in honour of the Indian middle order bat VVS Laxman, whose heroics with the bat after following on in Calcutta against the Aussies afforded him a unique kudos. Still no sign of Corkridge or Shackleton as the tension returned …

»

"Right, that's the first two pools done and dusted; two more to go with twelve teams remaining. Have you seen your school yet?"

"Pool C or "SK" after Warnie, the greatest leggie of all, may he rest in peace … Houghton Pinnacle … Marlborough … Corkridge Castle School for Boys …"

Pandemonium breaking out in the common room, knees raised above eyelids, Chad telling everyone to shut the fecking huck up, palms slapping the air, glares darting away from the screen in FOMO disorientation.

"(and girls)"

"I believe Clodagh, that these are the current holders of the Digners Cup, the defending champions. In fact, haven't they consistently won it for the last decade or so?"

"They have, Ramsay."

"Unstoppable force it seems. Led by captain and Head Boy Chap de la Ampetals …"

Clodagh flinched, just noticeable live on TV, stopping short of correcting her co-host while Wei Ping's lounge followed suit, the hilarity of Chad's name's mispronunciation and the wonderful Clodagh refusing to rectify, breaking the tension to drag them all back to their common goal. With so much released euphoria, they almost missed Shackleton being drawn last in Pool D, named "AB" as Chad nodded in pink-faced solidarity, proving he could easily handle contumely of any kind if the team were just having a laugh.

Down below though, the pressure gauge went past red, purple and black going where no man had gone before, the entity engorging itself to the point where one further smiling, jeering face in front of his might shoot the pile - pea shooter style - so ferociously outwards, it would tear through two layers of cloth - thick cotton underwear and the finest tailored trousers - and human flesh if he accidentally aimed or someone was tragically behind him.

Chapter » 33

Bounce

When Rufus pitched up at a Shaky practice session, his approach towards the team was a tense, nature programme predator meander in a slow deliberate arc, as the Shaky baby antelopes flicked their ears and looked nervously about. All that is except the Hanrattys, who both stung a glance at Yapa who they'd ask not to invite the so-called 'new recruit'.

As he arrived at the bag graveyard, his coffin hitting the earth with a thud alongside the assembly of backpacks, plastic packets, old fashioned parent-loaned zip-up bags, tennis racket cases and travel suitcases, he smiled. He began warming up himself which also freaked everyone out. Corin strutted over towards him, knees high, determined to nip this in the bud before it became any bigger; especially as no one else seemed willing, able or intrepid enough.

"Bit obvious."

"Eh?"

"You. Here. Now. Your little buddy Chad's mastermind plan sticks out more than ... you ... here."

"I seldom got to play for Corkridge."

"Precisely."

"Look ... if cricket was that sort of game, I'd be doing a disservice to the whole institution of the sport. Let me play ... then judge."

"A few token performances in the pool games are not going to change anything."

"Might for you lot."

"Ha, ha. Corkridge humility shining forth. Plus, not necessarily performances as your MO; how about spying on us or, depending how low your team is willing to stoop, sabotage?"

"You've been watching way too much Netflix. What exactly would I report back ... this team can't play cricket? Or as a master saboteur ... saw your bats in half?"

"I wouldn't put anything past ... your kind."

"This is actually where 'your kind' faulters ... you judge my kind before you even know anything about me. Is it the wealth, the gender, the way I speak, the school ... whatever suits you to categorise me so I can be the villain in any scenario?"

Corin bit her tongue with a reactive quip - a bit of a classic but that seemed all she had left at this stage: cutting come-backs. He made sound points which made her trust him even less, polish was a Corky-boy's sublime weapon of choice, the old boys decorating The House of Commons in equal measure to the boardrooms, court rooms and anywhere else where soapboxes beckoned towards grandiose statement makers like the backwards pull of a wave getting ready to break.

"You're not going to play," said Corin after a pause, adopting absolute-submission-batter mode.

"That's not your call," Rufus puffed, resuming his workout as though he'd had enough of the exchange. "You'd be blasting your nose off to spite your face. I can play. This is now my team."

Was this the ultimate soapbox slapback: going to the core of defending a mission or just good politicking? Corin, now genuinely at a loss for words, believed the fellow at this moment, his floppy umber-coloured hair bouncing upon his sunken cheeks as he pulled down on his forearm behind his back, stretching his lats.

"The big question has to be ... why? Why take on a barrage of abuse from your old team to join the enemy? What could you possibly benefit from joining a girls' Comp team, other than winning favour with your hero-captain to secure his rather sick bet with my sister?"

"It gives me a chance to play cricket for one; and two, if I get the chance to play against my old teammates, I could prove they'd made a mistake leaving me out."

"Play 2nds!"

"No Digners."

"It's that big for you guys, isn't it?"

"I don't think it's worth telling you what I truly think of Chad—"

"The double bluff moment?"

"No. I'm just not built to be the oppressor any longer."

"Oppressor! Wow! Did you and Chad practice that in the mirror while singing into your hairbrushes?"

The question forced a grin from Rufus, further messing with Corin's head: Was he beaming because she was right, funny or wrong?

"How about this?" Corin asked, attempting to return to form before this exchange backfired beyond irrevocable. "You're a bowler who fancies himself as a bat right? Aspirations to bat up the order ... regularly?"

"I'm listening."

"If we're so bad, pad up, and get into the far left net—"

"Let me guess, pinecones dotted around for good effect?"

"Okay, I'll concede: it is a bit livelier than the others but no hazardous impediments to speak of."

"Mmm-hmmm."

"If you go out - even once - you leave and don't come back."

"Come on ... you'll be throwing the arms up in the air if I middle one through the covers. Nets never work for that because you just can't tell, and relying on the biased bowling unit, well, that'll be fun. I'm already the pariah outsider - that'll do wonders for my acclimatisation, all you lot baying for blood if the ball is an inch off the ground."

"Only bowled. And caught behind. Keeper and two slips."

"One slip?"

"Why?"

"With your attack, the luxury of a second slip is something we won't be seeing this season. That or your captain sister has a level of illogical optimism not often seen - cricket's Eddie the Eagle."

"Okay one slip. But you've got to survive an hour?"

"What else? Score a double century while I'm in there?"

"Now that you mention it ..."

"Blindfolded, batting left-handed, facing the other way, one-handed, holding my breath, miming ... all at the same time?"

"You see, it is much easier to just admit what you're up to and head on out. There will be no tail between the legs, just an efficient acknowledgement that this venture is not mutually beneficial and is completely unnecessary given the gulf in cricketing class between our two schools."

"Far left did you say?" slumping down to put on his pads. "Tell you what ... during the hour I'll guarantee to hit six sixes - any less and I'll be back picking the grass and mud out of Chad's spikes before the sun sets."

"Your words. Confidence and masochism a blurry line at Corkridge."

"If batting proves my worth and loyalty, then the cricket gods (and years of private coaching) will see me through this minor challenge. Suggest you warm up."

The ball danced. Almost as though the lively net was in on cracking the conspiracy theory, balls nipping, jagging, skidding and bouncing. And the team bowled well above themselves when Rufus went into bat - which was great to see - a collective effort of grunts, bent backs, creative wrists, overt follow-throughs and ... ultimately ... frustration. Rufus hit his six sixes early then went deep into the depths of his defensive shell, playing at nothing that was anywhere away from the stumps. His sixes had been carefully selected, knowingly watchful and aware that these bowlers - as with all bowlers to be fair - would bowl bad balls and launching a six (none of which were disputed by anyone including Corin, whose pace and movement was impressive that day hitting Rufus on the helmet and on the chest on multiple occasions) looked assured and low risk. Once the sixes were in the bag, his entire posture changed: he took guard again, this time on middle-and-off which brought about a fair few vociferous LBW shouts, many of which looked dead in the water to which Rufus kept responding "Never part of the deal." Corin couldn't help but feel even more suspicious that he'd had the nous to exclude LBs.

When the bowlers became aware of the time running out, the effort balls countered the aching fatigue, most running in even before the previous bowler had vacated the net. Rufus though, a Bear Grylls survivalist cricketing masterclass on display hopefully for everyone to at least glean how the opposition thought, would stop the bowler if not fully ready, glove raised to a cacophony of guffaws, then resume batting. On one occasion Corin ignored his pull-up from the crease and bowled anyway, clean bowling him only to snag his smug shoulder shrug of "Wasn't ready." On 55 minutes, the flurry of bowling was frenetic, laser beams of red penumbras zipping towards Rufus who would resolutely bet the old Shane Watto big front pad out in front and block, so the balls came to a dead halt, fizzling out like a dud firecracker. Seeing it the way he was and now with a measure of the net's quirks and each bowler's strength, he knew he had them beaten but, on 59 minutes Corin got one to jag away and find a thick outside edge that was likely just between first and second slip. The whole crop of bowlers went up except Enid who shook her head to an incredulous Corin, palms duck-feet outwards, expectantly dragging Yapa in who also shook his head.

"Wouldn't have carried," was Enid's prognosis as Rufus fist pumped and hip-wiggled his way out of the net past Corin, now collapsed against the side netting, dejection not even close to doing justice to where she literally sat. Rufus towered over her, putting her in shade from the setting sun and stuck a glove out to help her up.

"Now let me have a bowl at you," he said.

Chapter » 34

Driven

The line of Range Rovers adorned the bank, conspicuous shooters from the grassy knoll, all seemingly the same colour, style and model, a cookie cutter procession of organic snacks, comfortable fold-out chairs and big shades. Corkridge's warm-up games drew impressive parental and scouting crowds, starved of outdoor cricketing action throughout the colder rugby months, a clinching of summer's inchoate warmth, opportunities to bestow the hibernated one-upmanship to fellow parents, be it vicarious success, business milestones or medical procedures.

The Corkridge XI warmed up with the ferocity of a fully-fledged, mid-season team; they looked fit, lean, driven, agile and opportunistic to take the season by the scruff, drag it through a painful exposition of the opposition's cricketing frailties and dump in on the carving slab, a carcass to be filleted, consumed and defecated out. Chad strode the team out, gathering a circle of young high-achieving men together, removing himself from the embrace and standing arms-folded in the middle, his cupcake's red hatted cherry in the middle, perusing his warriors in readiness for the carnage that lay ahead, his own distinction to be exultated on high, soaring past Icarus and the sun to attain deitylike immortality if possible. Didn't the school's motto of ***Excedere Summum Propositum*** extol that very dogma? The tips of Chad's hair, recently highlighted, twinkled in the sun, Pygmalion, the grandfather of Adonis, meeting Medusa, there ... that day ... and every day until the Digners final, the sparkled shimmer, unmistakably drop-away-angled jawline and perfectly manicured sideburns ready for ... well ... anything.

"That's the captain in the middle. Chad de la Ampelas. County Captain too. Well-rounded allrounder."

"Yah, I've heard loads of stories about this young man."

"I've watched him bat. He's this, sort of cricketing genius, this perfect functioning, thinking, acting cricketer."

"Do you mean like if a cricketing God had a baby with a cricketing Goddess, then Chad would be that prodigal son?"

"Precisely, but to go one further. You know how the cricketers on television have all this promise, prowess and potential?"

"Yah, the three Ps!"

"Precisely. Well, Chad sees what's going to happen before any other cricketers and is able to adapt instantly, scoring runs or taking wickets even before it has happened!"

"What, so he sees into the future? The cricketing future?"

"In a way, yah."

The cricket on display during this warm-up match would be the equivalent of watching a superheavyweight spar with a strawweight. Chad insisted the openers retire so he could get some game time out on the pitch, coming in at number 3 with his now iconic sideways, still-armed scissor jumps, alternating each side then a long stretch down with the bat parallel to the floor. His first few balls were more circumspect than one might expect, the bowler with the long run-up not as ungainly as he looked, landing the ball in good places with purchase off the pitch. Once Chad had a measure of him though, it was like producing a coaching manual of shots around the wicket, footwork, decision making, timing and technique, with no real threat of going out and a visual treat for the onlookers, the oohs, aahs, yahs and wows showing no signs of moderating as he made a hundred without one single strand of his highlighted hair tips darkening with sweat.

"Oh my word; I mean that boy has to be the most competently assured cricketer I've ever seen this school produce. Did you see his back foot drive past cover? Shades of Gower."

"His bat is like an extension of him; connected as a wooden appendage, an extension of his being almost, the way his elbow stays so high and hands whip through the ball."

"A cricketing Zorro of his generation!"

"Yah, precisely. I've enjoyed watching him more than watching my own child."

"Oh, gawd, yes. Mine's stumbling around for the 4ths on the outer fields … I think."

"Worth the admission price it seems."

"Well, this is the most expensive school in the land but, yes, totally supportive if they can produce sportsmen like this young man."

With the ball, the balance and ferocity of Corkridge's attack looked a notch up with the addition of the Neethaniel brothers, brutish, dense muscle bulging beneath the whites like sand dunes in the distance. One boy literally cried off, unable to handle the heavy ball pace, refusing to face another ball, the tears dripping from under his helmet in breathless jerks. Just as James wasn't required with the bat, neither was Danny with the ball, the brothers tearing through to batting line-up as Chuck hid in the trees to watch a succession of bails reaching the boundary, stumps cartwheeling, batsmen ducking, crouching, crumpling and backing away, sometimes as much as three feet outside leg stump, a tentative bullfighter reaching after the bull has charged past.

The game came to a grinding halt with the final wicket, bowled middle peg, the high five between the Neethaniel brothers making a louder noise than the crack of the broken stump. Chad trotted over to the opposing captain to provide the obligatory handshake, refusing to look the boy in the eye in case he engaged, likely taken by Chad's celebrity and eager to seize this propitious occasion. A limp hand too: noted by Chad who looked for a wash basin to get rid of the ordinariness as quickly as humanly possible. Just as he was walking back towards his team, already plotting how to create a berating tone for improvement to avoid any complacency as the season began proper, a flock of geese put him in tattooed shadow, one opening its bowels, the distorted white-grey globule arriving to Chad's right. He stopped, surveyed his luck, his good fortune that he'd probably coerced nature to land the poop away from his person, deriding those morons flying the 'lucky if a bird craps on your head' flag, a brigade of losers who always got dumped upon, be it birds, girls, teachers, friends, genetics, wealth or just society at large.

He was Chad, the one whose luck wasn't just given by a bird's butthole, staring dead down at the glistening excrement, now adorning his precious cricket field, the one blemish in an otherwise perfect day. He signalled to the ground staff to sort this out, pointing downwards, a man leaping off the roller to attend to Chad's inimitable hand gestures.

Not worth spending any more time thinking about bird pooh, strutting onwards as the geese, further on and spooked by something, unleashed a rainstorm of similar intrusions all over the Range Rovers.

Chapter » 35

Keeper

Never a more apt term to lodge within a sport without the deserved acknowledgement of the magnitude, and hence discernible duple implication. Just as Chuck had branded Rebecca not 'a' keeper, but 'the' keeper. The dictionary describes the strangely dated term of a 'wicky' as *the player in a cricket team who stands behind the wicket in order to stop balls that the batsman misses or to catch balls that the batsman hits*, which is either a sporting injustice of an understatement or a subtle difference between a wicketkeeper and a 'keeper'. Good teams were inherently built around a good keeper, the positives a worthy keeper brought often not afforded even a sideways glance: the unsung hero.

Keepers had to hold a contributory batting role in the team too, often relegated to the middle order due to the physical demands of staying switched on for every single delivery during the fielding innings, or pushed up the order in the limited-overs formats as the recent cliché of keepers being have-a-go-heroes was becoming difficult to shake. A keeper who could belt a quick-fire thirty now seemed more valuable than a keeper who refused to go out and build a soul-destroying rock in the middle order that sapped the bowling unit of any nerve, vitality or impetus. And the physical demands of staying alert half a day or more to wait patiently for that one mini-chance and have the body strength, balance, eyes and late adjustment to snaffle the catch, then start all over again the next ball once the batsman had taken guard. The keeper also acquired the unfortunate commission of being the presiding motivator, chirper and chief comedian out in the middle, the exceptions like Dhoni severely missed having been replaced by the all giggles and mockery Pant whenever a wicket fell at his little hands … or gloves.

The contradiction between Corkridge and Shackleton's incumbent keepers could not have been more severe across all elements of the ever-present presence behind the stumps, from batting to fitness to verbals to outlook. Larry was taking her time to fully acclimatise to the duties, mainly the static nature of the role and holding the squat pose for hours on end. The bespoke training take-away had been predominantly body squat based but with isometric targets which were challenging to the point of conscious impossibility. Larry though, undeterred, kept at it, helped along by Rebecca while their collective quads took on a sinewy strength as each tried to outlast the other, first in wall sit then low squat. Once it was clear Larry had the better of Rebecca, she'd fire off balls for Larry to catch to hone the coordination while holding the pose.

Corkridge's keeper was described by many an opposition as 'chopsy', his cutting hilarious-for-one remarks often called up by the umpire for being too close to when the ball was bowled, thus a potential for distraction for the batter, already smarting from a mum / physique / appearance / cricketing ability / mannerism / topical comment, sometimes so canned one could swear the audience laughed on cue. He was small but imposing as some small chaps are, his mouth and finger waving pulling many a six foot plus opposition down to his five-foot cough cough. He had more freckles than a person with orange hair and his own curly brown crown, a squib with swollen bee-sting lips and pisshole in the snow eyes to complete the Mr-Potato-head-on-crack ensemble. Unlike most of the Corkridge 1st XI, Stanley 'Stanni' Forthenstan had not played in the A team throughout the ages, languishing in the U14Bs, U15Bs and 2nds until a house match the previous year where he went after Chuck, hooking and pulling just about everything, his dominant right hand going from a liability to an asset overnight, or oversquareleg more pertinently. His glovework was unrivalled, a succession of one-handed swoop the bails off run outs and back glove stumpings when the batter overbalanced and stumbled out of the crease like a last order drunk from a bar. Chad felt he spotted something that day, a mongrel, cheeky-chappy-chirpy fighting spirit that might shake things up, jettisoning the new keeper directly into the 1sts. Nothing to do with the antecedent dropping a dolly off Chad's bowling the week before, meaning he only got four wickets and was deprived his Michele Pfeiffer ball award at assembly the following Monday.

As the season progressed last year, some of the other coaches and opposition had spoken out about lines being crossed and this simply not being cricket, but Chad was able to diplomatically smooth it all towards blowing over, especially as Stanni seemed to rile the right batsmen at the wrong time, key partnerships broken just after he'd lashed his caustic tongue to establish some doubt of either what was coming next or what had just transpired (including failed dates, hair combing fails, shirt tucking, parents absent on the bank, parents in full force 'what the hell is your mum wearing' on the bank and recent failures). Chad pretended to discourage a few times when exchanges came to a heated head, but it was an obvious doors open approach when results garnered throughout the innings. At 7 with bat in hand Stanni had also produced some swashbuckling quick-fire contributions, never really having to dig in to save anything what with Corkridge's top order, but when setting a target, able to add the impossible peak on a mountain to shut down any optimism from a chasing batting line-up. Now that he no longer feared the short ball thanks to Chuck, swinging wildly at just about anything a foot plus from his guard, his eye and bravado accumulated runs, albemostofthem fortuitous: over the slips, keeper or plopping between the boundary and inner ring fielders.

The pundits always sought a rivalry of positions, with keeper generating special attention given the scope for contrasting styles and uniqueness of the responsibilities in the game of cricket. Larry had the reaction speed of a mongoose but initially went hard at the ball, the gloves and mini-pads two foreign additions that didn't exactly compliment the day-long squat hold, which meant she palmed a significant majority of balls out in front of her. To address this Yapa had devised an exercise allowing the ball to come to her, permitting soft hands and pouching under the eyes. This involved a whistle where Larry was not allowed to move - even flinch - before the whistle sounded, in order to counter her quicker than the average human reaction time. With less time to react the theory was that the ball would reach her without instinctually going hard at the ball and the exercise worked initially with Larry's glovework trending towards the 'tidy' echelons. Batting for Larry compounded the awkward, extraneous sensation likely due to the golf swing her brothers had forced her to acquire over the years on the range. The slow, measured backswing and whipping hips through the ball in a nice deliberate arc with arms extended and hands soft didn't gel with getting the body into line, footwork then meeting the cricket ball to connect, find the middle and time the shot. Another of Yapa's scribbled notes – increasingly universal for each player and training drill – appeared for Larry to take guard outside the leg stump, sanctioning her improving eye to swing through the ball as though it was small, dimpled, white and stationary. The balls she did connect sailed far, even a slight draw on some of them, but with the stumps' exposure, they were often disturbed and like Yapa read from another note "You can't bat from the pavilion," so a core focus centred on defensive technique and the judgement when to get the old one-wood out to put it past the green.

So, depending on who was put on the spot, under the spotlight to commit to either ... he's a keeper or she's a keeper, would have to really understand that double entendre. Both were keepers – literal cricket definition, after the catching in a hat was outlawed – and all of Shaky's growing team, perhaps bar Rufus, what with his prickly, chary approach to acclimating to the team – would hand on heart swear in front of a live studio audience, high court of justice or deity that Larry was a real 'keeper', undeterred, positive, taking on any challenge with a wilful, disregarded blasé that only she could muster, Rebecca so often the lucky ogler of this spirit. Larry exuded being a keeper of the other sense: you just wanted to hold her and not let go, whereas Stanni was seen as a keeper by one person, his captain oh captain, and that wardership would only last if Stanni refused to drop the mic, kept scoring runs and winding up oppositions tighter than Corky's grip on Digners.

Chapter » 36

Top Order

Chuck's mental and emotional implosion began to subside, yet as no result of any collegiate sense of Corkridge camaraderie to help a teammate out of the doldrums when lying face down in one, the uppercut from a love interest too denting on the machismo to be acknowledged as anything worthy of support. The reason Chuck began to climb the path back towards self-respect had nothing to with acceptance, instead, good old fashioned internal house hierarchy and politics. Boys boarding houses at Corkridge held the innate, uncanny ability to sense weakness - they smelled it, the fumes unconsciously providing newfound bravery which belied natural layers of hierarchal respect - which, if left untended quickly became brazen disregard, disrespect and even taunting. When a younger kid named Toby flicked yogurt across the dining hall to splatter neatly between Chuck's eyebrows, the crossed line saw Chuck of old roar, tearing across the dining hall to ensure the flicker ingested more of his own yogurt than he cared to, the flurry of forced spoon feeding a Turkey Teeth 'before' picture. This small act restored at least a speck of

Chuck's kudos which eventually spilled back onto the cricket field where he performed well for the 3rds then 2nds and was invited back to the 1st XI net sessions so Chad and the coach could 'take a look' as part of a formal assessment.

The Corkridge top order batters would have likely played for any school or junior county in the world given the exceptional account of their skills, aptitude and game awareness but having Chad at number 3 upheld a double impact of bleeding in complacency, knowing he would always make the runs, and the unwritten rule of never showing Captain Chad up. If the openers did perform well, they might hold some back on say the strike rate so Chad could continue the heroics at a quicker batting pace or if Chad did happen to go out, the number 4 bat would sometimes lazily go out if the game was already practically won, leaving it to James at number 5 who would never technically be considered a top order bat, his bludgeoning in the middle order a perfect complement to Chad's epitomised strokeplay all around the wicket, the two styles clearly not of the same genre.

The Corkridge XI opening batsmen knew deep down they were the entrées, the main course chateaubriand dripping with goose liver fat pacing up and down the dressing room, only fair to unleash on a suspecting, adoring public. The opening batting pair complemented each other relatively well, having attended the same junior school and been coached from before they could walk by the same coach, a firm believer in making each shot look better than it actually was, prone to holding the pose after a cover drive or leaving with a bullfighter, sunny armpits French disposition, even if the ball was some way from their person. Fans called it 'stylish', haters called it 'all class and no arse'.

Of the pair, they were sometimes confused for twins: same height, same hooked nose, same non-descript brown hair, same bat grip near the blade, same bat brand, kit and same shuffled running style, refusing to allow the batting spikes more than an inch off the ground when trotting through for a safe single. In their entire career as openers, George Mildew and Harrison Plodkin had never once, not even during a house match or internal practice match, ever run each other out. This cautious approach bordered on vigilant insomnia with obvious quick singles turned down should there be a blade of grass's risk of being run out, the modern requirements of a run-getting mantra not deterring their obdurate spirit in any way, shape or form. And the two were so confident in the other's resolve, the trust and belief normally signalled with a raised glove, hoarse "No Run!" that when that hint of risk crept into the non-taken run, both sat back on their heels, growing roots while the fielding side lost any hope of a direct hit and resigned for the next delivery. With the additional scrutiny they did start taking runs when they knew they'd hit a boundary, the movement between wickets a subconscious message back to the dressing room, spectators and scouts that activity was transpiring out in the middle.

The insurance policy against runs left out in the middle was just one concentration lapse from entering stage right, teeth shining, bat ominous and heels kicked up the backside as he strode fresh from a few token throwdowns: Chad the wonderous.

Equally the number 4 bat, a prodigious talent at the junior performance level, suffered the same fate, his cardinal modus operandi to elevate Chad as opposed to filling his own cricket spikes. So much so that he'd been forced to change his name, his parents now even adopting his 'improved' Christian name. Bradley or Brad as he'd been since top scoring at U9 just sounded too darn similar to Chad, causing an unrest of confusion with scorers, parents and fans, the shocking implication an actual discombobulation of who made a hundred at U14 level. Chad refused to accept a substitute nickname either, insisting that these stats rotted on websites and scorecards until history was literally rewritten by those limited enough not to remember Chad's multitude of magical innings. Weak proposals such as Bradster, Bradass, Bradman ("as if" - Chad quote), Radbrad, Bradbro, Bradmeister and Be-rad were swatted away with head shakes, eye-balls and prominent "Nos!" as Chad's suggestion of Yannos, the polar second last letter of the alphabet a neat symmetry even if Brad wasn't Greek, didn't look Greek and had never even been to Greece, his only claim that he'd once thrown up tzatziki, believing it to be a healthier mayo.

So, Yannos Dalrymple batted just below Chad de la Ampelas with many of Brad's relatives and peripheral friends merely accepting that this generation was often unhappy with the identity they'd had thrust upon them, now identifying as a Greek, his father's role as an insurance broker for largely Greek shipowners attributed as the key departure point from the family's *1st Viscount of Stair* heritage. As a cricketer, Yannos was oft caught between a rock and a hard place (and susceptible to being caught off a length if you believed the chat) in that he came in after Chad so hardly anyone noticed he was out in the middle and prevented the pundits immersing in the big hitting fireworks of James Smith-Franklin who, when joining Chad, generated what locals in the area called a 'must see event' or 'Beauty and the Beast' - Chad's silky everythingness and James's bludgeoning burly power to lose the ball in places most felt impossible. Yannos was dubbed 'the advert' as the annoying commercial intrusion where you'd go stick the kettle on or take a tactical spend-a-penny so you were ready for the main event. In frustration once, Yannos - deprived of the strike by a fluid innings from Chad - almost ran his captain out which saw him batting number 9 for the next few games.

Once. People paid to see Chad keep the strike and his partner trot in vain after another boundary then fist bump him, not some kid from Greece use up valuable balls. Ουάου.

Chapter » 37

Huddle

It was unmistakeable. Even the most oblivious, naïve eye couldn't argue: it was the first thing that leapt into a person's mind, no matter how hard one tried to not see it or view it from another angle.

"I don't actually care," said Corin at the team talk days before the first pool game. "In fact, it strengthens my resolve. Let's all laugh at ourselves, together … here we go, one, two, three: ha-ha-ha ha ha ha-ha!" the forced outburst which sounded like each had acquired an 'r' on the end, echoed in the biology classroom, the plastic skeleton seemingly smiling only to shield his or her eyes every time he or she looked at it. The rest of the team clearly didn't share Corin's accepting blend of disregard and disdain.

"This has been done to us," Daughtry chuntered from the back, her head higher than the organ charts.

"Duh," Noel muttered, slumped in the corner next to the fake plastic nutritional display, grabbing an apple and pretending to take a bite.

"Let's Google and see if it looks different," suggested Rebecca, an honorary member of the team now that Larry and her were practically inseparable.

"It doesn't make a difference; it does strengthen our resolve and, if anything, we wear it with pride," Enid line drew, suspecting this might be fuel on the fire rather than a wet blanket to quell.

"That thing! With pride! You're so far past having a laugh your sides have split and all of those are all over the floor," tutted Rufus, motioning towards Daughtry's accompanying chart.

"I've been ridiculed with stuff like this my whole life," Jacob stammered, bringing a horrible real sense of permanence. "Can we get them reprinted or rebranded?"

"Too late," said Yapa. "We play with, no time to replace. Picture not change cricket. Or you."

Onka said nothing, staring down at his phone.

Wei Ping read a joke scrawled on the board, garnering no chuckles other than from the skeleton, Noel puppet mastering from behind.

Onka put his phone away and studied the emblem on the sleeve and the front of the trousers, addled that this was how English schoolboys chose to mock, the mechanics of a practical gag with such effort such a waste of time, energy and talent. If he'd known the lengths Chad had gone to ensure the sponsor's emblem looked less like a delighted chef slicing a giant doner kebab and more like a deranged horror slasher with a phallic hand-held protrusion, he'd have been doubly as shocked; where he was from energy was expended surviving rather than on silly childish pranks.

"We can fix this, maybe not fully before the first game but it can be fixed. My Mom is a seamstress and says she'll do her best."

"It is against the rules to cover up with a patch," said Enid. "So if your mother is able to let us focus exclusively on the cricket, without any distractions, then she is a goddess ... one of our team."

Onka smiled, knowing his mother, so accomplished in so many disciplines, would love the inclusion.

"And another thing," Onka said, looking more uncertain than usual, his eyes lowered, a sprinkle of excitement meshed with trepidation. "You guys rugby fans?"

Chapter » 38

Strike

On the same day - purely coincidentally - the Corkridge and Shackleton XIs (or more like VIIIs in Shaky's case) attempted to take fast bowling practice to another level.

Yapa, once again fumbling scattered pieces of paper between pocket, nose, palm and hips, would state functionally, matter-of-factly, that this was going to hurt. The fast bowlers in Corin, Daughtry and Noel eyeballed the white lines of the crease with a mix of uncertainty and animation. Yapa had drawn the lines at least five to eight feet closer than normal, so as Jacob took guard with Onka the other end, quizzical heads cocked to the side, canine confusion resounded in all directions along, across and around the pitch.

"Someone's going to die," said Corin nonchalantly measuring her run-up.

"Get your feet, hips, knees moving," instructed Yapa. "Bowl full pace. Duck, sway and move early."

»

On the other side of town, Corky hid from view with an internal practice match on a tucked away field, colloquially called 'The Graveyard' due to its bouncy pitch: a fast bowler's paradise to counter the sobriquet for any bats. The brouhaha that pinged between the Neethaniel brothers erupted in a series of fist to chest punches, the recipient not shifting an inch backwards and the ferocity of each looking like it would shatter a normal human's ribs. Chuck tutted from the other end, feeling as though he didn't need any shows of infantile machoism to get the ball to dance off this pitch. Chad had called this session 'Bowler on bowler' orchestrating the four quicks (Chad of course inserted himself directly into the quartet and was no slouch with his pace but no one would argue had a more nuanced and variety-laden approach; could the other three swing it both ways, bowl off and leg cutters and back of the hand slower balls? Not likely; well not consistently anyway) to bowl at one another to bring out the competitive spirit and gee up whichever two ended as the opening pair for the first Digners pool match. Chad and Chuck were padded and the brothers rocket ship departure ready to join forces with The Graveyard.

»

Corin's first ball to Jacob was a loosener of the loosest variety and Jacob did not react, letting the ball go through to Larry who neatly sucked the ball into her hips with an "Oomph!" Noel, spotting this might actually be some fun, encouraged Daughtry to have a crack with a "You're up HB: don't be gentle." Daughtry hobbled in, the approach of any lanky quick, her legs and arms looking as though they belonged to two different individuals. The closer crease threw her, as Noel grabbed the popcorn, her delivery from a foot wide of the crease and connecting Jacob squarely in the gut without bouncing. An apology and abortively fought back tears five minutes later, Noel still rolling around from his mark, Yapa mentally hooking the delivery for six, Jacob and Onka swapped sides meaning Noel bucked up, ready to seek the high prized wicket of Onka.

"Okay if fast bowler hit batsman," instructed Yapa, Daughtry still looking crestfallen. Noel, bowling left-arm over to a high backlifting Onka, got one to straighten and lift causing Onka to jump and arch, channelling anyone unlucky enough to face the Windies in the eighties. Noel faux smirked right in Onka's face, muttering "More coming." Onka blinked a chary grin back.

Even Chad was surprised at the pace and lift generated from the noxious combo of Neethaniels and Graveyard, one ball not quite beating him for pace, more so lift, so that his solid defence kept the ball out with the bottom of the bat's handle accepting the punch. Chuck on the other hand was a ruinous melange of pissed-off aggression and aware that one false move could kill him dead right there as even the sun hid from the twins. His approach involved swinging at anything short but with enough leg side safety, backing away and sending most of the balls toward and above the twitchy slip cordon. As was the modus operandi of the session, not much was expected to be length but with such a lively pitch even length balls could be threatening so Chad ducked and weaved best he could. After Chad found his stride, he kept Chuck on strike for the entertainment value, the gauge dialled up after every delivery until, after one particularly nasty bouncer, Chuck whipped off his gloves and tore after the approaching lefty Neethaniel brother, merging like ink dropped into water. The two got to it, fists flying in all directions until righty brother Neethaniel went in to support, meeting Chad's outstretched bat on his Adam's apple as he passed the non-striker's end. Fuming he empaled a pig-eyed warning to Chad who casually diffused his advance with a reassuring "Let them get this out; this is good for them."

»

Once the novelty wore off, both the bowling and batting units dug in, the most encouraging sign to other non-quicks padding up to at least 'have a crack'. And the bowlers in turn, not wanting to be shown up being filleted to the boundary from a significantly shorter distance, even more severe than the old back foot no-ball before the rules changed and quick bowlers were even further marginalised. Onka got the rub quickly - as you would expect - batting deeper in his crease and defending anything that wasn't a length delivery and Jacob, once those twinkle toes were shocked into defiance, was able to shift between front and back foot, sometimes even playing a back defensive elevated from the pitch, his body precariously the last barrier should the ball move late. There were, of course, a host of wickets - mainly caught behind fending - the slip cordon's stinging hands inescapable from first through fifth slip, the bowling trio starting a competitive tally which annoyingly Noel led from the outset. Corin was in second but started catching Noel as her variety and adaptation to the new length became settled. Daughtry lost a bit of whip, unsure whether to float it up or slam it short, the latter serving up a smattering of tennis ball bouncing balls to be dispatched with not-so-much consummate ease. She did, however, likely bowl the ball of the day to Onka, pitching middle and dislodging the top of off, a feather whisper past the top corner of the bail to dislodge, only Noel noticing initially to propel his feigned jumping high five, pretending not to be able to reach HB's outstretched hand.

tOp Of Off

»

When the fisticuffs had died down, after what seemed like an eternity for anyone but Chad, the game resumed with the Neethaniel brothers padded up and Chuck ready to serve a dish cold, medium or even Nando's hot to do more than lay down a claim. On the side of his temple a puffy swollen ostrich egg loomed, the corrie-fisted brother taking guard and even raising an eyebrow at how pink it looked from afar. Chuck held the line, held the wait, feeling his temple throbbing like a stubbed toe then blew a kiss towards the non-striker Neethaniel who pretended not to notice but patently felt the threat. Chuck's run-up had traditionally been rhythmical, almost languid, then jumping into the stride to fling down the ball. His control, balance and coordination gave him extra pace which in turn hid the array of ball skills he had in his bowling locker. Playing substandard and slightly-above-standard teams had meant beating batsmen for pace through the air was the quickest, most efficient way to notch up wickets and win games for Corkridge and Chad. And when all else failed there was always the cocked elbow to draw upon for that extra zip, jag or scurry. Chuck sped in, faster than Chad had ever seen, his knees a white blur of successive kicks followed by the customary jump and an elbow more bent than an Indian bookmaker - practically a baseball pitch. The pace generated off The Graveyard and lethal positioning almost killed his new northern nemesis. Chad nodded in approval, pushing the sides of his mouth down to acknowledge complimentary surprise. The ball having struck the helmet rolled back benignly, Chuck retrieving from his toes and returning to his mark as the non-striking Neethaniel signalled for medical assistance.

Chapter » 39

Variations

The night before the first Digners pool match, the girls couldn't sleep so Corin snuck through to Enid's room and the two made hand shapes against the iPhone torch on the ceiling to make the time go quicker. Enid was the more restless of the two, giving up on multiple occasions when evolving from crocodile jaws to something more elaborate became taxing. The evening was hot - too hot for that time of year - which meant the next day was bound to be a scorcher too, tweaks and adaptations of how to play the conditions and suss out each opposition player's weaknesses dribbling through particularly Enid's mind.

"Think we're going to be okay," Corin whispered.

"Is that a question or a statement?"

"Somewhere in between. Got a bit of a buzz on though, not sure sleep as a prerequisite for good solid cricket is going to happen; just be steaming in running like a drunk person!"

"We haven't really had much time. To get our games. Too busy organising ... cajoling ... coercing ... hoping ... praying. I can never get used to the precarious nature of cricket: two shakes of a Corky's cravat, and the game swings on its heels.

I keep trying to remember what Dad told us through the years, going over deliveries in my head ... shots ... tactics ..."

"Do you think we should talk to him again? Say we're in this now and need his help?"

Enid turned onto her side, disregarding the oppressive duvet to one side, only to pull it between her knees to stem the clamminess, the duvet as the snug meat in the sandwich.

"I don't think we can ... if he knew what this was all for and to dredge up a part of his life he clearly wants to leave hidden away, buried in the past."

"It will never be buried though ... and this is the redemption ... of sorts."

"The level we're at is beyond words too: we don't have the time to develop new deliveries. Jimmy took five years to introduce the inswinger."

"I've bowled most of the varieties, even in jest but I get it's worse for you leggies: matches aren't the time to experiment with new balls. What did Dad teach you?"

"Stock delivery is and was a classic leg break. Dad always said the groundwork of wickets for a leggie was built on a solid foundation of returning to your stock ball and keeping it tight to put pressure on the batsman. That and turning the ball."

"Which you've always been able to do."

"Not really. Started with an arm that came through at about three o'clock which got great turn but was about as easy to control as a fly you've just missed with a swatter. Then coaches forced me to come through higher and the spin disappeared, yet the line and length improved. It was Dad who suggested I come right around the ball - 'drawing a big circle with a paintbrush' he called it - and voilà ... well, not quite, but the turn came back, the arm went through at about one-thirty and a semblance of control was established."

"All I remember from those days was coaches going crazy for your wrist, trying to change everything you did but keep your wrist, the show pony leg spinner paraded for all to see."

"Without taking any wickets in the nets or ever getting to play in the boys' club teams though. Those little chumps would see a slow girl bowler and be skipping down before I'd taken my pre-delivery breath."

"I never liked facing you."

"Now you tell me!"

"Well I had to maintain some level of ascendancy being the little sister, always trying to match the mighty Enid."

"You did more than match," breaking the snug sandwich and tenderly kneeing Corin in the side.

"Don't injure your teammates before the game … afterwards maybe!"

"You were the one who used to try and injure me if memory serves."

"Dad always tried to get us to operate, to think, to behave as a team: a unit, but I suppose having an all-conquering sister meant you had to do a bit of conquering yourself and, to stand out, that meant conquering the all-conquering sister."

"I never begrudged your taking me down a peg or two; probably deserved it most of the time."

A far away owl hoot set a cat off, a caterwauling fade to black as Enid turned back onto her back, inadvertently dragging Corin onto her side to face her, the tit-for-tat timelapse choreographed as only sisters know how.

"Which other deliveries did Dad show you?" Corin asked, tracing Enid's profile with her little finger in the chestnut gloom.

"Well, obviously the marquee variation, the one that gets everyone ga-ga – the googly which, along with the top spinner, has probably been my shining light of late, ensuring the same action as the stock ball and getting either good turn in or bounce. Right-handed LBWs should be a factor if the umpires believe you've done it intentionally. Dad also showed me the slider which might work at this time of the year when the pitches don't turn and the flipper which I never really got to understand or try, snapping it out the front of the hand just too high risk. Steer clear of the arm-ball he told me unless the batsman is way far back in the crease and not looking to score."

"Jeez, bit more technical than in and outswing, off and leg cutters and back of the hand versus knuckle ball slower."

"Another sisterly bluff ... I know you have more in the locker."

"Just the beamer. For Chad's head."

"Unfortunately that's boundary bound with ease, unless you OD on Weetabix."

"Might be worth it, just for fun."

"Fun for their scorecard ... and supporters."

"What about the finger delivery? Dad always said you had long fingers."

"Oh my God, I completely forgot about that," said Enid, breaking the cycle and facing Corin head on, nose to nose. "My middle finger, that's right. He said no one knew about this - it didn't exist as a delivery other than some obscure ancient cricketer who made it work once in 1950."

"Once?"

"During one series he came away with a bowling average of 7.6! Then got injured and never played again. Jack Iverson was his name."

"How do you bowl it?"

"Well this finger - the middle - tucks behind the ball and you deliver it like a normal leg break. Theoretically it looks like a leg break and still turns unlike the flipper - a low jagged rotation. I could never get it to work though, the ball sticking and me overcompensating by flinging it high into the air with an invitation to smack the leather off it for anyone with an eye."

"Your version of a beamer."

"Indeed, but with the menace extracted so completely, a small cute furry animal would seem more intimidating."

Corin eventually found some solace in sleep when Enid became aware of the power outage. This was the time - stewing in the pocked murk like a death row insomniac - to get all the self-doubt out, splatter it about the bedroom, an oil painter using watercolours; make a right mess - don't tell Mum - and watch as Dad retreats when the admonishing drama ensues, winking as he walks out the room, secretly applauding the mess but inoculated with marital solidarity that he never really could back her actions. But he did - he always did, and this was for him, a veiled inwards thanks which could go so sour as early as tomorrow that would turn the longing gratitude upside down. She touched Corin's cheek with her middle finger, gently enough not to rouse her from a dream of taking wickets by the truckload and belting boundaries by the boatload, stopping short of jabbing her cheek and twisting as she might have when they were younger. She gazed upon her extended middle finger, lingering as the murk got invaded by a dusting of sombre grey needle-beams, the sun squelching forth behind terraced house blockers in the east, tapping Enid on the shoulder to let her know that today was game day and, save for shoving the sun back in its universal pocket like an unwanted used hanky, there was no going back. Now.

Chapter » 40

Powerplay

Out in the middle for the toss Enid could feel her eyes ache. She kept blinking as if to dispel the pulsing, each time coating her pupils in another layer of sleep-deprived grime, so much so that when she looked up at the umpire to call the toss, she couldn't tell whether he was smiling or not. He was, a big start-of-the-season earlobe-to-earlobe smile which might have given Enid and Shaky the assurances that this actually was a fun exploit, but all Enid could see was a film of creamy obscurity between her and the next phase.

"One of the oldest traditions in organised sport," the umpire began, revealing a pristine £2 coin, preserved in mint condition for an occasion such as this, almost fumbling the tender in giddy ardour. "It appears right at the top of cricket's rule book from 1744: 'The pitching the first wicket is to be determined by the toss of a piece of money'. So here we are the pregame coin toss."

Enid smiled in the general direction of his face while her opposing captain, a tall boy whose knees seemed to be above Enid's eye-level, muttered "Let's do it," with a hint of impatience at the umpire's elongating the sense of occasion.

"This is the first official match of the Digners Cup in Pool D. This will be a 50-over match between Flounders Witheringham School for Boys and Shackleton Senior. Who would like to call?"

"She can fill her boots, or heels, or whatever they wear."

"Might have to borrow a pair - assume you have to hand?" came Enid's retort, her eyes clearing in solidarity with her resolve. The umpire, oblivious to the early needle, gestured towards Enid, positioning the coin vigilantly on his thumb nail.

"The young lady will call," flicking skywards with a deft, practiced hand, the coin's flutter a uniform display of rotation perfection. So mesmerised was Enid by the shiny wagon wheel turns, she almost forgot the call, the coin comfortably heading downwards when she spouted "Ta— uh, heads," her dad had always said, go heads and with your head. The opposition captain looked miffed as though she was trying to pull a fast one, scrunching his lofty face until the coin came to rest on tails, the dry grass accoutring a dead cushionless landing.

"The call was heads," the umpire decreed with a tint of regret in his tone. "Yet the coin shows tails. What would Flound—"

"We'll bowl ... Sir. Should be over in a whisker ..." he said walking off before the hands had been shaken, leaning over to Enid to conclude "... get the fat lady ready ... she's going to be singing before tea."

Turning, the Shaky twelve looking on in eager anticipation, Enid played a wrist drive to signify they were batting which was what she was likely to have done regardless, the pitch not looking too threatening this early in the season, yet her face gave away she'd lost the toss. Corin gathered the troops in a huddle as Jacob, Rufus and Onka went to pad up only for Onka to abandon his endeavour after an angry stare from

Rufus. Corin began explaining how they should use the bravado against FWS, frustrating by keeping wickets in hand, the disregard for her own swashbuckling bravado surprising both Yapa and Enid who nodded in complete agreement.

Flounders Witheringham School for Boys was a mid-level private school not famed for academics but with strong sporting clout. Infamous for maintaining academic standards on paper yet allowing some of the dumbest jocks in the nation into the school on bursaries. Enid and Wei Ping had confirmed earlier that there were no real stars to target in this team, yet the overall consistency was good one through eleven, the captain an opening bowler who didn't really know how to set a field which meant there would be a potential disconnect between balls bowled and fielders placed, allowing conventional scoring opportunities. The game was being played on the FWS home 1st XI field, so Shaky would have to wait for their first home game. The pitch, although seemingly innocuous to both Yapa and Enid, did look greener that any others this time of year and the decision to bowl might be fifty-fifty arrogance-stronger bowling line-up. The Flounders opposition changing room had been awkward as they'd made no allowance for the gender split, so the girls and boys had been forced to change in shifts. Thankfully though, Onka's mom had deterred the unrelenting efforts of Chad and the Corky tricksters, to painstakingly fix the logo to resemble the wholesome products of a local kebab house. The team, though, still wore the kit with a level of circumspection, as the rumour was the local eatery would be serving from a mobile catering van at a reduced fee come lunchtime.

The decision to let Rufus open with Jacob had been chaotic. Rufus, tirelessly campaigning in a 'just let me get on with what I'm good at' intonation pipped Yapa and Enid's 'getting Onka in early' at the post. 50 overs was a long time, so the decision had been to allow Rufus to prove his utility whilst holding Onka back to his more accustomed number 4 position behind Enid at 3. With no real established opening pair, Shaky were vulnerable against what looked a solid if not varied attack - multiple quicks and some military mediums with one spinner on a pitch that did not look like turning, despite the green tinges. FWS had played most of last season with no spinner and won more than 80% of their matches, so the pitch was more conducive to up and down pace plus skiddy medium quicks in the middle overs.

"So it begins," Enid kind-of-asked Yapa in a rare, reassurance-required tone, resisting the urgency to pad up probably somewhere between blind optimism and nervous denial. Yapa, scrunching a piece of paper into his pocket looked assured, calm even.

"This team beats itself," he began. "Patience is key. Frustration. Strangulation. You must be there holding the bat at the end of the innings even if you've only scored small runs. Then we win easily. Outfield slow so lots of threes. Breath deep. Drink water. Energy sachets in your pocket. Your wicket vital."

"No pressure then."

"Never pressure. Fun game. Cricket. But win. Beat this team. Put okay score on board then they try win in first overs. Nothing fancy. Slow burn."

"Slow poison," Enid's mind filtering back to a park game with some local kids and her dad in North London before they'd all moved down south, a game out-outwaiting the opposition. And it had worked.

"Cricket's tedium can become its glorious resolve," she quoted back to Yapa, the memory now strong, Yapa shuddering his head upwards as though he'd heard it before.

Play started bang on the scheduled 10am start time, a healthy crowd already assembled, the spring's heat compelling most on and off the field to reach for the factor

30. The gangly captain didn't need to measure out his run-up as he'd dug a hole in the right spot, anyone unlucky enough to have a longer run-up risking ankle ligament tears. For such a tall drink of carrot juice, his run-up was uncharacteristically short, his long trunk arms still glistening from the sun cream application, the brown forearm, nose and cheek freckles all sent for refuge beneath the caked white water and sweat resistance cream. Jacob and Rufus came out to bat, Rufus a good few feet in front of Jacob, intent on facing the first delivery whether or not Jacob so desired (he didn't in fact, and was content to be the non-striker if only to quell the savage vampire butterflies chewing him out from the inside).

The inaugural ball was good - not crazy good but a nice line and length with a bit of lift off a length - Rufus defending but missing. In fact the whole first over was decent - a maiden - with Rufus losing patience around the third ball and bootlessly wielding an expansive drive or two for the remaining balls. Not one attempted shot found the willow and, luckily so, because this slip cordon had been pouching edges throughout the preseason and as a group for years before this.

"Flounders bread-and-butter," the third slip yelled upon completion of the over with another play and miss from Rufus. He wasn't wrong.

Then it was Jacob's turn to take guard, Shackleton yet to trouble the scorers or indeed open their account in the Digners Cup. The other Flounders opening bowler looked a carbon copy of the captain, only shorter and gingerer, already melting in the sun and with an easy, short run-up. His first ball had to be played at, Jacob fending without the required footwork, sending the ball bouncing at the feet of the chirpy third slip who misjudged the bounce to let the ball through for Shaky's first runs, a fortuitous boundary to give Jacob likely his highest strike rate of the season at a whopping 400!

He breathed a sigh of relief as the blood found his calves and feet, wiggling his toes inside his spikes to get them moving. The remainder of the over was negotiated with some concrete footwork and defensive technique, the only blemish the fifth ball which spat up and jammed his right hand's fingers against the bat's handle, eliciting an audible yelp and a hand rattling – Boyband / rapper in front of the eyes style. After glove removal, quenching the ubiquitous tears and an ice pack from Yapa, Jacob was ready to resume fancy-footwork battle.

When the first wicket fell, there was a discernible feeling that the sting had been taken out of the opening bowling pair, disregarding any semblance of line-and-length forcing the incredible, unplayable delivery only to mash out a few long hops, half-volleys and full bungers. Rufus in particular cashed in on the errant balls, mostly threes and twos, even after razing from bat-sweet-spot-central on multiple occasions. Jacob, less flamboyant, kept his wicket and dragged back his strike rate until pushing falteringly at a good ball, his anticipatory foot too quick to determine the pitch of the ball, resulting in an early weight transfer and short extra cover pouching a simple one. The ball, though, less shiny so job done, which is as much as Enid told him, striding to the crease, her eyes still milky and exhaustingly holding her tight in a wet blanket grip. A hush descended on the ground, the Flounders team bucking up a notch, as the first and second change warmed up, the two gingers flagging from the foamy exertion. Before taking guard she met with Rufus, who looked as though he may start perspiring if things actually got tasty. He had a different plan.

"We need to get moving here," he said. "This track is doing nothing and if these are the best two bowlers, there's nothing to fear."

"I'm going to take it slow," Enid stated, swallowing hard. "The bowlers about to come on might be better than the openers – they've held them back. Plus, our tail starts earlier than most teams."

"Heavens! We are twelve overs in and Channing Tatum over there has done nothing but move away from harmless deliveries. Either I'm going to have to up this rate singlehandedly or you can chip in – and I know you can bat … if pressed."

"Rather keep your wicket for now, then we hold out and get expansive later on."

"You bat your way if you want to lose the first game, and I'll bat mine. Going down swinging at least," he said returning to the crease.

"Two legs, please," came Enid's request, with one ball to negotiate, the benevolent umpire at the toss signalling with a serviceable nod, no hint of his affirmative carriage dwindling. Enid took a cursory glance around the field, the captain, likely at the end of his opening spell, chomping at the bit as the umpire's restrictive arm barricaded his attempts, the parking boom waiting for Enid to stand side-on, rectilinear toes facing forward and face. No third man, cover ring not full, an imbalance of surplus fielders on the leg and all-out attack with too many slips and close fielders apparent, yet the twinkle of their eyes – clear for her to see now even through the milky tears – burning to get this girl out, shut down this rebellion, quell this fad.

The umpire's arm went down in slow motion, an astronaut falling through space, the dot of ginger on the close horizon swelling, knees stabbing towards her, an approaching, attacking giraffe. The delivery of the ball was a blur, one false blink too many coating Enid's pupils, her foot planted down the track in hope more than awareness, the bat following to fend. The thud mid-way up the pad hurt, but not as much as the screeching appeal, denting an ear drum or eleven in the surrounding villages. The whole Flounders team, arms aloft, screaming at the umpire, height no issue, the ball having deviously skidded through, Enid's only hope the guard being more leg side than middle-and-leg, a Not Out signifying that the umpire got the guard wrong. Even Rufus looked anxious the other end, his eyes swollen but not fervent like the twenty-two other eyeballs all approaching the umpire as he pondered his decision, the smile eradicated for now. Enid looked up at him, after almost falling over when the ball struck, her pleading eyes intensifying the doubt that might exist. An age ensued – longer than any normal LBW decision – then he shook his head, signally down leg to a mire of protests and sought explanations. He couldn't look Enid in the eye for the remainder of the game.

The vanquished appeal did nothing to deter the vehemence on show for Flounders, the openers giving way to a fiery yet tight spell from the new bowlers, Enid hogging most of the strike. Rufus, increasingly frustrated, his firm belief that his eye was in, took a swipe at a wide one, trying to cut it over point only to toe the ball to gully, the bowler providing an effeminate gesture send-off. The score was 37-2 after 20 overs when Onka strode to the crease, the low total the primary chat factor for Flounders with comments like "Don't rush to trouble the scorers, girls" and "Hundred up … likely tomorrow."

Onka's calm was the tonic and the partnership between him and Enid blossomed as the bowling infuriation became infused with lassitude, more loose deliveries allowing the pair to play risk-free shots even if not collecting the maximum boundaries on offer. The heat told though and the deluge of three runs provided its own fatigue with a conscious desire not to get lazy and seek risky fours. Flounders tried their lone spinner who wasn't especially good, combined with a track that looked like year-old milk wouldn't turn on it, Onka bringing up a sensible eighty-strike-rate fifty in the 38th over with the score on 127-2, Enid's anchor generating some noise from the crowd even though she hadn't taken most of the strike. Her obdurate defence gave Onka more license to get on with it after the 40th over, but he fell to a spectacular keeper catch down the leg side. He might not have been given out, but like one of his heroes Hasim Amla, he walked, the other umpire's bemused face convoyed with the Flounders' headshakes and mocking chortles.

Noel was in next at number 5 as a Yapa-inspired pinch hitter, Wei Ping's intel showing that when the openers returned to bowl the death overs, they typically sought yorkers, which meant a healthy serving of full tosses. Unfortunately Noel missed what was simply a straight full toss and got bowled in the 43rd over, the score now 155-4. Corin skipped in, the distinctive side to side shuffle-hops and an exuded optimism no slouchy, sweaty, scolding, scowling Flounders' fielding unit could knock. She met her sister, visibly drained, in the middle, her hair plastered down her forehead seeping from beneath the helmet like butter on a hot white roll.

"You've done a super job, Sis," Corin stated, still checking out where the fielders might be sneaking towards. "Foundation is there, so we have a few overs to make hay."

Enid was too exhausted to nod, but smiled as Corin chewed imaginary gum and ran off to face whatever a pimply Flounders wannabe might have to throw at her. Excitement channelled can be powerful but the exuberance of this introduction to Digners might have been initially misplaced as the Flounders bowlers once again found another gear when bowling to a girl. Corin was lucky too, a few balls in the air just past fielders and narrow stump misses as she gave herself room. She did play a few powerful straight shots, yielding a handful of boundaries, not dissimilar to Enid, her energy spent but able to use the bowlers' pace behind square to rack up a few more fours. Both went out towards the end of the innings - in the same over in fact, much to the waning whoops of the Flounders boys, but some damage had been done. Larry and a younger boy in the team from the junior ranks saw the innings out, ending on a respectable 213-6.

What happened during the second innings whilst Flounders chased the target, was equally unfortunate and anomalous. The chat at the half-way point had been all about how Flounders' batting line-up was deep if not spectacular, with the bowling plan to emulate batting: frustration would win this match – seam on the money and tight non-scoring spin would see Shaky start the campaign with an against-the-odds win. Or would it?

The opening attack did kick off with aplomb, taking early wickets, and at regular intervals, but then something puzzling crept in, contaminating bowlers and fielders alike – they got complacent. Suddenly a winning total was 213 without the elbow grease, toil and wilting perspiration to actually bowl the team out and win the match. Wides, sloppy fielding, failure to back up and overthrows handed Flounders the advantage at the 30 over mark, their score an on-track 134-4, the middle order looking untroubled and gifted free runs easier than a Delhi vindaloo from a street seller. When the number 6 bat decided he needed new gloves, Enid took the opportunity to gather the team and unleash a hairdryer of reality to snap the team out of this slumber towards losing. Had they been through all this to throw it away? To this bunch of ... well, now they were the ones Floundering!

The captain's bellow worked to bring the team into tighter control, Enid bowling herself to set the precedent of regaining the ascendancy, yet regrettably for Shaky, the batsmen matched the strengthening of resolve and dug in to keep wickets, the run rate healthy enough not to panic, ticking along with the odd boundary and singles each over. For both Enid and Onka the instinct had rung true – not a smidge of turn anywhere to be found, a bevy of sliders served up and dealt with commendably. It was beginning to feel like something miraculous was required, a certain desperation creeping over the fielders as afternoon bed itself in and the tickle of chill displaced the warmth like an all-elbows commuter hunting out the final train seat.

With ten overs left to play Flounders required 47 runs to win, reaching 167 still with only four wickets down, both batsmen closing in on half-centuries, the punch-counter punch of their synergy and quick running between the wickets apparent, particularly for the Flounders parent who had by now disregarded any feigned decorum, praising in boisterous solidarity every fumble, misfield or scampered run. Noel was bowled out and Daughtry looked a tad out of sorts, the occasion and pressure an increasing burden; Corin had looked lively with overs in the tank and Rufus was struggling with his length the entire match which meant the death overs became perilous. The spinners were likely a risk too far in this situation and with this pitch, and there was no way on God's green earth Jacob was going to bowl. Enid stuck with the right and left-arm spinners in herself and Onka for the early part of the forties, almost yielding success as an edge sped fragments past the outer reach of Larry's gloves, en route to the boundary for a double-whammy gut-punch four.

Then came the miracle, well ... the breakthrough at least. In the 44th over Onka bowled a left-arm over googly to the number 5 bat, a right-hander, which constructed a semblance of grip probably due to the unnatural flight Onka had the guts to toss up. Without getting to the pitch of the ball, deceived by the flight and taste of turn, the batsman went through with the shot, slamming the ball directly to the left of Onka who stuck out a hand, the ball ricocheting onto the stumps, the team going up for the run out even though the number 6's bat was firmly in place behind the line. During the drama of the appeal with the ball squirting sideways into no man's land, the bat on strike wandered forward to either sneak a single or see what the heck was going on. Just as the umpire at the bowler's end shook his head, so Noel had the opportunistic foresight to retrieve the ball and whip it in to the keeper, a direct slam on the bails sending the Shaky team into their second appeal in as many seconds! This was unmistakeable though and the square leg umpire had no hesitation in delivering the index finger of death: out.

It took a while to calm the team down with the arrival of the new bat and Onka darted one in then dutifully threw another up past the eyebrows to provoke a double step miss, Larry doing the rest to sweep the bails off faster than any lamb's tail in either Kent or New Zealand. Two wickets down in that over; now it was time for the Shackleton XI to believe and deliver that ruinous blow. Flounders, however, hung in until the bitter end, the lanky ginger opening bowler captain coming in at number 8 to prod, poke and nick enough to take the outcome to the final over, requiring eleven runs. Enid flung the ball to Daughtry who seemed to move away from catching it, reluctant after not taking any earlier wickets and feeling like each subsection of limb was being initiated into its own gang, unconcerned with the other – quarrelling over turf even. She fitfully shook her head, pleading with Enid not to allot this burden, as there were other bowlers with overs to spare. Now Enid had a plan in her head from the outset, but this move represented her first ever captain's 'gut-call' as she'd noticed throughout Daughtry's earlier spell, although struggling for rhythm, there hadn't been much bat on ball for the balls that were in the vicinity of a good length. Enid had anticipated the captain batting 10 or 11, thus elevating himself to finish-off these little ladies struck her as an egotistical interchange that should be exploited. Corin ran over – dually concerned – motioning for Enid to throw her the ball.

"Don't get him out," said Enid, dragging HB and Corin

together in a huddle. “We’re not winning this with wickets - we’re restricting captain gingernut, keeping him on strike.”

“I don’t think I can—” began Daughtry, her hands wringing together to shut down the visible shaking.

“This is the faith everyone who has played with you has in you,” interposed Enid.

“Just let those limbs free,” supported Corin, knowing her sister well enough by now to gauge the fleeting mind change wouldn’t supplant the left-field theory (and stubbornness); plus this didn’t seem the time, occasion or moment of urgency to second-guess.

“Get the ball wide of off, that’s all. Any length other than full or too short. You’ve got this—”

Enid brought most of the fielders in, including third man as a bluff ploy to get the Flounders captain to win it with a few lusty blows. Daughtry remeasured her run-up as the Flounders batters raised their shoulders in defiant provocation. There wasn’t a calm soul within a mile vicinity and Daughtry felt the tears pool above her lower eyelids - a teacup overfilled - then the reassuring stating the obvious to dispel the horror from Noel, mouthing “You’re bowling the final over?” benefacted by a quizzical, crazy-eyed expression that instantly took the sting out of Daughtry’s torment. He concluded with “Don’t eff it up.”

The first ball was a leg side wide with the captain inches away from glancing a four down to a vacant fine leg. Enid and Corin and Yapa and the whole team breathed a sigh of relief while the Flounders parents cheered. Ten to win. Daughtry’s next ball was a peach, pitching and lifting past the fending batter - dot ball. Ten off five. The next ball, not as good as the previous, did the business again, missing the outside edge after a wild heave that saw the ball travel over cow corner in the captain’s mind. Enid breathed a mini-sigh of relief as Daughtry trundled in once again, an untimely full toss mistimed straight above a reaching Corin at mid-on, the ball spooning up – a dropped catch but a certain boundary saved as the batsmen scampered two to keep the captain on strike. Corin smiled, shaking her hand as Enid wondered whether she'd shelled the catch on purpose to keep the captain in. The rest of the Shaky XI looked unfazed so, either team spirit was rocking, nerves stowed in the denial pouch of subconsciousness or the team actually all gelled on the dubious strategy of restricting another batsman from coming in to win the game for Flounders. Eight off three required now, the captain shifting his stance onto middle and off, likely to try to drag one onto the leg side as Daughtry's wide of off tactic had been rumbled.

Daughtry went even wider for the third last ball, the batsman taking a wide completely out of the equation by Steve Smithing across to the off side and clipping it – a putridly ugly schlepp – over mid-wicket for four. It was a good ball and the right tactic, almost following the Flounders captain who looked like he'd played that shot exclusively with the right hand. He raised his bat in triumph, silencing the doubters in the changing room who'd protested when he chose to send himself in to bat. Four required off two and Daughtry, encouraged by executing a plan with her limbs that her brain had decreed, strode in for the penultimate ball, a standard length delivery that was met with an across the line swipe, the ball clearing cover point as Onka sped after it, making an admirable stop, bouncing on his chin near the rope, to prevent the boundary and restrict Flounders to two runs. Two runs needed. One ball left.

Enid resisted bringing all the fielders in and calling the team together for a chat, motioning for Daughtry to bowl the ball, conscious that any attention on the magnitude of the situation or too-technical a masterplan would send Daughtry over the edge – she just had to continue – run and slam the ball in front of the batsman. Daughtry duly went through the mechanics, desperately trying not to think about anything but landing the ball in roughly the area that'd been working for her - wide of a length and just short of a length. Her legs felt heavy as she strode in, sending the ball down past the whoosh of the captain's bat, missing yet setting off down the pitch. Larry took a cleanish catch, uncertain whether to run in to the wickets to restrict the second run or have a go at a run out ... her instinct kicked and she flung an underarm throw that smacked into the stumps, the non-striker having already arrived after a back-up that began days before. The non-striker yelled at his captain, who'd reached the other end, to get his skates on for the second run to win the match. They went, arms and legs sprint pumping, a blur of snowy gloves and pads as Onka underarmed the ball back, looping above the unsettled stumps to an approaching Larry who caught the ball with one glove and pulled the stump from the ground with the other, the team all up in appeal. No hesitation from the umpire, the captain falling to his face after being a couple feet short of his crease.

"Is that a draw?" shouted Noel, pelting in to ultimate fist pump Daughtry, passing flailing degrees of celebration.

"It's a tie—" responded Corin.

"That feels like a—"

Loss, thought Enid.

CHAPTER >> 41

CIRCLE

The train carriage was largely empty save for an old lady engrossed in a newspaper sudoku and a suited and booted chap, so loud and confident on his mobile in the silent compartment he had to be in Sales. The Shaky squad able to partake in the excursion were split right down the middle between unspecified anticipation and wounded regret from the last match. Onka, the instigator of the trip, had given up trying to put a positive spin on any part of it, preferring to let fate and inner reformism determine the veritable outcome.

The train seemed to shake more than anyone was used to, throwing bodies from side-to-side recurrently, conventionally just into and out of a tunnel, which made for comedic effect, the speed boat ragdolls adjusting to anxious wonky faces every time it happened. Rebecca was along for the trip, accompanying Larry as the two linked arms to lessen the jolting. Daughtry elbowed and kneed Noel on several occasions which provided him another opportunity to milk an audience, these reactions the meat in the football diving and theatrical death scene sandwich, until she actually caught him flush in the eye for a future shiner.

"Someone will actually think you play cricket," tutted Rufus from a seat in the corner on his own as Noel blinked in disbelief, struggling to focus from the bony angle at which HB flapped her wings onto his pupil. Jacob handed Noel his glasses as a weak attempt at humour, while Corin surfed the turbulence with natural authority. As much as Enid tried to shake the feeling of losing dejection and rise up to captain this side, dusting leadership in all the directions required - a cakemaker's calling for dry sponge - she couldn't. The mirth of the rollercoaster train further amplified her sense that she was the only one who really cared about the outcome of the matches, Digners and Shaky cricket in general.

The journey was longer than expected and when the trip became smoother a calm enervation descended on the team, especially when the salesman to the stars got off and the old woman disregarded the sudoku for a spot of knitting. There had been little time to reflect after the tied opening match, a hasty rat-tat-tat team talk from Yapa as the Flounders changing room cleaner stood impatiently by, eager to wrap up the Saturday shift. Enid had not said much either, the raw sense that they could have won that game itching her insides, outside and temple sides, caustic in dredging up small moments of the game that could have, should have, might have, if only had, gone differently. Her analytical burden had become her retrospective nightmare and, even with Corin's support, she couldn't shrug it and move on - and her self-awareness of this inability, this remaining too true to her emotions, further amplified her self-doubt and burgeoning self-loathing.

Onka had provided the exposition that this was a rare occurrence, facilitated by the changing global rugby calendar. Not many really got it, but went along with the added pitch of stalking an international team, a visit to Pennyhill Park and leftover food from the buffet if Onka could work his magic and discover an intrusive charm many thought he failed to possess. The visit of a southern hemisphere rugby team for a charity exhibition was only possible because the South African club sides had joined the United Rugby Championship, finally abandoning the All Black dominated Super Rugby which had become noxious for the game in South Africa with the travel, impartial referees and convoluted structure that lost fans after the heyday in the late noughties. In the URC the South African club sides now pitted their pace, power and talent against the best club teams from Wales, Italy, Scotland and Ireland, which meant more frequent visits to the northern hemisphere and a reciprocated spoiling from wet, windy mud to the spiritual glory of Cape Town in summer. Onka's mother, a woman of so many diverse talents the team was beginning to realise, had acquaintances to the South African World Cup winning captain – Siyamthanda Kolisi – a national and international icon, able to lead the barrier-breaking Springboks in a manner more befitting of a saint.

When the train journey finally ended, the seemingly infinite walk further dented any optimism in the group, even Larry's permasmile and Noel's dad jokes waning. Onka had insisted they dress up too – not quite dress suit and ball gown but enough to look respectable, so the added discomfort of what, for many, was a seldom worn sartorial proclamation, went beyond the camel's back, hay bales raining on the Shaky parade. Perhaps the timing of this venture was ill-conceived but, heck, beggars could not be choosers when stalking the Springboks. Or so Onka felt anyway.

Pennyhill Park didn't fail to impress though, lifting spirits ever so slightly upon meandering down the treelined entrance past the golf course on the right. The car park looked empty and ominous with no ubiquitous team bus to unnaturally hog multiple spaces, although this was not a team gathering for a match but rather a shake-and-smile or hopefully an exhibition training session for a good cause.

At the first sign of a prohibitory, officious, reception person, Onka strode forward to elucidate that, although not likely on a list in the vicinity, his mother had confirmed an audience with the team for a short period between formal commitments. With a dose of circumspection, the receptionist pointed them towards the breakfast buffet, his tone and conviction swaying her as opposed to the clunkily honest justification of why a superfan's mom was brokering a meet-and-greet. The breakfast hall was empty, so the team politely meandered through the corridors, marvelling at the oversized tapestries and obscenely high arched ceilings. If a team was wandering around Pennyhill Park, they were either deft hands at hide-and-seek or all on a word abstinence challenge, as the silence was so eerie even Jacob's feather draping footsteps sounded like a buffalo stampede.

After an hour or so, hope was all but abandoned even after a few visits back to enquire at reception, free reign granted but a line drawn for the guest's privacy. Onka's shoulders sloped, something none of the team had ever witnessed on a cricket field, so the team tried to cheer him up with an 'all is not lost' speech, even though there was nothing left to do but return to the train station. Corin put an arm around him as they walked out and Wei Ping showed him a YouTube clip of an elderly Asian woman being ten pin bowled down on an escalator as a rogue bag became unattended, barrelling down to ster-yike her, cartwheeling out of shot but funny enough despite the security cam footage. Onka cranked out an accepting no-teeth smile, appreciating the gestures but acutely disappointed that the quest had ended in failure, putting the small bat he'd brough along for signing deep into his side blazer pocket, hidden from the world until the next set of inspirational worldies decided to appear, and who knew when the heck that was going to take place!

Knuckles dragging, the group trudged back to the train

station, passing through a quaint, cobbled high street, the pigeon control admirable. Whilst meandering past an artisan coffee shop, a faint celebratory "Bokke" emanated from the depths, Onka failing to look up past the 2019 replica shirt badge he'd become fixated upon, a trance of green and gold, bobbling up and down on his chest with each step. Rufus tapped him on the shoulder, muttering "Your people," stopping him in his tracks to face the entrance of the coffee shop, the entire Shaky team staring in as though marvelling a modern miracle. As Onka clambered through his own team's crowd, he burst through the line of cricketers to come upon the 2019 World Cup Winning Springboks, enjoying an innocuous coffee, spread across almost the entirety of the coffee shop. The staff behind the counter beamed smiles, only neutralised by the rugby team's reimbursed smiles, grateful for the service, humble to the core. Onka felt a lifetime of not belonging, being pushed out, being let down and feeling uninspired come spewing out of his eyes, so he put his hand over his face to shield from both teams' view.

Simultaneously, Enid Hanratty, the captain and chief of the Shackleton Cricket Team and Siya Kolisi, the captain and chief of the Springbok Rugby Team, converged on Onka, both sensing the tightening body language was something that required attention. Enid put her hand on Onka's back and Siya placed a palm on his shoulder, the controlling of the shuddering futile.

"Is everything alright, young man?" asked Kolisi. "Nice shirt by the way."

Enid took a breath and stuck out her hand. "Mr Kolisi, this is Onkarabile Madonsela, an unwavering fan of South African rugby and a key member of the Shackleton Cricket Team."

"God has answered our prayers," responded Siya without intrusively forcing the boy to look up.

"He did," responded Enid. "We were a team in dire need of support and some cricketing talent and he came to help us when we needed it most. He stood up for us even with the opposition chasing him. And this is the rest of the team."

With the team sensing they were truly in the presence of greatness, fumbling iPhones for selfies and Enid's distraction towards the team, Onka raised his head, wiping the tears covertly with his forearm, now slightly embarrassed. Siya's smile only broadened as he graciously posed with each individual kid and the team, inviting them in to meet the rest of the Boks. The size of these humans shook most of the Shakies, apart from Daughtry who could at least maintain eye level with some of them. Despite the bulk and ominous shadows thrown all around the coffee shop floor as one behemoth after another blocked out a light or whacked it with his head - sending the bulb Newton's cradling back and forth - these men exuded kindness, decency, good manners and unassuming graciousness. The team were invited to share a coffee, no hint of problematic intrusion in sight, as the underdog cricketers interspersed to share a story from the archetypal underdog side, burdened with expectation and challenges to perpetually lift a country against the odds and often written off before kick-off.

Most of the Springboks had, in some shape or form, a cricket pedigree, albeit historic with many almost going the cricketing route but for the strong rugby call to dangle the incentive at life's fork in the road, yet still with a lingering fervency for everything cricket. The interest shown in the inaugural Digners Cup competition was conspicuous and the largely humble beginnings established a kindred coalition to tag onto the breaking the mould through achievement against all the odds. Duane Vermeulen, Eben Etzebeth and Damian de Allende swapped stories with Corin, Noel and Daughtry on the merits, shortcomings and afflictions of quick bowling, Doogz's marvelling at his three wickets opening in the first match of a double-header exhibition match against the Proteas easily quelled by Big Duane's solitary wicket in the following game, dismissing the greatest to have played the game: Jacques Kallis. Handré Pollard and Willie le Roux regaled further with the batters in the Shaky line-up, the Springbok flyhalf modestly never out of place as a stylish number 4 bat and the unsung fullback taking a rare paradoxical excursion to commemorate his leading 200 strike rate, lone six and one-handed catch on the boundary that got better and better with each rendition. Duane had the final say though, the only recognised 'allrounder' in the squad, much to the delight of anyone in the Shackleton team with designs on emulating his peerless actual allrounder display at number 8 – a man-of-the-match performance – on the biggest stage of all: the World Cup final.

Enid's brave face was put to the test by the felicitous distraction and colourful tales, the spirituality of the two sports finding harmony in adversity. She made every effort to shake the gloom, her appreciative smile hiding the despondence, until her cohort captain, no stranger to his own encumbrances, took a benevolent meander into her predicament.

"Captaincy never came easily to me; it still doesn't but I simply try to remain true to the person I want to be," said Siya sitting beside Enid.

"Problem is, I don't think we can get much better from here – despite all the will in the world. We've tied our first match."

"We lost ours. Then went on to win the World Cup."

"But you guys never stopped believing."

"Maybe not as a collective but as individuals, sure we did. It is natural to have doubt, question decisions, obsess over every element. The burden of captaincy which can also be a blessing."

"How does captaining a bunch of misfits when you're the one who got everyone into this mess in the first place turn out to be a blessing?"

Siya took a long, thoughtful sip of his coffee,

contemplating the true differences between the challenges faced and to come.

"I think that in a strange kind of way we are all misfits, trying to find and test ourselves in everything we do. Taking responsibility for your team is something you'll continue to do whether you are captain or not - it means you care about the outcome. We play every match for the South African people, to provide the hope in between the daily chores and tough situations most fans find themselves in. You might play for a different reason, but your message, your breaking of the opposition's stranglehold, your fight when all hope seems lost is what makes your team special - makes it more than just a game of cricket."

Enid could feel the back of her tonsils swell, blinking a molten film across her eyeballs that in no way tallied to the unsighted tiredness blinkers that blighted her first match. This guy, this leader of humans, his team so generous with their valuable time, was not sitting there to provide platitudes and hollow generic reassurances - he somehow understood her plight and associated juvenile troth, without judging or removing any magnitude of the confrontations ahead.

He got this and told Enid she got this too.

Chapter >> 42

On The Leg

The lead up to Saturday's match witnessed a concerted effort to make the school look neat, presentable even, only a handful of students allocated to cleaning there under duress. The pavilion began to resemble resplendence, but not as an *olde worlde*, arched, symmetrical pavilion might but rather if say a rave had a baby with a ski chalet and then that baby had a baby with the baby from a chicken outhouse and public library. Mishmash chic abounded but who was anyone to stymie creative expression even if the intent was bordering on sociopathic splotches of colour and decorative ornaments that made no sense in a school and had even less to do with cricket, the voodoo lounge result buoyantly unnerving any a visiting opposition. Most volunteers remained within the purple, sage and maroon guidelines, which might have contributed more towards the clashing monstrosity than any form of hindered control. One faithful student even left little numbers, shaped from discarded wax, each wrapped in alternating purple, sage and maroon wrappers on the opposition's bench, a cobbled together health warning that they were not edible instituted by Yapa just in time for the opposing team's arrival.

Unlike Flounders, this team - colloquially known as SanFran and formally known as Golden Gate Cathedral - was variable, volatile even. On their day they could likely beat anyone, which is why Enid, Yapa and Wei Ping all resoundingly agreed, getting on top early was vital. The nature of T20 cricket also meant that keeping the opposition down was harder, as small events quickly became seismic when defending or chasing a total. They also didn't have the depth Flounders possessed with half the team extremely capable and the other half invisible passengers. SanFran played a bit more fast and loose, unpredictable probably to themselves but, if there was slant either way, their strength lay in their batting, a top order capable of putting the ball far away and fashioning unorthodox shots that some of the other private schools may have shunned.

The Shackleton XI arrived to a raucous reception, a line of self-appointed cheerleaders and supporters lining their path into the pavilion, Enid feeling like Charlie as she approached Wonkaland, unable to resist letting Corin know that this made her Veruca Salt! Some of the fans had never even seen the players before, the occasion all too much for the likes of Daughtry who stooped in blushing embarrassment as she sped to the safety of the technicolour cricket pavilion. Noel lapped it up, raising an arm and bopping gangsta style, while Onka and Rufus kept stoic faces, shunning the weird adulation for the actual task at hand. Jacob couldn't resist and double twirled then mimicked a tap routine, even though the grass was too forgiving on the reverberation. Larry spotted Rebecca in the crowd and flicked an imaginary booger her way with Wei Ping and Yapa bringing up the rear, the contrasting approach polar in forearm balanced laptop and bits of scribbled paper respectively.

The Shackleton Senior Cricket XI ladies and gentlemen.

SanFran brough their own posse to counter anything Shaky mustered though, a snaking line of SUVs unable to find consistent parking or ground stable enough to protect their automotive wonderpets from either the elements or the marvelling eyes of the Shaky students, the first sign of shiny dragging at least half away from any supporting duties. The day looked fair as the tanks rounded on the game, grey-white cloud toggery covering all the blue above, a sharp breeze and unsettled milieu but with no consistent rain forecast throughout the day. As the match was T20, less time was required so the start time was afternoon which further subsidised the sense of festival and occasion.

Enid lost the toss and SanFran chose to bat which didn't seem disastrous even though Enid would have preferred to bat first as well. That said, the newcomer nature of the Shaky pitch had put some doubt in her mind as, although they'd played on a few of the strips, the pitch had not yet fully settled despite the groundkeeper's best efforts. The SanFran boys didn't seem like not-nice blokes but they came across so self-absorbed it didn't really matter what or who or how the opposition came at them, they were there to brush aside man, woman, child and cricketer alike.

Prior to the first ball a makeshift band formed on the sideline, orchestrated quite literally by Miss Hazard, resplendent in full supporter's kit, maroon tracksuit bottoms, a sage blouse and a purple-looking ski jacket that may have once been black. The cherry quite literally (again) on top was a Shaky team cricket cap, bestowed upon her in class by the sisters, a mark of the gratitude for the accretion she'd selflessly devoted much of her time towards. The band seemed like a good idea until it played, the trumpets so far off-key, pigeons in the area fled and a passing truck with the windows down nearly ran a red light. The triangle and recorders sounded okay as the lone trombone might have but the introduction of the violins – all three – the set more akin to an aggravated plaque removing flossing session than the harmonious subtlety of a crisp bow stroke, gradually saw the group disbanded until only the boy with the golden symbols was left to wait his cue, a wicket the most likely benefactor.

Shaky were out early, a spring in the side steps with waves to the crowd and unaccustomed adulation being lapped up from all directions. Enid decided to open with Onka, early left-arm wrist spin to either restrict the runs or take early wickets - both of which Onka was more than capable of producing. The field was an attacking one by T20 standards, a leg slip to disguise the potential use of the googly and a short square leg to pitch the googly, most of SanFran's top order right-handers. Rufus from the other end, much to Corin's dismay, which was probably just the enticement, Corin's variety and guile only matched by Rufus's claims of variety and guile; perhaps a short spell if Corin was liable to burst from mid-on. The SanFran openers looked strong, thick set the both of them with square pads to match their unrelenting jaws. Both strode with what looked like little purpose, the occasion to swagger forth towards the middle on an occasion such as this too good to squander. The directive from Yapa's paper to impassive face to one-word instructions was clear ... hurry. Quick on the over changeovers and rush between balls, giving them no time to ponder and railroad the deliveries. Shaky had a train to catch.

Play began and Onka rattled through the first six balls with little damage, beating the bat a few times, only a handful of runs acquired by the opposition. The opening bats' soirée in the middle took an age and Rufus was turned back after starting his run-up three times as the number 2 bat surveyed where he intended to launch the balls. Now, Rufus would likely argue that end gave little assistance to the seamers or perhaps they preferred the ball coming on, but the chunky opener with the zig-zagged eyebrows put the ball to all corners of the park, belting an unsolicited 22 from the over, Enid's rolling fingers signalling Corin would assume the bowling responsibilities from that end after Onka's second, the hint of a smirk distinguished from Corin's face when she realised this kid could bat and she might suffer and even worse fate.

Onka's second over took some more tap but he did pry out one of the openers, a googly which turned considerably popped up into the air after a misjudged sweep, the ball looping into Onka's hands. SanFran's number 3 was savvy enough to see out the over and wait for the destruction the other end, the confidence of the zigzagger on a 366.67 strike rate bleeding from underneath his helmet, his gloves and over the top of his white trousers. Corin opened with a slower ball which went for six back over her head, Rufus unable to stifle a giggle as he ran to retrieve the ball, Miss Hazard covering her head as the ball almost connected. Corin's next ball was quick but short and got pulled for a one-bounce four over square leg, his score on 32 before the ring of the symbol player's reverberation had died down after the first wicket. Enid knew better than to run over for some consolation or advice, which any other player would certainly have received, failing even to alter the field, the veracity of having a sibling in the same team made all the more real by the nature of said sibling. Corin was visibly fuming but dug deep to bowl a sweet off cutter, which beat the bat passing at Mach 3, followed by a groan - this kid didn't deal in dots.

Fourth ball of the over and Corin took a risk she knew no one except Enid and her dad would understand - she gave him a boundary, then again to set up a wicket with the last ball of the over. Balls four and five were bowled after square leg had dropped right back, the short stuff met with such venom, both sixes almost losing the ball in two separate neighbouring front gardens. Now came the moment of truth - the batsman was no mug so was either expecting another or the bluff as full and straight, a yorker if the accuracy was realisable. Corin's bluff though was not only balls four and five, and not only a flustered red-pink face when dispatched earlier in the over.

"Deception for a quick with the ball in your hand should involve all your emotions, creating an unconscious understanding in the batsman's mind of how you bowl and, most of all, include patience," her father had told her, playing the same trick on her in a family game at Highgate Wood.

Corin lumbered in, looking uncomfortable, beaten almost, her torso pendulating from side to side and her limbs all out of whack, a Medusa with four recalcitrant snakes. This ball was quick. Much quicker than the others, short and coming on to the batsman, surprising him but not before he'd failed to come through on the shot, the ball skying like a Macdonald's M arch into the clouds towards Noel and deep square leg. Enid felt it might clear even that, the longest boundary, but Corin knew all Noel had to do was take a sharp catch on the descent, preferably fingers up as the ball was still slanting over the rope for six, and the wicket was hers. Noel went fingers down and was cramped for room, his elbows pointing higher than natural, but held onto the ball, running back and mock wiping the sweat towards Daughtry, whose hand was still on her heart. The symbols clanged.

Although the total and in turn the run rate was healthy with only a smattering of wickets down, Golden Gate Cathedral's windy sails went from North Sea bluster to calm tropical sea breeze. Corin instantly came off, Enid saving her for the death with the level of venom she could extract from the home pitch, which resulted in the SanFran middle order swinging at ghosts and only ghostbusting some of them as Daughtry, Noel and Enid took a sizable chunk out of the middle orders. Noel, in particular, buoyed after his game changing catch, bowling left-arm over, straightening the ball up twice to get the only two lefties, both pouched by Larry.

Earlier, Onka had bowled through his allocated four overs, one of those prodigious spells that unbelievably produced no further wickets - the cruelty of cricket's injustice on display.

The top order of the tail wagged towards the middle of the teen overs, using what was now looking more like steep bounce to their advantage by going back and hitting behind square, the speed of the deliveries causing many a scrambling fielder to just miss saving the boundary. Enid, again surprised by her own instinct out of nowhere, sidled over to the diminutive Peter P. Trumpleton, the not out kid from the junior ranks, to ask if he fancied a bowl. She's spotted his ability - possibly accidental - to wobble and skid the ball at the same time in the nets, the trajectory from a low point and quick arm action making his deliveries all the more unorthodox and unsettling. Peter's eyes shook when she asked him, although one over couldn't hurt, could it, so he accepted, giving the ball a foundational rub on his trousers as Daughtry limped off.

The 15th over from Pete Trump-please-make-a-ton or Pete Trump-please-take-a-ton-of-wickets was nothing if not eventful. By now the middle-lower order had put San Fran in a more commanding position and, with a few wickets in hand, the nature of T20 cricket meant they'd earned the right to swashbuckle their boots to the brim, willow to ball at compound angles and points of contact the order of any T20 day. The first ball wobbled and skidded low, drawing a silence from all of the rest of the team bar Rufus, Peter smiling in disbelief. The next ball went towards first slip and was called a wide. The third ball found the boundary, a good shot over extra cover to be fair and the fourth found the top of middle stump, the symbols clash hastily clanged as Larry almost caught one of the bails. The fifth ball was also a wicket, Larry confident to stand up and stump the batsman, putting Peter on a hat-trick, something that was certainly not part of the plan. The final ball of the over really was a full bunger, gladly accepted by the new batsman and sailing over the bowler's head for a lofted six. Rufus shook his head and warmed up without instruction.

The last five overs for Shaky represented a tawdry fielding display with fumbles, a lack of urgency and some slovenly feet dragging histrionics. The SanFran total had clicked along, especially as the halfway point approached and the pitch started to look more concerningly variable, but this might have been the inconsistent bowling. 20 runs came off the final over bowled by Rufus and 16 off the penultimate over from Corin, something not quite clicking as each digressed from full and straight to either full or not straight, both believing they were doing more with the ball than was actually happening. SanFran ended on 173-8 after the allotted 20 overs as Miss Hazard had one last gasp attempt to get the band playing, having naturally selected who she thought wouldn't offend the refined eardrums of the travelling opposition supporters. The band ended almost as quickly as the SanFran innings had, a palpable shift in momentum now that runs were firmly on the board and Shaky had to hunt them down in this do-or-die clash.

There was a temptation to rip up the batting order, going with a brand-new combination, but this was tempered by Yapa who didn't want to divagate too far from what had almost worked in the 50-over format. He insisted on one tweak though, swapping Corin and Enid in the batting line-up, another piece of paper buried in the depths of his instructional fist.

Jacob and Rufus sauntered out to open, the familiarity of the opening pair symbolised by the lessening gap between the two, Jacob's flurried steps to keep up with Rufus not rehearsed. Some might have even argued Rufus slowed down to a snail's pace less than a strut but it could have just been the spongy outfield. Out in the middle Jacob looked lovingly up at Rufus – a dog's faithful gaze towards an owner awaiting instruction – as he looked the pitch up and down and pointed to the end Jacob should be, the striker's end facing the first ball. There was just something about facing that first ball and, despite Rufus's bravado, he'd avoid that at most costs, unless the opener was a 'turkey spinner' he recognised as a potential 'golden goose' from the Corkridge days. Both the SanFran openers were quick bowlers and neither looked remotely like poultry so Jacob had the honour of teeing up for the first ball, to be delivered by a left-arm quick from over the wicket.

From the boundary the first ball looked as though the bowler fell right over into the turf, but this was an optical illusion as the slingy nature of his delivery saw his arm come through almost parallel to the ground. The ball went past Jacob who did not have a clue what to do, the unorthodox nature of the bowler's action so foreign, Jacob just had no muscle memory to cope. Rufus, breaking etiquette much to the groans of the fielding side, trotted up the middle beckoning Jacob closer, sensing a form of intervention was required.

"Open your stance," Rufus hurriedly spat. "Ball's coming through low and skidding across your body so don't prod but commit all the way if you follow the ball. Good?"

"Not quite, but hey, let's dance!"

Rufus stifled a smile as he unapologetically returned to the non-striker's end, standing unnaturally to the umpire's left who shook his head. Jacob danced the Kozachok the other end, a nifty squat to stand double Dougie. The next ball, quite remarkably, went sailing over extra cover for a three bounce four as Jacob got his footwork just right and stepped across off to meet the ball and throw his hands through the shot. He beamed and Rufus – deep inside himself, nodded in approval, then outwardly frowned back at Jacob down the pitch as though playing a shot like that second ball of the innings, even if a T20 match, was plain irresponsible. Jacob though was undeterred as he'd never played a shot like that in his life and felt this was the beginning of something special, something groundbreakingly unique, something - like an impromptu dance move at a disco - had to happen now and look plain fabulous doing so.

The following ball got up a bit more than anticipated, likely propelled by the bowler's frustration, yet you would have struggled to spot Jacob's surprise as once again he threw his feet, pad, bat, hands and bodyweight in a synchronised direction to top edge this ball at a strange yet safe angle to the keeper's left for four. Ball three was an old-fashioned back foot drive through the covers, Jacob's anticipation now leading SanFran to believe they were up against a technically proficient, uber-footworked little titan of the openers game, prompting a field change to load the off side. A sensible single to the left of cover point, a soft hands Joe Root nudge down to third man, put Rufus on strike who nearly went out on the last ball of the over, a pea shooter which he dug out in the nick of time, his crouching demonstrative shock not dissimilar to Jacob's warm-up.

Cricket can be a cruel mistress and Jacob, looking better than he ever had with bat in hand, tickled one onto his pads which looked pretty darn close to a dead LBW even though the edge did make a sound. The deflection wasn't noted by the umpire at all, who might have still been fuming at the jamboree in the middle of the pitch after the first ball, his fellow umpire nodding in smug appreciation as the dreaded Out finger went up, an equivalent trajectory prostate exam less intrusive. Jacob was not keen to move and dug his heels in, even Rufus looking disappointed on his behalf, the popcorn view of a fellow opener making hay disappearing and shifting the onus onto the partner, the burden of a faraway total suddenly daunting. Jacob held up his bat in defiance to signify the inside edge and the umpire's resolve stiffened even further, shooing him off the pitch, approaching with harmful intent. Jacob, perhaps not well versed in the propriety of standing up to an umpire's decision - albeit woefully incorrect - eventually hauled his now leaden feet towards the gaudy pavilion, his bodily strangulations unable to stem the tears. Corin walked past him, coming in at number 3, and simply let him be, her now emblematic sideways hops passing Jacob's distraught figure as he kept his helmet on to hide this intensity of emotion he'd never experienced: life had injustices, yes, but this just felt like a heart-expelling, ripped from person, sucker punch which might take a decade or so to heal.

Corin and Rufus both played it cool with one another out in the middle, a little too cool for school though, Corin with her own plan and Rufus avoiding prescribing one. The run rate was slightly under the required rate, yet Shaky had nine wickets in hand with Yapa's plan to promote Corin likely the all-in gamble to win this match. Corin had to play. There was no point keeping her wicket when runs were the currency to win this match, another 150 required from this point; and runs meant risks which really didn't faze Corin in the slightest. Her challenge was when to go; when the bowling looked familiar enough to move the field around and pierce the gaps. Enid struggled to watch from the pavilion, every now and again pacing behind the building, a captain's hide-and-go-seek when the vested interest was her own blood. Corin took guard: middle and leg.

The first ball Corin faced was met with an assured defensive block, the ball dying at her feet like a dud grenade. She leaned down to throw it back to the opposition's keeper and was met with a quizzical stare as the ball might have not stopped moving, although the velocity with which it was meandering back to stumps was not threatening. Handling the ball was real, yet this SanFran team were unlikely to kick up a fuss and the umpire had thankfully not seen the ball rolling. The next ball sat up and Corin rocked back to slam it through mid-wicket, connecting nicely but finding the fielder who might have been slightly deeper than a usual mid-wicket - given this, T20's cavalier singles and Corin's post-middling eagerness, she called Rufus through for the run, setting off with intent. Rufus looked up at the mid-wicket who had already gathered the ball and screamed back louder than anyone had ever heard him articulate anything, letting out a child's favourite deleterious countenance. For a millisecond Corin kept going, the stubborn resolve and dislike of Rufus spurring her onwards through the charge but when she saw he was rooted to the other crease, palm raised aloft, she stopped on her heels and scrambled back towards her crease as the ball came flying in from mid-wicket. In slow motion the ball passed her visor and she instinctively dived at the same second, deflecting the ball away from the keeper to scupper what would have been a certain run out.

From the array of fielder's vantage points, it didn't look great, and the team didn't quite appeal but arms were thrown up into the air as the ball squirted away over the boundary rope and Corin refused to run, crumbled in a heap, the tip of her bat dutifully over the line of the crease, a chess player's refusal to let go when pondering a strategic move. The fielding team's dissatisfaction with the sequence of events spilled over to the umpires who gathered in a huddle, hunched shoulders scheming. Corin's face was one of genuine contrition as she got up, regathering herself and adjusting all cricket accessories which had relocated in the violent lunge: pads, gloves, thigh pad and especially helmet that had rotated almost to face backwards, Lego spaceman style. Yapa, sensing the umpires were about to cross a Rubicon that Shackleton would not be able to return from, strode onto the field with centred intent, even Rufus raising two eyebrows as he met the convened umpires head on.

"Accident," Yapa stated factually.

"Excuse me," responded the umpire. "You cannot be on

the field of play. That was an intentional obstruction of the ball to prevent a run out."

"Accidental. She was getting back to crease. No change in direction. Straight back."

"Mr ..."

"Yapa."

"Mr Yapa, this is a decision we need to make ... independently. Plus the ball before, she handled."

"That decision passed. Back to fielder when diving. No vision."

"These sorts of freak events don't occur normally Mr Yapa; how will these young cricketers learn if we skirt the rules?"

"Same way I learn when playing for Sri Lanka: fairness."

Umpire one with red face looked at umpire two with an even redder face, uncertain how to proceed from here. Neither had recognised the international cricketer, now of smaller stature and warier expression than the heydays of his playing career.

"No point making an example of this accident. Show spirit of game through fair consideration and rules. Plus no formal appeal now that the allotted time has passed so can't give out if no appeal."

Corin, Rufus, Onka and Enid clocked what Yapa had achieved - he'd taken the umpire's ability to give Corin out away through the time rule of appeal allowance. Had he not entered the field of play and stunned all into anticipatory silence, the fielding side might have lodged an appeal but as things stood they hadn't and the umpires knew they couldn't give Corin out. Once the danger was over, Corin walked over to Rufus to address the other elephant on the pitch.

"There was a run there, bucko!" said Corin, the entire front of her kit scraped with grass and dirt.

"Nope and nope! If you want to play Kamikaze cricket, you can donate your own wicket, not mine."

"We've got to get over this ... for this to work."

"Play it as it comes."

"I've been ... unfair to you ... from the beginning. Judged you."

"Is this your version of an apology?"

"Nope and nope!"

Rufus grinned.

"They've got some spinners warming up; left-arm finger spinners I think. I've played against some of them before. Not much turn but tight and hard to score off. Also a few wild card quicks they might try throughout the innings."

"I was told you were the quick single king of Corkridge."

"Ha-ha. I'll run and I'll back your call but there has to be a run there; or at least three-quarters of a run."

"I'll back you too. From now on."

The running between the wickets that followed was Torvill and Deanesque, the synchronicity unearthing singles, two and threes where for all money there were only dots, singles and twos respectively. As though when you just click and don't really need to even call, the wavelength one and the same, the earlier run out scare akin to flicking a light switch on within both players as the run rate continued just below required. Even when Rufus called Corin through safe in the knowledge that the ball was heading to the fielder's weaker hand, she trustingly went and made it home with about six whiskers to spare. It wasn't quite them smiling at each other after each stollen run, but the mutual respect began to ooze out through shot selection and placement, safe in the comfort of an able, willing, running partner. What certainly didn't dent the endeavour was that both were quick across the turf - sprinter standard - and when two plus were on offer, the ubiquitous competitive streak popped up as the two always checked when turning at the crease whether they'd pipped the other on the rotation. It all started to look too darn easy until Rufus fell with the total just shy of 100 required at 68 for 2, followed by a period of what should have been storm weathering but ended up being pelted by lightning.

Rufus wasn't run out ... thankfully, but he was looking decent and fluid when he skipped down to a lofty offie and got beaten for flight: stumped as he scrambled back to get his bat down. Corin gave him a nod of approval which he tried to ignore as he walked off, Onka in at number 4 to manage the delicate balance between steering the solidity of the ship while keeping the scoreboard ticking over like a wound that required bleeding, coagulated platelets not welcome for this flow. Every game he seemed to look taller than the previous thought Corin as he took guard, his unexpected right-handed batting stance generating a slavering exigency from the left-arm off spinner, eager to add to his tally of wickets as Onka's high backlift provided more incentive. Expecting *nog* an eyebrow tickling lofted delivery, the canny bowler darted one in at Onka's pads, the dull thud echoing through the band, pavilion and even reverberating around the school's corridors. The team went up as you would expect but Onka was quietly confident it was missing leg when the umpire gave it out. SanFran went into delirious meltup, channelling Diversity when they first hit the dance scene, a human pyramid of celebration instantly dulling the remaining Shaky support on the sidelines. Onka, an outstanding proponent of the integrity of the human spirit, showed no form of dissent and left, head stooped but not letting any further overt disappointment tarnish the etiquette of the game. When an umpire gave you out, you accepted the decision with grace, humility and sportsmanship. Even if the decision was more shocking than Eskom's ineptitude.

"Isn't he meant to be good?" a few of Shaky supporters muttered, those not versed in the trials and tribulations of the game of cricket.

So two became three wickets with nine overs bowled and

eleven remaining, Enid coming out to join the party - her sister's party - out in the middle, the SanFran tail now so dangled from a height, even a period of relative calm might not stifle this lot. Enid had to face a hat-trick ball and, despite knowing that her wicket was more valuable than most, she was safe in the understanding that a top order hat-trick in this pressure cauldron might just push SanFran's belief beyond the point of no return, rendering Shaky's Digners Cup inauguration one to be shelved in the forgettable section of the mental library. She felt more relaxed than anticipated and her sister looked set for a sizable contribution the way she was seeing the ball, which gave Enid more license to support rather than lead - welcome respite from the burden of captaincy. Now to just get through this ball.

The bowler took his time, ratcheting up the tension, bringing most of the field in to pressure Enid, a few chirps even starting to bounce about like water-balloons that refuse to pop. Was he due to emulate the wide armed LBW-generating dart or give it some air like the ball that got Rufus and see if this Shaky pitch could assist his quest for the first Digners hat-trick of the season? He spun the ball in his hands, motioning underneath the ball, foreboding and poised all wrapping into one ball of medium brown, flared nostrilled, wide stanced élan. He kicked at the turf, hoofing doubts down the pitch past Enid, the keeper, over the boundary and up the wild flower hill. He sniffed too, a loud guttural pull of air into those spectacular nostrils, forcing Corin to look away as she simply hated anything to do with snot, mucus or catarrh of any sort. She gripped her stomach, an instinctive self-hug which didn't fail to divert the bowler's resolve, so he did it again, this one more vehement, more voracious, more hat-trickish.

The blur of the awkward, arced delivery only attributable to left-arm finger spinners came fast at Enid, the blur of two fingers splitting towards her face, around the ball, the seam still and angled, the art of the dart disguised as loopier than a self-congratulatory politician. She got in line early … it seemed, watchfully circumspect, the bat angled back at no angle at all, determined to value survival over an opportunistic run or four. Then something clicked insider her, that realisation than although the bowler had given this a serious rip, his hat-trick glory excitement had pushed the delivery a few inches further up the pitch, overpitched and ripe as a black mouldy banana for Enid's signature and fast becoming archetypal shot, the old-fashioned front-foot cover drive. The ease with which she played the stroke – no broken wrists in sight and full makers name up the pitch – and the aesthetic beauty of the shot, slowly dissipating from the game, drew gasps and even an approving nod from the bowler. The ball skimmed across the outfield, the groundkeeper's crisp even grass stems throwing hands up in the air to propel the ball towards the boundary sooner than it deserved, which was some feat! Enid drew breath for what seemed like the first time in six minutes and Corin exhaled after holding hers for the same duration.

The Hanratty sisters were off and what followed was a quick-fire fifty partnership, complete with technical radiance and subtle innovation that habitually threw captain, bowler and fielder, individually and as a collective. Enid's watchful solidity nicely underpinned Corin's license to accelerate and the two generated the highest buzz of crowd approval as the game looked like nearing a tame conclusion in Shackleton's favour. Yapa's theory on bringing Enid in after Corin to symbiotically enhance each's game, tactics and role had worked … thus far.

Entering the 18th over, Shaky required an outwardly modest 28 runs off 18 balls with seven wickets in hand. There had been a few nervy moments as you would expect but both bats looked set, determined to finish this match off and register Shackleton's first Digners Cup win. The band was now in full swing, those able to play achieving some harmony and those not able to play still relegated to the cheering supporters stand, now in full fettle as the Hanratty girls readied for the final three overs. SanFran seemed to be going with the almost hat-trick bowler and one of the openers for the death, an expectation of full and straight from both, the Shaky pitch flinging the odd demon of variable bounce now that the first full match in its recent history was drawing to a rousing close.

The start went single-single, the left-arm spinner, choosing prophylactic restriction over any form of deceptive attack. The third ball, another dart, saw Corin give herself room on the leg side and open the face to target the vacant cover region, the ball not quite middling and angling more towards cover point who sped in to fumble the ball, leaving it behind. The girls, snap-necked at each other to test whether there was actually a run on offer, their dad's words of 'never run on a misfield' reverberating in both their skulls. Corin called Enid through regardless as the ball appeared some way behind the fielder, now scrabbling back to retrieve, yet both girls did not set off with virulent intent, an uncommon tentative misstep at both ends. Corin was a full quarter of the way down the pitch when she changed her mind about the run, Enid having backed up sufficiently to be almost halfway. Both girls stopped in the middle, frozen in uncertainty as the fielder, spotting the bigger gap, whipped the ball into the bowler who cogently caught it and gratefully slapped the bails off. Corin was staring dead ahead deep into Enid eyes and began approaching, attempting to pass Enid and thus cop the out from her call, appearing as though they'd crossed during the mayhem of the run out. Enid shook her head and mouthed "Finish this" before walking off.

Corin was visibly distraught having just run her sister out and Larry, in next, did her best to assure Corin that this was a minor blip which they could overcome if they focussed for the next two and a half overs. Corin kept looking over at Enid's disappearing figure, the slope of her shoulders, her stooped head, her trailing bat - this might have even been worse than scratching E all over the wooden banister when they were younger, the sword from the Playmobile soldier the weapon of framing choice which she'd never owned up to her parents about. Enid had copped the punishment and all these years later Corin wondered whether it was juvenile amusement, jealousy or some form of curious boredom that has spurred her to deface the banister and put her sister into solitude for the afternoon. That dollhouse she got all to herself that day was bittersweet - magical for the first five minutes then oppressively lonely for the remainder of the afternoon.

Corin just couldn't shake the shame and got clean bowled the next ball, lazily missing a straight one attempting an extravagant lofted drive. Larry, looking concerned piped out "Missing your sister that much?" as much to calm herself as hand Corin the benevolence she required at this moment. If the sisters had conspired to lose this game from this situation, this might likely be the complete end point for the Shackleton Cricket team. Noel's eternal optimism popped up in front of Larry and Rebecca screamed encouragement from the pavilion, a hush laying waste to the earlier celebrations. Noel was facing the last two balls of the over as Corin had kept strike after the run out and then been bowled. As it stood 26 runs required off 14 balls, the acuteness of the rate's increase not lost on Larry but perhaps lost on Noel who survived the first ball (only just) and went for a big heave-ho the following ball to find a fielder in the deep. Peter P. came forward and would face the first ball of the penultimate over as Larry and Noel had crossed when Noel was dismissed. Peter looked even smaller than normal, all laden with oversized cricket gear as though someone had poured a basket of laundry on top of his head. His bat looked like an ornamental mini, liable to break at the first breath of force. Looking at the width and height of the bowler he was facing, the bat might spontaneously shatter at the mere prospect of having to meet the ball dead on as it malevolently sped down the track towards bails and head, both apparently at the same altitude.

Peter's stance was wide which made his diminutive stature even lower, liable to be lost in one of the scarified taking guard grooves which crucified the crease in two primary lines: middle and middle-and-leg. As the bowler approached, Peter crouched down, almost exposing the top of the stumps, the ball fizzing up past Peter's nose, his evasive action nearly headbutting the ball. The ball thudded into the keeper's glove, a precious dot ball expended at Shaky's expense. Peter shook his head, trying to dispel the obvious pace through the air a notch up from his junior cricketing exploits. The next ball was a carbon copy, short and lifting, so Peter swung on his heels, got inside the line and hooked the ball for the maximum, much to the entire supporting team's surprise, Noel even forgetting to mock jump and high five Daughtry. 20 runs required off 10 balls looked a whole bunch more achievable and mathematically immaculate: two off each ball. Boundaries, in particular sixes, made such a marked difference in T20, especially at the end.

After one significant shot and a defensive stab, Peter felt a distinctive fatigue settle over him, making his arms lead heavy and his wrists stiff. The fourth ball came in angry – a straight bolt of lightning at Peter's toes which he failed to get out of the way of, so SanFran went up for a pleading "Howzat!". Even these umpires couldn't give this one as the inswing had planted Peter's toes outside leg stump which didn't diminish the pain whatsoever, needles of fiery javelins sprinkler-cleaning his calves, knees, thighs and most of his insides. Larry resisted going to check whether he was still alive. The next ball was a hobbled single, leaving Larry with one ball to face that over. 19 runs required off only 7 balls.

The last ball of the over was a length ball, maybe a tad lethargic, which meant Larry could go back and play an on drive past mid-on, the timing so good it beat mid-on, who was in, and a bolting cow corner fielder who was too wide. A welcome boundary with Peter to face the last over requiring 15 runs. A brief confab in the middle ensued, neither speaking of how the 15 runs were to be achieved, just that in a matter of minutes the match would be decided. The leftie offie wound up for one more trundle, the nostrils back to 50p size flaring, his being entrusted with this responsibility nothing neoteric.

Peter P.T. judged the length almost perfectly, sitting deep in the crease and going back to pull the first delivery for two runs, square leg coming around to cut off not a moment too soon for the fielding side. 13 off 5 balls. The next ball did something, turned and bounced and Peter had no choice but to play a sensible cricket shot around the corner for a single, bringing Larry on strike. Larry surveyed, pretending to know where the gaps lay and took guard with 12 required off the last 4. The bowler, either gutsy or foolish, chucked one up and Larry, relying almost exclusively on her eye and instinct, came down hard with a repulsive looking hoick across the line and against the spin, sending the ball top edging onto the leg side. As the first ball had seen the square leg drift behind square, he'd remained in the position, allowing this ball to drift safely to his left, skidding on the turf to intersect square leg and deep mid-wicket for four runs. 8 off 3. The bowler's next play was to dart one in at Larry's pads who just beat it pitching but only with the bottom edge of the bat, resulting in a single. 7 off 2 with Peter back on strike. The dressing room became a binary pick your side affair - those who could bear to watch and those where it was all just too much. Peter took a moment, a deep breath and waited and the bowler kept him waiting, making some final tweaks to the field, bringing mid-off up.

The penultimate ball of the match came fizzing through, the deathly silence from the sideline amplifying the noise, a piece of cardboard taped to a child's BMX. Peter, hitting with the spin, made room and lofted a drive over extra cover, mid-off instantly setting off after the ball. The shot was crisp and middled but Peter didn't yet have the off side power required for the boundary so he bolted knowing three runs could be on the cards. At the second run's turn the two looked at each other, assessing whether Peter having to hit a six trumped Larry having to hit a four, the latter trumping as the third run was attempted. The fielder, shying from a distance with a strong arm, narrowly missed the bowler's end stumps, a direct hit meaning Peter would have been shy of the crease, the bowler catching and breaking the stumps as a cartwheeling Peter cascaded past, ending in a heap but not out. So it came down to the last ball and shades of the first game's heartbreak at getting so close brushed over Larry's brow as she gazed past the outfield, her eyes rooting out Rebecca's orange-golden pupils, like two warm Halloween pumpkins flickering in the dingy distance. Rebecca winked at her, pumping a gentle rocking fist in her direction, just the encouragement Lauren sought.

The tension was all too much for the SanFran bowler who had visions of darting another ball down into the keeper's welcoming gloves and the game being all over bar the shouting, Golden Gate winning by three runs. The umpire held him at bay, while Larry absorbed the burning pumpkins one more time and got ready to face. As the ball came through, Larry shaped as she had earlier in the over, ready to strike predominantly with the bottom hand, only to adjust late using her nimble golf ball dodging reactions and flip the bat to reverse sweep with the spin, an extra fielder moved from the off to the leg in anticipation of a middle-order keeper with no perceived technique. She caught the ball with just enough timing, using the momentum of the spin to guide the ball past point and towards a despairing third man who'd lost the path of the shot from the unorthodox mettles to play that shot under this burden. That split second of flat-footed hesitancy from the fielder gave the ball enough confidence to emit with the rotations generated by Larry's rolling of the wrists and bobble up off the boundary rope, the fielder hopelessly catching the ball in one hand a moment too late, cupping the ball and staring at it like a dead baby bird. The non-batting Shaky team, supporters, band and pavilion dwellers went into a seismic meltdown, even Yapa cracking out a meagre yet bighearted grin. The team raised Larry and Peter high into the air, bouncing them about as Shackleton High registered its first ever win in the Digners Cup. Enid squeezed Corin's hand tight after coming up behind her then proceeded to congratulate the opposing captain and players for a truly heart-stopping yet now eternally memorable game of cricket. Oh, and thanked the umpires too.

CHAPTER >> 43

"That's an impressive draw, Daniels," muttered Horatio de la Ampelas through gritted teeth as the fourball teetered on driving over the female threeball in front of them.

"Any chance one of them would retrieve my balls?" chimed in one of Horatio's groupies, an oval man with a beard that a fifteen-year-old would be ashamed to put on the front page, sparce curly grey hairs hiding from one another in crevices, shadows and dark alleys.

Daniels knew he'd got hold of this one and it was about time, his game strangely off while Chad's father had continued the non-friendly rivalry that decorated every second Wednesday, come hell, high water or anything in between.

"Too many down with too few to play," was Daniels's faux humility wrapped up in an even more faux helpless blanket. A woman up the fairway waved her arms in desperation, pointing to the ball at her feet, perhaps even flipping a mild bird the fourball's way.

"Women on the golf course," Horatio began, emphasising

the 'the' to sound like 'thee'. "When did this rule come in at the club? Ah well, at least they force them to wear skirts, although frankly some of these mothers should be at the Natural History Museum rather than holding our game up. Not as bad as female cricketers though, eh Daniels?"

The comment stung like the end of a leather whip, Daniels being branded partly responsible for letting girls into Digners despite his fiercest efforts to the contrary.

"That's going to prove an embarrassment for any girls playing in Digners," Daniels eventually responded, forced to ride in the cart straight up the fairway as the other two went in search of their balls.

"It's going to backfire so spectacularly Horatio, that not only will we not be seeing a non-box carrying cricketer ever again in Digners, it will further bifurcate the genders into a little fun-and-giggle pocket for the girls and the big show for the boys."

"On what grounds? I quizzed Chad and he reluctantly told me they'd won their first match. You don't win cricket matches in Digners if you've a team of prancing ponies."

"Horatio, this is not something you need to expend a second glance on; this is a diversity distraction that will be shut down on safety grounds alone. And if that fails, we have other means. I'm surprised Chad is at all concerned after the displays we've been putting out."

"Oh Gawd, he's not. He cannot wait to get stuck in, but just not sure there's any possibility of them meeting through the knockouts so he'll be selecting this team as the warm-up when they get exterminated. You knew that, right?"

"Of course: a little pudding reward for all the hard work then back to the main course of winning the Cup."

"And you do know about the other added benefit, the real cherry on the pie?"

A whooshed hack bobbled one of the balls out just in from on the idling cart, neither acknowledging the ball's existence or the red-faced bungling cane cutter emerging from the undergrowth, the caddy following in tow after an admonishing incorrect club rant.

"Thanks, Mate!"

"You're more welcome than most Horatio; glad to be of service."

"Not you. The ball … Chad's always had … spirit," continued Horatio. "To complement the array of skills of course, both sporting, academic, leadership and entrepreneurial."

"His record speaks for itself. One of Corkridge's finest. Excluding present company of course!"

"Indeed. Competition much fiercer in my day though. None of this free pass LGBTQ bullshit though. Even though he's back of the queue as a white male—"

"Hmm," thought Daniels silently. "Not sure."

"—he'll make something exceptional of his existence. Cricket won't last forever but just the leg up into the national team, Oxbridge then run the family business."

"And business is booming I understand."

"I won't lie, it has been a fruitful season. Money prints itself while we sleep, but so crass to use the M word or even speak its existence."

"Let's just enjoy what it provides. Shall we," motioned Daniels, realising they were now lagging behind the other two golfers.

Horatio, sensing another delay as his counterparts dug out the fairway, lit his oversized pipe, the cherry-apple waft of burning tobacco alerting the female threeball, now alongside as the adjacent fairways top-and-tailed, a waved wrist or six not deterring Mr de la Ampelas in the slightest. Daniels, taking his own accidental secondhand toke, remained agitatedly curious.

"So Horatio, what of the Ashes ball you mention? What of it?"

"Ah yes – so a likely fringe benefit of lifting Digners for the umpteenth time will be the procurement of the actual ball that lost England the Ashes, courtesy of my son's endeavour and Duane Hanratty's suspect hands."

"He still has the ball? The actual ball he dropped?"

"Yes, my good man, he does. Hoarding with two teenage girls in the house … folly it seems."

"That is like a national icon! More famous than Red Rum … Frankel even!"

"It just couldn't get any better, could it?"

"How did this happen?"

At the precise moment Daniels completed the question, a bright yellow golf ball surprised the pair, dislodging Horatio's pipe from his grasp, a shower of lit brown tobacco embers exploding in a face halo of dull fireworks. Horatio's traditionally composed demeanour went, and by went meaning got smoked, trashed, obliterated as his face reached a shade of purple reserved only for the Queen's royal insignia. An unapologetic woman golfer – coincidentally donning a deep purple skirt and lilac shirt – stood behind a tree, more concerned with the state of the damaged tree than Horatio's expensive antique pipe.

"Tree is a hazard ma'am!" shouted Horatio, kicking her ball further away. "Something to be avoided, not aimed for!"

"You've put me closer," the woman laughed, hitting a pinpoint approach across two fairways, as Daniels mimicked the frown in solidarity.

"Not sure I'll ever get used to this," Horatio conceded, leaving the pipe debris, the anatomy now almost recognisable.

An annoyed silence transcended the group for the next few holes, Horatio smarting from the 'assault' and vituperative he'd had no clever retort to either mock female 'athletes' or draw attention to where he believed they should be … the old barefoot-kitchen chide with no real natural successor.

Daniels was still fixated on the Ashes ball, even aiming for Horatio's fairway lie every now and again to force a bit of one-on-one alone time to get the rest of the story.

Coming up the 18th fairway, the game long since over after the bright yellow lady-struck ball to pipe complete now with swollen upper lip, Daniels swooped one last brazen time.

"How did you get— erm, how are you going to get the Ashes ball into your possession? How did this unravel?"

"A good old-fashioned wager."

"A bet?"

"You bet! Some early season posturing from the abomination that is not only a cricket team with girls in it, but from the state school system too!"

"They were at Corkridge ... for a while," Daniels blurted then wished he could retract.

"You got rid of them I seem to recall."

"Well one of them - then the sister followed. Rules had been broken, along with your son's tooth."

"It had to happen back then, of course - not sure the wife and I would have ever cast an eye, ear or pound note in your direction again had you not gone with our ... recommendation. But alas, with the hullabaloo surrounding Digners now, hindsight's mistress might have encouraged a keep your enemies closer stroke of genius."

"You're not actually concerned about this ... this ... girls' team?" retorted Daniels, encouragingly bold and a tad indignant at being admonished for following instructions. "The team, our team - our boys - will sense we doubt them."

"Daniels. This has nothing to do with doubt. I didn't get to this station in life leaving anything to chance. Insurance policies don't always get redeemed but they remain for any eventuality."

"These two pretend golfers?"

"Exactly. A big slap-up meal at the plushest golf course in the county and an unrestricted drinks tab while I'm bombing home in the Jag will just about insure what we know won't happen."

"There is no guarantee they will be the umpires designated to the match – if it happens."

"Perhaps this is the difference between us Daniels. I don't acknowledge barriers or rules of any sort – if something is prohibited or frowned upon, I treat it as red during Pamplona. If you are not able to ensure this minutia is dealt with to seal the deal then it might be time for a change of leadership at Corkies. Your 350k salary was looking like trajecting in the right direction but can easily be waved in front of a younger, up-and-coming 'new money' private school head. These decisions are easily remedied and going from headmaster at Corkridge, there really is nowhere else to go. Perhaps the private sector if you don't mind licking envelopes and making sure the loo roll is topped up in the disabled."

Daniels looked beaten, a slapped puppy without the waggly tail or short-lived cuteness. To exacerbate the gulf in golfing class between the cahooting two and the prostituted umpires along for the day, the latter duo both played at the same time, the shots traversing one another across the fairway into the verging roughs, the etiquette of waiting for the furthest to play abandoned as the clubhouse's signature steak and pepper pie wafted down the fairway. Daniels, now no longer buoyed by the prospect of the ball trophy, bit his lip as Horatio continued with his game, the affable demeanour not even singed by the pontifical duress moments earlier.

"Horatio," beckoned Daniels as Horatio strode away to play his final approach, the gap between shots a lifetime with the hackers making up the fourball. "I will ensure it's done."

"You're up again," Horatio shouted down the fairway, abandoning addressing his ball as the adjoining lake welcomed another inhabitant from the rough.

He hadn't heard Daniels's reply, but didn't need to.

Chapter >> 44

Over Rate

The third Digners match for Shackleton was a walkover, an unnerving drubbing. Without being tested in any department the match was over in almost as quick succession as Corkridge's third pool game, a consummate demolition of a bridesmaid public school in a neighbouring village. Both were 50-over matches and both included tosses won and electing to field first, the batting challenge failing to reach two hundred collectively. Shaky's bowlers not quite tore through the top order but took wickets at regular intervals to nullify any momentum, the opposition apparently keener to not be seen playing against girls and return to their more favoured fives and le cross pursuits, the Digners entry the brainchild of a new sports head swimming against the tradition tide. The school - Emblem Diocesan - had a few bright sparks, a nuggety middle order partnership between the keeper and a spinning allrounder enough to at least flavour with respectability and set Shackleton a target that broke more than eleven droplets of sweat. Enid had been conscious that this was the weakest competitor in Pool D, so needed not only to win but win handsomely to improve the

Net Run Rate should the business end of the pool stages put the top teams on the same points. Plus the wicket had looked fruity with more grass than you could shake at a herd of Friesians, so she'd elected to bowl without hesitation when the coin emerged from the hairy pitch showing Her (peace be with Her) Majesty's head.

All the bowlers chipped in and the rotation of bowlers was a little more haphazard than Enid would have normally employed – short spells with a wicket or two evening out the spoils. A new swagger had emerged which Corin felt was awesome but Enid feared could be double-edged, with overconfidence preceding many a fall but letting it go in favour of expression. A few of the send-offs were aberrantly repellent, Noel's thoughtful directions back to the pavilion for the opening leftie case in point, Daughtry's beaming smile at getting a second slip fended catch not so. The previous win and uninspired opposition conspired to ensure Shaky's stroll through Emblem's park was clubbable, even if a jocose allusion ... this game was meant for merriment, Enid told herself, as she set funkily audacious fields, spurred by the lowering risk of the match situation as each wicket fell.

Chasing 147 in a 50-over match could have been sensible, turgid even to graft Shaky over the line but with NRR on the line and a bowling attack about as threatening as 'hold me back boys' David Warner tippy-toeing on a box to shake his little stubby finger at Quinton De Kock's elevated eye level after the latter retorted with some home truths after days of inane, immature 'banter' invented by Australian cricketers and blighting the game ever since. The openers were steady and decent but with little variety, which enabled particularly Rufus to fill his and the team's boots with an array of shots from someone anticipating precisely what was served up with no fear of the tricks, skills and deceptions most bowlers were adopting in the shorter formats. A few wickets did fall for Shaky, Emblem's celebration wake-like muted, but they knocked off the total in an impressive 20 overs with six wickets to spare.

Across town – towards the more salubrious end – a not-so-equivalent destruction was taking place, akin to a slasher-horror, the only difference being no eponymous anything (heroine, neek, good-timer or otherwise) left other than in pieces on the wet turf, at best huddled in the corner, rocking and imbibing on a secluded thumb.

Skittled for an embarrassing 50 on the nose (oh, btw, the number 8 bat did cop one on the nose from Chuck and was whisked off to hospital faster than a Corky parent assembling a mini-gazebo when Chad came in to bat) Chad decided to open with James and Yannos (a.never.k.a. Brad) so they could "Avoid the ice bath … muscles not even employed for this one, so no recovery required." As they went out Chad spat a glance at Yannos to either put out fast or get out fast so the 'grownups' could finish the job, Chad instructing Danny to clean his metal grille with baby wipes. Chad told George Mildew and Harrison Plodkin they could go home, the openers services not required today, such was Chad's bullish hauteur. James was likely to win this in two overs, as long as he kept strike, and kept Yannos as his plus one.

Ironically James missed the first ball, a long hop that should have been punished more than the pitch as his hefty frame swung around on his heels, leaving a WWI trench to peer out from the next ball. The next five though all went for boundaries, the ball's shine suddenly duller than the fielders' eyes, peering as the planes ascended, craning their necks in realisation that the thicket surrounding the 1st XI Oval was put there specifically to further punish the opposition.

At the start of the second over Yannos – facing his first delivery – played a sumptuous cover drive, miraculously cut-off by cover, after which an appeal was heard from the Corkridge pavilion. Yannos, slightly bemused yet feeling the pressure pinch, went for a big heave-ho next up and got an inside edge onto the stumps, Chad fist pumping himself as he strode out to bat, reaching the crease almost before the bails hit the ground. Yannos returned to the pavilion for a two-ball duck against the worst side in Pool C, dragging his bat behind him like a toddler admonished back to his or her room for a failed raid on a parents' bedroom, the monster under the bed licking their chops at the looming homecoming.

The applause was rapturous, delirious even, parents scrabbling for their iPhone 14s buried inside tweed jacket pockets, clambering for the front row boundary seat as Chad sauntered to the middle: his kingdom all before him, beneath him and surrounding him; star jumping above Maslow's apex without considering the landing. It was almost too easy too, the bowler overwhelmed by Chad's presence at the crease to the magnitude of struggling to lift his arm higher than his spiked hair. Chad had eaten at the buffet of kak bowling before but really preferred the finer bowlers on show, the ball coming on to his bat a better bedfellow for his flawless technique. When the bowling was this poor, a small adjustment Chad hadn't made in some time, strengthening his lower right hand grip: a baseballer coercing power when the ball was dying like a wilting flower.

The first ball went. Far away. Lost in the depths of the brambles, nobody willing to retrieve. Once the ball was replaced, this too went in the same vicinity, Chad making the bludgeon look stylish, Heston Blumenthal whipping up a Nouveau Big Mac for the masses to savour. Third replacement ball in and Chad even had the luxury of having his own fun, showing off to place the ball exactly where he wanted it - making it rain in the arid - avoiding the brambles and clipping a swinging delivery off his hip for a low six over deep mid-wicket, the ball coming perilously close to the fielder's hands, judiciously tucked under his armpits to avoid any mutilation. One of the adoring fans shrieked "We love you, Chad!" which was met with a raised bat and further low hum, chuckled mirth from the buffs and devotees. James, usually brutish and non-responsive to the death even managed a veiled complimentary nod of humour in lovely Chad's direction, walking off in mocked protest once the shrieking cascaded into full-on Boyband worshipping hysteria.

Requiring one run to win and desperately attempting to remain non-cancelled-slash-relevant, James hit the biggest six ever witnessed by anyone alive or dead, the ball sailing over the road to clatter into a window sill amongst the squashed terraced houses, the ball worryingly coming to rest alongside a kid's green, orange and yellow plastic playhouse. As the ball made contact with the residential dwelling, a brassy crack reverberating, Stanley Forthenstan channelled Bart Simpson with an exclamatory "So long suckers!" from the sideline.

Chapter >> 45

Out

There is no easy way to say this, through gritted teeth or wobbling lip, saccharine coat or titillate in any guise, overcoat, disguised velvet glove or otherwise …

The Shackleton XI lost their following match, the defeat a nasty concoction of overconfident meets calamity then gets introduced to nervy jitters who in turn marries shocking decisions (not least limited to shot selection, batting order, field settings, bowling spells, fielding displays and holding catches). All in all, the team as a collective dropped a dozen catches, at least eight chalked into the 'dolly' category, three of which looked harder to drop than catch. The spiralling out of control began gradually then, almost in freefall, the team implosion coincided with the opposition finding their strongest performance of the competition thus far.

In the end Shaky's total was chased with relative ease, a half-dozen wickets to spare and half of that in overs to spare, rapturous applause flooding the dusky ground as Enid fell to her haunches and Corin lay face first in the inner ring, a cadaver for the duration of the celebration. The rest of the team's swagger had been battered out of each, self-inflicted and the deportment of the XI was now one of 'not at the races' even patting themselves on the back for getting this far but resigned to the tournament being over for this year.

The world outside the clouded bus windows passed by at a slightly-quicker-than-snail's pace, the jolty bus clamping to a stop at unnecessarily regular intervals, propelling their heads forward each time to betray the anesthetised fixity. Enid couldn't look at Corin, needing to channel the blame somewhere and Corin couldn't look anywhere, tiring of mesmerising the stale slogan of the herbal tea billboard. This was the usual bus they caught after school but curiously empty, a big game of European football the likely thwarter. The bus driver, close to asleep at the wheel, could've mowed down a gathering hoard of zombies without twitching an eyelid, the corners turned with practised precision, occasionally mounting the pavement to avoid the back of the bus scraping a misplaced bin further back. Ohw, for an approaching, salivating, cricket bat wielding set of zombie Corky boys to exterminate, thought Corin. My kingdom, thought Enid.

"This is what happens when you let a Corky traitor into the team," Corin said, unable to stand the silence anymore and never any good at ruminating for more than ten milliseconds.

"Ah, okay, so you're blaming Rufus for this loss, not you as a leader acting like we've won the World Cup after one win and strutting about smugger than Chad's face when he hears of the loss?"

"There it is!"

"There is what?"

"I knew you'd find a way to blame this all on me. Since we were kids: the little sister's fault, never able to measure up to big sister, perfect pants herself."

"Perfect pants was actually something Patty was labelled with after a dress-up disco where he wore purple velvet Abba trousers … Patty perfect pants."

"I know! Catch the subtle reference with both hands next time … as they say, if you can get both hands to it, do it."

"Cricket metaphors? Nice catch! Oh, wait that's been used and, well, not much of any catching happening today."

"Maybe it's genetic," mumbled Corin under her breath, instantly wishing she hadn't indicated to get in that lane, in exact unison with the bus driver failing to signal at a deserted stop, the doors decompressing to let eleven invisible zombies on board without extricating any tension from within.

"You're going there? All the way down under to Dad's catch; that is a new low, even lower than down under," said Enid yanking her hoodie lower than it cared to go down her face, a stuck window blind.

"I seem to recall neither of us escaped the butter finger syndrome today," Corin sensing the ice had been cracked, so the ice road trucker hole in the ground should at least be explored.

"Along with half the bloody team! Job's not done … job's not done! Kept saying it but everyone was backslapping each other following their rebellious alternate leader to my left here."

"If it was up to you, we'd all reside in the nets … set up a little camp there, eat, sleep, breathe, ingest, excrete and 50+ sun cream caked on thick all day and night … there had to be a break … from cricket! It was fun celebrating that win - that's why we restarted playing the game in the first … well, second place again. To enjoy …"

"We've had so much fun today, haven't we? We're all loving this feeling - in fact, that's the most animated I've ever seen the team, immersing in all the cricketing failure fun. It was so much fun that when Jacob got sick in the loo from upset convulsing and Daughtry's parents left early, I just felt this full-on warmth fun glow, how about you?"

Their voice timbres had intensified, the final 'you' arrowed towards the back of the bus driver's flat head – a shaved rash of mottled skin sausages – causing a retaliating glance into the oversized rear-view mirror, dragging him from the dilation of zombie destruction slumber. The girls now faced one another, almost nose to nose, their teeth coated with angry saliva in an otherwise dry set of mouths, the impending home truths being locked and loaded, soon never to be taken back. Both Corin's fists were clenched, holding onto an imaginary pair of ski poles, Enid's eyes burning in disappointed vitriol, spearing right through her sister's pupils into the depths of her soul for the first time in forever.

"Let's go origins story for a second here," clamped Enid, not content to let the bus driver resume catatonic mode. "None of this would be … this way, if you had that smidgeon of self-control, that titbit of restraint, putting it back in your Asda jeans pocket and slapping your thrifty backside on the way out. But no, my sister has to make a stand, with a ball, at a school. Then my stupid loyalty and sense of justice follows her down the rabbit hole, with Alice and all the other inept cricketing inhabitants of Wonderland."

"Oh. Em. Ef. Gee. This is YOUR fault! Your ego, having to stand up to the class bully just in case your little sister outshines you even in that department! Little Corin claims Chad's tooth … I know! I'll go one better: offer up the worst possible symbol of injustice and grievance in our family's history to some spoilt toffy boy and challenge him at the one thing in his life he truly is the best at; and not just best in the class, or the school or even the county, but likely the country! Why have boundaries? The world. Your ego picks an unwinnable fight."

If the bus driver possessed earmuffs, he'd likely don them, a tinge of sympathy spreading across his obliging brow, having shuttled the siblings around for some time and acutely aware of their familial bond; that is until now, the bonds looking like a rogue untied shoelace, limply following retreating footsteps.

Both girls took a moment, a line on either side fender-bendered into oblivion but maybe the stipulated tonic, designated as the 'Gunfight on Route 402' the last accompanying passengers long since vacant from the vehicle. Neither spoke for the remainder of the journey, sitting on opposing seats, staring out the flanking windows, easing from spouted mad rage to a semblance of calm as the bus ended the longest then shortest then longest journey in history, a short walk from home. Strutting a pitch length ahead, Corin made sure to drag her cricket bag through as many puddles as she could see in the dark, the dry weather conspiring so her main targets were the remnants of overzealous car washes in the road.

When they got home, they both noticed their dad's car in the driveway, instinctually glancing at one another then away in protest - he'd been away for a while on some obscure business venture a million miles from cricket and the Volvo's presence startled them both as Corin almost scraped the side with her go-kart manoeuvring to get rid of the oppressive kit, opening the garage and propelling the cricket coffin to rest amongst the wood shards, spiders and expired wine bottles. Enid, just to hammer the petulant point, placed hers neatly in the designated rack, wanting to kick it in but forcing the orderly puzzle piece into place if only to irritate Corin. A few door slams and non-reciprocated parental salutations later, both were stewing in their rooms. Dinner on offer - stew coincidentally - without any reverberating assent from the bedrooms above was met with Bronwyn's volleyball bump to Duane, his eyebrows requesting setting but entirely aware that the only shot for this situation was to spike. He arose from the kitchen table, his suit looking more creased than when he'd left, dusted off imaginary crumbs from the carb-free trending household, took one more swig of the startlingly peng vegan African peanut stew with aubergine and okra and ventured upstairs.

The muffled sound of contrasting tunes snuck under the doorframes, the AirPods a place of genuine solace even if one sounded like Christian Rock and the other Base and Base. Duane had long since given up trying to indoctrinate his daughters into the exultations of nineties grunge - even noughties alternative punk rock - this phase mostly profanity laden female artists singing about bad break ups, but the small mercy of a Boyband free house. This was a tricky fork in the road: whichever door picked would likely get some sense of either favouritism or a perception that the parent had the 'problem child' pegged and in the crosshairs. So Duane decided a neutral patch was the best peace pipe smoking ground, but this would mean a double extraction to the welcoming yet never-used guest room. This was the first time he'd had to bring out the old guest room weapon.

A tender knock on each door and instruction to gather in the spare room, neither followed by a hustle of activity so a follow-on, this one more durable yet still munificent enough to invite the participants to parlay towards brighter resolution. The girls traipsed past Duane, walking without removing the AirPods or looking in his direction, the music worse than he'd conjectured, dry hoofmarks of spilled tears smudged across cheeks like muddy brushstrokes. Duane put his hand out to usher Corin past him and missed, Enid already halfway up the passage, her ponytail not bouncing behind her with its usual vigour. Enid sat on the far end of the spare double bed and stared out the window while Corin perched on the corner, closest to the exit should tantrums still be acceptable around these parts. Duane waited patiently while they both removed the earlobe assaults, Enid turning her face into the triangle and Corin sliding up the bed to settle while Duane stood blocking the door, initially folding his arms only to remember this was construed an aggressive pose so pliably letting them hang at his sides, awkwardly preventing his hands from hiding in his suit trouser pockets, his knuckles weather beaten from a lifetime of cricket balls.

"Something's happened ... clearly," he began, pulling them both into eye contact with him then each other. "Are you both alright?"

Neither responded, the sting of earlier home truths fresh, a new epicentre to direct towards not a fair option.

"Mum tells me you girls have been playing cricket matches again ... mainly while I was away. I'm happy you're both enjoying the game again."

"We're not," said Corin, looking at her unkempt socks. "Well, we were ... until today."

"You lost," said Duane reassuringly, moving to sit aside his daughters on the bed.

"We made ourselves lose, Dad," chimed Enid. "Everything that could have gone wrong today, did ... and it's no longer fixable."

"The important thing is that you both care about one another enough through ups and downs. The cricket and the match are supporting acts when it comes to family. Your bond as sisters is bigger than any game."

"Dad, this will never just be a game in our family!" hollered Corin.

"That's my folly ... and my fault; my burden, not yours. There shouldn't be a sins of the father in this family."

"That's not what I—"

"I couldn't deal with what the game gave me at the end; I'd got so much from what it gave me throughout my career and I felt like I'd given a lot back too. It wasn't cricket's fault - it wasn't anyone's fault. When we played the game - when I first put a ball and a bat in yours and Patty's hands - it was for the love of the game ... the complexities, the nuances, the thinking, the plotting, the tension, the chase, the defence ... it all added up and I just couldn't resist giving you both this gift of the greatest sport in the world."

"Dad, we're too deep into this, erm, Cup," admitted Enid.

"Nothing's ever too deep for you girls ... I'd follow you both to the depths of the Mariana trench! Don't think about the implications of what you've done – the only thing you can remedy is what's about to happen. Together, your solidarity and how you inspire each other and your mother and me will be the undoing of any opposition ... sport or otherwise."

"I'm sorry, Sister," said Enid, reverse engineering a tear up her face. "No excuses; you are my best friend and I want to be standing next to you (or at least telling you where to stand!) the next time we take the field."

"Losing hurts more when it means something to someone close to you," said Duane pulling them both closer in a wide-armed Albatross hug. "Double whammy for the team with both Hanratty girls in it!"

"I'm not sure why I'm the way I am," choked Corin. "Maybe it's both of your faults?"

They all laughed, just for a moment, a mini-release letting all but the residual air from the tyre.

"Girls I'm proud of the person each one of you is – irrespective of whether you win or lose – I can't go backwards but I don't want my legacy to drag either of you down. I know it has already and for that I'm sorry. I haven't been able to watch your games, but that is my problem, not yours. I'm there in spirit even if I don't want any part of my cricket to impact any part of your cricket."

"Dad, the reason we love the game is because of you!" contended Enid.

"We started up again because this was missing from our lives, from our family," Corin continued. "I'm glad you dropped that bloody ball! That sorted the ignorant hacks from the influences in our lives who understood your contribution and what you meant to the game of cricket."

"We feel you out there, the time and sacrifice you made to

always be there for us, cricket or not."

"This is getting like Dear Evan Hansen," said Duane. "One more track and I'm done for!" pulling back the stubborn lump that wouldn't shift from above his neck. "You know I love you guys to the moon and back and if you lead with your heads, play with your hearts and stick together through thick edges and thin margins, you'll emerge proud ... and content ... and most importantly ... together."

The girls looked at each other, the bus pistols at dusk vitriol all but vanquished, the quivery cartoon manga eyes holding back the tide, Duane taking both of their hands in each of his, a thousand ball strikes unable to dent their warmth and pliable softness.

"There's some lukewarm leftover vegan stew for you downstairs with something called okra in it ... Mum describes it as crisp, juicy and creamy whereas all I can smell are the lawn cuttings. If we carry on here any longer she'll hear the doorbell ring and know the complimentary Dominoes delivery was anything but, although we can't scoff hiding in the garage ... again!"

"You're the best, Dad."

"I know. But really it was my backup plan all along - ordering as I crept upstairs to coerce you out of your rooms and back to being besties again. When all else fails, there's always Pepperoni Passion."

Chapter » 46

Not Out

"Well. Well. Clodagh. This is all over bar the shouting. Well. For some of those budding cricketeers anyway!"

"Hello Ramsay," the disappointment in Clodagh's voice so prominent, the 'hollow' sounded like a German Netflix series, or it could have been the clamped down Irishness popping out for a defiant excursion on UK telly.

"Pool A looks sewen up like a handy seamstress's handwork ... try saying that ten times! Belchingham Bethel taking top spot irrespective of what happens with one to play, unable to be caught by the pretenders: the chasing pack."

"It might be worth positioning for our viewers: we have one pool game left in the Digners Cup, each of the four pools having played four of their five games."

"The top of each pool progress for those who haven't been paying attention to the knockouts, two semi-finals and a final at the home of cricket itself ... Lord's!"

"With the possibility of both semis also taking place at Lord's - Marylebone Cricket Club for viewers who ever wondered what MCC stands for - Middlesex's progression in the first division county championship determining whether that weekend remains available or hosting the senior match."

"Two semis or Middlesex ... that's what it comes down to," snorted Ramsay, even the producer lobbing in an anti-puerile eyebrow from the studio.

"Pool B looks a little tighter than Pool A," continued Clodagh. "WG sorted and VVS going down to the wire, the three top teams all able to qualify if they win, of course also depending on the Net Run Rate at the end of the games. The intention will be to play all three matches - 50-over format - at the same time to ensure no unfair advantage but the teams will be acutely aware ... a big win will do themselves no harm but many a team has faltered and lost by thinking beyond the result to the improvement of the NRR."

"So Clodagh you're saying Go Big or Go Home?"

"Uh ... not really Ramsay; more like Go Big AND Go Home."

"Onto Pool C and that has been a bit of a bloodbath really with Corkridge Castle School for Boys led by the effervescent Chaz del rey Ampelas flattening any opposition that dared to step onto the same cricket field, the margins of victory and nature of the destructions quite remarkable. These boys have a one-way ticket to the Cup in my humble opinion ... stand in their way at your peril!"

"Pool D—"

"Your little favourite Clodagh! Don't deny it."

"I won't."

"The plucky girls' team, punching above their weight and all that."

"It's a mixed team but thanks Ramsay for the insight."

"Anytime Clodagh; let's call them what everyone's calling them after their variable performances ... Shaky High—"

"The Shackleton Senior School Cricket XI fumbled their last game leaving a tricky home fixture against Testopony Tabernacle—"

"Eh, let's call a spade a dug hole on this programme Clodagh … they're done. They need a minor miracle to win this one, the Net Run Rate required severe or as my Granddad would say 'a bridge too far' even though this is likely a 'mountain too high'."

Clodagh turned towards Ramsay's grinning face, towering over the little presenter and putting his teeth into total shadow, leaning down with her eyes to his level, abandoning what might have been in the Sky's Guide to Sports Presenting Etiquette handbook. She put her hand patronisingly on his shoulder, addressing him, not the live audience or the seated cameraperson waving furiously from the dark depths of the studio.

"Ramsay," she said in a soft voice, gripping the top ridge of his trapezius, eliciting a noticeable wince. "I'm going to finish this segment on Pool D … on my own. With no further interruptions. Comprende?"

"Yes," said Ramsay, as Clodagh turned towards the camera.

"In Pool D – 'ABD' to many – Shackleton Senior School has played the brand of cricket many of us who deeply love the game respect … gutsy, bold, innovative and utilising the complete array of skills, quirks and characters at their disposal. They'll know they let themselves down in the last match, but sport is all about the unlikely scenarios, and whatever happens, they're already heroes to me, emerging not only to fly the flag for mixed teams but show that anything is possible. Of course the fans will only want a place in the playoffs but the margin of victory will have to be significant, Testopony Tabernacle's record impressive with one no result due to rain. Shackleton have to win and they have to win big yes, but belief is something that perhaps can make this team rise up from the ashes and smash whoever remain in their way. Over to you, Ramsay."

CHAPTER » 47

LEATHER

Why on God's green earth, a team like the Corkridge Castle XI required fielding practice was not only beyond the ten boys standing in a semi-circle but a planetary leap into another cosmos beyond the team's leader-and-chief, Chad de la Ampelas. These practices were not pleasant either, the coach – likely fresh from administering an actual Siberian gulag – took grisly pleasure in belting close range catches to the team, a broken hand or finger or few never further away than the spring hill in the distance should anyone shell a fizzing, arcing offering. In the previous match two catches had been dropped – touted as the first time this season Corky stooped to the 'double chin' drop, both by the same fielder (now playing in the 3rd XI), the second of which the mythical Jonty Rhodes would have been proud of, a ball that the unfortunate fielder turned into a drop catch by going for the impossible, better off just leaving the inconsequential boundary.

For this special punishment session, Mr Miller unearthed a dozen or so brand-new balls to ensure the outer shell stung with maximal inflexible velocity, the school's food and pastural budget now almost fully reallocated to cricket and winning the Digners Cup. The Corkridge boys had never seen Miller lean in harder to the shots as part of the fielding drills, his hips whipping through and wrists closing as though casting from a seaside rock, the ball almost speeding up as it arrived, the snap into (hopefully) fleshy palm echoing all the way through the classics to the science block. Chad had long since accepted his charm offensive didn't work with Miller, put down to a septic blend of Asperger's and ADHD as there couldn't be a human walking upright that was immune to those syrup-laden gold-plated charms, yet had one final go when the eternally tough right-handed Neethaniel brother went down clutching his right hand, an injury Chad didn't want to reinforce with some district level smiley face from the seconds, overwhelmed by the occasion to the extent he'd likely pass out. Chad offered to take the practice and Miller, unwilling to relinquish the slave master whipping, summarily sent Chad back to the edge of the semi-circle and aimed four consecutive cracks his way.

And the barrage didn't relent either, a target of no back to the dorms respite until twenty were pouched in a row, the level of difficulty upping like a thoughtless video game's level, the sixteenth to eighteenth catches bordering on gunshots. At one stage about an hour earlier, the team reached nineteen and a slightly off throw back to Miller's bat resulted in a skewed top edge, easily pouched by James. The return ball was deemed so poor, the team started the next round on minus ten. By now it was beyond dusk, the ability to spot the approaching ball so difficult in the gloom, Danny and Stanni both deflected balls into the other's face, a possible tooth relocation and bruised cheek both disregarded by Miller, now froth sweating down the front of his shirt and back of his pants. The floodlights eventually got cracked on as Miller realised he might not be home in time for dinner – an offence his wife's bulbous pot carrying forearms would not take kindly to, the contents once dumped on Miller's head as his own punishment.

When Yannos shelled what, under the circumstances, looked like a sitter, the direness of the situation for Chad reached DEFCON 2, evoked only under the most extreme circumstances where life - or even worse cricketing results - were at stake ... he'd be forced to call his father. Getting away from the barrage was tricky enough, any mention of a trip to the little boys' room or feigned sickness-slash-injury deemed worse than dropping the ball: at least you were in the fight Miller kept honking. Chad's desperation reached contemplation of just making a run for it, getting to the dorm, excavating his emergency iPhone (a 13 ... eghhhhh), hitting speed dial 2 (1 was Mummy Dearest) and locking himself in the common room but not before dragging a fresher hostage in with him to make the fire and rub his aching soles. But what would the team think - the captain fleeing the scene of the crime? They'd likely applaud him in the end, saved from the torturous target practice, but the visceral view of his spikes speeding towards the house would be a sight problematic to come back from. Plus this was looking encouraging ...

Twelve ... Harrison with a low stinger.

Thirteen ... Chuck with a confident one hander.

Fourteen ... Neethaniel mollydooker with a lunging shielded pouch.

Fifteen ... George with a precariously juggled snaffle.

Sixteen ... Stanni with an overconfident between the legs catch, true keeper style.

Seventeen ... James making likely the hardest under lights look like a rugby tackle, his swollen mitts reverberating in angry protest but significantly keeping the ball off the grass.

Eighteen ... Danny taking a bit of a miracle whip, not notorious for his fielding or catching, but employing all his life's reflexes to take a diving left-handed catch an inch off the ground.

Nineteen (and now the shots getting vitriolic almost, the ramifications of not getting hands to the ball likely to cartoon shunt the fielder Wile E. Coyote style clean across the field into the pavilion's dainty windows) ... the ball about to decapitate Yannos, his hands flying up to his eyes merely to protect, clipping the ball with the back of his hand - a slice of sorts - stopping the momentum so the ball floated up, innocuously spinning into Neethaniel dexter's hands. They all looked around nervously, anticipating a succinct disqualification from Miller who, staggering, motioned the ball back, Neethaniel looping it back across a diva-level stare from Chad to Yannos.

It came down to one more and it was clear who Miller was lining up ... it had to be and he unleashed living hellish fury down the line, directly back at Yannos. Chad needed this done, so shuffled across and took a flying leap across Yannos to take a fingertip catch with his left, bouncing on the floor and rolling back to a standing position, the team surrounding him, lifting him up and celebrating as though they'd won a match.

Chad took a glance from up high at his minions, adulating another feat of cricketing impossibility. See, knew the Chadster would make the right decision; let's keep running to Daddy for another day ... not this day.

Back in the dormitory, most of the younger kids already being harassed from the latest Machiavellian nightly monkeyshines, the fielders nursed their preponderantly hand wounds with a relay of Betadine, Dettol, ice, plasters, toasted sandwiches and tea. Chad's exultant poach could only dull the pain so long, a galling sting permeating on both thumb knuckles, manifesting in a direct order to get Rufus on WhatsApp this instance.

"Rufio, the boy who couldn't keep up with Peter Pan and ultimately couldn't fly," welcomed Chad, signalling for the door to be shut while he chewed on a lamb and chutney toastie.

"You saw that film?" Rufus chipped in quicker than Chad expected.

"Well ... no," said Chad, swallowing a chunk of lamb that should have had the fat trimmed off by the kakos on duty. "I just know stuff. Including films. Shall I call you Roofie instead? Probably more apt."

"What can I do for you, Chad?"

"Been a while since you checked in; having fun playing house with all your chicks?"

"We're done. They're done. It's all over. Undoubtedly you got wind?"

"Unfortunate result but everything falling beYOUtifully into place. We can't have them qualifying for the knockouts: makes a mockery of the game, our school and our sport."

"Well Chad, there's no danger of that happening now. If there was any wind in the sails, it's been blown away by the last performance. End of the road stuff so no need to be concerned."

"Never concerned Rubenstein ... never concerned. Feels like I need to reiterate what we're doing here or more specifically what you need to do."

"Lucky loser, right? You select us, erm them from the teams that don't qualify as a warm-up. Then you win your ball."

"And here's us thinking you weren't paying attention. I like that ... my ball ..."

"I've got to go."

"Somewhere to be? What's it like?"

"What's what like?"

"Playing in a girls' team?"

Rufus looked like a dog whose face had been blown into, never taking a moment to think what it felt like or articulate what being in the team meant.

“It’s … it’s … like being in a cricket team.”

Chapter >> 48

Late Cut

"No rousing speeches going to happen here. We've got to be out there fielding in five and this game couldn't come soon enough. We've let you down ... no, I've let you down. A captain plays for her team, with her team not above her team. The last game was the last game we're going to lose this season and not because we're all in this delusional fantasy about taking down the establishment but because we're better cricketers than anyone thinks ... than I think. I think we lost because you all sensed I didn't believe in you ... and you were right. But I'm only going to say this once - Noel put your phone away! - I've never believed in anything more than the cricketing ability, will to win and die trying attitude of this team. Whatever happens—"

"When we win!" interrupted Corin.

"When we win today, however the Net Run Rate ends up, we shouldn't be proud ... not yet. If we leave everything out there, take every risk we've ever wanted, drag every single last drop of blood out of this Digners stone, then we'll know we left nothing out; left nothing at the door. Today we go all in and we go beyond putting this team to the sword: we're relentless … when we've done something good, we go one better the next ball; if we fumble, we're up before the smirks hit our ears. Today we go all in."

"Agree," said Yapa, drowned out by the whoops, fist bumps and c'mons, the changing room reverberating. Not a soul roused, indeed.

The fickle nature of sport, school sport in particular and even more particularly a school without the arcane heritage woven into cricket more tightly than a seam, meant that the Shackleton support brigade was not present, barring Rebecca, Miss Hazard and a few students threatened with detention. The previous loss had gone so viral, so admonishingly tactless, that any fair-weather association with Shaky High XI's faltering cricketers was a poison chalice most teenagers were not willing to noose around their necks. Plus, the rapper Dwayne Tryumf was offering free attendance to 'work-out' his lyrics at a nearby warehouse.

The ground had an eerie feel to it as Testopony Tabernacle arrived without the customary fanfare of keen parents, siblings and stocked picnic baskets. The coach and the boys all looked snarly, teeth bared, noses scrunched and a chronic disdain for their surroundings – with young men like this perhaps the parents urged themselves to stay away. TT's cricket was fast, furious and forceful by all accounts, most of their opposition in the pool games swept aside by a barrage of going hard from ball one to the end. Rumours had long circulated that the school took boys of academic merit bleeding into behavioural issues and (hopefully) stopping just short of juvenile delinquent. Wherever they were from and irrespective of the academic proclivity, they looked terrifying: hairy, over-developed, knuckles dragging, bearded, scary quivering eyed humungosauruses arriving at a colosseum rather than a cricket pitch. Compelling danger surfaced that any female in the vicinity could be clubbed over the head and dragged back to a cave in the vicinity.

The opening bowlers for Shaky weren't altogether settled as a pair, no bad enactment given unpredictability was one of the few vices left at Enid's disposal. Enid and Yapa were split between a left and right duo and the fastest double act respectively. Enid fancied opening with Corin and Noel yet had to tread carefully with Daughtry who, if relieved of the opening reigns, might struggle to believe in her sole role of blaster-in-chief with the new cherry, the long limbs oft taking a while to warm up but when propelling, generating more bounce than anyone else. This sometimes served a further conundrum as a bouncy track (as Shackleton's pitch was fast morphing towards) was sometimes too elastic, the short deliveries consistently wided. Apart from the recent match-most-abhorrent, Corin's pace had gone up a notch or dozen making her the out-and-out quickest in the team. Her variety, swing and seam both ways made her the main strike weapon but again the poser of whether to save her for the non-eventful middle overs or the death. With a hint of moisture in the pitch, a greener than usual surface and Daughtry complaining of a niggly ankle, the decision went to open with Corin from the Cow Hill End and Noel from the Stinky Gutter End.

The two Donkey Kong openers were struck, quite literally, Noel and Corin setting about their statement blast like a snowball fight. Noel was swinging it around corners and Corin found that troublesome length but with real venom out of the pitch, nipping some back and swinging the rest away. The bowling was almost too decent and the openers, instead of weathering the storm, snarled harder and went at the bowling even more fiercely but couldn't make contact with a single ball for the first two overs, the only barrier a forearm, chest and helmet, the final blow even generating an out-of-place high-pitched yelp.

The jugular was exposed so Enid made an attacking tweak in the field from the third over which paid dividends, Onka at third slip pouching a sharp chance off Noel then a rattling of stumps the following over with a never-seen-before 'who me?' celebration from Corin. Two down without a run scored looked about the best possible start for Shaky until the less burley 3 and 4 bats tootled in - the 'architects' they called them, the strut of their approach and guard taking confidence implying that this wasn't their first rodeo, in particular following two tree hackers who seldom came off. More circumspect than palaeontologists dusting the fragile bones of a monumental discovery, these two proper batters played each ball on its explosive merit and saw off the openers without doing much damage to the score, but more importantly for Testopony Tabernacle, without losing another wicket. This prompted Enid to change both and bring on Rufus and Onka.

From the first ball Rufus was off - way off his game, wasting a supportive pitch with irregular length and balls into the pads that were clipped through mid-wicket with effortless luxury. Corin tried to look into his eyes from mid-off when she flung him the ball after another average delivery, yet he couldn't look her in the eye, turning away from his mark and lumbering in to bowl a no-ball, put over his head for another score. The knock-on impact hurt Onka too, the batters now set and beginning to accelerate, the air he gave deliveries met with footwork and follow-through to make his spell even more expensive than Rufus's.

"Everything okay?" asked Corin trotting over to Rufus as Enid discussed a more defensive field with Onka.

"Yeah. Fine. I'll find my rhythm," responded Rufus still void of his obdurate stare that told his teammates his bravado alone could win games.

His bowling improved to stem the runs but without any threatening deliveries to tempt a wicket, Onka's radar then shot to pieces as he went to all parts of the ground, including the Stinky Gutter. Enid motioned for Daughtry to warm up, ankle or no ankle swelling and thumbed up Peter who was already swinging the arms and twisting his hips, anticipating being called into action when Onka's final delivery went for six, his eyes unable to hide the disappointment.

"You've got to bowl yourself," said Corin when Enid passed between overs.

"I will, just getting them thinking we're fearing bringing on more spin," Enid responded, smiling to mask the creeping concern of the partnership getting more out of hand than Woodstock '99.

The runs had flowed by the time Rufus and Onka came off, the marquee bats looking smugger than a hungry kid locked in a sweet shop over Christmas. With the confidence came the chat, directed mainly at the bowlers but pretty much at anyone in earshot. The umpires had to step in when a verbal altercation escalated between Onka and the number 4 bat. Daughtry's first over looked like an entire loosener over but was still better than what Rufus had served up or what the batters had gorged from Onka's tragic spell. Towards the end of the over Enid signalled fuller and Daughtry found the right length on this pitch, her lack of pace in this spell working well to confound the bats with semi-loopy bounce.

Enid, without warming up, brought herself on to replace Onka, the batsman's sneering hitting attack dog level, enough slivery gums to make a dentist excited. She took a moment to run through some stuff her dad had said early doors ... no problem to sacrifice some runs for a long-term planned wicket. These were the two valuable wickets which were going to lose the game for Shaky, so her disappointed body language had to be pinpoint Oscar standard. The first three balls got flung up way too high, flighted out of sight of the eyebrows and duly all went for boundaries. The fourth ball was purposefully short to show the extreme turn - a stock leg spinner spiralling away from both right-handers - convincing the bats that all preceding full deliveries were the same. Enid kicked the turf, which could have been too much, then send down a flatter, nervous fifth which turned the same way but not as much, further confirming that her only play was leg spin with a smorgasbord of dodgy length and flight. Final ball of the over and Enid took stock, breathing deeply: were these batsmen good enough to warrant a two-over bluff or should she fire the lone Russian roulette bullet from the chamber this delivery? She eased into her delivery stride, the iconic large step forward followed by the cocked wrist past the apex of the bicep into the jump then the ball … flighted immaculately and a half foot outside off stump. The batsman's eyes lit up, a wide delivery which would turn towards the slips and be cut past cover point for a monstrously appreciated over. The ball pitched and jagged back – the googly – trapping him leg-before, Shaky going up in a desperate appeal, the 'zat' loudening from the 'how' to end on a crescendo of raised palms. The umpire had a think about height as the batter shifted his pad more towards the leg stump, gesturing an incredulous grimace, but he was given the raised finger. Enid bit the side of her tongue and breathed out as she concluded the high fives with the team.

The wicket seemed to break the batting side's spirit, a few soft wickets distributed between a barrage of sliders from Enid and metronomic accuracy from Daughtry, although the number 4 bat held firm, refusing to budge as carnage endured around him. Enid's spell in particular was thoughtful, unshowy, patient and tailored for each batsman. When TT were six down, the number 4 – at this stage having since raised his bat for a dogged fifty – realised he had to fill his boots before the malfunctioning tail emptied his Wellies without him enjoying the splosh-splosh of a country puddle meander. Peter was on and copped some tap before getting the batsman to play back to a flurry of balls, then put one full, eliciting an awkward lunge of needless defence and a tidy catch from Larry at the back. The two openers came back on and wrapped up proceedings well before the 50th over, that would improve the NRR and set up an unlikely run chase but one where they couldn't have hoped for any better with ball in hand, Testopony Tabernacle having never failed to reach the allotted overs in all the previous pool games. All out for 197 in the 38th over, Wei Ping furiously beating his keyboard to death as his Excel model simulated other results and half-way points came flooding in through the information sources he'd put in place, notably apps, websites and even his mother strategically placed at the game most threatening to Shaky's chances of qualification to the knockouts.

In the pavilion's changing room there was palpable optimism, not of the overconfident snatching defeat from the jaws of victory ilk, but one which wouldn't be deterred by any mountain, that is until Wei Ping broke the tension, peering over his glasses then instantly hiding his eyeballs behind the thick wedges of glass as though back to the comfort of hibernation.

"All other games going the distance - none of the other teams out cheaply which tells us that this is the game that will decide the winner of the pool," he said marvelling at his own unconscious use of cricket slang like 'cheaply'. "We need to chase the 198 to win in five-and-half overs," the words stunning the team's collective jaws to drop and bounce back up from the glossy floor, reattach, then flip open like a faulty glove compartment in a banged up old car.

"That's 36 off every over!" spluttered Corin and Enid in unison, some of the team substituting quick mental maths for calculated disbelief to challenge the hypothesis.

"Six a ball?" said Onka, saying more than asking. "One dot and we're out."

Wei Ping took a moment to survey the scene then, in an attempt to not let his waggery galvanise any further, confessed his gaudy attempt at wit.

"I'm joke ... make joke! Couldn't resist: the maths too

perfect! Bad joke! Wei Ping never try again!"

Everyone admonishingly breathed a sigh of relief but still remained trepidatory as Jacob and Rufus padded up.

"What do we need Wei Ping?" asked Yapa.

"By my 'truthful' calc - we need to chase down 198 in seventeen and a half overs at a run rate of 11.3 - this will give us a Net Run Rate superior to the opposition we are playing."

"T20 time," said Corin. "And we're chasing 200! Wickets don't matter in NRR remember, but losing ten does if we don't reach the total! Bat big ... but just don't go out!"

"No problem," said Noel knowing he wasn't batting anywhere near the top order.

"Kind of a simple game really, when you put it like that Cor," said Larry, safe in the knowledge she'd likely be batting today and even more likely when things would be getting tasty, salty even.

Jacob and Rufus strode out to the middle, Rufus lagging behind Jacob for the first time, Jacob side-step toe-tapping in eagerness to get those feet moving and the blood flowing to all digits before the first ball sped his way. Rufus, normally feline-like in his surveying of the fielder placings just wandered in, staring somewhere between his spikes and the horizon. The opening TT bowlers looked quick and they were, agitated to get going as Jacob laboured his guard. The first ball moved. Up and sideways and Jacob did well to leave it as it left him. The next ball he got solidly behind, a defensive push, nicely on his toes, bat tucked under his armpit. The dressing room gave no indication that two balls in he should be getting on with it, but such is modern cricket that the thought permeated into a resounding barrage of chirps from the opposition, that "this wasn't a five day game" and "he's secured the draw already" as to them, even though any slow rate was a ticket to the semis, taking intimidatory wickets was what they did best.

Third ball and another textbook defensive stroke, this one

front foot and the chatter ratcheted up as Shaky were zero runs with just over 17 overs to ensure their ongoing participation in Digners. The fourth ball zipped but so did Jacob's feet, coming down and lofting one over the inner ring for a magnificent boundary. Game on. Or so Jacob felt until Rufus turned a cheeky single off the last ball to keep strike into a send-back debacle as Jacob scrambled back and was run out. Rufus looked nonplussed, a blank expression void of contrition gazing through Jacob's lachrymatory eyes. Enid thumped her helmet on to go in at three when Onka put a hand on her shoulder and held up his phone. This was perhaps a moment when the phone server gods and the cricketing gods had tea and scones together and decreed timing as an important part of fate – it was an Instagram post from the Springbok rugby captain showing the entire team wishing Shackleton luck.

"I've got to make up for the bowling," said Onka as time pressured an appearance, Jacob reaching the pavilion with a new brand of tears: raging pin pricks in a pool tears squirting in all directions but down. "This will be my thank you to you for making this my home from home."

"You're one of us," said Enid removing her helmet.

"You're one of us too," said Onka, tightening his chin strap and making his way to the non-striker's end.

The first ball of the second over was a loosener even though the bowler's mouth appeared to be covered in actual froth, followed by an even looser shot, popping the ball back into the bowler's grateful paws. Rufus was out for a first ball duck and by way of celebration the bowler flung the ball into the keeper, just missing Rufus's helmet which he didn't even bother flinching away from. Enid, having just let her ears re-acclimatise to the freedom was forced to reapply the helmet and join Onka with Shaky two down after seven balls.

"Long time," she quipped as he met her halfway.

"From the one ball I've seen it's coming on nicely but not

much lateral. I'm going to bat outside my crease and hit through the line on anything that's full. Let me know if the keeper's creeping."

"Will do. Let's take a few balls to check this out. Our partnership is where this starts ... or ends."

Enid got through the second over with minimal fuss but even less runs and Onka took a few deliveries before deciding this was nonsense and that his batting skills were destined for greater than hopping up to look for third man or fine leg singles. What followed was like watching a batting coaching video, his footwork, timing and flourish of wrists at the end of each shot, leaving the growing gathering of Shaky students, curious at the sight of their team doing well all returning from the comparatively dull rap concert, applauding and retrieving the balls that hit and cleared the boundary rope with alarming regularity. Enid, without reneging on her immovable support rock duties, manipulated the strike so that Onka could tee up and deal almost exclusively in boundaries. Such was the bounty, they even started turning down easy singles at the beginning of overs if it meant Onka would lose most of the remaining strike.

As glorious as the shot selection was and as intuitive as the running between the wickets was, a required run rate of 11.3 was a peak higher than most cricket Everests. The score ticked along satisfactorily but never at the rate, so invariably the rate grew which made eight wickets in hand handy for depth of batting to score the runs but ultimately useless should Onka and Enid reach seventeen and a half overs without having reached the score. Testopony Tabernacle were no mugs either - well their coach wasn't - even if they looked like the biker gang cast from Tangled, and the instruction became clear: negative bowling. Giving up actively seeking wickets it became purely about restricting runs and this meant operating on the precarious edge of the laws - wide yorkers as acceptable but a left-arm orthodox spinner bowling exclusively down leg to right-handers was borderline. Instinctually Onka padded the first few away then left some which the umpire called as wides, but when the bowler started bowling wider and creating an actual risk of clipping the leg stump should a leave be misjudged, then tactics got trickier as padding away was not going to win this Test match.

When Onka fell it was ill-timed as the pair were just getting on top of the negative bowling, attempting to paddle a wide angled delivery and dragging the ball back onto the stumps. He'd made an impressive 63 off 40 balls with the total on 95. Enid remained not out on 32 off 23 when joined in the middle by Corin. To the cross over point of seventeen and a half overs, Shaky required 103 off 42 balls at 14.7 an over.

Corin, batting outside leg stump, instantly negated the negative bowling and when the offie tried a few wide darts Corin effortless dispatched each of them for fours, twelve runs off the remaining three balls of the over, one through cover, one reverse sweep past gully and one dragged over mid-wicket. The other end Enid discreetly picked up where Onka left off, using the full width and length of the field to work boundaries and a healthy rotation of strike to protect her sister at the start of her innings. The technical prowess and inventiveness of the shots given the field setting quickly shut the squawking mouths of close TT fielders, who ran out of derogatory things to say about girls quicker than Enid's feet to skip down and clip an inswinger over cow corner for six.

Above almost all else the girls loved batting together, partaking in each other's gains to embolden the other through intrinsic understanding, shot selection, instructional gestures and reassuring observations. It was as if whenever a gap appeared - a need or requisite - the other had the answer, in word or deed. Corin kept finding the fielder in one patch, so Enid signalled to open the face; Enid wasn't sure if airborne risk was worth it, so Corin pointed out the weaker fielders; Corin witnessed Enid play a textbook cover drive then emulated the exact shot a few balls later; Corin reverse swept which vitalised Enid to adapt and play more behind square, abandoning her comfort zone V past the bowler. As they passed each other during the fifty partnership, the wind seeping through the helmet grill, their smiles disappearing from one another's view out in the middle, there was a moment or few of genuine enjoyment of the game, the delight of achievements together and taking the game beyond the opposition; this was beach cricket with Duane, one or two more shouty clonks into the ocean enough to finish this chapter and return to the beach cottage with salty lips and sandy toes.

At the start of the 17th over Shackleton's score was 173-3, requiring 25 runs off 9 balls. Enid had moved onto 64 off 34 balls and Corin an equally explosive 42 off 15 balls, the two going at an almost identical strike rate since Onka departed. With the neighbouring concert a meticulous let down and the wildfire nature of gathering for something inspirationally monumental or generationally disappointing (both great outcomes in the eyes of the unwitting Shaky unfaithful) the support for the partnership to take the school over the line reached fever pitch, and certainly Yapa had never seen the school get behind a cause like this ever before. When the final over and a half loomed, the crowds fell silent as this was that moment when it all became real - the winning or being knocked out - and as the score required permeated around the ground, an unfeigned sensation of concrete nausea set in with some unable to watch.

Enid and Corin didn't need a mini-beano on this one: the job had to be done by them … right now. There were no other batters capable of getting this over the line from here, so they had to make the 25 runs before the tenth ball or … nothing! Testopony had one final ace up their sleeve, brought on to kick-off the 17th over - an unorthodox right-arm quick who bowled off the wrong foot. This was one of his first games having recently transferred from another school and Wei Ping went hurtling back into his laptop to retrieve any useful data but nada - he shook his head in disappointed disbelief. His first ball to Enid facing came quickly and unexpectedly, the strange sensation of letting the ball go early off his right leg startling Enid to catch the edge of her bat and drop centimetres short of first slip. 25 runs off 8 balls, but at least they knew, the element of surprise gone but a highly valued dot ball under the belt as the TT fielding side stopped chattering to focus in on the reality of keeping this game in their grasp.

The next ball was an unreachable yet welcomed wide that swung down leg, followed by an under the eyes middled on-drive for four, the ball slicing past a despairing deep mid-on who might have cut it off if he'd reacted earlier. Enid scanned the ground then gave up - sixes change the entire complexation of a match, a chase in particular. Whatever the cut-price Mike Procter served up next had to go the maximum … and it did, a glorious pull between cow corner and deep mid-wicket, picking the length early and smoking the ball for a low six. 14 runs required off 6 balls, the over halfway through and Enid deep into the seventies. A regrettable shot followed from Enid, trying to work the ball onto the leg from wide of off, the six having alleviated the situation such that a scampered two harnessing the vacant square leg would be valuable, but she came through the shot too early and front edged the ball back towards the bowler. The double-edged sword of bowling off the wrong foot meant the bowler was awkwardly wrong footed when the ball looped towards him, timing his jump too early and submerging on the downward journey just as the ball passed his splayed fingertips. It bounced safely but was a dot ball with the next ball achieving the desired two, concluding with deep square leg thundering in to almost run Enid out at the striker's end. The final ball of the over was merely a genuinely good ball, a slower ball from the back of the hand, the disguise augmented by the wobbly right leg release, Enid found wanting as the ball died past her bat, caught between going for a boundary and angling into the covers. Dot ball, the TT bowler looking about as chuffed as he could muster given the taut footing of the game. He blew Enid a kiss after the delivery, snatched his cap from the umpire and chirped Corin something horrible and not worthy of retelling as she prepared to face the final three balls.

The field was spread and it looked like the opening bowler who got Rufus out was coming back on, and it was difficult to deny that he was their best, nippy with a stock awayswinger to the right-hander, channelling Jimmy Anderson on roids. 12 runs off 3 balls - the maths simple enough, just to look for the spaces and decide in a heartbeat after the delivery whether to premeditate or let instinct take over ... Corin felt the salty air blow across her brow which told her which way to turn at the crossroads.

"Twelve off three!" she heard her dad calling, having fashioned an enjoyable ending to a game of beach cricket by hatching the 'Six ball' finale game, setting each of the kids a target. This morphed into twelve balls if the weather held and was always the way the Hanratty family chose to close out the Norfolk beach excursions. The bowler galloped in, piston-legged - it could have been Patty or Dad or Enid ... didn't matter; this was going beyond the breakers ...

An attempted wide yorker that Corin was lucky to reach and just get enough on it to skew past point for four. The bowler shook his head and spat, clearly admonishing the point fielder who could have done better. 8 off 2 and still Corin felt the chill of the North Sea breeze, the bat handle coarse from sand and worn from use as she swung again, this ball a lifting delivery that actually came in, top edging for a fortuitous four over the keeper. Had she not swung with such intent the game might have been over, but it came down to the last ball, four runs required and Corin heard the echoes of those memories: "Four off the last! Four to win! Corin Hanratty for World Cup glory!" This felt real and Corin closed her eyes then zeroed in on the widish delivery just short of a length, her right foot going across and opening her hips to play an old-fashioned back-foot drive through the covers. She got hold of it compellingly, middling it to the left of cover who stuck out a paw to deflect the ball behind point, the TT fielders all setting off in different directions. Corin didn't need to yell at Enid but did as a form of release, setting off like the clappers, completing one then two runs as the point fielder slid to stop the ball inches short of the boundary rope, Shackleton's deepest boundary. The throw was airborne, the trajectory too high without the forward momentum, enabling the girls to complete the third run. As Corin turned she failed to see an approaching TT fielder and got tangled together as Enid started the fourth run, the two battling against each other in vain efforts to stay on their feet, the supervening knotted roll akin to a clean out at the ruck. Corin excoriated the side of her face on the inside of the helmet, falling on her cheek then dragging herself back to her knees, freeing from the incumbering fielder as the original cover fielder who'd deflected the ball retrieved the wispy throw and set himself to shy at the stumps, witnessing a large chasm at the striker's end, Enid having reached Corin with no other option as turning down the final run would have been plain defeatist. She willed Corin up who scrambled up the pitch on all fours, leaving her bat and heading for the beckoning keeper, red-faced with gloves palm open and shaking like an Italian footballer. The Testopony Tabernacle team were not one to debate the merits of sportsmanship for an 'accidental' collision on the pitch, but the fielder did hesitate momentarily as he debated testing Corin's pace by lobbing it into the keeper or taking a shy at the stumps for Digners semi qualification glory. He erred towards shy but took enough pace off the throw, giving the keeper a fighting chance to gather and strike the bails clean off - a decapitated French aristocrat, Robespierre style. The throw came in, angling to the keeper's left as Corin's pace closed the gap, completely unaware of where the ball was or might be heading. In a flash she saw a haphazard brushstroke of red, the ball passing a few metres in front of her eyes, no bat to reach out with as she dived, near enough to reach her fingertip over the line given the urgent velocity she had attained, a long jumper spotting the board. As the ball sailed past her eyeline, the keeper moved to his left realising there was no direct hit to conclude this match, but given he was no taller than five foot, his levers would not reach between the errant throw's bounce and the stumps so he gathered and deftly flicked the ball from the back of his right hand as Corin landed and bounced on her front, just short of the crease. The momentum took her to where she could almost touch the line as the ball angled in towards the stumps, the distances between the ball-finger-stumps triangle scarily identical. Corin felt her hand slap down a whisker over the worn away line, a twinkling quarter-heartbeat before the ball dislodged the bails ... then a voluble appellate from the fielders, crazy eyed and in prayer before the square leg umpire ... then the taste of blood down the front of the lip and swallowed warm behind the nose ... then darkness ...

Chapter » 49

Follow On

The human body has the uncanny ability to adapt to a situation - evolve on the spot as a means of survival, acclimatisation or pressure. Equally powerful, the biology and specifically endocrinal system can go the other way, the opposite to just as swiftly shut everything down - the trip switch or grid power failure, the unexpected shock providing murky nothingness to shield the user from the violent storm, the extraneous prelude to what the brain, body, emotion and curiosity all wants in unison ... the result.

Corin didn't suffer head trauma; she didn't knock herself out inducing a non-existing HIA from her jaw clamping down in the confines of the helmet and knocking her unconscious for a moment while the decision makers above her ground eye level decided Shaky's fate with hopefully enough integrity to do the right thing. And in this case the popular thing was probably also the right thing - plucky underdog representing all genders, fully inclusive of all walks of life does good and knocks out juvenile detention centre. Yet the human sense of fair play means the cerebral decision should allow the full filtering of all visual data before raising the finger or shaking the head in the umpire's case. Oh, and by the way, Corin was knocked out, but it wasn't a good look to admit anything of the sort especially when she did come around, a semi-circle of some familiar some not faces peering over her, blocking the intel her awakening brain really craved … was she given out or not.

The pandemonium that filled her eardrums to the left and right couldn't be gleaned … was that TT whooping in celebration or the Shaky unfaithful joining in the celebration? Was Enid in a knotted huddle at the other end, bemoaning the loss through stoically fighting back the tears or was she being mobbed by the rest of the team while trying to make her way towards her partner in crime, her sister, her running/stumbling mate? Was the umpire's presence an act of follow-on guilt or vindication for the correct decision?

Corin clearly remembered sticking a finger over the line – Mafioso setting a rival hit on a smoky poker table style – scarcely before the ball swept through the stumps, the delta a nail clipping chomping through a normal, compliant fingernail. That said, her body was in the momentum of bouncing through the air and, from ground level and, with the absolute desire to make the run, it might have all happened the other way around.

Coming out of a trance, knockout or black out is never the slow blurry to focus cinema would have everyone believe; it is sudden – all of a sudden! There is a concept of time having passed as though while brains test pattern, deep space's exploration of time through black holes never ceases and the sudden awake feeling is tempered by the sluggishness of figuring out what the heck transpired in the interval, that extended glitch, that blank page of a book …

tOp Of Off

Corin's brain knew scant little as remonstrations continued like protest fires around her. There were raised voices, what looked like a fumbled phone in Miss Hazard's hand, coaches screaming at one another as the mayhem ensued. Corin sat up, now fully lucid and wanting resolution. There was no consolation in knowing that on a pure one-to-one cricket level, they'd decimated dangerous opposition, bowling the entire team out before the allotted overs and chasing the score down in under 20 overs at a wrenching run rate. All that mattered was what the square leg umpire did after Corin crumpled in a heap at the end she'd been batting, having either run the four runs required or … not.

The pockets of demonstrative sub factions dispersed to form a large circle around what looked like the two umpires, the two coaches, Enid, the opposition's captain and Miss Hazard, still fumbling with the phone as though it was the first time she'd used one. Corin thought she heard one of the umpires mutter "This is the equivalent of soft signal out," as everything went silent and the group's neck craned over the small screen, the muffled screams of the earlier shenanigans the likely viewing pleasure. Corin jumped to her feet and shot over, slipping under Enid's foreboding forearm, without disturbing her focus or even eliciting a "Oh hey Corin, thanks for losing/winning the match!" Corin was situated at a stubborn angle so couldn't make the video out but didn't need to, zeroing in on the umpire's face who held the device, his brow more the furrowed, each fold of skin oppressive on top of the sunken junior below, molten lava protruding out with each absorbed pixel.

As with most phone footage, the steadiness was closer to electrocuted than dolly savannah pan shot but Miss Hazard remained convinced the evidence was on the screen. When the TT boys were frenetically trying to prevent the fourth run, those crowding the striker's end had considerately cleared a path for the capture of Corin's finger jamming into the turf and sliding over the chalk, followed by the bails dislodging and the tide of appeals and high fives to confirm the umpire's doubts. Leaning over, hands on knees, the ump had semi-clearly seen Corin make her ground but took an age before shaking his head and stating, "Not Out!" The TT boys had instantly crowded the umpire, beckoning, pleading, imploring and the sudden swathe of antipathy had caused doubt in his mind. Cue Yapa and Enid joining the fray and ultimately Miss Hazard, who'd been approached by the Shaky supporter who'd captured the moment, sprinting into the trenches, waving the phone like a winning lottery ticket. The umpire handed the phone back to Miss Hazard and motioned for everyone to step away to provide his decree.

"My first instinct was that the batter had made his, erm, her ground. So the original decision was Not Out. This decision would likely have had to stand and not changed, but in the interest of fair consideration - to make one hundred percent sure - some footage has been reviewed and the decision stands ...

Not Out."

Chapter » 50

Castled

"It beggars belief that we've ended up here," said Corin stepping off the bus envisioning a man with white gloves and a tray of hot lemon-scented towels welcoming the players.

"Unavoidable. We'll have to adapt. Just as we have every game. Wei Ping is churning the pitch's history as we speak," said Enid lugging her oversized cricket coffin with practiced ease.

"Was it though, Sister? This smacks of foul play. They get to look at us more closely and whatever other hidden dangers await. This was ridiculously last minute."

The rest of the team filed off the bus and stood in amazement, the seventeenth century architecture looming above them in splendour and might.

"We're like the hobbits arriving in Rivendell here," said Noel.

Not many of the Shaky team had made the journey to where they were due to play the semi - none had the necessity or inclination to be there - but being there, in amongst the white bow ties, morning suits, chapel bells and tall spired buildings did generate a sense of awed foreboding. Larry instinctually spat her gum out onto the billiard grass of the outside quad then quickly retrieved it apologetically as Yapa's non-change of expression admonished her social graces. Daughtry's neck was craned higher than any of the team had ever seen which told everyone there was likely a Little Lord Fauntleroy channelling Rapunzel from Tangled in every tower: a fabulous boy wanting to get out and be his own person in the scary wide world. Jacob tripped over a pathway solar flame illuminating light in the shape of the school's crest - custom made and pristine until Jacob accidentally misshaped the darn thing into a dropped egg. Rufus - last off the bus - shook his head at the gawking newbies, still irritated at having to get a bus, his familiarity with this place chaffingly real.

In the lead up to the arrival, there had been enough last-minute shenanigans and plan changes to almost derail Digners. The lucky loser games that preceded the first knockout round were too varied and farcical, both Corkridge and Shackleton with the same idea in mind - pick the strongest opposition to play to hone the skills and test the players across all disciplines. Both selected the same team with Shackleton arranging the fixture early through Wei Ping and Yapa's proactivity only to be told on the morning of the match that the opposition's bus had been diverted to Corkridge, a veiled excuse of logistics interpreted as a wider, oranger, juicier carrot waved in front of the school, which they gladly munched all the way to the frond. Shaky attempted to hastily arrange a substitute but the mugging left them with a neighbouring school who were more convinced BatsMan was part of the MCU than a bit part player in a lesser school sport. The game was too one sided which provided no honing of match practice, while Corkridge summarily dismantled a team that was unlucky to not be part of the knockouts.

Then came the venue debacle, Daniels's behind the scenes jostling decidedly wangling the change. With Middlesex progressing, Lord's wasn't available, allowing Daniels to offer up Corkridge Castle School for Boys (and girls) as a viable alternative for both semis – one on the Saturday and one the following day on the Sunday. Yapa formally and vociferously objected, requesting a neutral ground but really there were no alternatives with that quality of cricket pitch on offer in the area, Daniels throwing in a host of added extras including additional stand seating, televising the match using new FrogBox 4K cameras, a Michelin starred chef doing the catering and a full orchestral band to play in the intervals accompanied by the robed and award-winning Corkridge Castle Choir – something many spectators would have made the trip for alone.

As the Shaky team approached the palatial visitor's dressing room, lines of Corkridge students had gathered to sneak a peek, a low murmur whispering throughout the tree lined avenues and adjoining boarding houses as their physical attributes were scrutinised down to the nth level. Daughtry, gliding a good stratosphere above the rest of the team, generated the most attention as Corkridge contemplated what those levers could do with a cricket ball in hand. Corin and Noel noticed the High Beam focal point early, Noel gesturing a frown and ghoul face to incite HB to be a bit more menacing. Daughtry coyly smiled and blushed as she tried an angry face that came across more like constipation than a quick liable to take your head off. Corin went the other route, encouraging Daughtry to just be herself, sure that the demure, awkward tall drink of water would freak the Corky supporters out more than an alpha big bird.

The team tried not to marvel at the décor in the changing rooms, the only missing appendage a mint choccy on a memory foam cushion, the latter actually present to comfort many and all tushies tired from a day's cricket toil and not wanting the introduction of an unsightly pile from the cool surface of the seat in front of the lockers. With Rufus out of sorts the decision was taken to open with Jacob and Onka and drop Rufus down the order, a move that, at the start of the season, would have riled him something shocking, but merely elicited a Corky version of 'meh' which sounded more like 'mah'. Enid really had to win the toss and elect to bat as Belchingham Bethel were notoriously good at setting a target and defending it, their gauge on what was a competitive total on an array of pitches always thirty to fifty plus par. Their bowlers were disciplined and stuck to their task, restricting rather than blasting through teams, something Shaky had not come up against in its purest form. Enid returned from the middle with a dismissive shake of the head ... she'd lost the toss and Shackleton were bowling first. Jacob and Onka reluctantly slid their pads back in the bag with Jacob applying another thick layer of blotted sun cream as his mother had insisted. Enid gathered the team for another unlikely push, another against the odds display.

"Speeeeeeeeeeeeeeach," sang Larry from the outskirts, the jollity out of place from her and the situation's perspective, but Enid insouciantly smiled and took the reins.

"I can feel we're nervous, but you'all want a speech, you'all gonna ged it!"

The laughter was nervy but enough to break the fostering tension. All eyes pinned on Enid as she looked to Corin for support, who in turn shook her head in a 'you're on your own, Sistah' for this one.

"Tactics first ... they'll go hard but they'll go sensible if they lose early wickets. Their tail is long: even the ten's notched up a fifty or two, so we can't relent, can't stop for one second. Every ball matters and every time the ball is near you in the field it matters. If any of our other games – or adventures – are anything to go by, then this will come down to playing the absolute best we can put out there coupled with a few freak moments of game-changing madness, so let's keep those in the locker and unleash at the right time – no huge confabs, you've all got this far knowing your own games so just back yourselves, let's back each other and I'll back the whole lot! When the crazy comes out the locker, let's make them feel it all the way back from whence they came!"

"Oh-ah!" yelled Noel, whipping out Pacino for no good reason whatsoever.

"We're going to play a bit scared in the beginning – no overly attacking fields to let the openers set and pace too slow as their middle order is able to stay long and score big. If we see them early, that's fine – then we attack so win-win – slow start versus exposing the middle order. Five, six and seven all play county, so the assumption is they have a few plodders in the top order to allow the middle to have some fun if they come off."

"Higher level of stumpings against this team than other dismissals," Wei Ping interjected. "So they like to use their feet up the pitch, especially to the spinners. Lauren, I hope you have glue in your gloves today."

"Every day, Wei Ping," responded Larry. "Every-single-day."

"Team ... gentlemen ... ladies ... people ... today is a day I refuse to give in, on the cricket field or in any tight situation with the opposition trying to get their foot on our throats. We are the only ones who decide where their feet go and on this occasion I'm mandating that for the next three hours, those feet go toddling back to their dressing room, bat tucked away for their last Digners innings.

Today ... I refuse to relent ... as a proud Shackleton cricketer. Proud to represent you all out there ... today."

The team huddled, the bind tight and true, clenched fists of cricket kit adjoining each member as no more words were spoken. The team emerged from the changing room to a crowd bigger than one they'd ever played in front of, the band in full throttle and the choir's sopranos beasting the tenors. Less party atmosphere and more grandstanding procession, the build up to something monumental, something Olympic: an epic trailer's score building towards a crescendo of heroic proportions. Enid contemplated whether this was all a ruse to freak them out; put cricket on a plane above their station, elevating the spectacle to a point where they feared reaching out an arm to chase the sun. Intentional or not, it was working, the team blinking like newbie celebrities at their first red carpet event, squinting in the flashlights, fish cavorting on a dry shore, evolutionary miles from liquescent safety. Losing the toss might not have been such a bad move - imaging batting in this cauldron, thought Enid, breaking into a jog to snap the team from the allure of the occasion.

The quicks were ready but Enid made a snap decision to open with herself, drag the spotlight onto a 'reckless' and 'vain' captain, the eyes of the Corky world fixated away from the team to let the pulses normalise and the arms feel lighter, disregarding carrying the buckets full of osmium. She'd bowl flat, unshowy darts - mainly sliders as they were less risky - mundane, underwhelming containment, until she tried to raise her right arm and a stampede of pins and needles went up through the elbow and down the back of her shoulder, a big-toed giant moonwalking over her grave.

Defensive field set and the batsmen came in, Enid mustering enough arm coolness to flick the ball up out of the side of her hand - as she'd done a million times before, the ball satisfyingly rotating in shiny seam-cherry-seam-cherry revolutions, loitering at the eyes for a howzit instance - only to fumble the ball, generating an audible snigger from the tweed-blazer sporting crowds. One thing was for darn sure

… all eyes on the girl captain of the S.H.I.X.

The first ball stuck in her hand, becoming an obscene drag-down, easily dispatched for four. The crowd cheered and the Shaky fielders grew restless. The next ball a bit fuller but not enough getting the same treatment.

"Hey, she's not so good after all!" rang out from the oak trees, the familiarity of the voice an unfortunate side-effect. Enid took the bait and glanced towards the group but couldn't make out any familiar faces, the brown hair collection a stew of clones atop grey tweed. The next ball was too full and the batsman incredibly missed it – a juicy full toss not dispatched but this gave Enid an idea so she turned towards Onka and motioned to warm up. The next three balls were decent enough, the sliders skidding on, close to the right areas, the bat up to the task to either keep out or work around for singles and twos. She was done: the first over under the belt which failed to quieten the hoards as more filed in, four-wheel-drives falling over one another for the prime viewing spots on the banks, but it did serve to break the heavy arm shackles and set Enid on a theory path for better or worse.

"These guys pick length," said Enid flinging the ball to Onka and raising a palm towards Corin to stand down from opening. "They are deadly in that regard – if you start even an inch short, it's gone but anything full, they're not scoring … or going out."

"So we keep them in?"

"And keep the score down."

"If the wicket presents itself?"

"We take it, but I have a feeling these two don't give much away unless we want them to ... and we don't. No power game between the two of them; no desire to take risky singles; just platform plodders good at picking out length."

"Got it, Skip!"

"Bowler's name?" the scorer yelled from the viewing

gallery embedded within the newly refurbished, high-tech scoreboard (known as a score 'capsule' complete with en suite).

"OnkaraBILE," a new voice emerged from the same tree area, emphasising the last syllable as the gastric juice that remains after a bout of gastroenteritis, a new ploy: the RIP ... rile, irk, peeve.

"It's Onkarabile," Onka shouted towards the scorers, conscious not to let the RIP take root, pronouncing the end of his name as two distinct syllables, enunciating the 'Bee-Lay' before marking out his run-up, preventing the bubbly blood with a coaxed injection of vein icicles. People had got his name wrong for time immemorial and he knew this was intentional, Chad and his band of merry sycophants doing whatever it took to get under Shaky's skin.

"Today I refuse ... today I refuse," he kept whispering to himself as he returned to the task of getting that left arm arced, the hip driving through the crease, staying on the front toes to pivot and not fall over.

The first ball was an absolute jaffa, ripping off an ideal length with bounce to buffet into the batsman's thigh pad, the thud distilling a hush across the ground. Any shorter and he knew he'd travel so the next few were flatter and fuller, all either missed or mistimed from both bats; Enid was onto something here, so Onka ratcheted up the consistency as the crowd lost interest after the magnificence of the first ball. Onka's action had always garnered interest, the lead up smooth but then exploding into a sautéed breakdancing octopus, every limb working against the other to eventually spit the ball out while incredibly leaving the bowler upright and not spider crumpled on the pitch after a whack with the proverbial slipper. The unorthodox action contrasted with a consciously boring spell of left-arm leg spin made for uneasy viewing for all those except the fielders, the supporters who understood the strategic significance of left-field tactics and

Miss Hazard. Wei Ping and Yapa gave the quadruple thumbs up after Onka's over, vindicating Enid's decision and kicking the licence to roam on this path gates wide open.

The two wrist spinners stuck dutifully to their similar tasks, the left right combo causing even more consternation from the Belchingham opening bats, as the open stance had to close then open again every six balls. By what should have been nearing the end of the opening spell or at least a change one end, the opening batsmen had struggled to middle a single ball and, without the dashing courage to go after either bowler, sat on a paltry 41-0 after 14 overs, the dressing room increasingly agitated and trees silenced into merely crackling from trodden footsteps. Everything had been either the model length or full - a twenty eighty split - with the line playing no real part due to the variations created by having six angles to play with: in, out and straight, from both bowlers. Yapa overheard a Digners aficionado comment on how he'd never seen a left right leg spin combination since the tournament's inception, let alone opening the bowling, let alone exhibiting the discipline, skills, application and concentration required to strangle the opposition. There was a hint of exhaustion from both bowlers though, the mechanics in the rotator cuff the primary concern as coming right around the ball to serve up a ripping, pure leg spin delivery required as much effort as any other bowler and the ache had begun to set in for both. Enid was also concerned that both might need to be saved to reveal the wicket taking deliveries when the firepower invariably came in to unleash.

They got to 16 overs - both two away from the allotted ten - when Enid was forced to make a change, bringing on Peter and Rufus, prescribing clearly to continue with length bowling to contain. Peter's first over took more tap than the spinners were being subjected to, the batters relived to have something coming on even if Peter's length was as instructed. The mis-hits simply went further allowing more twos and threes than the previous ones and twos. Rufus came in for his first ball and, completely against tack, dug one in, short and fast, with the batsman swivelling to hook, the ball getting big and top edging into the sky. Larry looked nervously at Enid as she got under the ball, checking whether the extent was to go as far as shelling a high-reaching sitter. Enid knew wickets from here on in were going to be essential now that the spinners were almost done, nodding in approval for Larry to pouch yet scowling at Rufus for forcing this decision at this juncture. Larry steadied herself and took a comfortable catch as Rufus gave a lone starfish celebration towards the trees, sticking his hips out in provoked protest.

The number 3 bat bounded in and once again the crowds got behind the match, the lure of wickets following wickets prompting a laying flat of half-eaten, seed-encrusted, lipsticked or moustache bristled cucumber discs until later, the bite grooves no local dentist's handywork. Rufus, bowling at the other opener as they'd crossed prior to the preclusion of crossing being instituted at men's senior T20 level, whipped down a barrage of defiant short stuff, some of which went sailing until the last ball which earned him his second wicket, a leg side tickle to the keeper. So, although wickets were not necessarily a bad thing, it prompted a rethink from Enid as the run rate pressure combined with the destructive reputation of the middle order meant either seatbelts or held horses.

Enid immediately made a double change, bringing on Daughtry and Noel much to Rufus's discontent. Through the spinners spell the ball had not been looked after and found the bat enough times to be scuffed which didn't suit either of the quicks, so the team got to working harder on the ball. The 3 and 4 bats accelerated the scoring, both looking accomplished enough but the bowling was sufficiently tight to warrant enough reassurance that this was a positive start to the match for Shackleton. Daughtry got the third with a decent cross seam that didn't hit the seam and skidded low to bowl the disgruntled batsman and Noel had a length ball caught on the boundary, dispatched with confidence but quick to the conclusion that the Corkridge 1st XI Oval was pointedly bigger than most grounds, so astute field placings in the deep morphed sixes into catches. When the ensemble jogging group ran out to high five Corin who'd taken the catch, Noel unashamedly assured everyone the ball was intentional.

With batters 5 and 6 at the crease the run rate had crept up to just under four an over with enough real estate in overs remaining to do some damage. From the way the two new batsmen surveyed the field, they'd been here before, undeterred and winding up, their forearms sinewed, sweatless and taut. Noel and Daughtry would suffer at their hands, not bad lengths but lines where the bats were able to shimmy around the crease and find boundaries at will. Enid resisted a knee-jerk replacement of bowlers after a smattering of expensive overs but at least one change happened as the number 6 bat in particular started dealing exclusively in boundaries. Corin replaced Daughtry and then Rufus replaced Noel, the former strangling out the number 5 bat to a sharp diving catch from Larry who no longer had accompanying slips as the coffers were being filled with wanton abandon. Rufus's spell in particular was troublesome as there was no semblance of consistency and the chances that were created weren't really chances which further agitated a spitting Rufus. Enid decided to give him one more over, conscious that Peter might not have the strength to bowl a full spell, Rufus and Peter now having to share the fifth bowler duties with the allotted ten overs between them. Daughtry was also limping and Onka rubbed his shoulder as many times as Enid wanted to but resisted.

Enid's 'walking wounded' policy would prove costly and potentially result altering. Keeping Rufus on to preserve

Peter – in hindsight of course – was the right call given Peter's fallibility but the wrong one considering the Rufus 6-7 bat combination. Rufus's final over this spell was more costly than a black cab on Saturday night, the first three balls going for the maximum, Wei Ping not incorrect about the use of feet. Rufus didn't bowl exceptionally bad balls, they were just consistently not taking account of the approaching batsman, first walking up, then skipping, then walking again, each ball turned into a half-volley and lofted almost to the brambles. Rufus's agitation only led to more boundaries and even though he looked like he was putting his back into it, Shaky's worst single over total with ball really woke the crowd, especially considering this was considered his home turf. With a no-ball to add insult to (an actual) injury, Rufus hobbled off, kicking his cap into the ground for an emphatic 34 runs.

Peter endured almost the same treatment as Rufus, who might or might not have looked relieved fielding on the boundary when the ball went jettisoning over his head on multiple occasions. After the fifth ball Peter ran over to Enid, tears forming in his eyes, stating he couldn't bowl another ball, a side strain of some magnitude cupped by his sheepish left hand. Enid called for Noel to bowl the last ball of Peter's over as he went off for treatment, a good ball, like the previous hour or so ending up being lobbed back underarm from the retrieving fielder as the batsman celebrated his fifty with much ape-chanting from all around the school. The game was fast slipping away from Enid, not least because she had to plug the allotted overs with either a misfiring Rufus or a non-bowler who'd yet to turn his or her arm over at any point in the Shackleton season. Enid rued not building depth in the bowling but when surveying her options from all the peripheral team members, recollected the thimble water depth she had at her disposal. Someone though, was going to have to warm up, or as a drastic measure she could bowl all the recognised bowlers out in an attempt to get Belchingham all out – they were already five down, but this was the highest risk strategy she would have adopted to date. If they got to the end still with wickets, the carnage that followed would make for embarrassingly soul-destroying viewing. One thing was certain though, they had to get a wicket and break this partnership … right now!

Onka knew. Everyone knew. A big dice role loomed, both leg spinners immediately back into action, a paltry two overs left from each to make this partnership disappear. This wasn't a time for containing, flat, full balls, this was the time for a magical delivery to completely bamboozle the batsman but without the luxury of a multiple-ball setup. Onka stepped up and beat the bat straight-away, a wariness creeping over the batting pair such that they took guard again, middle this time so covering more of the stumps than previously. Onka's next ball was the wrong 'un, turning past the bat like an orthodox right-arm leg spinner, the purchase on the pitch generating a groan from the crowd. The next two were also wrong-uns, bowling over the wicket and angling across the batsman's body, lucky not to get bowled off stump on the first ball and then lucky not to feather an edge to Larry the ravenous keeper. Four balls down and still no wicket but the runs had been stemmed, something that didn't concern anyone except perhaps Onka who knew four dots might just create enough pressure to fenagle out a wicket. The last two balls of Onka's penultimate over were two more beauties without reward, the number 7 surviving with Onka receiving a round of applause from a section of supporters that looked like OAP students of the game, their own scorecards open and glasses precariously balancing at the end of noble, elongated snouts. Onka rolled his shoulder and winced, pinging the ball to Enid who fumbled the ball, the pain in her shoulder equal to Onka's grimace. She signalled a 'one more?' query his way. He nodded.

Enid warmed up without shattering the illusion that she was anything but in tip-top shape, no ailments and ready to climb a mountain yet, upon reflection, bowling an intense eight over spell was her longest to date. She abandoned swinging the arms around when it became too painful and was just about to bowl when she noticed a shiny set of brand-new, milky-silver white Cheshire teeth blinding her from the boundary. There he stood, legs akimbo, arms folded, his grin lasering in her direction, an obtrusive sheen of perfect little rectangular replacement teeth, maybe from Turkey. Nothing moved on him, except for his blonde fringe which bobbled independently.

"Is his hair waving at me?" wondered Enid, transfixed for a time longer than was necessary.

He blew a winky kissy raspberry, then mock-bowled a slapdash leg break, swivelling to mock-smack it out the park then gripped his shoulder, Enid's hurt unable to escape practiced, prying eyes. Enid resisted the temptation to retort although it did cross her mind - tapping the tooth Corin chipped the only juvenile firepower she could muster.

"Thanks, Mate!" he mouthed as Enid directed her shoulders back up the pitch, ready to bowl to the well-set number 6 bat.

Her first ball hurt something terrible, the grind of bone on cartilage against the precarious shoulder joint making her effort grunt audible. The ball was well placed but didn't do much as the follow-through was curtailed, the batsman working the ball onto the leg side for two runs. She didn't rub anything, just went back to her mark to set again, a cold sweat indelibly descending upon her brow. There was only time for two more setup balls and, even if this ached more than an open surgical wound, she had to get it right and target the fourth as the wicket taking ball. It would be a slider to keep him in his crease and make him believe this was an over of darts, then a moderate turning shortish stock leg spin delivery to give him free licence to roam come the fourth ball. The second ball was flat - maybe too flat - but achieved the desire to root him in the crease, as the itch became a rash. Then the third, the ball turning merely from leg to off, the batsman pushing a back foot drive straight to the fielder, the feet now beyond itching and rash into full-blown hives territory. Enid resisting looking up at Chad in the same threatening eyeline position on the boundary, joined by the chief regiment of his supportive mates in James, Danny and Chuck.

This was the ball - it had to be - even if her last of the match. She came in, over the wicket, the fire sparks igniting beneath the number 6's bat almost as she released the ball, coming right around it, scrambling the seam and ripping the wrist through the ball as she'd never done before. The ball arched without a loopy loop heading a foot outside leg as the bat double stepped to come after the bowling, quickly realising that he wasn't going to make it to the pitch but remained committed to the attacking stoke. From Enid's delivery stance to where the ball turned towards shaped like a sparrow's beak, the ball gripping and spinning so much, the batsman couldn't reach it and played down the completely wrong line, inside the ball and at least six inches away. Even as the ball went past, he nodded in admiration, continuing to run up the pitch as Larry effected the perfunctory glove work, waiting patiently for the ball to pass the off stump, then swept the bails off with ease. Enid dropped to a knee in pain and relief as the square leg umpire didn't even bother giving it, the batsman tapping his bat twice with his glove in a sportsmanlike clapping gesture. He'd done some serious damage, but the best bat Shackleton had played against this season departed with a gracious mien. A standing ovation ensued, Chad and the lads bellowing the applause in the batsman's direction so as not to mistake the applause for Enid's bravura ball.

Noel was getting late swing, Daughtry some daunting lift - especially after Chad & Co. made what sounded like camel noises from their new spot right in the bowler's eyeline - and Corin got just about everything going: seam, nip, swing and bounce. True to form the tail were competent batsmen who did go skipping after most of the bowling to find a host of edges with some sharp chances going amiss. Larry was in direct action most of the remainder of the innings, shelling a tough overhead grab, the keeper glove webbing holding onto the ball just long enough for it to squirm its way out and bobble agonising in front of her as she fell. Larry looked up disappointed only to regain confidence through laying eyes on Chuck watching Rebecca watch her, then cheer her on with a conversant nod.

By the 42nd over, Belchingham Bethnal were 235-8, the number 7 still in batting with a left-handed number 10 that looked as though he could have batted anywhere in the order - bar number 6 of course. The spinners had both snuck an over each in the lead up, their remaining six balls dealt merely with circumspect resistance. Noel was bowled out, which left one each from Corin and Daughtry to get through their allotted ten overs, Peter being hidden from action at fine leg just to ensure he was on the field long enough to bat - even though this was highly unlikely given the extent of his side strain - and Rufus sulking at deep mid-wicket, not even pleading for the ball to make up for whatever happened earlier. Enid didn't even have a plan for those last six overs - it was in for a penny, in for a pound - the final two wickets had to go down in the next two as, even if she bowled Rufus, there was no one to bowl the three at the other end! These two batsmen would likely shut up shop to a degree now and wait for the invisible rabbit to be revealed from the empty top hat.

A brief conflab resulted, captain, keeper and the two quicks with overs left in the bank.

"Larry, stand up to the stumps," said Enid.

"Are you kidding?" responded Larry, then adjusted tact once she'd surveyed Enid's face. "It's doing stuff out there – lots! Lateral movement, bounce, nipping around. Can I have a long stop?"

"No long stop. Is the bounce variable?"

"Fair point. I'll stand up but we need clear signals from the bowlers."

"The signals we practiced," confirmed Daughtry.

"Baseball style!" added Corin.

"I'll give it a go, but ladies, when the byes rack up against my name, just know standing up to the stumps for you two is like sticking your face in a beehive!"

"Don't hold back," said Enid. "Full pelt. We'll live with the byes, but we need two wickets. Or else thirty-six times six will be the amount added to the total after you two are bowled out. Daughtry, how do you feel about getting out the slower ball?"

"Not good! I just haven't landed one properly even in practice, Skip. Not a good idea but appreciate the belief."

"With Larry standing up we'll force them back into the crease, so I don't think yorkers are an option; plus we don't want to contain. Girls, I'm taking all your leg side boundary cover away and crowding the batsmen ... slips, gully, short square."

"They'll know what we're up to," stated Corin.

"I know," said Enid. "Which is why just two balls of the twelve need to be unplayable, if such a term exists. These two wouldn't be used to defending and the lefty has a big stride across so LBW is a distinct option here."

"Let's make it rain," said Corin, slapping Larry's gloves with both palms and then onto Daughtry who was first up with the ball.

With the field in, even the crowd sussed the intent, the band laying down their instruments as an intensity veil covered the cricket pitch, enshrouding the gladiators to swell the worth of the next two overs. Daughtry's first ball was dug on too short and went flying over the bat and keeper's head for four byes, the lefty number 10 narrowly avoiding having to retrieve his head from the same spot as where the ball ended up, so agro pace and steep lift giving Larry scant chance to sojourn. The second ball was the same length but lacked any venom, so the bat threw his wrists above the ball, Larry gathering next to her face. The third ball was a sturdy length that the bat just managed to leave and Larry stuck a glove out to miraculously pluck the apple from the speeding tree. For the fourth ball, Daughtry decided to come around the wicket and pitched a quick delivery on middle but straightening up, flicking the front pad then the bat and into Larry's gloves to a rambunctious appeal. The umpire was convinced it had only struck the pad en route to the keeper and gave it Not Out, much to the dismay of the bowling side and in particular Daughtry who had not up until this point directly experienced an unjust, bad decision in cricket. This lit a fuse and the poetic sight Yapa envisioned all those practices ago came to fruition for real, the whipping of those limbs through the air in perfect harmony, the blur of HB's long arm of the law coming so far down the pitch it almost slapped the batsman's helmet peak. Remaining around the wicket the ball took off fast, the batsman taking futile evasive action, the ball lifting and clanking the side of the helmet with extreme force, the succeeding trajectory higher than most top edges. Larry pouched the ball and Noel couldn't resist appealing from second slip.

The number 10 bat was messed up, falling to his side then crawling onto all fours only to tip over like an imbalanced cow. The Shaky team showed genuine concern for his wellbeing as they helped him off, unable to continue batting. The number 11 walked in small strides, trepidation at the prospect of facing the final ball of Daughtry's spell, passing his teammate bound for the emergency helicopter. He took guard and looked like he went into prayer as Daughtry came around the wicket once again, firing down a yorker which was incredibly dug out and nicked for four. Daughtry was, in a way, relieved, and Enid could tell there was never going to be follow-on malicious intent by this cricketer – and that was just fine.

Corin warmed up, bowling to the number 7, well-set and already on a decent score as Larry once again crouched down behind the stumps, her nose so close to the bails she could've nuzzled one off. Even in the stance, his backlift looked non-existent, six balls to survive then the keys to the kingdom of bountiful runs, more prolific than a street kebab's afterparty. Chad and his minions watched carefully as this was the quick they most wanted to understand and most probably target to get the others' heads to drop: chop the leader of the attack down to size and the rest of the snake shrivels, he'd bestowed over a spritzer with his chums during a 'managed drinking' teacher student 'ready for the real world' event held at a pub called the Fox & Scratcher. Corin could feel her pulse was elevated – a good thing – as she steamed in, flicking her trademark left ankle at the batsman as part of the delivery stride. The first ball danced, angling in to the top of off stump then straightening, the batter forced to play and beaten by the seam away, an agonising pouch for Larry, stopping the ball with her collarbone. Corin knew she had to hold her nerve and go same again, a carbon copy of the first ball, again the bat missing with a defensive under the eyes attempted block, the only difference Larry stopping this one with her wrist, smiling in woe – a crazed, swollen eyed grin that helped her avoid the wrist shaking admission. Corin decided to go one more time – three of the same, aiming to miss the off stump, her signal to Larry preparing her for more body-stopping keeper-bodyline! If she strayed too far down leg to work it back and hit off stump, she'd be worked onto the leg and wider had no menace, so her hat-trick of length deliveries moving away ensued, the third the best of the bunch, jagging away and leaving Larry with no chance as it flew past the glove for four byes. Now it had to be: the magical fourth ball inswinger.

Corin tried to follow her exact routine, not looking anywhere different or handling the ball in another way - this was metronomic routine to lull the batsman into playing and missing in the same way, his awareness of the amount of seam ensuring confidence to play and miss as long as he picked the straight line. Corin's neck ticked a smidgeon as the Chad brigade tried to shift her off her rhythm, the word 'predictable' ricocheting from her eardrum. This ball - Corin's fourth - pitched in exactly the same spot, just outside off but instead of straightening, went on, following the angle and some, striking the motionless back pad of the batsman. Corin, almost stumbling to the ground, went up for the appeal with a yelp, the heels of her hands pointed to the sky, imploring the umpire to give Belchingham Bethel all out. He took his time, surveying the line and height of the ball ... then shook his head, Corin falling to her knees in disillusionment.

"It just did too much, luv," the Northern umpire explained as Corin returned to her mark.

"Now what," she thought?

"Don't just bowl the ball," she heard her dad's words ringing in her ears. "Have a plan every ball, even if the plan doesn't work, execute against what you had intended - your brain is your best weapon in cricket and good outcomes seldomly happen just because of a random fill-in ball."

Corin had two balls and after four dots this batsman was rooted to the crease, not likely to play an expansive shot ... unless ... one was served up on a platter, could he resist? She'd never tried this type of variation in a match and not many had been overly successful in the nets, Enid and Onka dispatching most for likely boundaries, but there was never a better time to be braver, come fortune or famine! There was no signal for this type of ball and she had no cover deep on the leg side, so she failed to signal anything, Larry's bemused expression pleading for some gesticulated data. In she ran again, same action, same arm speed through the air but dug this one in, dropping it shorter than anticipated, the batsman hopefully gleaning this to be frustration rather than the intended slower ball bouncer.

The ball dug into the pitch and accelerated, the batter at first shielding behind his shoulder then automatically opening up to pull as the ball started the final ascent of the top arch over the summit of the highest point it would reach above the batsman's eyeline. Normally slower ball bouncers would work to contain a free scoring bat, as they come through the shot too early - seldom a wicket ball but rather a containing non-scoring dot which, in say T20, can often be as good as a wicket. For this reason the confusion of the ball's place in this match and cricketing society in general scrambled the number 7 bat's cognizance, initially taking evasive action then opening the hips to smack the ball, then in a split second remembering he just had to survive two further balls, so re-closing the hips to defend whatever the heck this was from Corin Hanratty. The ball reached its final looping downward trajectory with the batsman unable to return to a defensive stance, swinging back around and nudging the ball with the back of his bat, the weird groove sending the ball scooping unnaturally to Lauren's left, narrowly missing the stumps. Having lifted her body from crouching but not so much as to prevent a pivoted lunge, Larry thew herself to the left of the stumps, low to the ground as the confused batsman tried desperately to follow-through with the accidental shot. With her glove no more than an inch above the pitch, and landing heavily on her left flank, an outstretched glove just (just!) managed to pouch the ball, the ball peeping above the webbing like a rising sun. Larry lay motionless as no one appealed, the unique back surface of the bat shot leaving everyone immobilised, stunned into inertia. Noel appealed from the slips, wanting to continue the theme, which then spread to Corin who did the same directly at the umpire, who looked at the square leg umpire who nodded uncertainly.

"The ball didn't touch the ground so, despite hitting the back of the bat, that's out I'm afred, yung mun," the umpire quantified before raising the finger.

"This is only the halfway mark," thought Enid, speeding in to lift her sister up off the pitch then join the team in mobbing Larry for the most unlikely of catches.

The changing room looked like a post battle civil war medical tent. Many a forearm covered both eyes in horizontal recline as each of the players assessed their own private ailments whilst Wei Ping sped around, computer in hand, breaking down the Belchingham bowling attack. Most crocked of all was Peter, who had a cacophony of ice and Voltarol patches attached all along his side with a melange of bandages, plasters and kinesiology tape. Sprays were also being liberally applied to shoulders, ankles, knees and wrists, ranging from cold water mist up to approved medical anaesthetic sprays, Yapa the gatekeeper to manage doses. Shackleton were chasing 243 at 4.86 an over, the latter damage limitation in getting Belchingham all out significantly reduced what was already a tough ask against the most potent bowling line-up they'd never faced. Jacob and Rufus padded up to open, as Corin went over to sit next to Rufus.

"Now that's how you bowl a slower ball bouncer!" she said, kicking his bag over to make room for her feet.

"Funny," he responded, strapping his pads without the usual precision.

"Hey, I just want you to know, we all get - I get - it must be hard to come to your old school and play for the enemy in front of all your buds."

"Yeah, well it's only a game, right?"

"Never for you … never for me. It means too much, for different reasons."

"This is the good luck pep talk where you tell me I'm one of the gals and to go out there and curtsey the hell out of each ball?"

"No this is just where I tell you the truth – everyone here backs you. You've made us a better team."

"Of late for sure."

"Everyone has their own patches … and demons. But just know that whatever you decide – however you decide to play – I back your judgement to make the right choices. You'll be a part of this team no matter what you do."

Rufus felt his neck muscles tighten, so he looked away from Corin and out towards the exit, slamming his helmet on as though arming a gladiator and grabbing his gloves. He stood motionless for a minute then looked down at Corin.

"Just don't try and emulate me," she concluded, reverting succinctly away from any actual sentiment. "Or you might actually make some runs."

Rufus walked towards the door, the clatter of batting spikes alerting everyone to the imminent dawn of the second innings, stopping at Jacob's station to put a hand on his shoulder and allow him to walk out first.

Out in the middle it was frenetic. Belchingham Bethel were a busy side, hustling left and right, bounding up and down, urging along and around. The spare ball was treated like a hot potato as part of the warm-up – which didn't seem to end even after Jacob had taken guard. Having observed the effect of early spin, they too looked like opening with spin, but only from one end, a left-arm finger spinner to take the ball away from both right-handed openers. He was canary-haired and lanky, so bounce would likely play a part too. Jacob's idiosyncratic superstition mounted, so he performed his quotidian Little Cossack squat-and-kick dance to loosen up the feet muscles and dupe the keeper that steps were-a-coming. Rufus looked towards where Chad was likely to be, atop his throne on the pavilion balcony, noticing none of the Corkridge XI were even watching, preferring horsing around and holding up phone videos for an ephemeral chuckle. The other opening bowler warming up looked like the number 6 bat who'd made most of their runs.

The first ball took place after a hush was ushered in around the ground, the almost conscious disregard for the match evident. The ball did nothing, straight on without turn or bounce, Jacob easily fending it off. The next ball went for a single and now, with Rufus on strike, his schoolmates all shushed one another to watch. Rufus was watchful for his first ball faced, his body movements looking more fluid and timing crisp. A few more average balls to conclude the over, one nipping through a little low but other than that just darts, and Rufus remained strangely chary.

"Is this the one we go after early?" asked Jacob as they convened in the middle. "Not doing much and I'm not sure I can hold my feet still much longer!"

"Don't hit the golden goose out of the attack; this team doesn't have many bowlers but the guy you're about to face is decent … be careful, we've got time."

Jacob, for good measure, completed one more squat-kick then went to take guard for the start of the second over.

The bowler was right-arm over and, first up, beat Jacob's weak fend outside the off, the lack of footwork irritating him, especially as the lead up had been so fabulously nimble and flamboyant. The next ball swung in, and Jacob managed to pivot and glance for a single down to fine leg. Again Rufus was circumspect although the bowling was mostly in the right place with more swing than Shaky had achieved, the swing though not complemented by any seam or bounce, banana balls moving from outside off to leg stump. The over completed and Shaky were none down but with not too many on the board. The crowd once again reassumed pulsating distraction, the game not able to finish in a turgid draw but feeling that way, until a Year 10 rebel sought to ensure Rufus lay down his arms.

"Hey Roof!" the boy bellowed. "Can't bat without your skirt on!" was met with braying hysteria from the pavilion's balcony.

Rufus was facing the off spinner, as the bowler gained in confidence through the containment role he was dutifully succeeding at, that is, unless Rufus broke his own shackles. The first ball was brambles bound, a crisp six, followed by a square drive for four and a cover drive for four. The crowd hushed and Rufus went further to town, belting the hapless offie all around the park, the golden goose truly defeathered, plucked and likely not to bowl again this century. Jacob smiled and tried to pick up the mantle the other end, but the bowler's skill was difficult to produce boundaries from, so he became intent on working it around and taking the scampered runs on offer. Every time he smiled over at Rufus, Rufus would scowl back, a reassuring return to form as Chad ditched his phone and stood, folded arms on the balcony, Nero seething while Rufus burned through the overpitched deliveries. The off spinner duly came off and was replaced by an out-and-out quick who hit the deck hard but did little else, so Rufus was able to shift to the back foot and continue to collect runs as his more-willing-than-able opening partner ran when he was told to run and stayed when he was told to stay. The smallest glimmer of relief flooded Rufus's cheeks as the aficionado section began applauding his quality shot selection and placement.

Rufus was the first to fall but to a good ball, the ironic cheer from the punters not doing justice to a solid innings. Jacob, almost as disheartened to lose his opening partner, went the next over to a bowler whose celebration was apparently a moonwalk. What ensued was a patch of effective medium-fast bowling and good catching from Belchingham. Noel was sent in number 3 as a self-proclaimed pinch hitter of sorts in an effort to get the rate up but fell cheaply thus rendering the Wei Ping-inspired experiment failed. The Onka Enid mainstay partnership was broken early with Onka unlucky to find the fielder's fingertips after connecting what looked like a six straight off the bat, the sound rich and crisp but not wealthy and crispy enough it seemed, the Corkridge extended boundary being maximised by Belchingham. This was a big wicket in the context of the match and Belchingham celebrated as though they had one foot in the final, the score 58-4 after 15 overs. Corin joined Enid out in the middle and both looked nervy, knowing this partnership would have to last as, with Peter crocked, there was only really Larry to come and still 186 runs to chase.

There wasn't much foot movement from either of the Hanratty girls as each tentative prod and miss or bouncing edge was met with a crescendo of boos and hisses from the galleries, so much so that a master who wasn't Daniels had to step in to institute some decorum as the wolves snarled at bay. Chad was quick to blame either his teammates or the travelling supporters, insisting and assuring the history teacher that he'd keep all the heathens in line.

Then came the short stuff and the girls struggled; strangely so. None of the bowlers - on show at that point - had yet shown any extreme menace with pace and lift, but a period ensued where they found a sort of skiddy length that would hold in the surface, a delayed tennis ball bounce that would reach the girls as they were going back to fend. From the galleries it appeared each were hopping around to avoid the chin music, the ball striking both above the ribcage on numerous occasions, to oohs, aahs and sniggers. Both, though, negated the threat of wickets by dropping the wrists as each ball ballooned towards them, but not many runs were flowing and the tactic embedded to the extent that Belchingham were unlikely to fix what ain't broke. If this was some sort of ruse for the final, it was indeed a risky one as this period was a painful corpus of bruises and helmet deflections for both Enid and Corin.

Eventually Corin had endured enough and took on the short ball, either sitting deep to keep it down in front of square or approaching to hit the balls on the up. The intent early on was kind on the scoreboard, not so kind on the purist's eye, boundaries soaring over the keeper, behind square and even a middled toe end of the bat for a four down the ground. Enid also started to get the measure of the length, uncharacteristically scooping, ramping and reverse paddling over the slips for a congregation of one bounce fours. Belchingham Bethel's captain was no mug though so switched up the tactics just as the short tactic waned, although it looked as though the damage had already been done. The change to spin one end and containment seam the other proved fruitful for Belchingham as both 'big femme-fatal fish' fell in successive overs, the luxury to shift back from evading to attacking to assessing not afforded to either of the Hanratty sisters by the match situation. Corin fell to a leading edge which spooned to cover and Enid played on to a ball that seamed in and stayed low.

Shackleton were six wickets down with over a hundred runs to get, the score on 117 at the exact point of the halfway mark, 25 overs into the match. With Larry already out in the middle, Enid having discussed keeping the strike to protect the dregs of the tail that would emerge after falling, she walked off as Peter appeared from the dressing room. Enid wondered whether she was making this up in her head, sure for all money he was laid up, crocked out of the game with the debilitating side strain that was close to impossible to function with, given the mechanics of body swivelling and how much the side muscles get employed with batting and bowling. Peter clutched his side as he strode out, holding the pain at bay, a bowl of runny jelly leaking over his forearm and through his fingertips. As he approached Enid, she noticed his eyes were swollen, red raw lids the balcony overhang above dilated pupils with an infusion of strong Ibuprofen.

"You don't have to do this, Peter," said Enid removing her helmet as the two met, Enid almost reaching the boundary given the sheepish, slow walk Peter was forced to adopt. "Your health is not worth a cricket match."

Peter looked up at Enid, his small frame quivering beneath her gaze, summoning strength, will and power from the depths of somewhere in the soul, intertwined with a thousand shooting pain needles sparking all the way down his side.

"Cap ... it's done, not me. I can bat. The run rate's not terrible so I'll just hang around a bit and chill, keeping Larry company for good measure. We can't have her winning it swiftly and taking all the glory!"

Belchingham set an attacking field knowing that one wicket won this match with the batting to follow more likely to hold the bat by the blade and face front on, French cricket style, that chase down 243. The ensuing half hour would prove to be the most nerve-wracking in Shaky's short cricketing history, Lauren giving a few half-chances in an effort to keep the runs tickling along and Peter hobbling through against a litany of shying at the stumps and missing, most leaving him stranded by a solid few feet. He endured though, running with everything he could muster and defending the end of overs to keep Larry on strike for the beginning of the next. Larry's fast twitch fibres required settling down, the knee-jerk happening too early on a pitch that was sticking, resulting in a perpetuation of body blows on all the female cast members. Not that this would have bothered her at all, golf ball bruises par for the course in her upbringing, the better than par on her course avoiding leopard spot bruises inflicted by her equality-enforcing brothers. From the supporters' stands, Peter looked pale, his shiny eyes bobbling around a motionless head and body, yet he kept glancing up at Yapa when there was a bowling change as Mr Yapa continued to fumble around with his archaic strips of paper, crumpled and emerging from hidden pockets every few balls.

As the final ten overs approached, the miracle, as the crowd became increasingly engaged, was that no further wickets had fallen, despite some moments hairier than the bin at a cheap wax salon. Lauren had endured and Peter had survived, but the summit loomed with Shackleton's score settling like a one-winged injured butterfly on a locust eaten flower at 171 runs, requiring 73 off the last ten and a bit overs. The Corkridge balcony, uncontained despite Chad's assurances, bleated unashamedly after each close call as the Shackleton support tried to counter the verbals without parading the obvious quavers in the shouts of encouragement.

"You think maybe we could have a match that doesn't go down to the wire, doesn't decimate all your fingernails down to the nub, doesn't leave childbirth preferable to the knots in your stomach! Maybe ... just this once," said Corin unable to keep still.

"Wouldn't be the beach if it wasn't Sis," said Enid, affording an exhaled smile. "Wouldn't have it any other way—"

"Take her head off!" vibrated an abrasive bellow from the Corkridge balcony, Chuck, swaying with drunken rage as Larry survived another gloved chance.

"You got this Lauren!" came the countered response from Rebecca, directly opposite the balcony. "Come on Shackleton!"

"You don't got this, Shaky High!" came a higher pitched

voice after an admonishing stare from Chuck, Danny this time, trying to quell his sister's support for the opposition.

"You got more than Corkridge will ever have, Shackleton!" came the now ping-pongesque tat to outsledge Danny's tit.

The umpired moved to quieten everything down as play commenced, Chuck and Danny clearly not seeing eye to eye in terms of commitment to the cause.

A new bowler emerged at the start of the 42nd over and Yapa gave Peter a thumbs up, who now took a new guard and seemed to instantly loosen up. The gloss expelled from his eyes disappeared and, as though he held the pain in a jar beside the bed, his knees took more of a bend, the bat now poised parallel to the floor as the bowler darted in, a sinuous action. The bowler's arm came through almost bent yet Peter was able to effortlessly step across and play a sumptuous cover drive on the up through the covers for four. The next ball was shorter but the same line so Peter went back, wincing a tad, and played a square drive for the same result. The bowler looked bemused as to what to do next and Peter simply went robotic playing an array of proper cricket strokes to pierce the field, on the ground, using timing and technique. The over was profitable, and Larry started to expand and settle in the same breath, getting out the reverse sweep early and turning length balls into short balls by sitting deeper in the crease for select deliveries. As the game squeezed towards completion, Shackleton started to believe, Lauren and Peter scoring with more fluidity than the match had seen since the Belchingham number 6's innings. Lauren's Swiss watch quick reactions combined with Peter's calm shot selection conspired to leave the opposition turning back to the hero with the bat to bowl the last over, Shackleton requiring 16 runs from it.

Peter was on strike and the first ball swung in as supposed yet got big on Peter who adjusted to swivel and hook the ball for an almost-caught four but crumpled in a heap on the pitch, the side strain dam wall pain barrier broken after a litany of cricket shots. He got sick into his mouth and swallowed it back down, determined not to show any further weakness as Larry came down the pitch to console.

"I'm fine," he said getting back to his feet. "Just slipped."

"Keep slipping if the ball ends up going the distance!" said Lauren, showing only the most complete faith in her batting partner's fabrication.

The second ball was the same and Peter knew he couldn't get on top of this so just let it hit him on the chest, his small stature being driven back by the swinging thunderbolt, scooting through for the single to leave Lauren on strike. 11 runs off 4 balls as the third ball was bowled and Lauren took aim then waited for the ball, leaning back and guiding it to inopportunely find deep point who took the ball on the bounce then fumbled to allow them through for the second. 9 off 3 and an attempted full wide yorker which, because of the slight swing in, Larry was able to get bat onto to the left of third man who did well to prevent the boundary and get the ball in directly over the stumps, Shackleton now requiring 6 runs off 2 balls.

Peter set himself as the ball came towards him, a misdirected yorker that sped through as a full toss, Peter's eyes lighting up knowing that he could put this away for a six! As he swung something broke inside him, the click-and-ping audible from the stands, as he stopped short of putting the ball away, only succeeding in paddling it around the corner. Larry went for the run and reached Peter at the other end, picking him to his feet as two fielders converged on the ball. Peter, regaining consciousness, got to a leg and hopped as fast as his ailing body would permit, as the throw went to the bowler's end, Peter launching from a distance on his functioning limb to slide over the crease before the bowler broke the stumps. As he peered up, some of the sick now coating his grill and the top of his shirt, he noticed the square leg umpire had his arm out ... due to Peter's small stature, an above waist height no-ball had been adjudicated.

"A no-ball!" Peter gurgled to himself, rolling over on his back before the stretcher came on to remove him for medical attention, a standing ovation from just about all attendees. The lanky lone figure of Daughtry emerged to join Lauren at the crease, her pads too small on her legs and the bat looking like it wouldn't reach the floor even if she leaned down. With Lauren on strike, Shackleton now required 4 runs off 2 balls.

Lauren glanced up at the Corkridge balcony, Chuck gripping the rail so tight the dilated veins in his forehead were visible from the middle. She looked behind her towards Rebecca, both her arms looped into her contiguous neighbours, Corin and Onka, unable to move. The majority of the field was in, those out in her favoured spots - cow corner, deep point, deep square, deep third and deep fine leg. She made an obvious point of adopting the ready to bat pose a foot or so outside her crease, the ground falling so silent that she could hear the bowler's heavy breathing as he headed towards her, grassed knees getting bigger like two green-brown traffic lights flashing on and off. As he rose to jump into his delivery stride, she took a step back deep in her crease then across to leg stump, opening the off side, but the bowler was wise to this and followed her, full and still swinging in. Lauren couldn't get inside the ball in time and plus, with fine leg deep, it was likely glancing straight to the fielder so she kept with her original instinct, putting all her weight onto the back foot and dug as hard as she possible could, scooping the ball out from under her eyes to the right of extra cover. She didn't really get it despite the wrists trying separately to force a four, so she set off in unison with extra cover and not at all in unison with Daughtry who had long since set off. They completed the first and turned for the second, the fielder's backside still working furiously to hunt down the slowing ball, then turned for the third, nodding in unison as their eyes met, the fielder leaning down. As the boundary was long Lauren was heading to the danger end and, despite setting off way after Daughtry, had caught up and some, so pinned her ears back as a decent throw headed towards the crouching bowler. No dive this time, just raw pace as she flew past the bowler who didn't waste time breaking the stumps, aware that the only opportunity was the other end, wheeling baseball style to go for a direct hit at the keeper's end. Daughtry, limbs, pads, fingers, helmet, hair, nostrils, sweat all heading in different directions - a scattergun of body parts and cricket appendages - had the foresight to legally change angle and run in the trajectory of where she thought the ball might be flung, even though her head faced completely the other direction. She felt the excruciating twinge of the ball strike her just below her calf then ricochet into a gap in the field, making her ground as the keeper threw his arms in the air, instructively turning towards Larry who instantly shook her head - Shackleton were not the type of team that could win this way; they wouldn't run to a deflection off the batter - that wouldn't be cricket. Once Belchingham acknowledged they weren't going to run - even though an easy run was on offer - the protestations died down for the final ball of the match, the scores tied on 243.

A murmur Mexican waved across the ground as no one was yet sure how the match would be decided if the scores remained tied; it was a knockout match so there had to be a winner and a loser. The umpires consulted as most of the Shackleton supporters chilled out believing it was wickets in the match so, with Belchingham all out, Shaky would progress having lost less wickets. Daughtry and Lauren looked anxiously towards their own dugout as Wei Ping, Yapa and Enid emerged with Google working overtime, their faces deformed with disquiet. The rules of the Digners Cup stated that should a knockout match end tied then the progressing team would be the team with the highest Net Run Rate 'including this match' so Wei Ping ran the figures again against the pool statistics and as much as he could swiftly glean from the scorers in this match. There wasn't much in it apparently and some busybodies and mathematicians around the field came up with a split of which team had a higher NRR. It seemed pretty darn simple to Lauren and particularly Daughtry who busied herself taking guard, not for the first time in her life, but undeniably the most important – she had to score at least a run off this ball. The field all came in, breathing down her neck, her bat a stick of fire against the imposing wolves, even if she was shaking so hard the handle felt like it would slip from her grasp at any second.

It had to be yorker time, thought Daughtry, a bullet fired down onto her pads, the big giraffe unable to get the bat down low and quick enough to bring willow onto leather. A wide ball yorker was out as all she had to do was reach out to make contact. Yorker or bluff and a perfect top of off delivery to bowl her, something easily within the reach of the talented Belchingham allrounder. The next ten seconds happened in complete super slow motion for Daughtry, the bowler's face not knees getting bigger, her crouching low and raising the bat towards the keeper, his two fingers on either side of the seam raising past his ear, the front arm coming up then a whoosh and a reddish blur coming towards her. She took aim as best she could and fended at the ball after it pitched, going past the bat and missing the bail by a papercut. Larry had long since packed her bags, reaching the opposite crease almost before the ball, as the keeper flung a glove to the ground and Daughtry mustered one more coordinated attempt to move those long limbs in unison to get her to the other side. She started slowly, as one might expect, but built up what would be remembered as her fastest ever head of steam, not changing any direction this time and diving full stretch from what looked like the middle of the pitch, her extended reach clocking up so much more ground than a few more steps. As she landed, a collapsing Jenga pile at the other end, Noel's unmistakable voice could be heard calling out ...

"That's all folks!"

Chapter » 51

Build-Up

Enid and Corin went to Yapa's office to talk tactics before the team dinner. They patiently waited outside until realising the door was unlocked as Yapa was stuck in traffic after a meeting. His office had reacquired the organised chaos the girls first remembered, yet as they were a part of the mess, they knew how to navigate between obstacles. Corin settled at Yapa's desk and put her feet up on an open drawer, clasping her hands behind her head to recline cautiously should the rickety chair snap backwards. Enid nosed around the latest whiteboard on Corkridge's scant cricketing weaknesses.

Corin leaned back, her feet slipping from the desk drawer, then in the scramble to rebalance she hooked the toe of her shoe under the drawer to yank it completely free, sending a confetti explosion of torn bits of paper all over the desk and the surrounding floor. Enid started gathering the notes, then stopped, staring at her fingers like the bloody hands of a first-time killer.

Establish bonded pairs – partnerships both on and off the field – working in tandem

Look for the core unique skills in selection – cricketers able to adapt – long limbs, reactions skills, ambidexterity, footwork

This team should be frustrated – do so by using their own egos against them

Bowl wide of the crease to this team

Aggressive field settings while padding the leg side boundary

Encourage each to have no fear and express their own cricketing character no matter what the situation

Practice session with high-jump mat to get the fast-twitch muscle fibres going and 100 consecutive tennis wall hits to build the next level of cricketers to support the girls and the left-arm leggie – without this there is no team, so invest time, effort and energy into these players

First home match v SanFran – rush them! Time

wasters of note so hurrying between balls and overs will unsettle

"What?" Corin asked, complete in the knowledge that something big was up, something substantial.

I love my girls – they're the best of friends but if the occasion presents itself (ie to up the run rate), bat Corin above Enid just once to shift the dial and get the best from each

To learn to face quick bowling – play a match or practice with a shortened distance between the stumps

Keeper leg stump guard – more room, swing through the line, golf swing

Belchingham bowler will play right into Peter's technique – look for county medium quick called Deranell

Clumps (of consistently good balls) > miracle balls against good teams

First match v Flounders to be frustrated with patience – let them implode and beat themselves by not blinking in stand-off, sticking to plan previously discussed

Enid dropped the remaining strips of paper, settling on her shoes, her legs wobbly.

"Dad … it's Dad … his handwriting."

The door's familiar creak, a whining engine cutting out, failed to break the scene, Corin rummaging on the floor to read the notes as Enid collapsed back, pinning a stray chair. Yapa entered looking flustered, then surveyed the unfolding scene in front of him, a tear cutting an unapologetic route down Corin's cheek.

"Duane Hanratty," began Yapa. "My friend, opponent and best ever player I play against," ushering Corin and Enid together to divulge everything.

"He wanted you both - his daughters - to rediscover your own love of the game without his interference but he couldn't stay away. He love you too much to not try help; not be part of your adventure."

"So, he's been with us this whole time—" said Enid.

"In the wings … watching from afar," completed Corin.

"He wants you two find your own destiny - not bound by his; not feel obligation to play for his belief in your cricket. Make your own … belief."

"You've been in cahoots—"

"All this time?"

"He know better than anyone that life never about certainties. All the best advice … planning … thinking in the world, doesn't change what happen on the pitch … in the field of battle. Like the catch he was certain he'd hold, he just wanted to help out in the background … move you - his children - closer to any possibility of certainty that cricket never gives; that life never gives."

> "Life is not always about certainties," Enid and Corin repeated in accord. "Despite your best … purest … most noble intentions."

Corin gathered up the scrap pieces of paper - mainly handwritten, torn at the edges, some post-its depicting field settings and cut-outs of printed emails with photos - crumpling them into a tight messy-haired ball before throwing overarm across the room towards the grubby square plastic bin in the corner of Yapa's office.

She missed.

»

At the other end of town, Chad sat mid-way, flawlessly dissecting his parents at either end of the distended chestnut-stained oak table, metres from both. He sniggered to himself, self-congratulating another hilarious gag, his only regret not being there to see the faces. Danny had eventually come through, rummaging through his sister's calendar to deliver comedy gold, Shaky's evening plans about to be curtailed ... mashed up and smelling like amoebic dysentery.

"Not sure why you're looking proud of your exploits, young man," censured his father without gazing upon his only child. "Seems you've landed yourself in a situation where you're either winning tomorrow or spectacularly losing in the most embarrassing of manners. Speaking of manners: chin up, back straight, elbows at your side."

"Father, I'm not eating here tonight remember? We have our team dinner with Chef Puant ... most grateful for arranging."

"Your father certainly pulled all the right strings for that little gathering," consorted his mother, her swollen top lip still recovering from the procedure. "Besides, even when not eating, you still embody the dinner decorum that defines you, no?"

"Of course, Mother."

"Chad," continued his mother, tilting her head to make her son out in the dim light, the contusions under her eyes hidden from prying eyes and likely preventing her making the journey to Lord's for her son's big day, lest she be seen by someone she knew. "Your father and I have not only made sacrifices for your schooling and appointment as Head Boy but all your cricketing exploits since you were four years old. So, this … this … this '*girls' team*' you're up against need to be silenced in a manner that doesn't reflect badly on your abilities, aspirations or future endeavours. Do you understand?"

"Of course, mother; and rest assured this is all handled – we are a better team, with better batsmen, bowlers and fielders, and invariably those teams win in cricket."

"Not always, Son" interjected his father. "Life can be a cruel lesson, so one has to take measures into one's own hands … even on the day."

"What does that mean, Father?"

"It means," his mother resumed. "Despite any best efforts in the lead up, you have not succeeded in preventing this abomination from making the final to play YOUR team and risk YOUR Digners legacy!"

Without knowing it, Chad's mother had cranked up her timbre, screaming, which alienated the new nose, new lips and crinkled the immaculately smooth sides of her face, rendering much of the surgeon's masterpiece momentarily derelict. "Look there, this whole cricket thing has set me off again," she faux sobbed, dabbing her cheekbones with a silk initialled napkin.

"It's alright, Dear," reassured Chad's father. "Our son will go to the ends of the earth to ensure when he walks back through that door, he will not only be carrying the Digners Cup but the heads of all opponents … the long-haired, eyelid-batting type most preferable!"

»

Everyone had chipped in as much as they could muster to hire the modest venue, a room off the side of an old church with rickety tables and mismatched chairs strews across the room. Half-drunk cold coffee remained in polystyrene cups, the church volunteers meaning to clear up before the next group, a 'generous' church donation the only prerequisite for the final supper on the eve of the big match. The Shackleton team arrived, some wearing their party finest, Jacob instantly sorting the chairs by shade of plastic colour.

"Micky D's in Tonbridge couldn't take a party of fourteen?" asked Noel, sniffing one of the stale coffees and reeling back, feigning a Matrix bullet lean in the process.

"They deliver," said Yapa, ushering everyone into the boxy room.

"Our dinner of champions!" said Larry, slapping her palms together and starting a fire.

"Confirmation of the vegan meal?" insisted Miss Hazard, the honorary guest.

"Yes Miss," said Rufus, appearing last from the back of the group.

As Jacob arranged the seating area and Daughtry cleared up the unexpended beverages, Enid and Corin remained silent, still reeling from the discovery. En route over to the church they'd talked between themselves and felt a sense of wellbeing that their dad had been involved and, of course, understood his motives but this was all tempered by the guilt of the ball offering, feeling even more pressure to win the match tomorrow. This was purely his only way to show he cared, they both agreed, and this assurance wore away the retrospective wistfulness as the team looked to their two leaders for inspiration.

While the team settled down in edacious anticipation of the gourmet 'underrated' McDonald's meal that was expectantly on the way via McDelivery, and Miss Hazard poured the lime cordial she'd brought along, a commotion ensued at the entrance and what popped his head around the door didn't look like a McDelivery driver.

»

The waiters appeared all at once – a restaurant's magician's trick – kitted in full black tie and each holding a bulbous cloche, poised, as the Corkridge 1st XI were forced to pay attention in case this meal was worthy of the reviews. As the nouveau portions were revealed, Danny wasn't the only diner who looked disappointed, James shaking his head in yearning for something more substantial, something meatier … a McDonalds perhaps? Once Chad had surveyed the array of drizzle encrusted dishes, he nodded in approval for placement then eviction so he could continue regaling the team with what was prospectively befalling over at the Shaky church dinner.

"Their sponsor, right," he continued, back on the podium as the team, like well-trained dogs, waited for permission to gorge the measly portion. "The one with the logo we had 'adapted' to look … well, let's just say more enjoyable that the slop they serve. The kebab place – local on the side you go to probably if you're looking for a disease or a cheap date – we've cancelled their McDonald's order and replaced with their sponsor's revolting nosh! If the E. coli doesn't kill them all the squits at 4am will mean they're not functioning at their best come time to fling ball down and we'll remove them from the planet. Oh my word, the indignity to have to dash off the pitch to 'go' at Lord's! By all means, do start …"

»

Confusion prevailed as the founder, owner and instore manager of Donna's Honours Kebab – beaming with thrilled rapture – wheeled in a stack of metal food trays and an assortment of serving utensils. The Shaky team glanced at one another, no one fessing up to changing the order, the alluring aromas distracting each tilted head in turn. Wei Ping checked the McDelivery order which now showed as cancelled.

"You very good cricket team and we honoured to provide food order this evening!" the man stated. "Tomorrow we invited to Lord's cricket ground and another big honour for our restaurant! Tonight we have usual kebabs and curry assorted dishes, Nepali and Bangladeshi regions. All fresh! All tasty!"

"Who order?" asked Yapa bluntly.

The man grabbed a piece of paper from his pocket and read "Best of luck tomorrow girls and enjoy the grub - assuming your stomach is made of sterner stuff if you're willing to face Corkridge at Lord's ... CdlA."

"Has anything happened to the food since you prepared the order?" asked Enid, circumspect until the bitter end.

"No. Order paid for on American Express and prepared fresh, straight from restaurant. Very best food just for you. No oil tonight as we know big game tomorrow - healthy, fresh spinach and free-range chicken always!"

Once the trays had been positioned and the servers poised, stationed at what looked like rice, side-dish, main and naan points, the trays came off, wafting an incontrovertibly deliciously spiced scent. Not one single person in the church offshoot didn't flinch, jostling for a warm plate to join the disorderly queue, even Miss Hazard, tempting a close angle into the chicken achari bubbling just below her tightly held plate.

»

"They're probably all getting sick right this minute," said Chad sucking down an Oyster with tabasco sauce. "Waiter!"

»

The meal felt more Henry VIII banquet than Christ's last supper, the church hall a convivial spectacle of a team that had knitted together, no longer inferior but about to play a cricket match at that sport's spiritual home. Once it was all complete, the owner, Mr Gurrehmat, keen to stress that much was still required to get his stall ready for Lord's, accepted the obsequious thanks followed by someone even raising a glass of lime cordial to Chad's misfired prank. Enid knew each player required whatever rest they could muster during what would be a traumatic lead-up night, her target of four hours shuteye not only downright optimistic but belying her assurances that she wouldn't spend the early hours of the morning obsessing over field settings, opposition player weaknesses and historic pitch behaviour. The evening had to end with a refocus on the matchups so that while each player stared at the ceiling, breaking down the sumptuous supper, their subconscious could break down their allocated paired opponent.

"I've got to get home to write tomorrow's pre-match speech," Enid said to quieten everyone down, an instant wave of laughter replacing the hum of conversation. "I know you've all spent the entire week obsessing over your 'PIN' or Paired Inadequate Nemesis, working with your teammates, your captains, Wei Ping and Mr Yapa to rain fire and brimstone to hit each one where it hurts most ... their weaknesses. So quick round the table to summarise for your teammates then we can all go clubbing!"

And so it began, no one looking around anxiously or with trepidation, each keen to initiate but knowing the working order, the efficacy of a congruous cricket team heading into the nine concentric circles of Dante's inferno, aware that each would increase in complex wickedness towards the centre of the earth where there could be only one waiting, this presence breaking the shackles of any restraint in bondage.

"I have two because I'm a bit more special than any of you," began Jacob. "The Neanderthal brothers although an insult to Neanderthals, finding a fight in any situation when the prey is weak, but confuse that killer blow paradigm and there might be a sniff of anything under 100 mph!"

"Not sure why I get the bloody keeper," tutted Rufus.

"Because you'll have to counter his inane chat!" guffawed Corin.

"Yes, indeed, so Stanley 'Stanni' Forthenstan, the standing crouching tiger, hidden fieldmouse. He's a busy boy ... like a dog doing his business but has a tendency to turn everything into a short ball; as he's likely to tell you, his prowess with the girls ... pulls at will!"

"Heeeeyyyyyy!" rang out across the room, each mini speech garnering crowd approval in the chanting custom, the only fitting brouhaha.

"What more can be said, bestowed, eulogised or sung from the mountaintops about our very own Corkridge Castle School for Boys (and girls) captain, Chad!" said Enid, rising slowly as she lifted the tempo even further, using the lime dregs in her stained church coffee cup emblazoned with 'Jesus Loves Sinners' to toast, generating the biggest screech-yelp-holler-wallop-table banging of the evening thus far. "He is too darn perfect, the prefect with the golden hair, batting, bowling, fielding, captaining ... turning water to wine and curing lepers! So how exactly does a team of no-hopers dethrone the greatest schoolboy cricketer of a generation? Wing it on the day? That's when we're at our best, right? How do we tilt that halo at just enough of a wonky angle to upset this captain of cricketing industry? He wouldn't have come up against a team like us in his illustrious life, so perhaps therein lies the answer. Kill him with ludicrous craziness! Every time we skinned the Chad cat we came up with another theory; every time the hypothesis made sense, it instantly didn't. There is no magic bullet for our boy Chad as he literally has not a single identifiable technical flaw, but somewhere in the top two inches lies an ego so nurtured, so developed, so matchless that, all that sticks, is play our game … exactly as we would to any normal Joe. No special considerations, for then, for once, Chad might feel a little less special."

"Big bad Brad!" Onka verified, nodding to an imaginary bopping beat. "Or Yannos Dalrymple: Chad's very own forgotten shadow, not daring to venture into the light where he might actually do something! This is different though; this is a final and even Chad wouldn't begrudge a match-winning innings from the underrated, a bit too much 'class over arse' number 4 bat. Beware the bridesmaids! Especially at Lord's, so test the attacking intent and showman desperate to come out and play."

"My turn: the middle order propping up you fancy top order 'feast or famine' glory hounds so the fans get what they paid for!" said Corin fully adopting the theatrical grandstanding that had established itself for the evening's conclusion, Shakespearian at best, mis-rhyming Eminem at worst. "My PIN or 'bunny' as I'd prefer to foil is none other than the bouncer, the brute, the power hitter in the body of a power hitter … Jimmy Smith-Franklin. There is nothing overly complicated about this fellow and feller of trees – he hits and the balls stay hit, so a long sailing time, Chad's right-hand, go-to guy when the water gets choppy and up until Shackleton High, they've been tropical island glass calm! With a big bat comes big opportunities so expect to be on your toes in the field as we move the chess pieces sometimes even between balls, as variation often goes the distance anyway, a swing and a nick or mistime bigger than most mortal sixes. It might be an endurance test – take the slugfest until your jaw dislocates, then pick it up off the floor and pass the hare at the finish line. Oh and he's slow between the wickets – not used to running singles as the ball is mostly in a galaxy far, far away."

"No Star Wars references please!" shouted Wei Ping. "There are no technology nerds here!"

"He's Ivan Drago without the doorstop sandwich slice haircut," Corin concluded. "And Rocky does the business in the fifteenth!"

"Could be fate or just my luck," Larry casually revelled. "My PIN is none other than Charlie 'Chuck' Hastings, a cricketer who has rediscovered his mojo of late, his bent arm nowhere to be seen unless of course ... well, he's bowling to me. I'm the weakness which makes him the weakness!"

"I get Larry's brother-in-law, containing finger-spinner yet to give the ball a proper tweak," Peter said, clearing his throat after the brother-in-law gag to allow the baying masses their barks of approval. "We thinks he's better with bat and ball than he's given credit for or has shown all season, so we tread with caution to prevent a marquee display in the final on the biggest stage of all. We're more watchful with his bowling, working rather than chasing and, with bat in hand, we test that weak bottom hand or bog him down to force a false stroke. When Danny holds up an end, the Corkridge faithful get that nagging feeling that if he's not doing the business, someone else could be out there in his place."

"My lucky bunny," sniffed Noel with aplomb. "Is Harrison Plodkin, a stickler for rules, order and feet cemented into the crease. As my esteemed colleague HB will attest to in a moment straight after this commercial break, Harry struggles to plod without his mild eew George – see what I did there – so early wickets puts the opening pair as Tango without Cash or more aptly, SpongeBob sans his best friend Patrick."

"His fellow opener," continued Daughtry, concerned that Noel's wordplay might be lost on everyone. "George Mildew. A decent player who doesn't often attack the short stuff, unless given the right incentive."

"It that all you've got?" Noel enquired and Daughtry nodded. "In that case I just hope you get a duff LB decision first up HB!"

As the base layer of sickly, undiluted lime cordial went down the hatch, everyone mucked in to help clean up, the church hall now closer to show home than the dystopian looted site upon arrival. Everyone said their goodbyes, a serenity replacing the antecedent speeches, the farewells less perpetual and more stopgap, a halcyon of tight camaraderie stretching as each Shackleton ambassador went to find a comfy pillow or room dark enough to shut out the imaginary ball by ball endeavours that lay in wait. Enid ushered Corin second last out of the room and the two stared back at the orderly pristineness of the room, the tables in symmetry with the walls and chairs tucked in, facing one another, motionless in servitude. They'd done this, created this order, this harmony for a few blinks but would it be good enough to surmount the insurmountable, ascend where no woman had dared to tread, sport's hallowed turf, all green and watered and pristine, the lords of Lord's gnashing their teeth at the intruders. Enid closed the door behind her, pulling it tightly shut, the click of the dilapidated lock securing the four walls until the next bible study or support group.

"Gentlemen, gentlemen," said Chad tapping the side of his glass to establish order. "The modus operandi is simple … if there's a girl in front of you, bludgeon her out of the way and, by girl, I mean anyone in the S.H.I.Team."

Chapter » 52

Dolly

Butterflies become winged beasts, flapping their sinewed, clawed wings so forcibly, the heart palpations are drowned out, the rabbling swarm beneath the chest cavity not only taking the wheel but double footing the passenger out onto the road, not upon the underwhelming North London arrival nor the turnstiles at the gates; not even passing the big quoted picture or the vacant nets with a clonus when spotting the outer shell of the stadium. The actual moment when the butterflies turn on each other, jostling and gnawing and belting in haste to get out of the stomach's cavity is when a cricketer walks onto the field at Lord's. Perhaps it's the greenness of the grass or the billiard flat precision of the blades' height, but more likely the grandiose flanking stands, dissected by the august, symmetrical, orange-bricked pavilion, Thomas Verity's gift from the Victorian era to all those fortunate enough to stride out onto the hallowed turf. As the Shackleton XI Cricket Team were consummating the moment the butterflies attacked. As each cricketer got further away from the boundary and closer to the pitch, it was as if the magnitude of the venue and the occasion exponentialised, each step scooping another dozen or so voracious butterflies until it was all just too much for Jacob and Onka in particular, the former dry-heaving and the latter merely letting the tear slide down his cheek. Corin looked wide eyed and pale, and Noel couldn't even muster a smart-alecky wise crack to ease the situation. Enid tried to absorb everything, the history, the majesty, the task at hand until she too got floored into quiet submission, the ground holding sway over every member of the side.

Corkridge arrived later than Shackleton, the plush bus getting stuck in the notorious St John's Wood traffic, unable to better Shaky's Jubilee Line with a gazillion changes in the lead-up, a hopeful omen to come. Without a hint of the occasion or the venue lowering the fever pitched bravado, the Corky Boys strode and strutted out – to the manor born, almost oblivious to the opposition's presence out in the middle. Chad took a minor peek at Enid as the teams passed each other, Enid affording a glancing reciprocal peek back: more boo than peek!

"They look bigger in real life," said Jacob, pushing his glasses higher with both thumbs to focus on the swollen heads of medium-brown haired creatures: a game drive.

"They're not," said Noel. "Bad day for your specs to malfunction, that's all. There's an optometrist around the corner if you need an emergency change in prescription."

"His eyesight is just fine," said Daughtry, holding fingers up in the clouds while Jacob tried to focus, repeatedly cleaning his glasses until he could make out it was merely her index finger, pointing in the 45-degree 'Out' pose.

Noel applauded with a golf clap.

The ground began filling up, cricket watchers trickling in at first then a steady stream powerful enough to cause a backlog as the security teams went through bags, purses, rucksacks and picnic hampers. The Digners Foundation had long been supporters of cricket countrywide and, with the opportunity to front its wares at the home of cricket simply too big to leave alone like a delivery wide of the stumps, through a funky campaign, had lured young cricketing fans with free entry for registered cricketers, reduced admission costs for schools north of the river and a host of competitions putting groups up at hotels with a day at Lord's the marquee event. Interest had also swelled through social media, the battle of not only the contrasting cricketing styles but also the antipodal path to the final, socioeconomic standing of the school and characters involved garnering an itchy attention that could easily be scratched at these Lord's prices, fully departed from a typical international Test match. Both teams though, remained largely unaware of the ground filling up, huddled unnecessarily in the immaculate dressing rooms, one team using every ploy available to either not let the occasion get the better of them or marvel exclusively at how this was the lushest ablution facility they'd ever rested any of their clenched little heinies on ever before.

The second good omen on the day of the final had taken place before each Shackleton player found a home on the black leather seats in the England dressing room. Corkridge had selected England's dressing room – a right they felt deserved as defending champions – but were sent to the opposition's quarters by a studious-looking operations assistant who insisted that the dressing rooms were identical so as to never be accused of home ground favouritism. Chad was bristling and left an unsightly dent in the travelling team's locker, his name also spelt incorrectly on the embossed nameplate.

In the dressing rooms, the new bespoke kit, designed exclusively for the final, hung on the coat hooks in orderly unison. Asics had gone for contrast with Corkridge insisting on their customary midnight 'All Black' black with dark blue trimmings and thus lightened Shackleton's purple, sage and maroon palette, reallocating the colours to make the trousers sage and the tops a mosaic of burgundy-hewed maroon and a lighter grape plum. As the Shaky cricketers stared up at their designated kit, hanging motionless above the black leather seats, no one had noticed the balcony, nor the makeshift barrier which would allow the different genders to change in privacy. Out in the corridor, Yapa's voice became raised which jolted everyone from the kit-induced stupor. He was arguing with Daniels, the Lord's operations person mediating and heading towards adjudication. Enid shielded everyone back from the dressing room's entrance as the voices went up steadily, the aggravation from Yapa's throat never encountered by any of the team before this day. Enid closed the door and the team proceeded to get changed.

Emerging one by one, some with a twirl or seven (Jacob), the battle armour slid into comfy and lambent, the Shackleton team avoided getting into a huddle in fear of creasing the new kit. Yapa knocked then walked in and closed the door behind him, his cheeks an uncharacteristic grape-purple meets burgundy-maroon.

"We have problem," he began, his tone ever the same.

"Your exchange … outside?" Corin asked, pleading for it to be something else.

"Yes. Cork head Daniels," without even a guffawed "Cork Head Daniels!" from Noel. "Raised breach of rules by Shackleton … by us, to Lord's director and rule adjudicator which either mean disqualification or player forfeit. She had no choice."

"What does that mean?" asked Onka while Daughtry looked longingly at the uniform she almost got to wear, the end of the bottoms dangling as close as could be hoped to her laces, a three-inch gap … progress … real progress.

"Peter can't play," said Yapa sternly. "He too young when registration."

"I'm old enough now," said Peter through the tears, his

bottom lip taking most of the flack as Corin took his one hand and Larry the other.

"You've done wonders for this team," said Enid trying not to get on the driverless emotive train, bolting through stations despite the red-light warnings. "Your contributions got us here!"

"They must rate you, Mate," continued Noel. "They fear the Trumpeter!"

"Cork head Daniels want us disqualified but Lord's say we have to play as the crowds want see spectacle. We play with one less player."

"So, the rule states that anyone registered at the start of Digners can play?" mulled Enid. "Peter, what size are you?"

The heads all followed Enid's, slowly rotating to face a preoccupied Wei Ping, his head still buried in his laptop, plotting how to play a match with only ten people until he realised the attention being coxswained his way would negate that completely. This was his moment but there was nothing in his notes to account for this scenario!

"Here we are Clodagh – the time has arrived! We're into the build-up of the Digners Cup final – for the first time ever at Lord's and for the first time ever on your television screens; every ball, shot, catch, howzat, dive, boundary and wicket televised live as it happens here on Sky Sports Cricket!"

"Well hello to you too Ramsay and, yes, as it happens tends to mean it's live, so you and us will not miss a heartbeat. It's the battle of the opposites; the clash of styles, of philosophies, of methodologies; girls v boys—"

"Who rules and who drools, Clodagh?"

"That should be blatantly obvious Ramsay."

"Do you know Clodagh, that the famous Lord's pavilion used to be a garden shed!?"

"Well, Ramsay, there's a little more to it – Thomas Verity

designed the iconic pavilion directly opposite us in the Media Centre over here and it was the third structure to stand in that position yet remains the oldest building at Lord's."

"Not like these plush modern surroundings we find ourselves in now – bet the coffee's not as good over that end of the ground!"

"The first pavilion burned down in 1825 and its successor, much tinkered with and extended over the years, was pulled down in 1889 and meticulously reassembled on a Sussex estate – here is specifically where the garden shed association originates."

"Bigger than mine!"

"Undoubtedly"

The time to run, hide, scream or flee was waning as the toss loomed, no warm-up permitted to maintain the outfield for an upcoming Test against South Africa. Corkridge had, of course, had a pre-travel light net session but were put out they couldn't get the obligatory rubber wickets and cones out to put a dose of fear into the opposition; plus it broke their usual routine which Chad hated. The Shackleton dressing room descended into huggermugger hysteria post Peter's expulsion then once the balcony doors were opened, taciturnity struck as they ventured towards the balcony. They approached as a solid line – an approaching regiment wider than the balcony doors – getting stuck at the entrance, which popped Jacob, Larry and Onka out onto the balcony's ledge like a Pez dispenser. A huge roar went up across the ground as the others filed out from behind to greet the balmy air, the roar intensifying as the groundswell became a swollen ground with little or no white, empty seats. They all looked at each other in complete disbelief, until Jacob and Larry simultaneous waved at the Donna's Honours Kebab manager doing star jumps in front of his makeshift food stall far in the distance. The cheers turned to mock jeers when the panto villain Corkridge boys also accessed their balcony.

"These people have come to see us play cricket," said Corin, not quite able to comprehend her own statement, her hand frozen static over her mouth.

"And it seems we've won the crowd over without bowling or hitting a ball in anger!" responded Enid. "Nothing like a purist, fickle crowd turning on you though, particularly if the cricket's not up to scratch!"

"Best we get out and play then, Sister," said Corin, removing her hand and smiling at the crowds, forcibly snapping herself from the spectacle that awaited.

The Shackleton XI made their way out of the dressing room and down the wide flight of stairs, greeted by an eclectic array of abilities splattered onto canvas in the form of famous cricketer portraits. Some were instantly recognised, others either too far in the past or not in the tabloids enough for select members of the Shaky line-up. The team went down three flights of stairs past a bemused gaggle of members, donning the unmistakably garish egg and tomato ties, some even going full-on dual-tone test pattern with the blazer, mostly pressed out a fair distance and straining the buttons, liable to bust at one too many quail eggs or rambunctious puns. When they reached the toilet, it was apparent they'd missed the designated turn-off on the second floor and skipped back up one flight to applause from the members. Making their way across the 93-foot polished wooden floor, a genuine sense of occasion smacked in a different way, surrounded by some of the greats of the game and some of the not so greats off the field.

"Nice if you sent a few down like that lovely Australian galah," Noel said to Enid, pointing to the Shane Warne portrait. "Even I know who he is!"

"I'll start by just batting better than he did," responded Enid.

"Seems fair; who is that?" asked Noel motioning his chin

towards a large oval head.

"That's Viv Richards," said Daughtry. "Even I know who that is, for all the wrong reasons ... didn't exactly cover himself in glory as a gentleman with the young ladies if rumours are to be believed; especially during his time at Somerset."

"Check out the big tall brain on HB! You're probably eye level with him up there," said Noel showing no signs of his heightist catalogue of bad gags waning. "Might be why he looks like he's smirking – got away with it!"

"Was Gooch's drawn by a five-year-old with Crayola?" Corin chimed in to Onka, lamenting the dearth of South Africa cricketers, none of his favourites cracking the nod. "They've made him squint."

"We're almost through the most famous walk in cricket," said Enid opening the door.

"Thank God for that," said Larry. "Couldn't breathe in there for all the aged testosterone and morning brandy stench!"

"Now for the actual main attraction," said Enid ushering all her team through onto the stairs, angled downwards towards the pitch. "Time for the big show."

As they stepped onto the field, the crowd provided a politely rousing, welcoming ovation as the loudspeaker introduced the team. Corkridge were already out in the middle, breaking the rules to a degree by chucking a cricket ball about, side-stepping, scarpering around scuffing a section of the outfield, until they suddenly formed an orderly line, facing the crowd.

"Would everyone please stand for the anthems of both competing schools," declared the voice from the loudspeaker.

"Shaky has an anthem?" catechised Noel, turning the least whitest shade of pale as Shackleton reluctantly lined up, an orchestral, trumpet-heavy prefatory salvo gambolling forth.

There was a collective, unified intake of breath, the Corkridge boys' diaphragms lifting as they pushed their shoulders forward, hitting the first noble line with ease. Shackleton were forced to stare straight ahead, Jacob involuntarily lifting alternating heels as the hymn's octaves oscillated. Elements of the crowd began to sing along too, which seemed odd until Larry happened to glance around and notice the words on the big screen. She nudged Noel and the nudging went all down the line until the team were aware their anthem might not be the most awkward public silence in history, but the angle of the big screen was slightly behind them, which meant somehow they'd have to break the military, stern face forward procedure exemplified by Corkridge to their left.

"This is the West Indies cracking out their first anthem all over again," whispered Noel. "There's just no place for anthems in cricket!"

The Corkridge anthem ended on a rousing crescendo, every boy in the team able to go from tenor into falsetto, the piercing peak shaming Rufus who could never get that high.

"Consider me from Ulster and this is the rugby section we just don't sing," he said, looking down the line.

The start of the lesser-spotted Shackleton anthem was almost as surprising as the completion of the Corkridge chorale, an extended drum intro Royal Blood would have been proud of. Most had a peak at some point during the frenetic drumming, to at least glean the first line then get away with a combination of mouthing, looking down and sneaking a line or two here and there. The first line was a double-edged sword: easy to remember but the hidden archive abyss where this ditty had been exorcised from wasn't exactly Andrew Lloyd Webber.

"*Sha-kle-ton, Sha-kle-ton, Sha-kle-ton, Sha-kle-ton, your children greet you well … like an eagle o'er the mountain, rising up for you, our school.*

If it's sport or the classroom, we'll always play the game …"

This was all too much for Corkridge who just couldn't hold it in any longer, the less assimilated Neethaniel brothers almost hunching in convulsed hilarity.

"*Win or loo-ooo-se, we can take it, rising up for you, our school.*"

"Can you though?" Chad was heard uttering as even Noel went beyond chuckling into mortified wanting this to end before he did!

The next seven verses got progressively worse invoking specifics like when Shackleton raised funds to fix the water fountain and the visits one student made to a care home. The lack of the school's pervading history presented scant material, yet this hadn't deterred the hymn writer in the slightest, the suspicion growing that Miss Hazard was the culprit unearther when spotted singing with hand on heart in the crowd. Verses nine through fourteen proved as much when values such as kindness, integrity, courage and humility intertwined in a funky pop meets operatic fusion, Mizzard's paw prints all over this section. The Lord's crowd played ball beautifully and by the final line, most had joined in to drown out the early jeers.

Despite the positive conclusion, Shaky were blue-faced relieved to have the anthems done and dusted, creaked necks now a real factor of the day from craning to digest the increasingly syllabic verses. The crowd hushed as anticipation of the coin toss beset all but one section who continued singing the Shackleton anthem.

The two captains walked out towards the strip following the match adjudicator, the coin crumpled in his palm upsetting his stride, the other arm a useless tentacle. The pitch selected was alongside the worn main pitch, so greener than a chameleon piggybacking on a red-crowned amazon parrot, the grass fatally lush and smooth to the touch. The pitches in the lead up had been nuanced, some lending more towards one of the cricketing disciplines yet ironically this one, at the home of cricket, was partisan, leaving neither captain, coach nor team members with any doubt … this was a bowl first pitch.

The match adjudicator - a serious looking man with a horizontally compressed moustache and an ill-fitting straw boater - opened his palm to reveal the oversized silver coin, a commemorative 100 Years of Lord's piece of cricket memorabilia. The coin caught a clump of the sun's rays, illuminating Chad's greedy eyes while Enid's sensitive speckled pupils forced her to shield away, raising a forearm to thwart the glare.

"The team with the highest points tally accumulated during the qualifying pool stages gets to call, so Corkridge, your call, heads or ta—"

"You know what, Sir," began Chad, walking in a little circle to lap up the atmosphere, circa sixty thousand eyeballs fixated on him minus those partaking in an early tipple or kebab for brunch. "Corkridge Castle School for Boys (and girls) is all about collegiate equality for all genders, sizes, orientations and proclivities. I would be honoured if Ms Hanratty called the coin toss. She deserves it."

"My, my, young man, that is a magnanimous gesture. Ms, heads or ta—"

"I couldn't sir," said Enid. "Shackleton follows the rules and procedures of the game and the Digners Cup so I would not want to take anything away from my esteemed opponent and deny him his … birth right."

"I insist … Enid."

"It stipulates … Chad."

"This is my chivalry … on display. I'm opening the door for you madam. Please … I insist!"

"You can insist and persist all day; I'm not calling. I'm fine to open doors all by myself this year too; and if they don't open, they can always be kicked in."

"All you need to say is one … word."

"No."

The match adjudicator looked nervously about, the cameras trained on the three out in the middle. He'd edged away from the two and the avowals persisted until it was clear neither captain would relent and the only way to get this match under way was to decree. His moustache concertinaed in as his lips pursed to interrupt, unable to find a gap as the volleys became smashes.

"Team captains," he eventually interposed. "We are due to bowl the first ball, so this coin toss needs to take place. If there is no agreement, we will revert to the rules and rule the Corkridge captain to call. Now ... heads or tails?"

"Flip it, I'll do it," said Chad his faux charm having alarmingly flown out of the stadium and somewhere towards Muswell Hill. "If she doesn't want a leg up, then that's fine. This will be the only part of today you win."

"Uh, calling a coin toss has no advantage: it's random."

A throat was cleared beneath the moustache, the coin going up higher than anyone at Lord's had ever seen, even the upper stand punters catching a glinting glimpse of the rotating scintillation.

"Never had to chase tail as it always chased me," muttered Chad. "So ... heads!"

The coin landed on the pitch and nestled below where anyone could see the result. The adjudicator leaned down aiming his moustache at where he believed the coin sojourned.

"That's heads," said Chad guessing.

"It appears that way," said the man, still squinting into the pitch.

The coin appeared to be lodged at an angle, neither facing up nor down, with neither heads nor tails clearly pointing towards the sky. The official was loath to touch the coin should his action disturb the outcome, as he slapped the top of his pockets for an imaginary pen.

"We can't see where it has landed," said Enid. "It's almost vertical so we should flip again."

At that moment Chad bent down onto his haunches and flicked at the grass shrouding the top of the perpendicular coin, nudging the coin flatter, toppling over to reveal the Queen's head."

"Are you kidding me?" said Enid, with protesting pleading eyes as the match official acquired his first full view of the coin.

"Heads it is," he said.

"We'll bowl," said Chad.

"Just in, Clodagh, Corkridge will bowl first."

"Seemed a no brainer looking at that track; the ball will be dancing!"

"Ha yes - like Strictly! Do you watch?"

"No."

"Oh. Okay."

"There was clearly some consternation out there at the toss as it took longer than usual and the match adjudicator did not seem best pleased when they left the field."

"Neither did Shackleton's captain; some glum faces teeming out there but not from Corkridge. You know someone once described that Chad de la Hoya as the perfect cricketing product, as though if Don Brandman and Ricky Ponting were able to have a baby together, Chav de lam Baste would be that little tyke. He has no weaknesses."

"Other than he's from Australia."

"Ha yes - another belter from our very own Clodagh in the media centre here at Lord's. This will be the first schoolboy match televised on prime Sky viewing ... ever!"

"Let's just call it 'the first cricket match' shall we? And, another first, the use of televised DRS for both teams, just as would be the case in an international or county match."

"Two each - and the review is lost if unsuccessful."

"Correct, Ramsay. Umpire's call and the review is retained. These captains will not be used to referrals of any type as this has never been used at this level of cricket before."

"We are moments away from the start of play. The two umpires are coming out now. I'm giddy with excitement!"

"For once Ramsay, you and I are in complete concord!"

As the umpires fiddled with the stumps, supposedly checking they weren't about to shoot out of the ground and fly away, the Corkridge XI emerged onto the field at Lord's, led by their mesmerising captain, to a courteous round of applause. Chad took a moment to drink it all in – he was at Lord's after all, leading out his team in his Cup, representing his school. This was his ground now as he scanned the members stand for his parents. He clapped back at the crowd above his head as he ran ahead of the team to establish some distance, his arms now waving in the air like Justin Trudeau. When he reached the middle, now way ahead of his lagging team, he recognised both the umpires who affirmed a plausive nod in his direction. These were his father's cohorts, round the house on a few occasions, slouching deep into the leather armchairs in his dad's study, slurping the finest English whiskies from the Cotswold Distilleries and stinking out the house with cigars fatter than their fingers. This didn't sit right with Chad, a line crossed, and his shoulders sloped wiping his smile dead.

Chad set the most attacking field he'd ever assembled, the slip cordon rammed like a bus stop queue as Jacob and Rufus came out to bat. The umpire at the bowler's end underarmed the new cherry to Chad past Rufus's nose as the right-handed Neethaniel brother measured his elongated run-up. Rufus at the non-striker's and Chad at mid-off were in close proximity and Rufus noticed Chad admiring the Kookaburra ball.

"Meant to be a Dukes," Rufus said to Chad, the corners of his mouth down in either resignation or admiration, but not both.

"Late change. Defending champions pick the ball," said Chad, shining it before lobbing it across to the opening Neethaniel, little pointed mounds festooning his swollen traps, pressing out underneath his shirt.

"Less swing. More bounce. Harder ball. Pronounced seam. Lasts longer to delay spinners gripping," said Rufus shaking his head and tapping his bat on the ground.

"You can take the boy out of the team, but not the team out of the boy," said Chad. "Once a Corkridge champion, always a Co—"

"Let play commence," stated the umpire signalling towards the scorers.

Jacob facing, his feet welcomingly itchy and his hands shaking like leaves in a blizzard. Neethaniel bowling right-arm over, bull snorting and falling just short of ripping his hooves back in the turf. The final of the Digners Cup was about to witness its first ball as the bowler set off, the crowd instantly hushing even further below church mouse gossip level. Neethaniel strode, his bulbous quads hitting each other as his legs pumped, two slabs of meat slap-slap-slap-thumping past the edge of the pitch and into his delivery stride, a great long-jump leap forwards rather than up, landing with a thunderous jolt and delivering the first ball with his feet placed close together. Due to his muscle density and squat frame, the expectation was that the ball would skid through fast and heavy, his height masked, yet this ball rose up from the green surface and skimmed the side of Jacob's helmet as Stanni took a stupendous one-handed catch above his head.

Jacob had not moved, not even a step or twitch, his backlift still parallel to the turf as Rufus's eyes swelled. The ball had accelerated so fast and with suck quick steep bounce it could have hit anywhere and Jacob would not have had the time to react. The crowd skreiched, the thud of ball into keeper's glove dense and unyielding as Stanni shook off a tingling palm. Neethaniel enjoyed his first ball at Lord's following through to the point where his shadow loomed over Jacob, their noses a vertical foot apart. He snorted at Jacob who smiled benevolently back, unsettling Neethaniel who could only snort even louder, turning and lumbering back to his bowling mark. Jacob looked at Rufus pleadingly who shrugged. Just as was the nature of cricket – for the split second when the next ball arrived … he was on his own.

The next ball was slammed down even faster but a morsel shorter and, due to the unforgivingly lively nature of the pitch, went flying over Jacob's head, clearing the keeper for a one bounce four, Stanni not even bothering with a showman leap in the air. The ball hit the sightscreen and came vaulting back, rolling back past Jacob at about the same time he first reacted to the delivery. To compensate he played a few air drives, coming up the pitch to imaginary deliveries as Rufus forged mock approval then instantly shook his head, confusing the daylights out of Jacob. Rufus then ducked and swayed and seemed to mouth "Survive."

The third ball of the day was a quick inswinging yorker that exploded on Jacob's toe as he tried to pull his feet down leg and out of the way, falling over and clutching his boot as though he'd stood on a landmine. Neethaniel went straight up, appealing, his fists facing the heavens with bent arms so that his biceps strained against his shirt sleeve, goitres in the wrong spots. The umpire instantly gave Jacob out despite daylight between his toe and leg stump as the 15 second countdown began on the screen and Jacob looked imploringly up from the verdure at Rufus, who could feel an equal set of eyes on him from his old captain at mid-off. Rufus took about 10.5 seconds then gave Jacob the go-ahead as Jacob looked in too much pain to make it towards the middle for a debate, the umpire contemptuously tracing the old-fashioned TV box shape with 2 seconds left on the clock.

The footage popped up on the big stadium screen, first confirming Neethaniel hadn't bowled a no-ball, his size 17 shoe making everyone in the stadium glad not to be the crease line; then a redundant check on Ultra-Edge to see if Jacob's bat had made any contact before the ball hit the foot, the designated LBW standing as the official mode of dismissal. With Jacob's bat frozen stiff solid and a distance from where the ball struck his toe, there was no edge, deflection or miracle of physics at work that Lord's final day. Then for the real determinant ... the ball tracker. As it was a yorker there was no pitching outside off, so the next factor became where the ball struck and was Jacob in line with the stumps. It had happened so fleetingly and the ball so fast that DRS showed a red dot confirming the ball had struck Jacob's toe in line with the stumps, the only remaining metric with the ability to save Jacob, the trajectory of whether the ball would have hit the stumps, with umpire's call making even a feather of a nick on the stumps out. The graphic muddled the order showing the ball precariously neighbouring the stumps then an aerial view over the stumps before the green dot shone next to the imposing red and a gap the upright toss coin might not have fitted through confirmed the Not Out. The umpire confirmed a reversal of his decision through cricket's version of that nineties dance move when hands would alternate between wobbly knees, as Jacob hobbled to his feet to fist bump anyone and the 'Shaky section' of the crowd in the cheap seats provided the obligatory ironic benign boos to express discontent at the poor officiating.

Half the over dispelled with more incident than most full matches and Jacob hobbled back to face, a steely resolve holding back any tears, his smile replaced with a taut jawline. His feet were where his whole game as an opening bat resided, so this was that time when the pain had to become a passenger while the twinkle toes did their job, ensuring his body was in the optimal position for the bowling onslaught he'd never experienced or, for that matter, thought he would experience. The fourth ball came fizzing towards Jacob, a good ball that leapt off a better length, beating Jacob all ends up but with one resoundingly good result: he'd moved his feet, coming forward but beaten for pace by a good length. The last two balls were back to type but Jacob survived, the first dug in at the throat with Jacob jumping, arched back, to avoid and the second a straighter ball which Jacob was able to duck after splitting his feet to balance. The end of the first over was over, just four byes but at least Shaky were on the board without a change to the wickets column. The two batsmen convened in the middle, Jacob's hobble without any hint of pantomime this time, the flinch-step-lift-fling routine one he'd never had the need to practice.

"You going to be able to get through when I call you through for a quick single?" asked Rufus.

"If you call, I'm there," said Jacob, raising his eyes up towards the lids as the craning of his neck too far up sometime caused his oversized helmet to fall off his head.

"I've got the other brother – left-arm over. Chad's saving Chuck for later – that'll wind him up a treat."

"Our presence alone is enough of a wind up for these brutes. These bowlers would break my dance instructor's resolve with their heavy feet."

"You've got yours moving which is good; and you've survived. I'm going to call you through for some cheap runs when it goes to the keeper – look how far back he's standing."

"I'm in – all in."

The Neethaniel brother didn't need a warm-up as he was already piping. He was the younger brother but a bigger, badder, more bizarre, more bulbous, bad-tempered version of his opening partner brother. His left arm looked double the size of his right arm and there was no discernible neck, the full-size men's Kookaburra ball looking like a ladybird in his palm, liable to be squelched into a paste of entrails at any second. His stats from the Digners tournament appeared on screen with a bowling average of 11.62 and a strike rate of 24.6 and, when his picture appeared, he became strangely transfixed - a monkey staring at its own reflection for the first time - broken by the funky splat freeze-frame graphics of his season's wickets. Rufus and Jacob didn't fail to notice the clip of a batsman being stretchered off after being hit in the head. He swivelled back to face Rufus, appearing a way left of the umpire, channelling full-on Disney villain by getting out the most muscular pose from the bodybuilder's handbook and letting out a wild yawp before steaming in to bowl.

Rufus sat a bit deeper in the crease, opened his stance for the lefty and readied himself as Neethaniel's left arm came roundhouse kicking from behind the umpire's back, almost decapitating him in the process and shunting down a heavy ball that got big on Rufus but he was able to pick the line and jump high off his back leg to get bat on ball - well at least handle on ball - the bat's handle quivering from impact right in front of Rufus's nose. The slip cordon was interested for a second as the ball squirted in their direction, but with the impact being handle not bat, the ball failed to carry, taken one hand one bounce by Yannos at fourth slip. Lacking any true originality, Neethaniel number two (frankly not dissimilar to a number two, all brown, furrowed, globular and charred) also followed through to get into Rufus's face, who stared directly back and didn't smile.

"Gonna snap that handle next ball," sledged Neethaniel. "Ball's going to get through the grill if you're not careful. Traitor."

"Only thing you're snapping," pondered Rufus, followed by a lengthy delay. "Is if your card appears and it's the same as mine."

"Don't get it."

"Didn't think so," said Rufus shooing the bowler back and regretting being too elaborate with his kiddie card game sledge.

Neethaniel had to outdo his brother's snort of intimidatory defiance so concluded with a grunting self-inflicted chest pounding brouhaha, determined that he should have the final 'gesture' before returning to his mark.

Rufus was barely ready when the umpire's arm was lowered and Neethaniel southpaw charged in once more, this time with more venom, more intent and more ill-feeling, his ears pink from toil. Once more he surprised the bat by slinging his arm out from behind the umpire, the ball digging in and moving away across the right-hander's body. Rufus felt he had the measure of this length and went back with his right foot, an attempted pull. With the green track and the bowler's fiery pace the ball took the top edge and went for six over the keeper's head, a crowd catch fumble caught in exhaustive detail on the big screen. Chad glared at Rufus who merely looked straight ahead as the third ball beckoned. This ball came in wider of the crease than the previous two, into Rufus's ribcage but he was able to get right up on his toes and inside the line, glancing the ball almost under him armpit, a clipped four with fine leg having zero chance to cut-off. Ten off two balls and this over was looking half-decent for Shackleton and their mismatched opening pair. No rotation of strike as yet which, to a degree, negated the ill-effects of facing a left right quick combo and with both batsmen right-handed, the field could entrench more solidly, even though Chad was considering fortifying the back boundary without the ignominy of putting in a long stop, something Corkridge would never normally contemplate and doubly so at this level. The fourth ball was fuller which meant no time to swing back in at the right-hander, Rufus going back and playing a slightly edged backfoot drive past point. Chad needed to downscale the attacking field to plug some gaps, so used this as a ruse to approach the stumps while directing traffic. He was near Rufus and out of earshot of anyone including the umpires.

"Roofy, that's quite enough of that now," said Chad continuing to wave his hands at deep point to move across. "You've made your point, now do your duty."

"Is this the 'sweep the leg' moment?" asked Rufus, standing tall.

"Let's remember where you're from and our little agreement."

"I remember an instruction as a bribe to get back into your team; the same team that shunned me for five years, relegated to be a bit part player, a supporting cast member never making any real difference to the team. I'm making a difference for Shackleton now."

"Don't just take it from me - look around. You'll forever be the traitor who, at the moment it counted most, forgot his Corkridge principles."

"Corkridge's principles would celebrate giving your all on a cricket field; it's your messed up sense of winning at all costs that will end up costing you."

"Wrong call Rufio ... wrong call. You may live - or not - to regret this error in judgement."

"I'm just fine with my judgement, thanks Skipper."

Chad called the Neethaniel bowler over for a quick briefing, Rufus suspecting targeting his front foot play where he was considered to have a weakness, so he inched forward to bat out of his crease, aware that he was closer to the pacy barrage but that good length balls could become half-volleys. It could have, of course, been a Chad double-bluff ploy to continue with the short stuff, although was it possible for left-arm Neethaniel to get any faster or more aggressive?

Wrong! The fourth ball came hurtling, likely the quickest of the innings thus far, catching Rufus on the gloves and squashing his fingers on his bat handle, a notoriously painful blow in cricket. Rufus dropped the bat instantly, unable to do anything but shake his hand as Neethaniel mockingly aped the reaction. Rufus could feel his finger was broken but couldn't let anyone know, least Jacob, who stood motionless the other end. One ball of the over remained and Rufus knew this was the time for bravery, the time to go on the attack as his finger might not last that many more overs. On the sixth ball - another short-pitched delivery - Rufus took an almighty hoick, missing the ball by some distance as the bat jarred in his hands causing further painful splinters up his wrist. Jacob called him through for the run as he'd backed up in anticipation, setting off as Stanni took the ball with both hands then flung his right glove to the ground to have a shy at the stumps. Despite Jacob's backing up, he'd likely have been out if the ball had struck the stumps, missing by a plume as Shackleton added a precious run to their total and Rufus remained on strike. 15 runs off the over and a broken finger put Shackleton on 19-0 after two overs.

The Neethaniel brothers had engines that not only didn't seem to have an off switch but also seemed to increase in velocity as each ball rained down with bestial fulmination; there was no tiring, just that feral, frothing desire to bowl another ball and bowl it faster, bouncier, skiddier, more threatening than the last. The opening spell got wilder, the barrage enough to decorate both Jacob and Rufus with bruised dots that would be trophy leopard spots for weeks after the match. The brothers were drenched, the black of their shirts shiny with sweat, foreheads a motley braille of chorbs and sweat beads. Rufus was in trouble, each shot - middled or not - triggering a shooting pain now all the way up his arm as batting with a broken finger was really not feasible. He could feel the snapped middle phalanges of his left hand's index finger, the fragments floating within the unbroken skin, yet he avoided fiddling too long, lest he give away the weakness the opposition could exploit. Jacob at the other end got the dancing shoes working but predominantly in defence as Rufus's daring kept the loose balls sailing and the scoreboard ticking. After four overs, Shackleton still hadn't lost a wicket despite a few close calls, the two openers battered and wounded but still standing, as the crowd got behind the plucky resolve. On 35-0 off 5 overs, Chad had had enough, his fill of peeved infuriation spilling over to prompt a bowling change, bringing himself into the attack to replace the left-handed Neethaniel, despite an intense previous over that troubled both batsmen. The crowds had come to see Corkridge - Chad specifically - take wickets, not two overgrown monkeyboys flinging their excrement for show.

"This would be a good time to take wickets," Ramsay stated, sipping on a single espresso.

"Any time in cricket is good for wickets," retorted Clodagh, focussed on the match. "If you're the bowling team."

The ovation to embrace Chad into the attack was rousing, his reputation as England's premier young cricketer with more potential than any schoolboy in decades inculcating even him. Chad took longer than normal to set a field for his own bowling, as the applause looked like never abating, his stats and pedigree just too crazy impressive to print here, only belonging on the Lord's scoreboard or a Wisden almanac. There was no arm swing, no stretching, no jumping jacks or double knee-lifting leaps, just the halcyon poise that he'd done this a billion times before and been successful a billion times before, so why should this outing at the home of cricket in the biggest final of his career be any different?

The blonder-than-usual mop began seagulling towards Rufus on strike, an indication that the Corkridge captain was about to deliver his first ball of the match on a pitch offering anomalous assistance to bowlers - at least in the morning before the surface dried out and hardened for the team batting second. Chad had often taken a breather when Rufus batted in the nets, deeming him not worthy to face the might and guile of his balls, even though he held back his marquee 'king of the ball' deliveries for matches. Chad's run-up wasn't as hurried and frenetic as either of the Neethaniel brothers, replaced with a metronomic steady rhythm that looked poetic, gliding on soft clouds, each stride a handsome replica of the last. Chad's first ball pitched wide of off stump on a length dangerous on any pitch let alone this landmine track, hitting the angled seam and coming back on Rufus who tried to drop his gloves and protect his throbbing shattered digit. The ball took the glove, dislodging the index finger from the bat's handle and flying through to Stanni who took a simple catch. Chad made a point of looking at all his team's bowlers as he coolly waited for the adulation, the 'that's how it's done, lads' expression an attempted galvanising gambit. The umpire gave Rufus out as he tucked his left hand under his right arm, and departed for a sound 25 runs at well over a run a ball. Chad put his finger to his mouth as Rufus succumbed.

Onka headed in, the lanky figure with an extended stride reaching the crease far swifter than his languid pace suggested. The Corky fielders were suddenly alive, busy in the outfield, chirping, skipping, hustling around their commander in chief who'd hopefully pried open the wicket floodgates for this charade to end and Corkridge to raise the Digners Cup and all get onto the sporting honours roll.

"Here's their number 3 boys," came a chirp, likely James. "Too good for us, so the little piggy went all the way home to Shaky High without any roast beef - sorry Zebra meat - or maybe he should go back to his real home, all the way back to the African plains."

Onka ignored, surveying the field setting for Chad's over but thinking of how the mean streets of Durbs were pretty darn far removed from the idyllic plains. Onka tried to push the thought out of his head that he was an impetuous starter early in his innings, opting to weather this storm first by truncating his high backlift. A leg slip was now in place and short cover, both attacking, giving Onka no uncertainty that his wicket was prized. Chad made him wait a few seconds longer than normal, splintering any ice in the veins and tipping the heart rate above techno beat.

Onka's first ball faced did very little, which might have been Chad's ploy – a straight ball that skidded a bit but had enough lift off the billiard table to just miss between middle and off stump, yet kept rising as it reached the keeper, likely a cross seam delivery that didn't hit the seam. Onka got back to defend but missed the ball, beaten by the unexpected bounce and heavy hard exterior, the ball still shiny. Chad smiled and shrugged his shoulders while Stanni added "Not even good enough to hit those chaps; here's our walking wicket."

Chad's next ball was more ferocious, angling in and straightening, Onka having a crack at an expansive drive but not getting to the pitch, missing again, playing down the wrong line to the groaning celebratory knock-on chirps from the entire slip cordon. Onka was not happy with himself, resisting the urge to slap his pad with his bat. What would be served up next – would Chad continue to make best use of the surface or do something funky, a variation at the time least expected? The next ball to reach Onka was the former, a seam up delivery that jagged in and rose, Onka getting behind the ball to defend awkwardly into the groove between his pad's flap and thigh, the ball lodging. Stanni, ever the obnoxious optimist ran up to the batsman and grabbed the ball from the groove appealing, jumping up and down, the umpire flinching to almost give it before realising the ludicrous nature of the appeal. Chad, motioned for the ball back to him, a semblance of irritability enshrouding his demeanour. Three balls – no wickets, but three dot balls which would place Onka under some pressure for the remaining two. Chad's next ball was just short of a length on middle stump, straightening enough to clip the top of off, forcing Onka to play at the ball. Soft hands and straight bat combined with the lift saw the ball catch the shoulder of the bat without spooning up for an easy catch, spinning back on itself and dropping short of first slip, a fortuitous escape and perhaps fate as Onka looked at his misshapen bat, the shoulder dented in a previous match. Onka wasn't that religious but was the ghost of Eddie Barlow's optimism providing one more chance? Chad's final ball of the over was another tricky customer to negotiate but Onka managed to, leaving him still at the crease and Chad with a wicket-maiden in his first over, the crowd acknowledging the early feat.

During the seventh over, perpetuated by the right-handed Neethaniel brother retained in the attack, Jacob and Onka managed to rotate the strike, predominantly playing back, using the pace to find gaps and exploiting the extras on offer. Onka was able to get his drive going on an overpitched delivery without middling the ball while Jacob's use of footwork to gambol around the crease was admirable. Chad kept himself on for the eighth over and the same continued, the two batsmen playing as late under the eyes as was feasible, the over going perilous-nudge-perilous-nudge-perilous-nudge. The run rate suffered but after the eighth over, Shackleton had kept their wickets intact, the score 42-1.

Chad persisted with Neethaniel for the ninth over, no sign of toil yet also no sign of discernible rhythm, the erratic deliveries worked around for bat-on-ball singles and twos. At this point Jacob was yet to hit a boundary and chose this over to open his account, picking length early to open his stance and paddle the ball around the corner. 50 up for Shackleton from the final ball of the ninth over, generating an applauding balcony as the two out in the middle resisted shaking hands, instead opting for a modest glove bump.

Chad faced a dilemma at the start of the tenth: keep himself on and risk another over without a wicket, even though he'd only conceded three runs in two overs and taken the priceless wicket, or succumb to a bowling change, even though the argument to save himself for later was plausible. This was the first bubble of self-doubt Chad had ever experienced in his life, casting another glance towards the members stand without any sighting of his parents. Chad turned to James to take the baton and have a trundle, his medium seam a possible asset on this track. Plus, he needed to hold all the quicks back and let one side of the ball scuff as he tried to execute the more clandestine plan B, signalling to James to start working on the ball while he bowled, a tiny piece of blackened sandpaper concealed in James's pocket and the thick sun cream trowelled across his nose and cheeks not amiss on a sunny day at Lord's.

At the other end Chad replaced a fuming Neethaniel with Danny, finger spin looking more likely to contain than attack, a move surprising most, especially on the Shackleton balcony. James bowled a heavier ball than it looked, the bat twirling in Onka's hands on a few occasions and he also had more variety than his lumbering run-up suggested, his leg cutter beating both batsmen in successive overs. Danny held up an end as he had all season, typically miserly and not conceding many runs even as Onka started to loosen the shoulders and play through the line. The pitch still had enough bounce to make this a factor which prevented scoring, then about halfway through the 16th over – James's fourth with the score on 90-1 – the ball began reversing. This was early by any cricketing standards for the ball to start reverse swinging and Onka had a few goes to retrieve the ball to assess its condition. He purposefully played down into the turf and casually picked it up to politely lob it back to the keeper, who instantly protested, noticing the one side bright and gooey and the other rougher than a badger's arse, the scuffed lines like a desolate planet's scarified surface. Something was amiss so Onka approached the umpire to request some form of investigation and was instantly dismissed, told to just get on with the game. Chad signalled for the lefty Neethaniel to warm up, his sulk at only bowling a two over opening spell without any wickets for the first time this season, more swiftly dispelled than Onka from the umpire's sight.

Neethaniel's first ball of his second spell was a loosener which Onka was able to pull in front of square for three – the first leg side shot in front of square that day. The bowler kicked the inviolable turf, leaving a gouge mark in the pitch at an inopportune spot for a right-handed batsman and he returned from over the wicket. The next ball went out towards first slip then hooping back into Jacob, the arc following a line that looked certain to be glanced off the pads for a few, but in fact slowed as it reached Jacob, holding up a straightish line to befuddle the batsman and clip off stump, Jacob playing around the ball and beaten by the reverse swing. The Corkridge team went up louder than they had in a while, Jacob's dejection at seeing the bails on the ground not in any way dented by the adulation at being given such a rousing send-off as a prized wicket. Jacob had been at the crease for sixteen and a bit overs against the most feared attack in schoolboy cricket, held up his end and contributed 30 valuable runs – all to be mightily proud of and Enid stopped to tell him as much as he strode up the steps towards the Long Room. Enid made her way onto the field at Lord's, the number 4 bat and captain of Shackleton receiving the biggest ovation of the day so far.

"Keep it together," she whispered to herself as her eyes blurred once again, the discernible blades of grass melting together in a brilliant billiard-felt smooth paste.

The strip was far out in the distance, appearing further away with each step, the realisation that she was following the same path her dad had followed many times, walking out to bat at Lord's. Flooding through her thoughts were his shots she remembered here from old footage, raising his bat for fifties and helmet off for hundreds, his generous smile without any overt celebrations characterising his life as cricketer ... team, enjoyment, love of the game with adulation shunted to the back of the queue. Her footsteps sunk into the turf, treacle making every forward momentum laboured, until it felt as though she was waist deep, unable to move, glued in immobility. Then her dad's dismissals entered the fray - bowled, caught, stumped, LBW, run out all assaulting her consciousness at once, a hacked together montage, his glazed eyes facing forward as he left while the fielding side celebrated, sometimes looking down at his feet, never raising the bat - all the low scoring innings at once. Then the dropped catch ... again and again, a screaming in her head amplifying with each fumble, his eyes wincing, the first sign of crow's feet and the ball hitting the ground, an echoing thud that forced her to stop, remove her gloves and stick a finger in her ear to rattle out the ringing.

"Oops, do we have an early problem here from the Shackleton captain?"

"There's no problem here, Ramsay. This girl knows how to play cricket and she knows how to stand up to bull— I mean, the opposition."

"She's fiddling with her ear Clodagh; seems in distress."

"Maybe nerves, maybe a small acknowledgement to her father who used to touch his ear when he scored a hundred, a tribute to his deceased parents."

"That's actually getting me all welled up! I'd better have another coffee to snap out of it!"

"She's fine now; let's just hope and pray her innings is a good one ... you go, Girl!"

When she reached Onka he placed a hand on her shoulder ditching the ubiquitous fist bump once he saw her face. Her eyes appeared varnished and her lips looked parched, cracked, flaky even. She kept blinking to focus and pressing at her ear from the outside of the helmet, which achieved nothing.

"O Captain, my Captain!" Onka said. "You've got this … always did and always have. I'll follow your lead … always have and always will. Oh, and by the way, it's reversing."

Onka's speech seemed to snap Enid from whatever nostalgic physiological trance she found herself consumed by, the technical detail of early out-of-place reverse swing forcing Enid to focus on how to counter.

As she walked away from Onka to take guard for her first ball the Stanni motormouth went into overdrive …

"Walking wicket, boys, walking wicket!"

"This one takes a while to get going so have a snooze in the outfield – less big shots than a Sopranos episode!"

"Snooze fest dot C Oh dot UK, lads – no point in patrolling the boundaries as they'll be quieter than Shaky High next week."

"Captain goes, they're done … there's less tail than a Shaky social."

"I'll shut up … she might cry."

"Drop it like it's hot, Sister … just like your dad did!"

Enid took guard on leg stump, opened her stance like her dad had taught her to left-arm quicks and waited for Neethaniel to charge at her. The first breeze of the morning cooled her brow beneath the heat of the helmet, and she wondered whether this was nature or the displacement of air from the storming bowler. He'd moved directly behind the umpire now so the only indication she had that he was approaching was the umpire's lowered arm, so she bent her knees a tad and set herself. As if not scary enough, Neethaniel suddenly appeared above the umpire's right shoulder, his tumid face a winner for any Halloween mask, steam protruding from his nostrils, his face contorted, squashed cabbage mangled, an ugly new-born with pocked blotches, the left arm like an axe being raised to strike down on one of Henry VIII's wives. A red arced blur brushstroked across Enid's vision as she stayed rooted to the crease, the ball beating her all ends up and tearing past her outside edge to the safety of the Chatty Kathy's gloves at the back. This animated the Corkridge players as a hush fell across the Lord's ground. Onka nodded some needed reassurance Enid's way.

The bowler then decided to come around the wicket to Enid, Chad orchestrating the immediately unsettling move. Enid closed her stance and, instead of taking a new guard, shifted her toes over a few inches to rest on middle and leg. After the umpire announced the change, Neethaniel still ran from behind his back, obscuring himself until the final stride then appearing but, as he was around the wicket he could fling his powerful left arm back with more abandon, a slingshot coming down at Enid from two o'clock. He dug it in and the trajectory surprised Enid as it took off, hurtling towards her head but again holding its line to make it more threatening: easy to duck your head directly into the ball's path, so Enid swayed, leaning back to let the ball pass her nose without following her.

"Man's game," Neethaniel hawked as he followed up the short delivery with some more sophisticated chat, nose to nose with Enid's face.

For the remainder of the over, Neethaniel continued around the wicket, the sling action not finding Enid's bat once as she did well to survive with her wicket intact.

"They've done something to the ball," said Onka as they gathered, relieved the over was over. "I'm sure of it - I had words but was shooed away. Think the umpires might be a bit bent too, so keep your pads away from anything full."

"Thanks. Without Peter we've not got much to come after Larry so best we set up camp right here, right now."

"Agreed: we sit tight as, although I don't believe in the word, with the ball reversing, the green track and the raw pace, these are about as close to 'unplayable' as I've ever seen. Oh, and your boyfriend is warming up."

Enid looked behind her to see Chad with ball in hand – this was personal … he wanted her scalp.

"You sit tight. Hold up an end," she said. "I've got something slightly different in mind for Chad's overs. Like my dad used to say: Die Trying. What do you do to a cricketer with no apparent weaknesses … get him believing he's invincible."

"This is your Barry Richards play, isn't it?"

Chad's first ball to Onka was neatly played down to third man for a single, bringing Enid on strike for the clash everyone had paid to witness … captain v captain; boy v girl; incumbent v upstart. Enid was yet to get off the mark, a milestone that troubled any cricketer, but this didn't seem to trouble Enid: this was a final so it had to be feast or famine … big runs or lose the match. There was no difference between a duck and a twenty here, so she relaxed and played her game. Chad enjoyed his first ball to Enid, a wobble seam that also swung late to beat her all ends up, Stanni's gloves already doing overtime. Enid acknowledged the good ball which irritated Chad as he waited for the ball to be recycled back to him down the line of slow fielders. His next ball swung conventionally in but straightened off the seam rather than reversing, Enid trying to prod down to short mid-wicket only to push a leading edge over Chad's flailing arms for two runs, opening her account in less than fashionable style but this didn't seem to perturb her in the slightest. The next ball was venomously short, hurtling up to her throat and she looked as though she was getting into position to hook only to pull out of the shot and play a casually awkward flick with the outer edge of the bat over her left shoulder, the ball catching the edge and dissecting the keeper's raised in vain left arm and leg slip, a charging fine leg retrieving the one bounce four.

"Lucky," said Chad following through.

"Yeah, I need some, don't I?" responded Enid, drawn into the verbals for the first time.

"You never had an edge until now, if you get me."

"Pesky edge," responded Enid, looking at the cherry mark halfway up the edge of her bat. Chad walked back, bemused, shaking his head and chortling to himself.

Enid survived the remainder of Chad's over without troubling the scorers any further and Onka did an incredible job to keep Neethaniel out the following over with the ball doing a lot more than seemed feasible on a cricket field. He rotated the strike but received the brunt of what might have gone down as the most tasty spell of the match, the ball reversing around corners and Neethaniel's arm height variations keeping both batters guessing as the ball skidded, bounced, swung and seamed ... sometimes all in a single delivery! Onka noticed that Neethaniel was consistently overstepping, bowling savage no-balls to get his release even scarily closer to the batter. After the over Onka decided to raise with the umpires.

"Excuse me, Sir, but would you mind keeping an eye on the bowler's front foot? He seems to be constantly overstepping and the no-balls are not being called."

The umpire was eye level with this lanky teenager and unable to hide his disdain when responding.

"You're a bit of a busybody, aren't you, young man? First the ball's being tampered with, now we're missing no-balls. What next ... alien craft abducting their fielders and returning them as superhuman cricketers? Just get on with the game for Christ's sake, or I'll have you sent home!"

"I am home, Sir."

Chad was back on Enid's case at the start of the 20th over as she audaciously walked up the pitch to him, reaching the pitch then twirling the bat in her hand to pull out of the cover drive and play another shot with the leading edge, the ball squirting between cover and extra cover for two runs. Chad's next ball was full, and Enid splayed her legs playing a Chinese cut through them for four runs, this time off the inside edge of the bat. The game was up - the message clear as the horrible reality dawned on Chad that his opposing captain - a girl - was just toying with him. She was playing shots with the edge of her bat on purpose! Mocking him, Chad the Magnificent, in front of all these people on his stage on this day, his coronation as King of Lord's. The boundary brought up the Nelson - 111 - an Admiral Nelson legacy symbolising one eye, one arm, one leg even though Nelson never lost a leg. Swathes of supposititious fans raised their feet off the floor in solidarity with the batting side. For the remainder of the over Chad bowled wide yorkers, unlikely to take a wicket but at least preventing this imposter getting her edge near the ball. The Nelson remained as Chad snatched his cap from the umpire: 111-2 after 20 overs.

"You're not that good," he muttered as he passed Enid.

"You're right," she responded earnestly.

Port side Neethaniel's fifth over was just as treacherous as any he'd bowled but, as is the nature of cricket, an extended period without a wicket characterised by Onka's display of solid defensive technique and low risk scoring shots, saw a slow withering of resolve. Chad restively made a double bowling change, replacing himself with some further finger spin from Danny and swapping to starboard Neethaniel from the end providing the most assistance to the quicks. Still no sign of Chuck into the attack. Chad had played the game long enough to know that at 121-2 after 21 overs with more than half the innings remaining, the game could easily swing the pressure back on the batting side, either through containment or wickets, but panic was an unattractive trait that any captain – especially at Lord's – should avoid. His demeanour – on the big screen for less time than he'd have preferred – needed to be ice cool, calculated, with every move as though the plan was going according to plan. He smoothed his golden fleece just as the camera cut away to an aerial shot of the food stalls surrounding the field, the queue to get a taste of Donna's Honours Kebab snaking beyond the complete length of the Media Centre, outstripping the beer queue and giving the Pimm's queue a real run for its money.

Danny came on and was looking innocuous until he went around the wicket and started pushing his deliveries across the right-handers without any turn, the balls skidding but with enough surprise bounce, Stanni taking a host of low screech-laden catches which beat the outside edge. From over the wicket Danny had given the ball a bit more air, yielding him the odd ball that turned more than the batsman would expect from this finger spinner, but easy enough to negate with the ball safely negotiated off the pads to the left and right of mid-wicket for ones and twos. For the final ball of his fourth over, Danny got one to grip and bounce, the ball moving into Onka and perhaps tickling the closing face of his bat, onto his pad, spooning up so that Stanni vaulted the stumps and dived at Onka bundling him out of the way to stick out a glove. The ball landed squarely in the glove and, before the umpire flinched with his decision, Onka walked.

"What an idiot," Stanni slurred as Onka walked off and the Corkridge players engulfed him and Danny, the desperation for a wicket dispelling high fives, not passing go and cascading straight to hugging euphoria. A key partnership had been broken and Enid knew and respected this about Onka; this was his way – he always walked, part emulation of his hero Hashim Amla and part decency of him as a cricketer. No one had even mandated walking in the Shackleton squad; neither had anyone judged Onka's decision on the biggest stage of all which didn't overshadow his core principles and the way he embraced the game of cricket. He'd made a gutsy if slightly less flamboyant than his usual style 41 and got a standing ovation from most of the crowd and particularly the Shackleton balcony, where weathering that bowling storm had provided enough of a foundation to at least compete.

Larry was surprisingly sent out at number 5, the third wicket down in the 22nd over with enough real estate to build an innings and disrupt the field placings as only Larry knew how. Corin was being held back, hopefully to blast at the death but there was still the small matter of Chuck to bowl, his arms salivating as they wind turbined in opposite directions. Chad signalled for Danny to stand down, but persisted with starboard Neethaniel as Larry resided at the non-striker's end. Enid started looking more fluid as the ball's reverse swing got dulled with each bat on ball connection and the grass flattened so bounce was a smidge more consistent and less potent. Enid hit two consecutive fours in the 23rd over, one a timed front foot glance in front of square and the second a hybrid cut-ramp that was more of an upper-cut over the slips, initially seeming too cramped to play the shot but bending her back almost to the floor to deflect the ball past Harrison's despairing dive at deep point. Larry was yet to face a delivery when Chuck entered the fray, going over the wicket as was customary for Corkridge's premier fast bowler. Chad gathered the team in a huddle while Chuck harangued the lot of them, fingers, arms and spittle flying in all directions to leave little doubt that this was where the game was won or lost.

Larry looked unfazed as she took guard after a discussion with Enid. The brief was simply play your game: if the funky shot or opportunity to unsettle the bowler's length by moving around the crease was there, then take it, but have a brief perusal of the surface first, feeling bat on ball to get settled. Chuck's run-up looked double anyone else's, almost at the boundary rope and wishing Graham Dilly has been more bullish with the boundary extension. Larry could just make out his bobbling brown hair in the distance as he catapulted in, his head dilating in menace with each stride. What happened next would go down as one of the more deplorable moments on the pitch at Lord's as Chuck reached the crease and leapt into his delivery stride, his arm unashamedly bent at the elbow as he flung a full toss beamer at Larry's head. Her years of dodging her brother's golf balls on the range might have saved her life as she reacted just enough to avoid taking the full force of the ball on the side of the temple, swaying so the ball caught the grill flusher than any body blow thus far in the match. The crowd shrieked in horror as the umpire reluctantly signalled a no-ball and Larry crumpled into a heap, Chuck instantly crying accident, the ball merely slipping from his grasp. The medics were on instantly as Enid protested with the umpires to no avail as Larry was stretchered off for a head injury assessment. The crowd started booing when Chuck appeared on the screen and he dismissively shrugged it off, his teeth bared as the adrenaline fuelled by hatred pumped deep and thick. Corin, her pads and gloves not fully attached, joined her sister out in the middle.

"You've got your pads on the wrong way around," said Enid. "Strap flaps on the outside, remember?"

"Ah well … Hanrattys love challenges; wouldn't be any fun if there weren't a bunch more self-inflicted obstacles in front of us, would it?"

"Dad did the same thing; against New Zealand … think he made a duck. At least your first blast at Lord's is a free hit!"

"Dad would complain there was no such thing as a ball bowled at you without consequences—"

"'Risk-free cricket: all the rage'"

"I'm not honouring the old days by blocking this one, that's for darn sure, Sister!"

"Would expect nothing of the sort."

"Fire with fire."

"Puff the magic bent arm dragon is working up a bunch of steam over there, but just hope Larry is okay. Let's do it for her, but be careful the umps are bent so they'll give it if there's a hint."

"Gotcha: pads out the way; nicks and run out remedied by DRS but umpires call and on field 'out' looms large."

"I'm so glad … to be out here … with you Corin. Dad would be proud."

"I'm not even going to call you by your name – you're still co-captain to me! Save the speeches for when I've actually done something. You might rue your faith when Noel is out here with you in two minutes!"

"Classic Corin," Enid would hear her dad's words reverberating in her ears as Corin dispatched Chuck's latest bent-arm chuck for the first maximum of Shackleton's innings over long on, the no-ball sailing for a six about six rows back into Shaky's corner much to the delight of the patrons, one of whom dived across the seats only to shell the ball into his empty plastic beer cup. A 600 strike rate was something to be fleetingly proud of but wouldn't get close to beating Corkridge, so Enid shot a few big sister 'responsibility' glances Corin knew oh so well, imploring 'be sensible' rather than 'be da woah-man', Corin's shoulders slumping like a child whose favourite toy had been confiscated. Chuck once again started from the horizon, the lonely shepherd steaming towards his sheep and – of course – Corin could not resist … this ball went even further back, hitting the middle tier of the stand for another six, Chuck's earlier beamer goading his subsequent overpitched deliveries delightfully in Corin's slot. Twelve off two, so the 600 strike rate persisted as the crowd sprung to life, a new Lord's fans' favourite discovered after only two melted bashes. Enid could only smile, resigned to any sibling of a stubborn sister's true place … advice meant nothing, landing so hard on deaf ears, each pearl likely to remain in the fleshy folds for infinity, snuggling the ear wax into a duvet and refusing to ever get out of ears.

Chad glared at Chuck who in turn glared at Corin then his teammates then the crowd, looking for anyone but himself to blame. Again he returned, liable to do anything to prevent this girl dispatching a hat-trick of sixes back over his head. The arm was the same, bent as an incumbent political party promising revolution after years in power, but the ball came out differently and Corin failed to spot this, true to her cavalier character, another smack with the stance open and the back leg lowered, intended as a heave over long on once again, only this time coming through the shot early and getting struck on the back pad, Enid thinking this was about as plumb an LBW decision as she'd seen. The umpire's finger was almost up before the appeal, sending Corin packing after only three balls, the angle of his finger and tension in his arm vitriolic. Corin approached Enid as the 15 second DRS countdown started on the screen.

"You had to go for it, didn't you?" Enid stated, resigned to Corin's fate and that of the team in general.

"There's not time!" responded Corin. "Shall we leave it? Felt dead as a doornail."

"Slower ball. Over the wicket. Off cutter. Pitching on off. Halfway up middle. You've more chance of ever listening to me."

"Sister, I had to have a go, if only to avenge Larry – I'll leave the rest to you, just make these smug fu—"

"There's no batting to come and we have both reviews remaining …"

The countdown hit 3 … 2 …1 before Enid snapped forth the 'T' gesture, Corin not quite believing her sister had actually gone for it.

The umpire – even more reluctantly than the first – tutted

before signalling with the finger box as Corkridge all mocked the referral, throwing T shapes at a bunch of horrendous angles.

"Third umpire to Control; we have a referral from the batsman for LBW. On field decision is out. Let's check the front foot first please ..."

The picture took a while to come up as Chuck's delivery rock-and-rolled too quickly to make the foot out, his bent arm and the speed of the back-and-forth glitch making him look like he was at an Eminem rap battle in Detroit. Eventually the playback slowed down and Chuck's planted front foot could clearly be seen over the line, enough daylight between the back of the boot and the line to drive a toy truck through. The crowd went into ballistic meltdown, their hero spared for another ball at least, so Corin, after sharing a breathless reprieved moment with her captain sister, rewarded the faithful with another maximum, this six off the no-ball squarer, perhaps taking a hint of the bat's top edge and just clearing a stretching George at deep square leg, elongated so far skywards it appeared he'd been apprehended by the sheriff's best guys. 20 off the over and Corin wasn't quite sure she was done, with five balls bowled and still three remaining. Enough was enough ... or was it? Showomanship and cricket were long-standing bedfellows – weren't they?"

Chuck's panic was apparent, immortalised as the bloke who got spanked to all parts of Lord's by a girl. He asked Chad for more boundary protection who rightly refused on the grounds that sixes couldn't be stopped by anyone but the crowd ... and the bowler. Corin was solidly confident that Chuck would go back to what had worked, his slower ball but perhaps with a back of the hand or knuckle variety, although taking that sort of risk under this pressure was unlikely from a chap who dropped the ball three times en route back to his mark. Corin forced herself not to have any sympathy for the fellow who'd put Lauren in hospital, as he reared in once more, the ball nipping away to beat Corin's outside edge and instantly restore Chuck's bravado. This took the wind out of the crowd's sails and two sensible dots later, Corin was able to restore, reinstate and relay her active listening faculty at the Hanratty family Christmas gatherings for years to come. For the first time since the fifth over, Shackleton's run rate was above six, on 154-3 with Lauren retired hurt and one over away from the halfway point in their innings.

After a tricky stint from Danny and more 150kmph plus deliveries from Chuck, the game paused with an official looking commotion in the outfield, Harrison sporting an exaggerated hobble carried by two teammates, Shackleton on 161-3 after 27 overs, with Enid on 28 around a run a ball and Corin on 22 with her strike rate returning to a semblance of normality after her initial spate of sixes.

"Looks like someone's going off," Corin said to Enid taking a breather.

"Did you see anyone get hurt?" Enid asked.

"Nope."

"Some more devilry at work."

A picture of a girl popped up onto the Lord's screen as the crowd politely ushered Harrison off, eager to get on with the drama.

"Corkridge Castle School for Boys (and girls) twelfth man: Celestia Osborne-Jackson," appeared below her accommodating face, decked in midnight black.

Chad put Celestia at short cover, as Chuck initiated his third over, her made-up face directly in Enid's eyeline. The ploy shouldn't have irked Enid, but it did – their token female to field a few overs, not bat or bowl to show the world what a progressive team they were, when in reality her addition only increased the testosterone rather than levelling it out. Enid was mature and kind enough to realise she should be collegial to this young woman who was probably a keen cricketer sidelined by her male counterparts, but if they were better, Enid felt they should play irrespective of gender. After the second dot ball, Celestia shot in to retrieve the ball at Enid's feet as it bobbled, preventing the standstill.

"You're not doing us any favours, with this whole show; these shenanigans, girlfriend," tiffed the new girl.

"What does that mean?"

"You don't belong out here; neither do I. This is a boy's game."

"I'm sure you don't really believe that."

"You're making us look more pathetic, more in need, more inferior than if you'd have just stayed at home."

"This game is not about gender – it shouldn't matter – it's about the enjoyment of the game, competing at whatever level is right for each individual's aspirations. Making everything about gender rather than ability is where society is tripping everyone up, let alone you and me. We're playing this match because we want to win and we enjoy cricket, not because we're girls with an attitude shoving our brand of chick cricket down everyone's throat!"

"I'm not in your little Shaky sisterhood of rejects; sooner you're back on the hockey or netball field the better!"

"As a human being I wish you well for today's game and hope you field well; as an opponent I'm looking forward to driving the next delivery past you, through you, at you … the end of you."

Cricket never seems to go the way anyone, any coach, any captain or any ardent fan plans, but this ball – the third of the over – Chuck served up a juicy half-volley which Enid obliged to cover drive off the front foot between mid-off and extra cover, a magnificent cricket shot from the highest echelons of any coaching manual, the full face of the blade 'makers-namedropping' without any closure of the wrists to generate extra power, Celestia whipping her ankle out of the way in fear of a broken bone. Celestia was moved to a less accountable position behind the keeper immediately after that ball, her job seemingly done without avail for Corkridge, yet Enid was ruffled at the sudden realisation that this whole game might become about her being a female rather than a cricketer, sparking a couple of rash shots in the over, one across the line misreading the length and another trying to cut a ball too close to her that cramped her, sailing over her gloves, mercifully without a noise as the umpire's trigger finger looked itchier than an eczema sufferer in a sauna. Now it was Corin's go to be the reassuring presence to drag the Enid train back onto the tracks.

"Don't let some little token psycho plot – likely originated with a few kegs, chest thumping and dumb jokes – upset your game," said Corin. "This is how they roll, not how we roll. You've got to be here at the very end – that's the only chance we have. Leave the dashing brilliance to me … I'm better at it anyway," Corin resolved, winking.

Thanks, Sis," said Enid, fumbling for her fleetingly out of reach steely resolve as Danny waited to bowl. "I left out pride and family honour when lecturing the 'pick me' about why we're doing this … my bad."

After Corin played a majestic old-fashioned hook off her left cheek for a one bounce four, the Hanratty girls reached their fifty partnership, completely unaware until the achievement popped up on the big screen and the hordes acknowledged. Since joining her sister, Corin had scored 35 and Enid 14 with one extra from Chuck's GBH upchuck that wadn't no ball. Chad began remonstrating about the ball to the umpire as the sisters blocked everything out to drink in the family moment … a fifty partnership at Lord's, an involuntary hug and stern attempt to keep it together.

"Job's not done," said Enid. "Love you by the way."

"Like Dad says: 'can't bat from the pavilion'; let's keep going, I don't want this to end."

The umpire requested the metal circular ball measuring

contraption from off the field of play once Chad contended the ball was out of shape. It went through easily enough upon the first few goes but then the umpire managed to jam the ball at a funny angle, stopping the follow-through. A request ensued for a box of balls and the new ball that emerged was a fair deal shinier than the old one, Chad waving it in Enid's direction. Enid, present at the assessment throughout, protested as best she could but met the same dismissed fate as Onka, a better ball for Corkridge a brick-walled forgone conclusion.

With a firmer new cherry in his hand, Chad caused problems, zipping both ways, the pronounced seam and harder leather fizzing through an array of shots caught between implacable defence and all-out attack. With the newer ball though, any bat on ball meant boundaries were easier to come by and Enid accumulated a fortuitous nick past the now dwindling frown of slips, Chad kicking the turf in protest. It had been a while since Larry's demise and this partnership grated at Chad to the point where he was about to do what he called 'thinking outside the stupid box' but what most cricket aficionados would term 'unsportsmanlike'. With Enid still on strike Chad strode in, his usual metronomic glide and jumped to deliver the ball ... yet he didn't, stopping and looming over the stumps before knocking the bails off with the ball in his hand, appealing to the umpire a metre away. As Corin clambered back after supposedly backing up, the umpire gave it out, almost sticking his finger up Corin's nose as she stared up at him in dejection.

"Mankading, Clodagh, Mankading! You don't see that very often!"

"Unlike mansplaining or manterrupting eh, Ram—"

"That is such a nasty way to go out but if you're going to sneak up the pitch when you back-up, you run the risk. That will be a valuable wicket for Corkridge."

"Many in the game frown on this method of dismissal as unsporting - just listen to the crowd express their disapproval."

Enid sped over to Corin as the counter headed for zero.

"Were you in?"

"Probably not; didn't think of it, just strode forward in case you got another nick. Wasn't thinking!"

"This is not something you should have to think about - dirty low blow tactic ... I'm going to refer."

With the countdown quite firmly on 1 second remaining, Enid raised her bat to horizontal and punched her glove upwards, the umpire at first reluctant to refer a Mankad.

"Third umpire to Control, we have a player referral for ... for ... Mankad. On field decision right under the umpire's nose is out."

The slow motion review started with Chad leaping into his delivery stride only to fake the delivery and stop, the camera behind his back. The angle of the square camera could not see clearly past Chad as he obscured the stumps and any part of Corin that could be behind the crease. The third umpire shifted to the other camera facing Chad, with the same issue, James's large frame at mid-on obscuring a clear result. From the DRS technical room commentary being broadcast at home on televisions it looked like the third umpire had given up looking for a reason when suddenly he halted proceedings, asking for a zoom into a white blob between James's thick calves. A long silence ensued, the rock-and-roll footage lighting up the bails as Chad dislodged them with the white blob touching the right side of the crease appearing to be Corin's boot. Press-light-press-light-press-light then boot's pressure on the ground danced with the lit bail. The third umpire seemed happy that it was Corin's boot but not convinced the boot was over the line, the squashed edge potentially not exhibiting enough wrinkled compression to be deemed down over the line. Everything went silent as the screen shone "Decision Pending" the whole of Lord's holding their collective breath. Then a word - or was it two - appeared behind the bat and ball graphic in the sponsor's trolley.

Enid couldn't make it out.

Corin couldn't make it out.

No one could make it out.

Then the trolley got bumped over by two words and the crowd went ballistic when the words "Not Out" appeared in green and yellow.

"Three's not a charm," Enid said to Corin who made her eyes as spherical as they'd go and laughed.

Chad protested with both umpires for some time before returning to his bowling mark, a cacophony of unfamiliar boos ringing out around the Lord's ground, supporters unable to shelve their sense of injustice.

To escape the Manchad hang-over - with 18 overs remaining and Shackleton having stockpiled 189 runs - Chad reunited the opening Neethaniel freaks for a four over stint as they neared the end of their allotted overs. The brief was if they couldn't get these girls out, then just kill them - music to the pulped ears of both brothers who were yet to dip a hair below rabid in their pursuit of captain pleasing, pain and or wickets. By now though, Enid and Corin Hanratty were well up to the task, set and seeing the ball not quite like a watermelon but let's say a cantaloupe, Enid whipping one ball off her right hip onto the leg side in front of square for an exquisitely improvised boundary. Corin started ramping and playing down the ground to full deliveries, finding golf chip space onto greens all over the place and taking on the short ball but with awareness of where deep square leg and mid-wicket were lying in wait.

Enid reached her half-century in the 35th over after a scampered three from a mistimed drive that beat the field but couldn't quite make it to the boundary off Neethaniel port side, and Corin an over later from a cracked under the eyes cut, squirting and accelerating off the turf to beat point off Neethaniel starboard. At the end of the 36th over, Shackleton were 219-3 as Chad flung the ball to James, his trusted lieutenant through thick and thin after an expensive spell, his despair at this partnership between his two primary nemeses far beyond embarrassing and well into the trauma realm. The sandpaper in James's pocket might still have some rough purchase but this was unlikely so, with primitive pace being hoydenishly dispatched to all parts and spin at this stage an even higher risk, it was either himself, Chuck or James, the latter with a trick up his sleeve … for sure.

"You got something brewing?" asked Chad handing James the ball.

"What do you mean?"

"Pull something out of the bag to get these little you know whatchamacallits out."

"You tell me, Skip and I'll do it."

"Okay, run over and tackle one of them to Kingdom Come."

"Okay, Chad," James dutifully accepted and almost broke into a sprint before Chad grabbed him by the collar, his feet kicking forward like an overeager dog on a leash.

"No, you dummy! I'm asking you for a nugget of an idea in that thick skull of yours to help us wrestle this match from the annoying grasp of those soft delicate hands! You feel me!?"

"Uh … no, Skip, what do you want me to do?"

"You got nothing?"

"You still want me to tackle them?"

"Just bowl the ball and … and … try to take a wicket?"

James lumbered in to Corin, the ball wobbling and unsteady in his hand, plopping a half-tracker down which Corin duly accepted and dispatched for six over deep square.

That felt so good, she mused, the crack still ringing in her ears. James's second ball was the opposite - overpitched, so Corin sat back in the crease without much footwork and heaved another six back over the bowler's head. The third ball was probably a cross seam that sat up like a cherry pie on an American diner counter, reaching Corin's bellybutton before she walloped this one for the maximum as well, the crowd going into hyperdrive having reinvigorated her earlier failed hat-trick of sixes. Chad couldn't look James in the eye, who trooped back to his mark, his shoulders sloping him into a human rocket, and speaking of which, yes ... the fourth ball went over extra cover as Corin went down on one knee to hit one of the most complex cricket shots: a low daisy killing six lofted drive over extra cover. This situation now went full throttle into 'beach six balls' game, without the need for her father's eleemosynary insistence that a mistimed kiddie plough had reached the sea for six, an attempted knuckle ball which appeared as a slow full toss dispatched into the upper tier stand for the fifth six of the over.

"That is brutal!" Clodagh screamed in Ramsay's face.

"Yah! Wow! Great fun out there and fun for the viewers too - six off six beckoning ... can she pull it off?"

"Yaaaaaaahhhhhhhsssssssssss!"

... as Corin scooped the final ball over her left shoulder for the final six of the over.

"And you thought I'd just researched him as a batsman!"

"Sister, in that mood I think you'd have done that to any bowler!"

The adulation went a bit overboard, all of Lord's rising to Corin's 36 off a single over as James at one point looked like he might resort to violence and tackle her into the ground. In the mayhem it was missed that the girls had shared a hundred partnership, as the momentum shifted towards

Shackleton, James's devastating over leaving Chad with scant options to pry out a wicket and break the Hanratty family stand that looked more solid than James or Chad's furrowed brows. Chad did not want to bowl himself from that end – now with bad juju – so brought himself immediately back on with the intent to bowl defensively and keep Enid rooted to his end. Plus, deep in the chasms of his self-doubt saying 'hi' from behind rocks and brick walls, creatures he'd never laid eyes on before, was the solid credence that there was only one cowboy on this high plains' pitch who could arrest this development. Darwin had laid it out … this fluky charade with his withering bunny boys diving for cover and quivering in fear could only be ended by the one – the only – Chad de la Ampelas, Corkridge Castle School for Boys Head Boy, Cricket Captain and epoch owner of the Digners Cup ad infinitum.

"If it's going to me," Chad scolded himself as he clutched the ball with both hands. "It's up to me … not me too!"

The first ball went completely against script as Enid effortlessly waited for the ball and played an under the eyes on-drive, so well-timed mid-on started jogging back to retrieve the ball from the boundary before it was past him. Enid and Corin then swapped three singles between them leaving Corin on strike on 91, within single figures of a fanciful century that might have been dreamed up by an author better suited to fantasy novels. Corin tried not to think about the nervous nineties, the previous over's exploits still a fresh drumbeat against her heart, the penultimate ball a wide yorker she couldn't reach and not called a wide. For the final ball of the over, Chad attempted a slower ball bouncer which Corin was up for, swivelling back and cracking a low six that almost killed the square leg umpire, rising like a fighter jet as it reached him then continuing to clear deep square and dent the billboard. The problem was when Corin looked behind her, one of the bails was on the floor and

Stanni was furiously appealing to the umpire in a puckered heap on the floor as he raised his finger from a seated position. Corin figured she might have slipped on the green surface and tickled the stumps with the back of her spikes but couldn't be sure. When she looked across at Enid she knew as Enid shook her head, having kept her eyes on her sister rather than the six that wasn't. It was heartbreaking to watch Corin walk off, but the standing ovation drowned out Chad's Flintoff celebration, thrusting his crotch out and standing decussate, his arms raised and legs splayed, waiting for his team to surround him and elevate him in exaltation. They took a little longer than normal to reach him this time around.

Four big Shackleton scalps under the belt with one in A&E, so really five down, Chad rediscovered his mojo and, in celebration, rewarded Chuck by bringing him on from James's near-death experience end, the total and paltry batting in the Shaky chamber an instant relief for Chad who felt he could reach the total on his own. Noel sauntered in, waving at the crowd given any opportunity, while Chad subtly pushed the field out to permit the single. Chuck's first ball allowed Enid to play the ball into any of the vacant death traps and she played this one down to third man which Noel took as his cue to call her through for the single as it was behind square so well within his rights as the non-striker. Initially she sent him back, her glove raised, but his eagerness to bat was unquenchable so she trotted through for the single. Noel's first ball, he took a whoosh at a wide one which missed his bat by a mile then he made out it was a leave. The next ball he flat batted back to Chuck who angrily shied back at his stumps only to ping Noel on the ankle with no apology and no hopping from Noel who remained determined to win the mind games. He could feel the welt rise with soft pliable skin spilling over the side of his boot as it swelled, exhorting him to casually lean down and retie his laces, looser this time.

The next ball he got hold of, middled from middle, a swipe across the line that went to cow corner for four. That was more like it, so he played the same shot to a ball nibbling outside off, this one looping over the vacant slip cordon for another boundary. This batting gig is pretty simple, Noel thought before another fresh air waft, connecting his pads to seal the over which Stanni fumbled, allowing the pair to zap through for a leg bye, the timeworn umpire almost overbalancing when lifting his leg to signal.

Chad kept himself on and Noel couldn't wait to face him, salivating at the prospect of introducing Sir Chad to his special brand of nuanced, uncoachable technique. The first three balls of Chad's over were old school, pre-playing-against-girls-in-a-final-at-Lord's Chad but ultimately lost on Noel, two inswingers followed by a leg cutter to generate the edge only generating a huge swipe that would have missed the ball even if it hadn't jagged away toward first slip. Noel still looked proud of himself though and Chad felt he needed to dumb down this spell as he wasn't bowling to team Hanratty anymore and a simple on-stumps-hit-stumps might account for this number 10 bat masquerading as a number 7. It did. Nothing more than a straight ball wobble seam that nibbled about saw the end of Noel's optimistic innings and Chad's second wicket. Chad, now brimming with swagger, considered bowling himself through to wrap up the tail and get Shackleton all out before their allotted 50 overs, leaving their ailing captain stranded without a partner.

The kid who walked in next was from Wales named Gwyndaf, his small steps taking an eternity to reach Enid. To Chad these were his lambs to the slaughter and the crowd sensed a gross mismatch, getting the slow clap going on the bowler's approach, the abject, freckled face beneath the fortified helmet likely with eyes wide shut. Straight shooting was the order of the day, Chad bowling a length 'net ball' which cascaded into off stump. Chad was on a hat-trick and the Shackleton innings, so promising throughout, looked like it might falter at the final hurdle. The next person in was another boy, this one Irish from Lower Sixth named Gary to tally up the Celtic representation and taller than Gwyndaf, but not by much. His stride was more purposeful then, within ninety seconds, he was heading back the way he'd arrived, Chad taking an easy slower ball caught and bowled, the French cricket they'd wanted to play in the warm-up on display for all to see. Chad dropped to his knees after the wicket, a Lord's hat-trick in a final immortalising him FOREVER, wiping whatever leadership yips he might have toyed with earlier and establishing his legacy right in front of this lucky crowd and for all television viewers, great and small. Corkridge were now going to win this match … handsomely and his hat-trick would be replayed in schools, bars, montages, movies, television series all over the world. He instructed everyone to move away from him so the camera could savour this special moment, remaining on his knees, his hands together in prayer, being grateful to whatever deity had bestowed these wonderful gifts upon him, the Captain Fantastic!

"Clodagh, I can die now, as I've seen it all!"

"Alright."

"Six sixes, Mankad, medical drama, unbelievable referrals, sibling partnerships, fast-fast bowling, bouncers, beamers, now this … the real pinnacle of cricket in my option … a hat-trick! And it had to be him, didn't it? Questionable tactics in patches but when it counted most he stepped up as captain of this team – Chat da le Lama – and only took a hat-trick!"

"That's all."

A gasp percolated across Lord's as Daughtry entered the fray. Her protective ensemble all moved in different directions as she strode, as though she was a transport camel eager to shake off the load and run free into the desert, leaving behind this obligation. A long handle was the tallest bat they could find for her but it felt too heavy, so she dragged it behind her, not wanting to devour the energy lugging it towards the crease. Coming in at number 10, she was put out that Wei Ping had usurped her on this occasion, although with ten overs remaining there was little chance to avoid the ignominy of either slot. Noel's pep talk of "Don't die" and "They should make that bowling illegal as someone could actually get hurt ... oh wait ... someone did!" did nothing to dispel the nerves but when he mentioned "No quick bowler in the world able to get it up at that noggin in the clouds HB, no matter what the track was doing," she felt better and inspired for about three seconds until 30,000 sets of hands clapped and clapped 60,000 eyes on her march out, some believing there were two people in her frame, one on the other's shoulders.

Daughtry was spared the indignity of facing the next ball as Chad's over was up and Chuck resumed from the other end to Enid, determined to keep strike. For the final two balls of the over the field came in so Enid bunted one over the cover region but only took the single, leaving Daughtry to face the final ball of the over from Chuck. Taking guard looked laboured enough as she could barely lean down to mark her stance with the bat, so used her spike instead. Daughtry bent her legs as far as they could muster as there was little doubt what this ball was going to be. Chuck fired in a decent inswinging yorker which Daughtry was able to dig out, even squatting further as she sought a run which was declined by Enid.

Chad's tail was so up if someone had tied a balloon to it, he would have floated away and Enid had the additional burden of shielding Daughtry from any bowler, let alone Chad, but knew at some point it was inevitable. After her first ball yorker successfully negotiated, Daughtry looked ready to get those levers windmilling. Chad's first ball was carefully watched then with the second Enid gave herself room, Chad following her down the leg, so she once again played the Chinese cut through the legs for two runs. The next ball she got out the yummy on the eye drive and drove through the covers, but the fielder got a hand on it to restrict to two runs. For the remainder of the over Chad made it impossible for Enid to reach the ball, one swinging down leg side and a wide yorker on the off, neither called a wide. Enid's restraint spilled for once, raising her palm to the umpire who shrugged it off, even calling the over one ball short after five balls, to ensure Chuck had a crack at Daughtry.

Chuck tried another yorker to Daughtry first up which she was equal to, then went short which only seemed to get to about her lower ribcage, as she got beautifully behind the ball to play a defensive stroke which the crowd enjoyed. The next ball came back at her and rapped her on the top flap of her pad, the ball so high no one even bothered to appeal although the umpire might have given it anyway. Then came Daughtry's moment with bat in hand – to a full inswinger she elegantly slid her feet out of the way and played a leg glance off the toes for four, her timing impeccable and long reach to the floor nice and fluid. The crowd's new darling had served up a single-morsel treat and there was nothing cricket fans appreciated more than a quick bowling tailender playing a proper cricket stroke. The next ball she defended admirably, pushing one down off her hips and the final ball of the over saw an easy single turned down instantly by both batswomen.

Chad took a bit longer to elect but eventually kept himself on, even though this would be his ninth and penultimate over. He just needed to muzzle Enid, keep her quiet this over then chop off the tail and throw in the recycling bin the following overs. He really wanted a crack at Daughtry so left huge single gaps in the field – easy runs that would be difficult to spurn. The first few balls were simply good balls that were easy singles but which Enid refused, then it became about how far Chad could bend the rules until a wide was called, a bouncer ending up a few feet above Enid's head without ducking. The second last ball of the over was an above waist high full toss way outside off stump that caught Enid by surprise, so much so that she missed it but so did Stanni, gloving it behind him enough for Daughtry to call Enid through for the run, one ball remaining. Chad had been waiting two overs for this opportunity and didn't waste it, nipping one up the slope to catch a valiant straight bat from Daughtry, Stanni hyena cackling even before he'd taken the catch. Daughtry's heroics were over, but the runs Enid had been able to accumulate while she held up her end were invaluable at this stage and given there was only Wei Ping to bat. Enid knew he was NEVER going to miss this opportunity but feared despite the most ardent optimism, she had to go huge the next over and, frankly, Shackleton were one ball away from being done and dusted.

At the end of the 44th over, Shackleton were 284-8, so Chad thanked the cricketing Gods for their extended practical joke but ultimate mercy in ending these shenanigans before they got to 300. Two girls appeared at the exit door of the Long Room, one with her head heavily bandaged leaning on the other who guided her down the steps and onto the field, letting her go gently like a carrier pigeon. The crowd clocked who it was but not all at once, a gasping undulation as Rebecca ran onto the field, stepping in front of Lauren to hug her around the shoulders before she went back to face the death metal. Chuck spotted Rebecca first without fully comprehending, then hurried Chad to retrieve the ball so he could ready himself for another onslaught.

"Again," Chad mouthed as the noisy clapping crescendoed up until there was no discernible slap on palm, just a constant swell of deferential espousal.

"Abso*******lutely!"

Larry had passed the HIA … only just, the medical practitioner on site almost putting his foot down as the cognitive responses were not all as they should be. She'd taken a boat load of Ibuprofen as her head did hurt something horrible, but behind her eyes still ached and the area where the helmet had jolted hardest on the side of her skull was numb to the touch and liable to explode if tickled by a feather.

"I don't even want to ask," began Enid. "But are you okay?"

"I'll have mine with a side of fries, thanks so much my captain of industry; do birds usually fly upside down?" responded Lauren looking skywards.

"Good to have you back!"

"Completely my fault! I was slow; if my brothers are watching I'll never hear the end."

"Not many cricketers get baseball beamers from jealous ex-boyfriend psychos first up; I think you did quite well to header it using the grill – skills in the vills."

"Let's get to 300, then bust out da rhymes, shall we?"

"Larry," said Enid stopping her from leaving by holding the shoulders. "You really don't have to follow through here: walk back off, no harm done, everyone gets what happened to you. They'll come harder at you again now, that's how they roll. Is your health and wellbeing worth all this?"

"Enid, this is the only way I know how – where I'm from there is no option to give-up or back down. Even if I felt like it a teeny, weeny bit, there is just no way I would know how."

"He's bowling around the wicket to you."

When Larry took guard, her thighs felt wobbly, her bottom lip drooped, the pounding in her head ripened into a looping drum solo, the ends of her fingers tingled and she realised in all the mayhem she needed a tinkle.

"Bit pathetic it led to all this hullabaloo," she thought to herself. "Just hurry up and bring it!"

As Chuck hurried in, she opened her stance and leaned over without collapsing, ready for another beamer, so getting into position to get outside the line. If the ball was a beamer but misdirected away from her head on the off, she could always upper-cut it over deep point. There was no beamer but a vicious bouncer outside Larry's eyeline that lifted, aiming directly for her head once again. She went back onto her heels, now unable to duck so chose to launch into the air, aching her back spectacularly, lifting her right ear to the sun. The ball skimmed her helmet's trifling peak, unerringly as a photographer captured her elevation, both heels almost touching her backside and the ball - an oversized rigid clown's nose - passing inches from her face. She landed on her haunches and stayed there breathing heavily as Chuck followed through to remind her of her earlier 'mishap'. Chuck persisted around the wicket, conspiring with the umpire to afford Lauren no further rest time, the arm going down without her stance being set, this ball delivered from a lower slingy position directly at her head ... the beamer's higher budget, less worthy sequel. This beamer though was what Lauren was waiting for and plucked it from in front of her nose for a monster six. Enid pumped an innocuous fist down towards the pitch then looked at the umpire presumptuously, the ball not called a no-ball for being above waist height. Lauren was dizzier and almost fell over, but Shaky had another maximum!

For the next couple of balls, Chuck reverted to the most bent arm he'd ever deployed, the masses still dining out on the six, which dragged the puff from Chuck's sails as his attempts to generate more pace did only that, the throwing style unable to harness the guile, swing, seam and variations requisite at this stage of the match. Chad came on to bowl his final over, mustering all scheming and skill to whittle out the last two wickets but coming up empty handed, the final delivery dispatched by Enid past his floundering right boot. The boundary brought Shackleton's team total above the three hundred mark to 302-8, with four overs remaining and Enid on 79 runs. Chad lapped up the warm applause for his six-for, putting his cap on then removing it again in succession to brandish it at the crowd while his hair refused to settle down, the humidity puffing it out at the sides so much so that when he caught a shufty of it on the big screen he kept his cap firmly on.

With four overs left the girls targeted the next two to bunt and run, Larry confident that her legs could carry her, even though unable to run in a straight line. Chuck's ninth went largely to plan, six singles with two cheeky steals to the keeper, Stanni hitting with the second but Larry safe enough to avoid an ensuing Out from square leg and DRS. Neethaniel Labour came in with the usual demonic verve, hitting the turf hard but seemingly annoyed Chad sufficiently by going off script to warrant Neethaniel Conservative to warm up for the final over.

At the 49th over's outset - Chuck's final six pitches - Shackleton were 316-8 with Enid on 85 and Larry with an indominable 14. Cricket can be the cruellest of mistresses often without the princess in the tower kicking the prince's ass, embodied by Chuck's first ball - a full awayswinger heading for the base of off stump, that Larry looked to reverse sweep. With the additional pace generated from the skew arm, she was just too late on the shot, the ball thudding into her back pad firmly enough to then rebound off the edge during her follow through, back towards Chuck in the process of going up for the LBW appeal. Upon seeing the ball spooning up towards him, he abandoned the appeal and lengthened his stride to make a meal of diving for a ball that probably could have been pouched upright, but the unmistakably crisp bat sound without the ball anywhere near the ground meant Larry was gone. Chuck celebrated his first wicket of a tough day at the office by giving her a send-off, then taking an ersatz bite out of the ball, spitting the stray chunk of apple back at Larry, the sophistication whether this was a biblical message questioned for months thereafter. Rebecca was waiting in the same place she dropped Larry off and, as she collapsed into Rebecca's arms, Wei Ping came vaulting past them, a full-blooded spring onto Lord's, the crowd buoying the foray with a "Heeeeeyyyyyyyyyyy!"

Wei Ping's face was a divergence of blustered eagerness and complete self-belief, the antagonistic fielders looking him up and down as though he didn't belong out on the numinous turf at Lord's ... at all. But he knew he did - this was where he belonged ... right now and, of course, he had a plan. Enid held out a fist to greet him which he missed.

"I've got it all planned," he bestowed upon Enid. "I'm going to move around the crease to upset Chuck's line then target the vacant cow region then maybe a ramp shot and a drive over the ring. It's likely I will secure us a few boundaries at least, but be ready for any runs against my name!"

"Just get your body between ball and stumps with your bat dangling anywhere in that trajectory," said Enid, noticing he was holding the bat with the blade facing out. "If it's not near the stumps - which I highly doubt - run! I'll call you through."

"Captain Enid, I make you this solemn promise on all my honour ... I will not go out; I will be with you at the end."

"Eleven balls ... we can still do some damage."

Wei Ping took guard on what looked like off stump, the bat's blade still facing so Enid signalled for him to turn it the correct way. He laughed and placed his glove on Peter's ill-fitting helmet, dropping the bat so it dislodged the stumps, the umpire agitatedly stepping in to rearrange. He stuck out a glove to shake the keeper's hand saying, "Good match so far, eh?" only to be dismissed as Stanni stood up to the wickets scuppering the stolen run plan, so he approached the nearby fielders for a fist bump, all of whom left him hanging, some muttering slurs in the puerile realm of "We Pong today."

Chuck's first ball to Wei Ping looked as though it grazed the top of off stump, Stanni taking a sharp stop-catch standing up to the stumps as the bail wobbled back into its groove without lighting up. The appeal was stifled as Wei Ping's bat came through so far after the ball had reached the keeper, it was almost back in Chuck's hand again at the supposed moment of impact. The umpire looked away, praying not to be in the conundrum of giving out followed by an easy referral and made to look even more like a clown versus the explanation to Chad's dad. Chuck dug the next one in, Wei Ping almost catching the ball with his body, the ball rising to hit him in the chest which saw him drop the bat, clutch at the ball and fall on his face, smothering the ball beneath him as the fielding side willed him to stand up and check the ball was still alive. Chuck's fourth ball was full and straight, and Wei Ping spectacularly got his feet out of the way, appearing to do a handstand on the vertical bat which miraculously was in the ball's line, spinning the bat and squirting to the vacant short square leg region. Wei Ping landed like a maladroit gymnast, his eyes lighting up down the track towards Enid at the prospect of his first run. For a breath Enid hesitated as she'd only have two balls to face before the next over but the prospect of giving Wei Ping a run after all he'd done to espouse the team since the activation of the Shaky XI was too great, so she jogged through while Wei Ping went past her, both hands in the air, no bat in sight and junketing beyond the bowler's crease. Chuck's fifth ball was a mile wide yorker - not called - then the field came in, so Enid popped it over the ring for an easy single.

Neethaniel right-arm over was about to bowl the final over of the Digners Cup final, Shackleton Senior on a commendable 318-9, Enid on the dreaded Aussie bogey number of 87 versus Corkridge Castle School for Boys (and girls). At the tail end of Enid's marathon innings there was nothing left to do but throw willow at ball, her measured accumulation interspersed with some critical strokeplay adjudged during pivotal phases, would render this an innings for the purists, irrespective of what transpired off the final six balls. The first ball was an out of reach bouncer that looped over her head, not called a wide, the second the same so Enid rose into the air to slap the ball, a one-handed tennis ball smash and still she couldn't reach it. No wide called. For the third ball he came around the wicket, bowling the ball outside the side of the crease - another no-ball not called - the ball pitching a foot outside leg and sailing over the stumps, Enid unable to meet the anomalous angle. This was getting ridiculous, so she took a deep breath and thought back to all the weird and wonderful deliveries her dad had unleashed on them as young girls, the spirit of the game's fun filling her veins as the crowd voiced their discontent at the tactics and dodgy officiating. The third last ball of the match was the same wide of the crease delivery, Enid getting down on one knee to play a crouched hook off her left shoulder, a formidable one bounce four that got the crowd to their feet. Neethaniel switched back to over the wicket for the next ball, attempting a wide ball worker but Enid came walking up the pitch and met the ball on the full to hit the rarest of cricketing sixes over extra cover, as she moved onto 97, one ball remaining. Enid dared to dream for merely a gulped lungful, of scoring an actual century at Lord's, Wei Ping's determined face the other end to spur her on to greatness. Chad and Neethaniel remonstrated before the latter snatched the ball and steamed in, eager to finish this over and the Shackleton innings. The ball hightailed one last time, a wide bouncer, but again Enid had sauntered up the pitch, this excursion more to the off side in anticipation. She got high enough to slap it down in front of square but without fully middling, so the batters set off for the first two runs as deep square and cow corner converged on the ball. At the turn for the third run, James had the ball in his hand, cocking to fire it in at the keeper's end, Wei Ping lagging behind Enid's headway. Enid looked up as James's strong arm released the ball with vituperation, safe in the knowledge that Wei Ping would be run out. Wei Ping turned for the third and was willing but Enid held her hand up, stranded on 99 not out but not willing to burden her teammate against his wishes of staying in until the very end. The ball came in and Stanni broke the stumps in frustration as the Shackleton innings came to a dramatic close. Wei Ping ran over to hug Enid, spouting, "I'm not out! They didn't get me out! Knew they couldn't rattle me! I'm not out at Lord's!" as Enid stumbled into his meagre embrace, exhausted from her exploits to the point where she was suddenly struggling for breath. Wei Ping let go of her to continue his celebration and she collapsed onto her pads. No one from Corkridge came to stick out a congratulatory paw or help her up.

"330-9 Clodagh! That's a decent total but likely falls short against this Corkridge batting line-up?"

"It is a power unit that bats deep, Ramsay, but let's just take a moment to savour this batting performance and, more importantly, this innings – a masterclass of poise, technique, judgement, hitting and game management. What a warrior!"

"That 99 will irk her some though? One away! Could've made it?"

"There was no third run on offer … at all. She chose team over her own glory; just take a look at what it means to her teammate and super-sub Wei Ping Tan …"

"He's not stopped celebrating, has he?! He's high fiving the entire perimeter of front row seats now."

»

"Weez gotz ourselves a total to chase! I mean its preferable we didn't and it's not unfair to say our, uh, your bowling was some way below par but maybe it's about time we had something meaty to chase. While I was taking hat-tricks you were letting a girls' team put 300 plus on us, so the only way to eradicate that from the annals of human history is to wipe that smile off their faces and chase this target down relentlessly like a fox in the woods. Be bloodhounds today ... sniff them out, hunt them down and rip them out of their hidey-holes by their bushy tails! Gentlemen, this is going to require a team effort for once ... not just me picking up all your slack, but rest assured if we lose this game ... its going on your tombstones."

»

"We find ourselves in this incredible situation. We've all had different journeys to get here and different reasons to want to win, but our collective solidarity remains the same. Know that whatever you decide to do out there will be backed. There's no getting more out of each of you through a few words of bluster. I've seen you play cricket; I've played alongside each of you, and I'm just simply relieved to have you all by my side as we go again. However you decide to go up to that next level of your ability is up to you ... be it digging deeper, taking a risk, laughing off a niggle, using the intel, shrugging off a boundary, misfield or dropped catch, or standing tall when a Corky boy stands over you with a bat in his hands seeming taller; do it for you, your family, your friends, your values, your integrity, your team. I've already got so much ... and more."

The Shackleton team came together in a tight huddle, the tightest bind any scrum coach would be proud of. No one said anything, they just held the circle, ineptly holding back the tears as the roar of the crowd awoke them from gripping slumber, the second innings about to commence as the umpires made their way out and the balcony doors shook as 30,000 decanted, watered, nourished cricket fans willed the Shackleton XI out to take up their positions.

The plan was to open with Daughtry from the Nursery End and Corin from the Pavilion End, letting the slopes contradict each's stock ball: Daughtry's in drift would go down the slope towards the slips and Corin's natural awayswing would come back down the opposite slope. George Mildew and Harrison Plodkin were out in the middle shortly after Enid had set an attacking field, two robotic doppelgangers with identical ticks, gestures, air shots and authority. Shackleton felt if they could nip one out early, the other opener would follow suite, getting the likes of Chad and Yannos facing the new ball.

Play began and Daughtry loped in, a loosener disguised as a long hop that George let go through to the keeper, less threatening than anything dished up by Corkridge on that pitch to date. Claps, energy, caterwauls, and encouragement followed as they all got behind HB. The occasion was a big deal and proved a bit too much for poor Daughtry at the outset of her spell, plopping innocuous ball after ball that just slid down the slope, looping and popping into Larry's gloves rather than filling the palm padding with a venomous thud. She looked close to tears, but no boundaries had been chased, small nudges and technically proficient opening batsmen shots to unclip the shackles of the scoreboard rather than shatter them. Corin in contrast was doing too much with the ball, her opening over looking as though there was little possibility of the batter getting any bat on ball, the slope and her pace almost telegraphing where the ball would reach the crease and with little danger of disturbing the stumps.

Corin resisted going too full as she knew these openers could drive and the over would have been a maiden but for the four byes that took off from middle over first slip. Daughtry's second over was marginally better than the first with a bit of zip appearing but the score continued to accumulate as the openers grew in stature with an increasingly sussed measure of the pitch and the attack. Corin's second was borne from frustration, so she pushed some of her quick leg cutters too full allowing George to score Corkridge's first bat-induced boundary. Enid had seen enough and promptly took her sister out of the attack; there was no ideal length Corin could hit with the new ball doing more than anticipated, changing ends potentially creating even more extreme movement off the seam. Bringing Noel on seemed to calm Daughtry who found a nifty patch of tight cat-and-mouse with George who looked troubled at times even if Daughtry was yet to unleash anything vitriolic, none of her short deliveries getting above bellybutton height. Noel's first over was a maiden, also tight but somehow unthreatening as the crowd got restless and distracted at the lack of spectacle, Corkridge plodding to 20 without loss after six overs, Shackleton's bowling bravado some way behind their batting's histrionics.

At the start of the seventh over - Daughtry's fourth - the intended cause and effect caused but didn't effect. Daughtry finally got one to lift, digging it in shorter than anything served up already, the bounce looping past Harrison's chest as he swayed out of the way and the umpires called it a wide. Her next ball was inside the markings as it passed the crease, but flopped down the slope with Larry taking a diving catch in front of first slip and another wide was called. Enid's protest took place in earshot of Daughtry's whose shoulders acquired more worldly weight with each delivery, her inability to contribute to the team more prominent than the mediocre balls crookedly called wides. The last two balls of her over both went for boundaries, one pull behind square and another back foot guide past a diving Onka at point, both

George, unveiling the first expensive over of the innings.

"Please take me off," Daughtry said to Enid, wiping the already smudged tears from her jawline. "I can't do this; I just don't have what it takes."

"This is not about whether you do or don't have what it takes - you clearly do; this is about getting everything you're doing with your body in sync through accepting that you're meant to be here, you're a fantastic bowler and this team needs you. Think back to all those spells when you just clicked ... away from the crowds, just you and the ball, putting it in the right place. You're one cracking ball away from this right now ... I can see it," Enid said, wondering if 85% belief and 15% doubt meant you were actually a false teller of tales.

"Please just let me take a break?"

"How about this - one more over? You put everything you have into those six balls and then, if you want, you can chill at fine leg the rest of the match, but those six balls are going to be remembered. I don't care where you put the ball or what you do with your wrist or the grip, I just want the ball to hit the pitch or the batsman as hard as you've ever hit anything in your life! Okay?"

"Okay. Six balls. Then I'm done."

"No matter what."

Noel sensed something was up with Daughtry and chose to bowl his next over too full in the hope that these batsmen would be prone to getting forward to aid HB's one short ball that was about to emerge from the shadows of self-doubt. Enid, Onka and Corin clocked what he was up to after the third ball was driven for an easy four straight down the ground, and nodded in approval, Enid pushing mid-off and mid-on back now that the Powerplay's fielding restrictions were complete. The remainder of the over was expensive without conceding a boundary, the protection cutting off fours in exchange for cosy twos as the batters settled. After eight overs, Corkridge were 38-0 as word reached Enid that the requested heavy roller had not been used - in fact no roller had been used after an inexplicable instruction from somewhere - going some way to elucidate the benign nature of the pitch this innings.

Daughtry's first ball was a straight long hop that got spanked for four immediately through mid-wicket, George now likely flicking the switch to get going and push the run rate up in anticipation of the explosive batting to come. A solid start was what Dr Chad had ordered and by gawd a solid start was what they were delivering. George took the uncharacteristic step to emulate Chad's fortune-telling haughtiness, pointing towards cow corner to indicate where the next ball was headed. Daughtry, never willing or able to abandon her accommodating and genteel nature, dutifully looked towards where George was pointing, not fully understanding the implication until she reached her mark. Her run-up that ball, although not the finished article in any contrair manner, was a half gear shift up in co-ordination alone, the first delivery where she had a semblance of fluidity. The ball looked to be fading to leg again, then straightened up the slope and clonked George on the pads, going back to cut despite the boast of the slam over cow's throat. It looked a decent shout and Daughtry aberrantly led the appeal, skipping into the air. The umpire, appearing to have dozed off, awoke with a jolt and instantly shook his head belching, "Not out! Now calm down!"

Enid consulted Larry who confirmed their joint concern about height but Daughtry was insistent it was out, still indignant at being told to calm down for what was really just a mildly fervid leap with conviction. With only two reviews, Enid had to make a snap decision between a dismissal that felt Not Out and breaking the team's rut to get their bowling innings underway for real. She was conscious of umpire's call sparing the review but had watched enough referrals on television to know that tall bowlers and height almost always lost reviews, the ball tracking over the stumps and "Review Lost" appearing to a dejected Broad, Morkel or Starc. With three seconds left of the countdown, she backed her opening bowler and signalled for the review. Front foot was (just) okay, the third umpire checking this relentlessly to confirm a bulge of boot rubber behind the worn line, and the easy one of pitching outside off was a forgone conclusion. The ball tracker showed George hit in line, so that too was red with only the point of impact remaining as the screen glitched at the moment of truth and everybody let out a collective groan.

Pitching ... In Line.

Impact ... In Line.

Wickets ... Umpire's Call!

The dreaded amber warning accompanied the ruling, where the centre of the ball struck just outside the area delineated by a line drawn below the lower edge of the bails and down the middle of the outer stumps, possibly 49% inside on the x and y axes. The review was retained but Daughtry refused to accept this was the authentic outcome, muttering to herself and anyone within ear shot as she returned to her mark. All eyes were fixed on her for her third ball despite Noel's best efforts to gesticulate eating popcorn out of an imaginary cinema box in anticipation of the show to follow; and Daughtry didn't fail to deliver. Her run-up, smoother than twice refined peanut butter, fluxed along the ground's surface, ghosting towards her delivery stride, then a full ball that got right up without a hint of the floatiness that had blighted her earlier balls, pinging George flush on the elbow - the funny bone, not so funny for George as he dropped his bat and himself, hugging his knees rocking on the floor as he cupped his left elbow, stopping short of screaming for an enforced amputation to remove the pain. Daughtry's benevolent nature sought to check he was alright until a firm forearm from Rufus ushered her back to deliver more of the same please.

The next ball was the whip Yapa had been searching for all season, the long arm of Daughtry's law dissecting dead straight down the pitch, lovely and high, zipping in back up the slope to fold George into the folds of a compressed concertina, the only indication that the ball wasn't buried somewhere within him, the reassuring, warm sounding thump into the keeper's gloves, Larry a good foot off the ground when taking the ball, instantly ushering the slips back and asking Enid for another. Following up with anything worthy would be nothing short of a phenomenon, yet Daughtry bowled the same ball from the same decadent height only with more whip and wrist and, if the erstwhile delivery cut George in half, this samurai sworded his entire torso, his legs appearing to kick up aerobics style, hitting the top of his handle and lodging underneath his grill. His nose didn't quite bleed, but created an unmistakable Rudolph glow, lighting the way for any teammates brave enough to follow him from the North Pole and directly into Daughtry's hostile line. George got through the over quite literally by the skin of his teeth, the final ball an almost overpitched delivery that rose from an impossible angle to strike George on the underside of his grill – no handle to slow this one down – so much so that he bit down, slicing a feather of tongue off and chipping a sliver of his front tooth before seeking solace in the middle with his guy-pal Harrison.

"Ready to come off then?" asked Enid, clapping as she ran past Daughtry.

"I'm anti-violence and certainly anti-guns but I'll give you the ball when you take it from my cold, dead hands," responded Daughtry, doffing her cap.

Noel continued left-arm over but couldn't quite get his length right immediately as the ball wasn't swinging much, Daughtry paving the seam and bounce path as the fielders legally worked on the ball. Harrison's continued rotation brought George on strike, determined to stay that end. Harrison motioned for quick singles but George was more likely to dive face first into a field of stinging nettles than return to face Daughtry and ended up lazily chasing a low bouncing wide ball to get a thick edge through to Jacob at first slip. Noel followed through with the aeroplane celebration to celebrate Shackleton's first wicket of the Digners Cup final, the melancholic doughnut in the wickets columns updating with a protrusive '1', the score 47-1 after ten overs.

The team gathered in a mini-huddle, giddy with excitement, Noel adamant that Daughtry had done nothing to claim credit for him getting her bunny out, even though, she knew precisely that any mocked admonishment from the mouth of Señor Pothas was a deeply veiled compliment. He held his hand out for a low five and she still fell for it, whooshing past his palm as he shimmied away, her good-natured chuckle a million miles from the bowling destroyer and chief six balls earlier. A wicket in cricket has that uncanny ability to lift spirits, speed up walking in, remove fielders' hands from thighs and increase the commotion, the chat, the umph and oomph, all of which Shaky now exhumed, determined to keep it up for as long as it took to take another wicket and acquire that fix all over again.

James Smith-Franklin barrelled in over the Lord's turf, a surprise as Shackleton were expecting Yannos Dalrymple, unaffectionately unknown in cricket circles as 'Brad'. James's bat looked like an oversized club, the only thing missing from his ensemble an unconscious cavewoman being dragged behind him by her hair. Whatever destruction or intimidation he had planned, he'd have to wait for at least a ball while Daughtry took aim at Harrison from the other end. Daughtry picked up where she left off the previous over, troubling Harrison with each ball to the point where he got ironic cheers for any bat on ball, a fortuitous leading edge that squirted past cover for two after intending to work it through the leg side. Such was the combative fight in James, he wanted to only take the single and be in position to take Daughtry on, but the run got called through by the balcony, Chad not willing to sacrifice a single run even if to reinforce an already steady ego. Might have been folly though as the next ball Chad was making his way off the balcony to enter the battlefield, Harrison getting trapped LBW in front from one that tailed back up the slope but kept low, missing the seam. The shout looked dead for all money - plumber than the depths Corkridge would go to to win this match - but of course not given. Daughtry did not even wait for Enid's blessing, signalling for the review herself, her two elongated forearms meeting perpendicularly like the tangled wings of a Quetzalcoatlus. It did not take long for the three red dots to send Harry packing and, as Daughtry walked back to her mark with the esteemed honour of bowling the first ball to the Corky captain, the umpire rubbernecked down at his own shoes, unable to face up to yet another dubious decision.

Chad coming out to bat was like witnessing something commemorative, for the ages, many of the crowd with phones capturing the moment - all portrait which would have irritated Chad if he'd have noticed. Chad's batting stats for the season and his career were obscene, antagonising Bradman's final innings led failure to well exceed three figures, a record he intended to build upon as he entered the senior ranks. You see as good a bowler as Chad was, the money shot nowadays more so than the old days was batting. The big IPL and CSA T20 money, the awards, the man of the match, the captaincy and the general adulation, kudos and respect always lay with the batsman. Chad knew that flinging a ball down in weird and wonderful and fruitful ways had its own cult and certainly supported his real prowess, but with willow in hand was where he was captain of his industry, armed and taking his name, like Bradman, to be heralded by

'The' so that all the world knew The Chad could be only one sportsperson on the planet. He'd initiated a hashtag (#TheChad) previously only to be told that The Don was an abbreviation, hence adopting #TheCha which didn't really suit the direction he was headed or wanted to head. With each step towards the middle his aura glowed brighter, illuminating all who had the courage to point their eyes in his direction, the closest to cricketing omnipotence many had witnessed as lifelong cricket and Lord's fans.

This was his house and no way a girls' team was bringing their brand of whingeing cricket to dethrone The Chad ... #NotInMyHouse.

With Harrison – true to prophesy – joining George back in the pavilion, two new batsmen assembled out in the middle at Lord's, undeniably Corkridge's top two in the line-up and perhaps forever. Out in the middle it was a cauldron, yet Chad and James lapped it up, two accomplished prizefighters waiting for the smorgasbord of circling creatures to try something. Daughtry had a lone ball remaining, Chad facing and, despite bowling what looked like her best ball of the day – a menacing length that got a hint of swing away but seamed up the slope – Chad nonchalantly got high off his toes and drove the ball mid-air for a stylish four. That shut the Shaky-supporting crowd up for now and took the smallest fart out of Shaky's sails as Noel and Daughtry still dined out on swapping opening batter targets as Enid tried to pull everyone back to the real double threats that snarled at each end.

With Corkridge 67-2 after 13 overs, it became clear that James was fed up with nudging, stopping his shots and being Chad's bridesmaid to help rotate the strike, Noel sent back over his head for Corkridge's first six of the final. It wasn't a timed big six but more of a blunt force trauma six that landed in no man's land between the first row of seats and the advertising billboards, Chad giving him the air fist bump, not bothering to run as was always the case when James went 'postal'. James possessed technique but opted for brutality, the hips open and confidence high enough that his eye was in and the bowling innocuous enough to hit through the line with impunity. Noel was not happy, his perpetual cheeky-chappie grin wiped off his face like removing Mr Potato Head's mouth altogether, his pursed puckered lips lost on his face. Peril loomed, predominantly in the chunk of willow brandished by Corky's number 3 for the day bat, yet this was no deterrent for Noel, the fight he'd been wanting to pick his whole life. His next ball went across James, defying the slope to zip up it as James took a wilder swipe at this one, getting enough on it to nick over the slips for four, the bowler's moral victory no solace for the damage to the scoreboard. Noel was now searching for something more than was spouting from his wrist, so the next ball came from an odd angle around the wicket, wider than James expected so he stopped the shot, the ball pitching outside off and clean bowling him, Larry coolly catching one of the bails as it tumbled towards her. James shook his head then then screamed, first at Noel then the umpire, while Noel continued to celebrate albeit in a muted fashion.

"He's bowled that ball with his right arm!" James continued to remonstrate at the umpire, as the words became audible.

The umpire glared at Noel whose innocence would have held a thick chunk of butter in his mouth that whole time without a hint of melted warmth dribbling down the sides of his tongue.

"Young man," the umpired barked. "Did you bowl that ball with your right arm?"

Noel knew there was no other option than truth as any continuance of the scheme would be checked and reflect badly, not only on Shackleton's integrity but his own honesty. Bowling the ball with a different arm was one thing, lying about it was another.

"Yes," responded Noel without any culpability. "Is that not allowed?" he asked embracing the 'new to cricket' ignorance.

"No, young man, it is not," spat the umpire. "That's a dead ball!"

"It's not … Sir," added Chad. "It's a no-ball. Free hit."

"Yes, or course," the umpire concluded, brandishing the horizontal 'you're crazy' version of the circling helicopter with his rigid finger.

Enid sidled up towards Noel, "This was something we were holding back, right? You have to declare right or left-arm to the umpire first."

"I know," said Noel. "I'm sorry … impulsive frustration got the better of me … and I didn't know the implication was a no-ball."

"Don't sweat it; fine to try stuff, let's just keep it ... within the laws."

"I'll make this right."

James was loading up for the no-ball, the sparks from a space launch splattering around his feet, as Noel informed the umpire he'd be continuing right-arm around the wicket, to which the umpire retorted there was no 'continuance'. Noel's slingy action followed the same path mechanics but this ball was thrown up, a juicy full toss that James was going to smack the leather off of, until he didn't. The ball was some form of slower ball, likely knuckle or back of the hand, that started at James's eyeline then died and dipped as he swung wildly, clean bowling him … again; a dot ball on a no-ball making some amends from the previous show of petulance.

"I'm on a hat-trick now," Noel couldn't resist jibing as he followed through under James's nose.

"Nice ball," said Corin as Noel ventured back to his mark. "Think you could do it again? It'd be the first ambidextrick in cricket!"

"And who says only boys get all the funny lines?"

Chad was looking fluid and untroubled, which prompted the introduction of right and left-arm leg spin to stem the tide, Corkridge sitting pretty on 90-2 after 15 overs. The ball turned extravagantly from the outset, so much so that, aided by the slope, there was a surfeit of wides from both bowlers, some unlucky to be called but the line could not be settled on even with sliders and flatter deliveries. Enid's were spinning down the slope from the Nursery End, some pitching outside leg stump and turning so far across the batsman, they'd have the luxury of watching it without playing a shot as the umpire went into albatross meets Christ mode the other end. Onka from the Pavilion End had the same yet inverse issue, his stock left-arm leggie going down the slope into the right-handers to be left as leg side wides, James able to sweep a few for boundaries. For the balls that did look like sniffing out a semblance of the stumps, Chad in particular was able to negate through his big front pad blocking any chance of connecting with LBWs safely off the table. Chad didn't go after Enid ... yet, and Enid held back anything with a hint of set-up variety as she wrestled with how to switch ends, falling back on Corin to warm up for the fill-in over. Between them, the spinners conceded eight extras in four overs - all wides - allowing Corkridge to keep the scoreboard ticking, reach the 100 team total and end the ninth over on 118-2, nicely in control of proceedings with Chad on 32 and James on 28, Shackleton's equivalent at this stage of their innings lagging on 105-2.

Up until now Rufus had been unobtrusive, out on the boundary, his broken left finger heavily strapped. With both batsmen looking increasingly untroubled and nearing half centuries, Rufus limped into the attack to bowl to his old captain first up, who tried to help him set the field for his bowling then fell about once Rufus and Enid had settled on most of the big boundaries blocked and only one slip. Chad didn't dilly-dally and duly hit two fours off the first two balls, one off the back foot, then off the front to bring up his fifty which he celebrated right in Rufus's face, taking longer than Lord's would have expected for a half-century, prompting a slow clap to get on with the match. James was salivating at the prospect of getting after Rufus and got his opportunity at the end of the over, a good length flat batted from deep in his crease towards the umpire's head at the other end, enough on it to decapitate the official, at minimum embed in his corrupt skull. Rufus, in the follow-through and more unbalanced from the effort ball, stuck his left hand out and clutched, the ball striking his bound broken finger so hard, a helpless yelp escaped from his lips as he fell, the ball ricocheting for four runs.

"That's the Shaky effect, my man," said Chad, looming over Rufus as he held his left hand close to his belly, hyperventilating. "You'd have not shelled that simple chance had you remained in the Corkridge fold. James thanks you though … he'll give you unique appreciation when he makes his ton."

"That's the hundred partnership between these vibrant, brimming, talented young men, Clodagh! Chaz de le Ampelast and James Smith-Franklin … what an outstanding performance under the circumstances."

"Let's spare a thought for the brave bowler Rufus, who stuck a paw out to try and catch that thunderbolt; and with a broken hand!"

"Indeed, what a soldier! They're carrying him off now—"

"You wouldn't know it though - the crowd still applauding the partnership! Are they doing a lap of honour?"

"Feels like the game is slipping away from Shackleton; might have already slipped if these two fine sportsmen kick on from here."

"It's going to require something special, that's for sure, miraculous even."

Cricketing tales are not cricketing tails nor are they fairy tales, the bounce of the ball or physics of a bat swing (not of the bowtie variety) not following sentiment, popularity or will, so it would be remiss to mention that at this alleged 'rock bottom' for Shaky, things got worse, a whole lot worse, the level of shakiness or adversity no one in the team had ever faced before. With Peter permitted to field as twelfth man for Rufus, the bowling rotation went Onka and Noel in tandem, bowling six collective overs, followed by a re-introduction of both Hanratty sisters. With each unrewarding ball and gap found, the Shaky heads drooped lower, a real sense of the game being done permeating across the team, despite everyone's best efforts to put on a brave face through hollow words of encouragement. And it wasn't that the bowling was bad, it's that the batting was superior without the bowling rhythm or nutty good delivery remarkable enough to pry out a wicket and send one of Chad or James packing. Onka bowled a tight line and length and got sound turn but the batsmen had this covered; he even set up the googly which Chad announced he'd seen out of the wrist a mile away and cut for four. Noel was getting impressive swing back into the right-handers with his left arm and across them with his right arm, but the variety only served to disrupt his line more that the batters as they feasted on errant deliveries throughout the spell. Neither bowler could be faulted for effort, strategising or skill - it was simply a case of masterclass batting on show for Lord's and a dejected fielding side. Even James felt he didn't need to get out the big shots, the canter of slow poison enough to drown Shaky in their own aspirations at the big boy's table. Corin and Enid's first over in tandem also failed to deliver the emotive 'sisters doing it for themselves' grandiloquence, both following suit to set up wicket taking balls and execute soundly, only to be scuppered by the cruelty that only cricket knows ... an inside edge ... a stopped shot ... a fielder drifting from position … a single in the ring … a harsh wide.

At the end of the 32nd over, Corkridge's score loomed on 206-2, Chad coasting on 84 and James teeming on 59, 108 balls remaining with only 125 runs to get, the required rate below seven with no sign of abating and eight equally willing batters to follow and potentially hit the winning runs at Lord's should either Chad or James be so kind as to relinquish that honour … not likely if they could bloody help it!

"Is this the end of all things, Clodagh?"

"My head says yes but my heart says no!"

"They've put up a good fight these girls – this team, but they've come up against a powerhouse cricketing institution, not easily dethroned."

"I detect a hint of sadness in your tone, Ramsay."

"You detect correct, Clodagh."

Corin the bowler, James the batsman as the business end of the competition approached, the 33rd over, a slight breeze darting between the thickets of seats becoming gustier as the sun hid for bursts, shy behind brisk clouds. Chad and James had taken a long time to pontificate this interval and Corin waited impatiently as James took a new guard on leg stump, such was his confidence that he was seeing the ball like a beachball. He smiled at Corin, a malevolent freeze-framed mouth, lest she forget that the chilly revenge for her six sixes embarrassment could and would come in whatever fashion he chose from now on, be it winning with overs to spare or completely ending the match with a fusillade of fatal whacks.

Corin's first ball got an ironic block, James in position almost before the ball had been bowled then, as if toying with her, mowed the remainder of the over for 17 runs, including a single off the last ball to retain strike, Chad reluctant to spend a whole seven balls off strike, yet dragged through as

James swapped words with Corin until the umpire stepped in to separate the verbals.

Enid ripped-off her fourth over to James, chucking down a slider outside off to keep James quiet, even if just for a lone ball. James went after it, a thick inside edge onto the pads, yelling "Stay!" even though Chad had backed up halfway down the pitch. With no fielder in close on the leg side there was no real peril and James was forced through so Chad could get a piece of this action. Enid did not change the field for Chad, which seemed to make him a tickle indignant as he waited for the bespoke 'let's block up what we believe to be big bad Chad's strengths' field alteration which he would marvel at being 'impossible unless you build the Great Wall of China around the entire boundary ... even then though ...'. Enid waited to bowl while Chad pat-patted the earth, noting there wasn't even a fielder moved to deep cover for his signature shot ... the exact same field as James? James! Enid tossed one up, more flight than she'd permitted in this match, as Chad got to the pitch but stopped the shot, still smarting from being treated like any ordinary, old teammate batter. He took two runs, still convinced that his personalised field would ensue. Nothing happened, Enid still waiting behind the umpire's arm to bowl, giving this one even more flight so he helped himself to another two runs. Third time's the charm, but no one budged!

"Perhaps she just wants this slaughter over with," Chad muttered to himself.

Then came what Chad believed to be Enid's googly, so he went down to sweep without any intention to hold back on this one. As he stretched out his leg and swept from outside his pad, the ball failed to move along with his bat's flightpath, holding its line and bouncing - a top spinner - the ball catching Chad's top edge, ascending higher than anticipated, the ball's upright seam having sprung off the pitch. This represented the first and likely only chance Chad had and would bestow upon Shackleton, as Wei Ping's wobbly legs reluctantly tried to find the right spot on the 45. Chad refused to run, watching intently as Wei Ping shifted left then right then left then forward then forward some more then back then right, only to end up about where he had been fielding in the first place. The ball was now looping in the downward arc beyond him, his position too far forward as the entire stadium froze. At the final moment where one imagines an easy pouching cue celebration, the ball sailed over his head, although he managed to dive backwards and get a hand to the leather. The ball hit the tips of his fingers, bobbling up to allow him to twist in the air and get the other hand towards the ball, but alas the ball had the beating of Wei Ping as it splattered onto the grass and Chad whoop-whooped taking the single.

Wei Ping was distraught, lying face down on the turf, his face buried deep into the blades, hiding his shame as his body convulsed on the surface. Enid was down on her haunches, fighting back the tears as the stadium's noise bucked up again then died down as though they were witnessing a Greek tragedy. Wei Ping didn't move for a while, every person at Lord's dead silent, willing him to get up. Even the wind abated for that moment, not even a clank or clap of relief coming from the Corkridge balcony. Wei Ping Tan stopped moving, his inanimate trifling lifeless physique the human embodiment of where the remainder of the Shackleton XI stood … until … someone was heard calling from the outfield …

"Today …" the words echoed around Lord's, the team turning to face the origin.

"Today … I refuse to relent … as a proud Shackleton cricketer … and a proud sister," Corin hollered from the depths of deep mid-on.

"Today!" shouted Daughtry from the other end. "I refuse to relent ... as a proud daughter ... proud to represent you all out here ... today!"

"Today ... as a proud dancer ... I refuse to relent!" yelled Jacob, then Onka, "... as a proud South African ... proud to represent Wei Ping Tan ... my Shackleton teammate, brother from another mother and *tjina* for life!"

Wei Ping slowly lifted his face out of the crater mask he'd fashioned, the wet grass beneath his eyes, mushed into a Thai curry paste.

"Today ... I refuse to relent ... as a proud member of the society for the open acceptance of people who love fantasy novels, television and film!" came Noel's profession, the ground's riffraff devotees saluting with a drawn sword. "Proud to represent you all out here ... today ... okay!"

"As a proud granddaughter and sister to five brothers ... today, I refuse to relent," came Larry's cry.

"... as a defecting son who picked the right side," came Rufus's edit, a lonely figure alongside Yapa on the home balcony. "Proud to be a Shackleton cricketer!"

"Today ... I refuse to relent ... as a proud Shackleton cricketer. Proud to represent you all out here ... today ... and tomorrow!" came Peter's riposte.

All eyes fixated on Enid, who back on her feet, strode over to Wei Ping and put a reassuring hand on his shoulder, crouching down then slowly rising back up.

"Today ... we won't relent ... as a proud Shackleton cricketer, daughter, sister, teammate, and friend. Proud to represent you all out here … today!"

As the Lord's crowd went into overdrive, Enid could barely hear Chad mutter, "Great speech," as she walked past him to resume bowling. Enid elected to bowl around the wicket this ball, James looking quizzically back, opening into a complete French cricket stance for this delivery. The umpire's arm went down and still Enid waited, until he rotated to hurry her along, so she departed her mark, punching her right hip through the crease and ripping this one miles outside leg stump. Before the ball had landed James simply stepped back to block the stumps with both oversized pads, no chance of an LB pitching outside leg and wide for sure, unable to reach the ball, his bat tacked up on his right shoulder. Enid's ball gripped and spun farther than any wrist spin ball before, that day and since, the ball fizzing across James's torso at a sharp angle, catching the toe of his bat on the way through to bobble away from Larry and towards Wei Ping, who saved the single to rapturous applause from the empathetic galleries. Enid suddenly looked taller, loftier, stronger and reverted back to over the wicket the next ball, the around the wicket version her beaten chest show of strength. Then came an absolute beauty, James more wearily reaching out to prod, beaten all ends up as was Larry, allowing another skittered single, keeping James on strike at the other end and Chad back to resume non-striker duties as he witnessed more pats on Wei Ping's back or what he termed 'negative reinforcement'. The dropped catch had somehow galvanised Shackleton which Chad neither understood nor cared about, celebrating shelling a dolly all the rage with losers nowadays.

Corin was raring to go, James the other end, equally chomping at the bit to get closer to his century and win the game for Corkridge. She came steaming in from over the wicket, a vicious delivery that looked the fastest of

Shackleton's innings thus far, James swinging forcefully but only finding thin air as Larry took the ball at eye level. At this stage, Corin didn't give a monkey's about anything other than generating real, raw, unadulterated pace, the second ball shorter and lifting to whistle past James's helmet, another unfulfilling hook stroke. The third connected James squarely in the chest, his bulky frame absorbing the hit and expelling a hint of a farted groan, the thud onto exposed ribs unashamedly satisfying. "Don't you dare rub it!" thought Chad and James didn't. Three dot balls - all short and all quick - was about the respite Shackleton had been in search of all afternoon, allowing Corin to mess with James for the last three deliveries - a fuller length that seamed away beating his bat then an inswinger that clattered into his thigh-pad. Now came the moment all of the team and most of the crowd had been waiting for - the final uppercut in the fifteenth, James shaking on the ropes bleeding in front of the politburo - a fierce, whipping, mad delivery … that wasn't … a knuckle ball that saw James swipe in desperation and the ball die on him once through the shot, ambling into the stumps, his thick front pad too late to scoot back and kick the ball to freedom. Berserk scenes ensued.

"Shackleton have their third, Ramsay! In the 35th over after a beautiful piece of quick bowling by Corin Hanratty!"

"She doesn't do moderation our Corin - it's either six sixes or wicket-maidens from this girl! Quite an over!"

"I'd love to say a long time coming but this has all just happened between everyone throwing the towel in and now … literally seconds ago! Where has this Shackleton bowling unit been?"

"Ever the killjoy I have to stress, Corkridge remain in control of this match with plenty of batting to take this final over the final hump."

"Whatever happens from here on out, I don't care and

don't read into this, Ramsay, but I'm going to hug you … just this once!"

Enid to Chad; Captain to Captain; one's tail lifting from dragging along the pitch, the other's so high it loitered above his head like a feather boa, but Shaky had a sniff now, their last chance saloon still serving happy hour drinks so they had to temper the optimism. Enid wanted this over to happen … this was what this match was all about and, of course, Chad too wanted this to happen – get on top to quell this minor rebellion and the game was as good as won. There was no wasting time and Enid opened with a threatening googly, Chad not picking it at all and lucky not to edge it or get bowled, Enid stoic in avoiding celebration … nothing achieved with merely a dot ball. The next ball was more of the stock variety, but gripped and prodigiously ripped past Chad's outside edge. The crowd hushed as Chad had been beaten twice in a row, the quality of leg spin bowling on show at Lord's upping the ante to the point that something had to give. Chad called Yannos through for a quick confab in the middle of the pitch.

"You're going to go after her," he said to Yannos, fresh off the boat.

"Go after the leggie? Bowling those balls?" asked Brannos, incredulous.

"I'm going to chase the next ball then you'll be on strike … go for it, get the run rate up and I'll anchor."

"Are you worried about facing … her?"

"I'm on 85 … what do you think? You're on zero, so pull your weight for the team and don't let me down Yannos."

"It's Brad," but Chad was already out of earshot.

As foretold, Chad came dashing towards the third ball so Enid dragged it wide, looking for a stumping. In a comical double footed slide tackle, Chad went at the ball with both feet to prevent the ball reaching the keeper, only just getting the toe of his boot to connect as the ball spewed away, allowing for the single. Brad took guard yet watched the next ball, unwilling to charge from the outset as instructed, another gorgeous delivery that drifted in and turned past his bat, retracting the blade just in time to indicate it was a leave. Chad looked fuming, his eyebrows darkening his face so Yannos came after Enid's fifth, getting a messy edge over the slips that ran away for four. With the final delivery Yannos again went at Enid, the googly befuddling him such that the ball collided with his pad but outside the line, preventing any notions of a review. On 231-3, Corkridge required exactly 100 runs to win the match, with 14 overs remaining.

"You've misjudged this pitch," Chad chirped as Enid retrieved her cap. "Not a Bunsen at all."

"I must be that good, then?" responded Enid. "Or maybe you're right and you're just not that good? If I'm the turner on the Bunsen Burner, then why are you missing everything?"

"Two lucky balls doesn't make you Warnie."

"Takes three to play this game."

Corin was hopefully the incitation, the quicks still able to extract something from the increasingly flat track of a pitch, the swirling wind adding to the level of bowling complexity. Corin beat both Chad and Brad's outside edge with balls that jagged off the seam, yet both were able to grab a few runs by utilising the pace and holes in the field now that Shackleton were all out attack. Enid had informed Corin she was saving her for the death, so Corin knew this was her last over of this spell, putting her back into the deliveries and holding back any further extreme variety as the Corky batters didn't look like wanting to do anything other than guide. Onka was re-warming up and due to replace Corin after another over from Enid, and Corin's last ball freebie single ensured the captains were again matching up, the crowd chant-clapping Enid's delivery stride to amplify the clash. Enid was convinced Chad would try to come at her again, signalling to Larry that she'd have to go really wide this time with no danger of an overturned stumping from a wide. Chad looked uncomfortable for the first time in the match, fidgeting like his hero Steve Smith, an imaginary rash engulfing his body as he'd once experienced when using the Economy Class toilets while all were taken in Club World. He was only twelve runs away from his debut Lord's ton but that seemed an eternity away now with his indecision between going after the leg spin or sitting back to survive and wait for other bowlers to present easier opportunities. He glanced down the pitch at the umpire who held Enid back, comfortable now that his father had such, such … influence, after earlier designs that Corkridge would cake walk this with more than crumbs to spare. As the umpire nodded in return, Chad settled on using his pads as LBWs were off the table, but tucking your bat behind your pad when playing a stroke wasn't a tactic he was accustomed to at any stage in his illustrious career. Getting off strike looked too perilous even if Yannos delivered upon his instruction, so he'd give her the moment in the spotlight she so craved at Lord's - a maiden - as this would all be forgotten once he won the match for Corkridge and lifted the trophy after this … this … minor blemish.

Enid, when finally permitted to bowl, chucked down two innocuous sliders which Chad was proud to nullify, followed by two googlies which Chad padded away, the bat tucked safely behind his front pad. The fifth ball pitched on middle and leg and Chad, wary that it could clip the top of off if it turned enough, was forced to play at the ball, the ideal length negating any pad only endeavours. The ball took the faintest of Chad's outside edge, no discernible deviation, but a brittle sound that scooted into the warm safety of Larry's keeper mitts. The whole team and all the front sections of the stands went up for the appeal … Enid had her man … finally. She didn't even bother turning to the umpire, just ran up the pitch to an approaching Larry whose facial expression suggested something entirely incongruous. The umpire hadn't raised his finger, so Enid, without flinching signalled for a review, Chad looking forlorn and resigned to his fate.

"Third umpire to Control, we have a team review for caught behind. The on-field decision is ... Not Out. Front foot fine – it is a fair delivery. We don't need ball tracker as the ball has clearly missed the pads so let's move onto Ultra Edge for a potential caught behind."

The graphic appeared with the straight line and the ball poised in front of Chad's pad, the side-on angle zooming in to the conceivable point of impact and, in the process, lobbing Chad's head off out of the frame. As the ball neared the bat, frame-by-frame – an agonising wait – a flurry of lines appeared as the ball passed the bat which many believed to be conclusive, a cheer erupting around the ground until ...

"I see the spike, but the batsman's bat appears to be striking his pad simultaneously."

As the crowd settled down to further immerse in the drama, it was unmistakable that Chad's bat had clipped his pad on the way through, the distortion of pressing on the white pad enough to convince everyone that the pad had indeed been struck. To the naked eye though, there was some daylight between nicking the ball and striking the pad, yet the sound wave spikes appeared as a collective clump, even if the early protrusions were higher and more extreme to signify willow with the latter lower and more widespread as that of a dull struck pad might appear. The third umpire deliberated for an abnormal period until a conclusion was reached.

"The ball has either struck the bat or the bat has struck the pad and there is no clear evidence as to which, so I am forced to go with the on-field decision of Not Out," the words jumbling out on the screen as Chad rubbed his pad to rub it in further. For the final ball of the over Enid let her emotions get the better of her, flinging an extempore arm-ball at Chad, the full toss welcomed to the boundary with ease, a help yourself freebie that might have bowled him he was so dumbfounded.

"No maiden for this maiden," Chad congratulated himself then reused the line on Brad who didn't laugh, then Yannos did, when Chad force-laughed him into accommodating submission.

Onka's return to action was met by comedic replays of his ungainly action put to a dance track, the media director's montage funnier to him than anyone else in the ground over five years old. Chad looked expectantly at the boundary then back at Brad, a clear sign to get on with things, so Onka purposefully served up some loopy left-arm leggies to coax more of Yannos and less of Brad. An expensive over resulted but Onka trusted the final ball of his over as he gave the ball more air than the previous deliveries but with more of a rip to reduce the loopiness, pushing the ball wide to make Yannos come get it, the inside of his right foot colliding with the inside of his left foot as he came skipping to meet the pitch. The ball suddenly dipped on Brad, so he had to shift what was looking like an off side drive, as he followed the extreme spin by swatting the ball in the air towards cow corner. Noel was out in the deep but the ball was surging over his head and towards his less favoured right hand. Noel instantly jumped behind the boundary line, the front of his feet knocking the boundary foam but not enough for him to fall over, an arm on the ground to steady himself drawing gasps from the neighbouring stand's front row. He could judge the arc of the ball to a degree, initial instincts correct in that it would easily sail over the boundary for a six, unless … he intervened. He'd always wanted the glory of those catches he'd seen on TV where the fielder catches the ball mid-air and either pops it back to another fielder or lobs it skilfully enough to regather, but when in the caldron of having to actually pull this off, his balance and coordination seemed to desert him in succession. As he stumbled forward, tangled in the foam boundary, he propelled himself up with all his might. He was airborne as the ball neared so, without any time to adjust, let his hips fly forwards and kept his shoulders still, becoming fully horizontal in mid-air. He heard the fizz of the ball loudening as he reached his right arm out with every sinew, hoping he had enough to pouch the ball. The loud assuming slap happened suddenly, and he clutched the ball securely but his descent back to earth had begun - an elevator dropping - and there was no way to contort his body away from landing on the foam. At the final second before his rigid horizonal posture clattered back down to earth he adeptly flung the ball skywards, letting out a helpless screech in the process. Out of nowhere Daughtry appeared, but Noel's throw was angling over an adjacent part of the boundary at mid-on, Daughtry getting her most complete almost two-and-a-half metre reach aloft, thrusting up in perfect unison for some serious hangtime, tucking her legs up so that the camera captured three rows of stunned fans beneath her body. She too caught the ball - an incredible plucked apple snag - but she too was destined to land over the boundary and hand Yannos a six, so as she fell, she pirouetted in mid-air and flung the ball out of the back of her hand - rugby offload style - as Noel regathered his composure, untangled himself from the interfering boundary foam and took a Jonty Rhodes run out dive forward towards the dying ball. It would be checked ad nauseum for the next twenty minutes, but Noel took the catch in the field of play.

"I had it covered," he said to Daughtry as she lifted him off the turf like dirty laundry. "Don't you dare claim that catch HB … the scorecard is reading c Pothas not c Turner!"

"Fine by me. Exactly what the fast bowler's brief is all about … showing the rest of the team how to catch," as the rest of the team mobbed the pair to revel.

Yannos was on his way and Onka, with a little help from

the juggling circus act of fast bowlers in the deep, had his cherished wicket at Lord's. Stanley 'Stanni' Forthenstan was in next, busy and restless even on the approach, dragging his freckles and curliness in a sack behind him as he spat out his old gum and plopped a new one in for the occasion. En route to the crease he hid behind Daughtry, attempting an obnoxious practical joke of sorts, her shadow subsuming the little fellow, but gave up when she failed to take the bait and he was left crouching behind her, his jaws furiously masticating to get the sweet rush of gum flavour into his bloodstream. As much as no one wanted to admit it, he was the perfect type of batsman for this occasion, hustling, bustling, finding runs where there weren't any or bringing the worst out of the opposition. Before he'd faced a single ball, Stanni had done the box-helmet-wedgie fiddle routine so many consecutive times, it appeared to be on an unremitting loop and would later become one of Twitter's top GIFs.

With Rufus out of commission, Enid was forced to stick with spin for the next five overs. She considered holding herself back, especially the problems she was causing, but decided to stick with pace for the death overs and try to nab a wicket or two in the lead up. Chad avoided facing Enid like the plague, preferring Onka's into the right-hander stock balls and Stanni charged at just about everything, while Chad camped at the other end with his glove perpetually raised. Onka received a warm ovation from the crowd at the end of his spell; he'd bowled incredibly well and adapted to a batting line-up cluttered with right-handers as Enid got one more shot at Chad who sat pretty on 99 not out. Larry, anticipating fireworks, removed her helmet for this over, breathing down Chad's neck who would have given his kingdom for one lowly run, the field brought right in to intimidate him and his golden fleece.

The wind had picked up to the point where the swirling in the stadium collected stray plastic beer cups and relocated contorted pie base foil receptacles down adjoining steps, the scrape of tin on cement failing to distract even the lowest attention span punters. Enid had the ball in her hand, the field was ready and Chad was waiting. Her first ball produced flight where the seam remained benumbed still at a forty-five-degree angle, pointing towards the slips, pitching on leg stump and ripping past Chad's tentative poke, Larry elegantly taking the ball, holding her hands still, inches from the bail should Chad decide to overbalance. For her second ball, she landed it on middle stump, putting a further conundrum to Chad: Was this another serious ripper moving extravagantly towards off or a googly that he could paddle or glance for that day's maiden century? It was neither: a top spinner but with a cross seam, the ball rotating as if God had flicked Saturn's ring whilst horizontal across the planet, his or her or their middle finger catching it sweetly enough as Gods just wanna have fu-hun. With this delivery the desired effect took place, the ball not pitching on the seam and skidding onto Chad who was JUST able to get his bat down in time, creating a last gasp barrier between winning delivery and broken stumps. Enid had her hands on her head now as either Chad was going to ride his luck all the way through her spell or something was going to give. She was owning him but that meant nothing unless a 'W' appeared next to his name and he was banished back to the dressing room. It was Enid's third ball that would generate some more controversy, as clearly this final hadn't had enough!

Chad seemed content to still be there, the end of Enid's lethal over a mere four balls away - he could do this; this was within the realms of the mighty CdlA! Enid started her run-up, entering the delivery stride as she had previously, yet this ball seemed to come from lower, her cocked wrist whipping through and around the ball, appearing to give it more revolutions than ever before. The ball instantly angled far across Chad as his eyes widened believing she'd strayed a savage wide, the drift accentuating this even further, so Chad motioned to leave the ball whilst simultaneously protecting his stumps, back in the crease. When the ball pitched – a good few feet outside the leg stump – it gripped, ripped and zipped, startling Chad on the way through such that he pushed his wrists down at the ball journeying towards the top of off stump. The ball caressed his back pad, narrowly missing off stump, beating Larry and bounding behind her only to clank into her stray helmet. Chad, not caring about anything other than getting away from the leg spin minefield, had already set off calling Stanni through for the run irrespective of what happened, hearing the odd noise of ball striking helmet before he'd crossed in the middle. Most in the team knew the ball striking the fielding side's rogue helmet was not a good thing, the umpire relishing the opportunity to show his partial understanding of the laws of the game, specifically Law 28 'The Fielder'. He awarded Corkridge five runs for the ball striking the helmet – as was the rule – and another extra from the run, deeming the batters had crossed prior to the collision, the dead ball signal following suspiciously late. He also called the ball a no-ball, meaning the next ball was a free hit and ignored Enid's case that a leg bye negated the '5-run Penalty', claiming it had missed everything. Chad muscled in to insist he'd got a feather on the ball, so the umpire reversed the leg bye extra and gave Chad the run, getting him to a ton at Lord's.

The disappointment swarmed amidst the fielders and bowler to accompany the swirls of wind, hands on hips, heads, haunches and mouths. The crowd dutifully applauded the century as Chad did a complete tour of the inner ring, helmet off and punching the sky as each section of the stadium's clockface was fortunate enough to receive his gratitude. At the end of the celebration, once he was back at twelve o'clock where he'd begun, he drew back his face, rumpling his features into a screeching, "Come On!" then

"Let's Do It!" and finally "Not in my house! Whooooooo" slapping both his gloves on his pecs, bouncing adroitly into a double arm raised V for Victory.

It felt wrong, it felt nasty, it felt desolate but Shackleton had to avoid throwing in the towel and use whatever they had left, their resolve and sense of fairness having taken a proper pounding. Enid's no-ball delivery caused no further damage as Stanni was not up to the wide slider, Larry's dejection for the helmet incident etched all over her face. Corkridge were now 289-4 in the 44th over, with only 42 runs to get and a whopping six wickets in hand. Enid had two balls left to bowl as, even though she had an over spare, she'd long since decided that irrespective of what happened in her ninth over, she'd be reverting to pace for the final six overs. So after some agonisingly close moments, Enid was due to finish her bowling at Lord's in the Digners Cup final wicketless.

Enid bowled the penultimate ball of her season, spotting Stanni coming after her again, but sticking to her intended delivery of a stock leg break with sick revs, her shoulder almost dislocating from its socket as she pivoted off her front toes and swivelled, her back leg rising up above her head as she stayed upright, driving her right hip through without falling away. To the crowd and Enid this happened in slow motion: Stanni's rendition of Swan Lake, as he skipped down the track and tried to work the ball through the leg side, not reaching the pitch and the ball beating him, traversing the gap between backside and stumps and reaching Larry behind the stumps. The ball had turned so much that Larry was now standing with her body fully visible down the track, away from the stumps and her immaculate glovework took the ball on the bounce and broke the stumps in one fluid movement. Larry's appeal was angry, as all three stumps got flattened and she motioned forcefully downwards at the gap that still remained, the umpire with no choice but to give it out. Enid was the first to reach Larry and picked her up as Larry's crazed eyes kept on revelling, her typically cool demeanour somewhere in a nebula where cricket doesn't exist, revolutions away.

Stanni traipsed off, passing Daughtry just as he had on the way in, his burst of 20 runs off 5 overs enough of a contribution to win this match for Corkridge.

"Any more fiddling and you'd have been arrested," Daughtry snuck in without riposte.

"Girls never get the funny lines," Noel insisted from within earshot. "Unless it's boy related!"

Danny Hallow-Jensen was next in, visibly anxious, the business end of this match baring its backside like a baboon in mating season. Danny held his bat like a right-hander yet Enid had already begun altering the field for a left-hander, his father having the foresight to coach him with his dominant hand at the top of the bat. He had one ball to face from Enid who stayed over the wicket as she boldly put a leg slip and short square leg in place, indicating a 'more of the same' extreme ripper. Danny took guard on middle and off to stifle this ball by dragging Enid wide, then smother the spin before the magic happened. Enid took one final breath and launched, a ball heading strangely down the leg side, markedly wide of the left-hander. This ball was flatter than the miracle ball to Chad, not allowing Danny any decision time so just as he was motioning back to leave, the ball pitched and went the other way … the googly! Well disguised and ripping way more than most googlies, this ball bent from wide of leg, around Danny's legs to clout the leg stump as Danny lifted his gloves in vain. He'd been bowled around his legs! And Shaky had their second wicket in as many balls, Enid on a hat-trick. The viewers at home had the probability percentage cut after that wicket but still Corkridge as the firm favourites to get this over the line with a 76% win probability. But Shaky had a sniff … a double nostril snort in fact with the dangerous Danny removed for a first ball duck, Noel having waited the entire Corkridge batting innings to unleash his one-liner that became a two-liner in all the excitement, "No ducks given! No ducks given!"

With six overs of the match remaining, Charlie 'Chuck' Hastings strode out to the crease, the only mercy for Larry being that it looked like no further spin in this match, so they'd have the 'space' Rebecca sought ever since their breakup. Larry had a serious and violent bone to pick with Chuck, but her way was not to get personal either on or off the field, so she chose to let the cricket do the talking, avoiding any trash talk bait. As her brother strode off distraught, Rebecca was there to give him a consoling hug as he was family after all. She hadn't switched sides, of course, extolling a hefty rat-a-tat-tat for Shaky, unable to simulate Larry's sportspersonship from the sidelines.

Chuck was handy with the bat and would have batted top four in most teams, his lowly number 8 status a constant irritant that today he would eradicate. Like his bowling there were no half measures but he had enough technique to judge when to go and how to get his body into a bludgeoning position; he wadn't no slogger! Out in the middle it was great to be back with his old pal Chad, once again in favour after the small hitch of the Rebecca pining incident and subsequent loss of bowling form, confidence and technique. It would all be right again, once he and Chad put the nail in Shaky's coffin!

"The quicks are back on," said Chad looking like his swagger had fabulously sprung out of a cricket coffin in the dressing room and returned. "Two big overs and we're gods."

"I mean, we're at Lord's FFS ... this is what we dreamed of all the way through the junior ranks, age group, district, county, national. We've done it! We've made it! Great to be back with you, brother ..."

"Let's see."

"... to be sharing this moment with you."

"You cock this up, I'll dump your bitch ass faster than the keeper's girlfriend dumped yours!"

Chuck's smile sprang off his face into his top pocket, burying its head behind the woven Corkridge castle.

"Do. Your. Job."

Daughtry came on to bowl the 45th over, once again from the Nursery End, looking calm, composed, even indomitable. Chad at the other end, appeared back in the saddle, twirling the bat handle, drawing upon his high scoring, untroubled period against Daughtry earlier. The first ball showed Daughtry was not there to just serve up any old slop but Chad was equal to it, premeditating a shot for two runs, then again to the same place the second ball for three runs, running hard to effectively transfer the onus onto Chuck to avoid a spectacle right at the end by breaking Shackleton's spirits this over. Chuck was tall - not tall like Daughtry - but tall enough, able to take on the short stuff and with enough of a fluid front foot to not be in trouble if the balls were full. Chuck watched the first ball, stepping forward, the ball travelling under his eyes, then felt he had the measure, swiping at one, which looked nasty but went over cover for four. The next ball Daughtry drifted more into the slot and Chuck was able to get hold of it but with a trajectory high and up rather than a forceful guaranteed six. Jacob at deep mid-on moved to his right, steadying himself for a possible catch, finding the time to push his glasses back up his nose as the ball descended. He felt he was in the ideal position, glancing down to his heels that were less than an inch from the boundary foam, as the ball held in the air longer than seemed reasonable, an upward buffet of air knocking it slightly off course and further towards the stands. Jacob stood firm and the ball's audible fizz accentuated, a bottle's top being forcibly removed, as the ball plunged into his cupped hands, the sting of stopping the missile pulsating into his fingers.

Jacob stood frozen, not sure what had happened, his glasses back to their customary position at the end of his nose, as Chuck sped past Chad and the umpire, scramming towards Jacob's fielding position at a serious lick.

"You've stepped over the boundary, four eyes!" Chuck yelled in Jacob's face. "There's no way that wasn't a six!"

"I ... uh ... umm ... not sure ..." said Jacob looking down as Chuck grabbed him with both gloved fists by the collar and pushed him through the boundary's barrier.

Then all hell broke loose, the rest of the Shackleton team descending upon the scuffle while the Corkridge balcony emptied to join the affray. Larry arrived and struck down on Chuck's arms to release Jacob while Chad held Onka back to let the scuffle rumble on. The Neethaniel bouncers arrived, so Daughtry stepped in to stop them, holding one's collar in each hand and extending her arms out, as they pushed forward without regard for anything or anyone. Stanni was yapping at Corin's heels so she gave him a shove, sending him flying backwards, tripping over the foam onto his backside. Noel and James had ended up nose to nose exchanging pleasantries, Noel's feet dangling off the floor no deterrent for any of his kamikaze chat or shoving. George, Harrison and Danny ushered from afar, not overly keen to get into the thick of it, while Onka wrestled Chad to the ground and Larry finally smacked Chuck's grip from Jacob. Enid was trying to calm everything down and separate factions of tension when she too got knocked to the ground, so she sprung back up and threw the nearest Corky boy to the ground who happened to be Brad. Wei Ping went slithering beneath everyone, bravely popping in between skirmishing pairs to stop the madness and avoid any punches being thrown. Corin ensured James put Noel down by following Larry's party trick, while Enid threw Chad off Onka, the pair getting to know one another more intimately rolling around on the turf. Daughtry still had both Neethaniel brothers pinned, her grasp lodged and arms locked straight as the officials arrived and even the mascots got stuck in, a human kebab that had only recently suited up for Donna's Honours Kebab, outnumbered by the Corkridge golden eagle and chess castle, but nonetheless undiscouraged, cleaving the eagle's head off to reveal a sheepish looking Daniels and toppling the castle with a little known chess move: kebab takes castle off the board.

"Complete pandemonium, Clodagh, the match so tense it has descended into violent chaos out there!"

"There comes a time, Ramsay, when you just have to stand your ground. This is one of them!"

"The mascots are even getting into it ... looks like the kebab has decapitated the eagle and the castle is down for the count!"

"Sense will have to prevail shortly to stop this and get the match back on track, but for now let's just put this down to passion for the game and your teammates, shall we?"

"Clodagh, you can call this whatever you like, but from up here it looks like Wrestle Mania got a makeover from full colour cricket! Confident the members would have preferred a deliberate removal of the white glove and clip across the jowls to settle this score."

"Handbags, pushing, shoving ... all marginally acceptable; let's just hope no one does something they'll regret."

Once Yapa stepped in, he managed to separate the sparring duos and calm everything down until the match referee berated both teams for unbecoming conduct. There were a few red cheeks, ruffled hairstyles and grassy outfits on both sides but apparently no serious damage. The small matter of what had actually happened with Jacob's catch was referred upstairs by the umpire with a soft signal of Not Out, Jacob's honest uncertainty of where he took the catch shouted down by Chuck's insistence that it had to be the maximum, as the pre-trial openings were heard. The angle of the footage was not clear or especially conclusive as Jacob appeared to take the ball cleanly and away from the boundary but then after a delay his heels did shift back to press against the foam, the top half of the captured footage cut off, so difficult to determine whether Chuck's assault had pushed him over the boundary. The third umpire employed just about every angle available to him, even employing split screen from the moment Chunk arrived to grab Jacob. Jacob's feet had been shifted back over the boundary, what remained unclear with no further clarity on offer was whether he'd moved them or Chuck had moved him, so once again the on-field decision of Not Out stood. And the six was awarded, taking Corkridge past the 300 mark, needing only 27 runs off the final 5 overs to win the match. The ball was passed to Noel, safe in the portending knowledge that a bad over here was the game.

With Chad on strike, Noel went back to basics, electing to bowl his ninth over left-arm over the wicket, every run a precious gem as the fielders walked in crouched, their senses heightened by the juncture's plight. Two Chad boundaries off a decent over from Noel later had the smell, feel, taste and touch of Shaky's coffin nails.

Corkridge required 18 runs off the final 4 overs with four wickets in hand, the team balcony already high-fiving and getting ready for the victory lap around the Lord's perimeter. Daughtry was on for her tenth and final over, the calm composure replaced by a hyperventilation of angered injustice.

"Even if we don't pull this off," said Noel handing her the ball between overs, "just take his head off, as I think he'll look better without it."

"He's going to do nothing rash," said Enid. "To him the game's won, so any additional ball we get to bowl is bonus.

Take each ball as its own special beast and, Noel's right, make him play everything, with his bat, his head or his body. Be careful the wides though, the umpires want to get off the pitch before they get lynched."

"By us!" said Noel resuming his fielding duties.

"Ball by ball. If we get to the next over, we're still in the game. Make him play. I'm giving you a slip."

Daughtry tried to picture Chad without his head then headed in to bowl, her knees nice and high and body upright. She dug in her first delivery and Chad smirked as he swayed out of the way. Her second ball was fuller yet still lifted off a length, Chad dropping his hands, the ball thudding into his midriff. He was winded as the ball had tucked in just below his ribs but you wouldn't have known it. The third ball was another unlucky sequence, Daughtry – to everyone's surprise – retrieving the Steve Harmison to Michael Clarke Ashes 2005 slower ball from the depths of an unmarked locker, the ball looping up then savagely dipping on Chad who hadn't read or expected that at all. He managed to jam the bat down and just catch the ball before it landed, squirting it past the despairing slip for another four. That could have been the moment for Shackleton where victory was snatched from not the jaws but oesophageal region of defeat, Corkridge now needing an insignificant 14 runs off 21 balls. Chad uneventfully defended the next ball then scanned for gaps, the field once again encroaching in as, only over his dead body was Chuck going to hit the winning runs off the next over. Daughtry didn't give up and another cracker of a delivery rose up to Chad's chest which he was able to get behind and inside edge onto the top of his hip bone for a single, calling a reluctant Chuck through for the single to face the last ball of Daughtry's spell. That hurt Chad but the sweet taste of imminent victory meant he could trot through with his helmet held high as Corkridge impended on the precipice of victory.

Daughtry strode in - one last effort ball, then she'd done all she could - bowling to Chuck who adopted a slugger pose to dispatch this one with force. Daughtry went short but not too short which Chuck met with a middled flat bat back at the bowler, the ball striking her flush on the side of the temple as she tried to arrest the limb explosion and take evasive action on her follow-through. Behind her the umpire had hit the deck and lay face down with his forearms covering his head. Daughtry crumbled like pick-up-stix being emptied from their cylinder as the ball split her head and blood seeped into the pitch. Wei Ping had the guilty task of retrieving the ball and hovering over the stumps to avoid Corkridge pinching a run, as the medics flooded onto the field and Daughtry's Shaky teammates crowded around her lifeless corpse.

"Oh my, that's a horrible turn of events, Clodagh, the poor girl."

"That didn't look good did it, I hope she's okay. Vicious shot back at the bowler. I've been predicting this for years with the quality of bats and explosive hitting in the game - such a shame it has proved accurate."

"The game will probably be called off I suspect; can't really continue after that."

Daughtry was semi-conscious once they loaded her onto the stretcher, her teammates placing their palms on the vast expanses of vacant limbs before they wrapped her in a blanket, as the batsmen pleaded with the officials not to cancel the match. They placed an oxygen mask on her face after they'd got the bleeding under control - the flow of a headwound difficult to control - and were almost off the field when they stopped, motioning for the Shackleton captain to join them.

"She's refusing to go off," said one of the stewards. "We

have head injury protocols, so she cannot continue, but she has agreed to go off if you agree not to forfeit the match."

Enid looked at Daughtry's drained face, her own eyes welling up in unanimity with her fast bowler.

"You just have to promise to win the match," said the steward, lifting her up to remove her from the battlefield, her thumb raising as she got carried off, the crowd hitting noise levels Lord's would likely never witness again … unless perhaps India played Pakistan in a World Cup final at the venue.

Shackleton would have to finish the match with only ten players on the field, a fielder short leaving a potentially crucial gap under these circumstances, but they had no choice … not only did they have to do it for Daughtry … this was for just about everyone in the ground, at home, at the end of being written-off and told you couldn't do something you'd set your mind to. The camera crew picked up someone wearing a stubby replica members' tie in the cheap seats, having procured a Sharpie and scribbled on a cardboard panel …

"*I'm fielding for Shaky*" the sign read.

All around the ground the crowds began chanting and fashioning their own signs with lipstick, sun cream, ketchup or whatever was available, signage popping up all over Lord's like lighters at a concert.

"My Twitter and Insta are blowing up, Clodagh! #FieldingForShaky has gone not even viral but mental … look at this!" Ramsay held up his phone as Clodagh completed writing the slogan across her shirt.

"No, Ramsay … look at this!"

18 balls. 13 runs. Corin on to bowl to Chad, her second

last over, the field predominantly in to prevent a slow death of singles, running the customary risk of Chad ending the match with a collection of cogent strokes, but really, Shackleton had no other choice. Enid and Corin deliberated over which positions would be in to save the single and which out to block the earlier route should Chad wish to book that plane ticket. As Chad made it clear to Chuck the plan from here to the victory salute, the two pairs accidentally sidled up against one another in the middle of the pitch as Chuck leaned down to examine Daughtry's blood stain, his pride at being the cause unmistakeable.

"You girls can take your losers' medals to your big boned friend, when the zoo's hospital opens for visitors," said Chuck, as Enid held Corin back.

"Now, now, Chuck," said Chad. "There's no need for that. The only thing I'm concerned about is honour."

"Honour!" said Enid incredulously. "Not an abundance of that on show today, from Corkridge anyway."

"It's like my father says," Chad retorted. "It's not the journey that's important, it's where you start from and where you end up. No one remembers the in-between. And I seem to clearly recollect a certain ball on offer, dropped by some loser has-been as the origin of all this ... you'll be honouring that commitment when we're on the podium."

"My memory 'recollects' a different origin Chad," piped Corin. "Your tooth playing hide-and-seek in the school corridor. Might be time for the sequel ... that helmet secure?"

"Just make sure you get me that ball ... the one your dad dropped."

"Thanks, Mate!" Chuck threw in to score brownie points but in fact usurping the line Chad was about to spout as everyone returned to their positions for the third last over of the game.

Corin needed to be on the money early, and she was, her first ball tailing back into Chad and slicing him in half like a seafood butcher lopping the head off a bighead carp. Corin's next ball danced to an even merrier tune, angling into Chad but then straightening like a leg break, Chad prodding down the wrong line as the ball went thundering through to Larry who juggled the ball, late further swing and sudden velocity producing a misjudgement. Corin felt Chad would be expecting a wicket taking variation, adopting a defensive stance, so she tried to sling the awayswinging yorker, well executed, but an inch shy of the stumps, Chad digging at another one that went through to the keeper. Three dot balls would normally elicit some form of concern verging on panic, but Chad still looked assured with the low target as he eyed his next single to retain the strike. The field remained the same as Corin bowled another dot ball, this one an off cutter that completely deceived Chad as he jabbed at another that drifted through to the keeper. The fielders out all came in, giving Chad the tantalising option to secure a boundary off the last two balls, even though he was intent on keeping the strike the next over and getting away from Corin for at least one ball. He'd played and missed at her first four balls so adopted a tiny backlift as she fired in another, this ball swinging away then coming back at Chad, his motionless bat held in front of his body like a shield, desperate to just let the ball hit the bat. With a little extra bounce off the seam the ball spat and hit the splice of Chad's bat, enough of an indication to run irrespective of where the ball ended up, calling Chuck through who, initially reluctant, set off. The ball spun the bat in Chad's hands and trickled out towards Wei Ping on the 45, his walking in bursting into a full pelt sprint, as his eyes zeroed in on the bobbling ball, dull, scuffed and worn at this stage of the game. Chad was gone, heading down the pitch away from danger towards the non-striker's safety zone as Chuck pinned his ears back to make his ground. Wei Ping swooped, picking the ball up with one hand and diving simultaneously, releasing the ball towards the vacant and exposed stumps. Chuck, nearing the finish line to glory, stuck his bat out as the ball tumbled towards leg stump, Wei Ping bouncing on his face after releasing the underarm shy at the stumps. This Wei Ping's remedying his earlier drop, his chin lifting off the worn turf as the ball disturbed the bails and Chuck cannonballed through past Larry who had her arms in the air. Not Out was the umpire's call - Enid, Corin, Larry and Wei Ping all signalling the "T" in unison, this one of little doubt. Chuck kept running, understanding his fate as Wei Ping was held aloft, his moment to shine never at a more opportune time, a direct hit run out claiming Corkridge's seventh wicket. The match was poised at exactly a run a ball - 13 off 13.

The Neethaniel brothers were not classic number 11s but, in Corkridge terms, not that far off. They'd never been required to bat in a match so had been limited to the odd slog and giggle in the nets, their raw power and eye for a ball meaning they would still waltz into most top order schoolboy teams around the country. The eleventh member of the Corkridge team would be in next, batting above both the brothers for the simple reason that he was a recognised batsman. The week before he'd transferred from another school for this very reason, Daniels wanting to bolster the batting line-up just in case a crisis struck, and this was about as darn near to an apocalyptic crisis that Daniels could have fathomed, the 100% sports scholarship worth every penny as Sham Peakpasture joined his latest captain for what would hopefully be one ball before Chad steered them over the line. It was. Corin cleaned up the pretender with a magnificent wobble seam that flicked the top of off, leaving Daniels wondering whether it was too late to cancel the grant.

The Shackleton team gathered in a huddle as the wind picked up to a level bordering on unpleasant and a Neethaniel entered to a cacophony of cheers, boos and delirious screeches, the crowd almost unable to handle the drama.

"Enid, you've got to bowl yourself next," said Noel, abandoning any hint of irony.

"You don't want to bowl?" asked Enid, concerned that Noel might have an injury niggle or peculiar crisis of confidence.

"No, I want to bowl, um, I'm fine to bowl, it's just that you are the best option right now. You're on a hat-trick for heaven's sake!"

"My intention was always for you and Corin to bowl the final two overs and I haven't changed my mind. Unless you're not up to it, unleash the alternate arms. Your rhythm looks immaculate."

"You'll have to give me loads of boundary cover; protection all around."

"I only set fields for good bowling. This over's for Daughtry."

Left-arm over the wicket Noel continued bowling to Chad. He looked back at the balcony, only Rufus and Yapa in attendance, Daughtry likely in the medical tent protesting her toughness and wanting to get back out, split head or no split head. He looked around the ground and the *I'm fielding for Shaky* adorned most chests, hats, placards and signs as the crowd burst into a slow clap, willing a conclusion to this, willing Noel to take care of Chad's ninth life. Noel started this one on middle, Chad anticipating swing either way, but the ball died, an off cutter that went past Chad's edge. Noel then elected to go right-arm over and bowled a leg cutter, the ball in exactly the same place and beating Chad in exactly the same way. It not so suddenly dawned on Chad that there was still a smattering of runs required and his knuckle dragging partner at the other end sure wasn't going to score them, so he had to do something other than defend. Noel went back to left-arm, electing to go around so staying the same side as the previous ball, this one coming from a much lower slingy action, angling towards leg stump then straightening. An inch further up the track and Chad was done for, but he manged to get inside the line and account for the seam, clipping the ball off where his belt buckle would have rested for a four, splicing deep square leg and deep mid-wicket. He breathed a sigh of relief ... 9 off 9 ... this was his to win now. Noel shifted to right-arm around, coming in wide of the crease and digging it in short, Chad attempting a pull at chest height but missing, beaten by the pace and lower bounce, the cross-seam delivery from Noel's locker of tricks. Noel then went all the way back to left-arm over, running in tight to the stumps and coming down higher than normal, the ball floating away from Chad only to pitch, straighten and bounce, finding the edge of Chad's bat towards the vacant area between third man and deep point. Chad took off, calling Neethaniel righty-tighty through shouting "Three! Three!" as Jacob lunged full stretch to stop the boundary, getting his fingertips on the ball but pushing it past an approaching Onka, who flipped on his heels to head in the other direction and retrieve the ball. The throw was commanding and put a spring into Neethaniel's lumbered stride but he made his ground. Six runs required off seven balls, two wickets in hand.

Noel had one delivery remaining so opted to go left-arm around the wicket, Enid rolling the dice setting an attacking field to prise out another wicket. He had one final glance up at the balcony and there she was, her head wrapped like a mummy, raising a thumb, his HB. Noel adjusted his arm to come through at a higher angle, kicking his right toe out, wide of the crease, the ball angling inwards towards Neethaniel's giant front pad that looked like a boogie board then straightening splendidly to jangle into off stump as the batsman thrust down the wrong line. The delivery struck with clipped precision, dislodging the stump and sending it cartwheeling backwards as Noel followed up his wicket with a less elegant cartwheel himself, pointing up at the balcony as he landed and stumbled into the adulating throng.

"Whatever anyone paid for this match … it's worth more and some! There are no refund requests happening today, well, not from this cowboy anyway. Clodagh … still conscious? Clodagh …"

The final over of the Digners Cup beckoned, Corin Hanratty poised with ball in hand, Corkridge requiring 6 runs off 6 balls with a lone wicket in the locker, Chad on strike, having dreamed of this situation ever since his butler dropped him off at his first private coaching session. Enid, in the captain's perch of mid-off, dropped herself deeper, offering Corin a final glance as the sisters locked eyes on one another for the last time before the final would be over. Neither said a word. After days, weeks and months, this was the end of all things, six whirlwind arm movements with a battered old piece of red leather at the home of cricket standing between that bonded, locked-in scene and the outcome of the contest.

Corin took one final breath and ran, the crowd clapping so loud, gusts from the wind and her buffeting pace drowned out completely, as she unfurled a wide yorker, easily within the markings that was called a wide. Corin, unable to restrain herself any longer, let out an exasperated wail, the bonanza of one-sided rulings from the on-field umpires no longer practical to contain. Cricket, long cherished as a sport where disdain should not be directed at the umpires, was predicated on fair adjudications but this had got to a point where one more rakehell call would cost Shackleton the fixture. Corin almost let it slip in the umpire's direction, then masked the outcry by screaming into her cupped hands as a form of self-admonishment for bowling the wide. The double-whammy effect wasn't lost on Chad: one less run and one more ball … 5 runs to win off 6 balls.

Chad made the decision then and there: he was going to smash a six to win the final. There was no more spectacular way to win a match than with a maximum, and looking across at his batting partner, the number 11 Neethaniel lefty-loosey staring down his bat's blade as though he was aiming a rifle, there was no choice other than to hit the winning runs himself. Corin, her cheeks pinker than a puppy's pig chew toy, scooted in, delivering a ball that jagged in off a length and caught Chad flush in the box. Pain is a funny thing in that, there are types that a man is able to mask, but getting caught crisply in the nether region from a delivery as speedy as that, there is no hiding. Chad's eyes filled with water as his golden complexion shifted to milky pale. He took off a glove to surreptitiously check whether both were still in place then resumed fighting back the debilitating concoction of nausea, pins-and-needles, cavernous aching and humiliation. The unforgiving cricketing public, initially groaning in sympathetic solidarity, then reverted to guffawing, a brief resolve from the entertainment's preposterous tension. Chad tried deep breaths and hyperventilating, debating the ignominy of being whisked off for any injury such as ... this. It was stiff upper lip time even if it felt like hugging knees and rocking in a dark corner time, so Chad took about as long as was feasible before the crowd initiated a relevant chant, then reset himself to win Digners.

The next ball Corin chose to bowl was a wobble seam, pitching in the same ominous place as the previous ball but instead of jagging back it nibbled away, Chad giving himself room and whooshing past the ball, the quivering orb missing the stumps by an inch, Corin's hands behind her head as the bails stayed put. Chad's pain was almost gone now and he got hold of the next ball, smoking a straight drive all the way down to Enid who came around to cut it off, the middling of a slightly overpitched delivery resulting in only one run being on offer, so Chad turned it down, sending Neethaniel back to gaze back up the pitch at his batting masterclass. The stroke's timing and acceleration off the bat gave him confidence though: this was all heading in the right direction, a metre left or right and it would have been a four which would have tied the scores. Three balls remained and Chad momentarily doubted the six to win it glory, establishing that an invigorating four then a single would do just fine, just dandy. The next ball from Corin followed, a back of the hand slower ball meticulously executed, Chad forgetting all technique to smother across the line, an ugly wild display of batting, throwing a wet blanket on Alicia Keys's hit. Two balls left to score the five runs. Everyone was in the deep now bar a couple of fielders, the crowd fully *fielding for Shaky* in voice but unable to plug the gap of the eleventh fielder that, under these circumstances, could prove more costly than a term's fees at Corkridge. Enid called from her lonely position, getting all fielders on their toes, the wind loud yet the stands louder, Corin racing in to bowl the penultimate ball. Chad setting himself deeper in the crease as the ball arrowed towards the base of the stumps, full and straight, Chad using all his manly might to dig it out … dot ball.

Chad dealt with the disappointment by convincing himself it was fate – he'd hit a magnificent six off the last ball and his legacy would be secure, fastened and ready to propel him onto the next level of glory, if that even existed! The equation was simple … with Corkridge on 326-9 with five to pass Shackleton's 330, a six won the match … anything else was complete failure for the defending champions.

As Corin hit her delivery stride, the additional effort caused her front foot to slip a little, the ball released without the usual zipping venom, and floating up towards Chad. His eyes lit up as he felt he easily had the measure of this one, clearing his front foot and opening his hips as the space in his 'V' was vast, only Enid at deep mid-off to cause any concern. It felt nice as he whipped his wrists through the ball, no jolt of the bat or shock up the handle, just the sweet music of a certain six.

Enid set off to her right, the largest part of the Lord's boundary presenting a distance challenge of some stature, her pace after 84 overs out in the middle forced to be quicker than ever, the beach sand in between her toes coarse, each plunged step giving way to toil, the sand becoming sludge becoming green Lord's outfield grass as she neared the proximate region the ball was due to land. She looked towards the pitch in the distance, Chad's arms aloft, Corin immobile along with the rest of the team, a collective lung pressure of held breath bursting at the seams. For all money at that point the ball looked to be sailing well over the boundary, the game lost despite a valiant effort, then the cricketing gods surely stepped in to provide a not so freakish natural milepost, a resilient gust goading the ball downwards. Enid spotted the ball dipping way in front of her and despite the intervention would still require some stopping, her dad's dropped catch replaying in her mind as she shook her head yet kept running. Her eyes went glazy as she neared the x marks the spot buried treasure of where the ball might land and all she could see in front of her was her dad's hands grappling at the ball but ultimately shelling it. With all the will and all the strength and all the endeavour and all the skill in the entire cricketing stratosphere, this was not a catch, bouncing just short of Enid's outstretched hands, her body elongated and contorted to defy all laws of quantum mechanics to take this catch, dismiss Chad, win the match and avenge the injustice against her father. She flew … at the ball, willing her fingernails to grow a couple of inches that she might flick it up, pouch it but to no avail, the tribulation of the trial now just to stop it going for four, as the ball slewed on the ground, striking the base of her straining thumb and deflecting over the top of her outstretched body. After she'd planted her armpit painfully into the outfield's turf and as her legs curled up over her back, she felt the ball strike the underside of her spikes, then dribble unbearably past her eyebrows to nudge the boundary foam and stop dead in its tracks.

Enid remained motionless, wishing for her body to be swallowed whole by the lush Lord's outfield, her mind playing every permutation of what could happen next. Chad had hit a four off the last ball which tied the scores on 320 a piece. Would it go to wickets taken, where they were both level on nine? Would it go to run rate during the pool stages which would award Corkridge the Cup? Would it be shared, and she'd have to lift the Cup, smiling though gritted teeth in heartbreaking torment next to Chad?

"What the heck! What the hell happens now? Clodagh? Clodagh ..."

As much as Enid felt like languishing in a stew of her own self-pity, she knew something was amiss when she spotted Corin slapping both her thighs in a dismayed outburst. The crowd's chatter had gone into overdrive, as no one really knew the outcome until Chad jumped in the air and hugged his batting partner after something the umpire had decreed. Enid, surely sick to the back teeth of bombing around everywhere, sped up as the umpire's words became audible, most of her Shaky teammates crouching around the pitch, hands pressing down on their heads, peering between their clenched elbow perforations.

"The laws of cricket clearly state," the umpire repeated once Enid arrived. "That if a fielder intentionally kicks the ball over the boundary rope, five penalty runs are awarded to the batting team! Therefore, this game of cricket is awarded to Corkridge Castle!"

"It wasn't intentional," Enid stated, heading straight to the point, banging out the key fact as a matter of fact rather than conjecture before all hell broke loose, which invariably it would if the decision stood.

Corin had taken herself off, avoiding the line she was looking not to cross but oh so desperately wanted to; Enid too felt her blood boil but understood the only way out was calm assurance and alternatives that would seem to lead to the same outcome.

"Sir, you are most certainly right," began Enid. "But what's the harm in making sure the rest of the world is in perfect unison with your decision? Your on-field decisions have stood all day; how about one more but with a final helping hand from the third umpire ... no harm getting the tick in the box?"

The umpire took a moment as the crowd refused to buy into Chad and Neethaniel's celebrations as they ran the length of the field to be mobbed by the remainder of the approaching Corkridge team. Eventually the umpire signalled for a referral while most of the backroom staff Googled the hell out of the MCC laws and flipped through the Digners Cup rules as a backup.

"Third umpire to Control," came the now fully proverbial primer. "Umpire review with the on-field decision of five penalty runs for intentionally kicking the ball over the boundary; can we see all available angles please?"

For the next eleven minutes Enid had to suffer multiple slow motion replays of her mashed up diving expression - eyes, mouth and nose contorted in strained effort - and her gymnastic bow pose, the arc of her legs dangling boots above her lower back like Christmas ornaments. The base of her spikes were clearly shown kicking the ball over the boundary line, so there was no question there; it was just whether there was intent on her part and the conclusive and far-reaching consensus was that, with her face that constricted and pointing away from her feet, there was zero possibility of the act being deliberate.

"On field umpires, we have a decision ... the act of kicking the ball over the boundary is deemed accidental so please overturn your decision of five penalty runs and award a boundary four."

"Clodagh, I've been to Lord's more times than I care to admit, but golly, have you ever seen a crowd react like that? The media centre is shaking! Clodagh?"

"We're going to play a Super Over!" Clodagh was heard screaming through her newly emblazoned #FieldingForShaky shirt that was now over her head as she charged around the media centre, dive bombing other reporters as most tried to hug-tackle her irrepressible euphoria.

"How do you know? Isn't that just for T20s?" Ramsay shouted across, joining in the clapping as Clodagh jump-fived three consecutive people.

"Digners Cup rules! Added back when the competition was reduced to only T20s due to a shortened rain affected season. One over each! Following the same order as the original toss. Shackleton to bat first, then Corkridge, with the highest score lifting the Cup?"

"The way things have gone today, I have to ask … what if the scores are tied … again?! At the end of the Super Overs?"

Clodagh calmed down, sitting back beside Ramsay and pulling her shirt back from over her head, the question an instant sobering up reality.

"Extras conceded in the 50 overs."

"Crickey, that Digners Cup really has to have a winner, doesn't it?"

"It does."

"Have we checked who conceded the most extras in their innings? Wides, no-balls, byes and the like?"

"We don't need to, Ramsay, that has been decided for us … today … out there … in the middle."

"Clodagh, I should remain as a commentary neutral on this, but I have to climb firmly onto that bandwagon … the umpiring out there was abysmal. Come on

Shaaaaacklllllletoooooon! Oh my word, did I just say that live on air?"

In the Shackleton dressing room, there wasn't much deliberation about which batters would be walking out for the Super Over. The two top scoring sisters padded up in taciturnity, Onka next in and Larry on standby should two wickets fall in the over. Initially Enid has asked Onka to open with Corin but he'd replied, "Captain, this is your fight - you need to be out there with your sister. Just happy to be beside you and ready when you need me," so Enid reunited the beach batting partnership one last time. The dressing room was serene but not sombre, as each player tried not to make sense of the day's histrionics, shelving replaying each flareup, episode and unprecedented occurrence until some meaningless post-mortem or fireside chat with a relative. There was still a job to do - one of those jobs where everything that has gone before needs to be folded, neatened and placed in the too big/small shelf for future generations - and the Shackleton spun out of the madness onto a halcyon destiny where the batters understood the discreet credence and, as a fielding unit, there was no limb, joint, or tendon too precious to sacrifice to prevent Corkridge ascending Shackleton's eventual one over target. The Corkridge XI, in contrast rallied around one person, the transference of partial responsibility both relieving and supposing in equal measure. Chad believed, therefore Corkridge believed and, if for one second Chad stumbled it was more a case of help him back up and step away as opposed to raising him onto shoulders. Corkridge were already out in the middle, Chad ball in hand, when Corin and Enid stepped out to bat, the welcoming crescendo the Lord's faithful still had in reserve remarkable.

Corin was going to face Chad's first ball, but not before Chad was able to get a few final discouraging words at Enid while he pretended to choreograph his delivery stride.

"Really unlucky with the drop off the final ball, hey. Such a valiant effort."

Enid tried to block it out, remaining laser focussed on where the gaps were as each run in a Super Over would be like gold dust, but Chad wasn't done.

"Shades of your old man out there … fumbling, bumbling, tumbling. That would have been the Cup."

"Wasn't a catch."

"It was a dolly. Anyone in our side would have taken that with some to spare."

"I suppose that is the difference between our teams, Chad: in mine, we give our best and accept if there's a difference between that and the outcome, but we're honest; your team is about a false sense of what could've or should've been. I am at peace knowing that I gave everything I had to chase down that catch … and it just was simply … not a catch."

"Is that what your dad said too?"

"You're a great cricketer, Chad, I just hope for your own sake you let your character catch up a bit."

Chad had nothing. He left, forcing out a sinister chuckle as he played with the ball he'd selected earlier from the box of spare balls provided by the umpires. This ball looked sweet as a nut, Chad felt, better than what he'd bowled with earlier, still hard but with enough of a contrasting smooth and rough verging the seam to generate some undoubted swing.

The umpire signalled for play to commence, and Chad raised both his arms towards the crowd, took one last drink of whatever was being hurled, bestowed and endowed his way, then immediately shunted in, a weird ploy to unsettle Corin at the start of the Super Over. From the first ball, Chad to Corin, it was clear swing was the order of the over and countering this ball would be troublesome, a normal length ball that started on off stump and which Corin felt she had the measure of to launch over Chad's head for six, only to swish at fresh air as the ball swung towards leg, passing directly over the wide marking line. Corin shook it off and Enid gave her an encouraging nod from the other end, Chad walking past an inch or so taller. Chad's next ball was tighter on Corin's body but a better length, pitching and swinging away, Corin lucky to get anything on it, a wild slash that went directly to deep point on the bounce, the Hanratty girls through for the single. With four balls left and a ball that was not likely to settle down before then, Enid perused, noting mid-wicket was up and square leg deep. Enid, far more comfortable on the off side and not much of a premeditator, decided to force Chad to adjust late, so she shimmied to the leg side then across to the off, but Chad was wise to this, following her as she got her back leg across. The ball again exhibited some extreme swing, going right across Enid, who was able to play an exceptional shot off her right hip, clipping the ball for a sweet four to deep mid-wicket. The gap was instantly plugged as Corin clapped her sister on from the other end. Halfway through the Super Over, five runs on the board for Shackleton. The next was a menacing yorker - fired in at her toes with punishing inswing - that Enid did well to dig out, Corin calling her through despite the peril as short square leg embarked on a foot race that Corin was able to win through effective backing up. Just a single but not much most batters could do with a ball like that. Corin set herself for the penultimate ball, the crowd's cheer so loud it drowned out the thump of her heart - it felt to Corin that the entire season depended on what she did with this ball and how she anticipated Chad would bowl it as, the way the ball had moved this over, the only tactic could be prognostication. In came Chad, so out went Corin hoping Chad would follow her down the leg but swing the ball away to bowl her, giving her room to channel her sister's signature shot. Chad got the length right once again, Corin getting her back leg down and poised, making enough room but half expecting the clatter of wickets behind her as the ball did swing away yet Corin was able to meet it with the full face of the blade, a low humming shot that cleared extra cover and went sailing into the stands, the aesthetics of the shot under that pressure sending the crowd into delirium. Enid punched her bat in applause the other end - but not too hard - Chad somehow finding a way to blame the fielder. If ever a maximum was 'needed' to post something decent, something defendable against a quality batting line-up, that was it, but Corkridge and Chad in particular would have the last laugh and end the Super Over on a high, clean bowling Corin as she attempted the same stroke off the last ball. With a boundary a piece and not much else, the Hanratty sisters departed from the arena, mentally preparing to defend twelve runs for the Digners Cup.

During the brief intermission in the dressing room, there was no denotation that anything had been left at the door, countering the acute swing and pronounced seam to acquire twelve runs only seen as an amazeballs achievement, the treacherousness of facing up to that uncanny movement clear for all watching to recount. Corin, who might have fallen into that perfection, self-admonishing trap as well, was stoically resolved to get back out there and defend the total. As Enid ripped the Velcro of her pads free that final time at Lord's, she changed her mind on three separate occasions between Corin and Noel, settling on the former as word reached that James would be opening with Chad. As she placed her kit aside and wheeled around to lead the team into battle, the entire team was staring at her with Corin, Noel and Onka the tip of the human spear.

"You're bowling the last over, Captain," said Corin.

"Everyone in this team is acutely aware," began Onka, "that you have always looked after your teammates, putting each of us first before your own interests ... you bowled one less over – under your quota of ten – yet you were the pick of the bowlers, particularly to Chad."

"I appreciate this," said Enid. "But spin in a Super Over, it's … it's …"

"Gutsy," said Noel.

"And the right thing to do," said Corin.

Yapa nodded in agreement.

Shackleton took the field for the last time. The box of balls presented to Enid was a different colour to the one Chad had selected from as the umpire held out a sad collection of dull, reject apples making the ugly fruit section in the supermarket look the belle of the ball, the decision to bowl spin vindicated. It didn't matter so Enid just closed her eyes, stuck her hand in and retrieved a furry, rough, almost misshapen cricket ball that might have been used in her dad's day. She gave it a quick twirl out of the back of her hand for good measure as Chad and James approached to meet their fate, fairy tale or sobering real tale. Enid hoped for some mythical moment when everything would become clear, the field setting, the balls to bowl, her vision, the aching in her shoulder, the use of the howling wind, the prevention of the raw exposed blister on her ripping spin finger, the dry taste in her mouth … but everything remained the same, even if every move, motion and gesticulation felt in slow motion, the noise of the crowd just a humming as the world shut down, tacit and unvoiced with a lacklustre assuaging covering, just like the ball she held in her hand. She didn't even notice Chad take guard nor the umpire's arm lower; she just knew this was the time to bowl the first ball of the last over.

She felt herself up on her left toes, nice and high, driving her right hip through, releasing like drawing a circle on a whiteboard with a thick black marker over and over again, the ball releasing and flying as she stayed upright, the seam as still as a camouflaged insect, getting smaller and smaller as it made its way over to Chad, his backlift going high for a big shot to end this succinctly … firmly … without doubt. The ball pitched an ideal length and ripped along the seam, turning out of the imaginary rough as Chad launched a serious across-the-line assault, the turn so extreme he got nowhere near it but obscured Larry as he swung, the ball beating him, the stumps and most of Larry's glove, catching the rubber inner of the thumb just in time to dull the impetus and save a certain four as the batters scampered through for two extras. Corin clapped encouragement in Enid's direction from the adjacent mid-off, Enid's trance allowing Corin to rally the team into full blooded, all-in, white-knuckle, cheek-biting, buttocks-clenching, bottom-teeth-baring espousal. Enid went again, bluffing the arrival of the big-turning googly, going wide of off, but giving the ball less revs should the umpire's hair trigger finger step in with a wide, a slider of sorts. Chad wound up again as the ball skidded on turning just enough for him to reach as he went for the slash on the off side, catching enough of the ball to get a thick edge over where gully would have been, beating third man for a disheartening boundary four. Corkridge needed seven runs to win off four balls and Enid went again, no choice in the matter but to keep putting the ball in good places, doing good things … something had to crack, had to give, had to pay out! The third ball was the googly, Chad befuddled and beaten all ends up but once again surviving, a charmed batting life of the most zealous breed, the ball tearing back at him, forcing him to take evasive action, hitting his gloves and sliding down the leg side past Larry for what looked like an easy three, fine leg up and charging back, the ball with not enough on it to make it to the boundary. Chad ran the first two slowly with a view to remaining on strike, but James - still reeling from the 'every run is worth each one of your whole lives' speech before the Super Over - instinctually lumbered through for the third, only comprehending his mistake once past Chad and too late to turn back. Corkridge had nine runs with three balls remaining so James felt safe to steal a single and leave the glory of hitting the winning runs to Chad. Once Enid saw him swinging his arm in a huge revolutionary ruse, she knew he'd defend, so bowled her broadest turning delivery to date, a special delivery that pitched outside James's leg stump and bowled him top of off as he lunge-prodded forward, beaten by turn, flight, length and loop. He was off and Stanni was in in no time, Enid lost in her senses, unable to process anything, instruct anyone or hear anything, Corin vice-captaining to protect her sister and maintain this spell of bowling. Stanni's hustle, gum chewing and wasted effort fidgets did not even feature in Enid's recollection of the moment as she unleashed the full repertoire of leg spin bowling on show, a bouncy top spinner outside off that Stanni charged at, realising he couldn't get to the pitch so tried to smother both his pads over the delivery as it exploded up into his stomach, Chad calling him through for the run, no one in the inner ring able to threaten with a run out. Chad was back on strike with one ball remaining, Corkridge on ten runs, requiring really only two runs to win as Chad was safe in the understanding that if the scores were tied at the end of the Super Over, Corkridge would walk off with the Cup based on extras conceded in the match, Shackleton's imposed total more punitive. Corin brought the whole field in for this delivery, everyone on their toes, their lungs taut, ears stinging, and jaws clamped to contrast the 30,000 plus mouths open, jaws splattered on the floor, eyes watering from yelling. If Enid had waited another few seconds, everything might have come into severe focus again, the noise would have retuned and the serene expunging droning rendered obsolete, the nirvana of what pundits loved to call big match temperament shunted to the part of the queue behind Corkridge Castle School for Boys.

So she didn't wait. She went for it.

Bowled the ball.

"Dad, that's impossible!"

"Impossible is just a word that sounds better in French but is really just a frame of mind. Just try it! What's the worst that can happen?"

"Patty could smack it for six! Into the cold sea, then I'd have to go get it! How about you get it if it doesn't work?"

"Sounds fair."

Enid and her father stared at Patty on strike, the Norfolk beach groins serving as barricading stumps which always prevented assigning a keeper, an energy saving obstruction that saved many an errant delivery's retrieval.

Enid felt the North Sea wind splash a salty jet stream up her nostrils as she adjusted the glabrous tennis ball in her hand.

"Ball between the first and third fingers, with the second underneath?" she whispered to her dad, shielding her mouth so Corin couldn't lip read.

"Yes," her dad whispered back. "Flick up one side of the ball with that gangly finger of yours."

The ball looked wobbly at release, maundering up to Chad whose front leg was coming out across the stumps to meet the pitch. As the ball deceptively marched up the pitch, it was clear Chad was sweeping this one no matter what, the ball completely confounding him as never before, drifting, dipping and even coming back into him, only to shake, rattle then find the seam *tjoep* still and Mohican upright, accelerating into an impossible bounce. Chad was almost through the shot when the ball, after speciously holding back, took off vertically rather than at the stumps - a yoyo going back up the string - catching the irregular edge between the toe of the bat and the side, Chad putting his full power allowance into this shot, swinging emphatically and following right through, willing the ball somewhere ... anywhere ... away from him ... for two simple runs ... separating him from his birth right.

The ball went up fast, an accelerated ascent into the heavens as the wind played silly buggers with the ball, hand tennis between impish clouds, the ball lost forever in obscurity, hanging, holding, as Chad and Stanni completed the first required run. As fast as the ball went up, once reaching the apex beyond where Icarus feared to tread, everything slowed down even further, a sleepwalking dream recollected months later, the sun angrily awoken from his or her slumber for that cumbersome second to shine around the ball and sear any who dared to peer up's pupils, a leaden red cherry thrown into a blinding reflective custard, subsumed, swallowed, and flushed away as the elements drew their swords for one final battle with providence. Enid raised her chin slowly at first then snapped her head back as the sun's rays invaded before the wind went to work with its grubby line-altering hands, the ball metamorphosising through all states of matter while spiking, curling, darting, electrocuting then, shaping to return to the planet, freed itself from nature's embrace and descended with a new complexion, all the while wriggling free of the knocks, lashes and rays, each objectifying as an acquired appendaged hindrance. To see the ball, Enid closed her eyes, the black dot from staring straight at the sun indelible in her darkness, the tiny shade in the middle, the ball's location ... its destination ... its end point. She waned backwards and took a few steps sideways bumping into Corin, the two tangled, intertwined, arm in arm, shielding the sun as mister wind splashed pitch dust in the sisters' eyes. Their eyes met as first Enid motioned 'yours' to her sister, then Corin completed the same instinctual flinch ... yours Enid! Neither dared look away, lest the other not be clear on who was instructing and who was listening, the ball soaring earthwards, a magnet returning to hibernation immortality upon some ornate stand in one of two schools. Then they both looked away from one another as everything but the ball paused, their attention drawn to a place in the stands, every single person in the crowd frozen, faces contorted in screaming anticipation ... beer fluids suspended in mid-air, fingers splayed on taut raised hands, eyes bulging out so far they were liable to plop out of their sockets and onto the Lord's turf ... all except one. There he was, a duo of parallel saturated secretions framing his smile, a comfort of still confidence monopolising his features ... their dad. Then not even the reminiscent Norfolk beach enough, a kaleidoscope of early memories inundating the girls' senses ... held hands on park excursions ... butterfly kisses ... the adventures of Sir Wigglin Wigglingbottom ... garden treasure hunts ... elaborate beach castles with 'fire in the hole' moats ... the security of sitting on his shoulders ... plasters and a soft kiss for a harvested thorn ... an arm across the chest for a casual road crossing ... the generous smile ... the enveloping hugs ... the never safer feeling.

As their eyes wormholed through the Lord's crowd detonating, Duane Hanratty - flanked by hands-shielding-eyes mum Bronwyn and cupped-hands-spectator-catching brother Patty - quelled whatever implosion either Enid or Corin believed he was diffusing, no doubt etched anywhere, his face plucked from the convulsing throng with only one message ... belief.

Then that sick, permanent whirr of the ball fizzing through both of their outstretched fingers - the reality that not all cricketing misadventures have Disney endings - the deliberate insolence of the ball in front of their eyes, dropping into the grass and popping up (one hand one bounce?!) then falling back down and rolling to a standstill, nestling in between their boots. Then a cerebral rewind, pressing buttons in the brain to re-grasp reality, reaffirm the happenings, re-control the controllables, the rewind too far now - years back to the Ashes - their dad dropping the ball, his eyes wincing in pain as the Thanks, Mate! slips through his hands, no tears like he has now, now real pain, no parental pain of watching his daughters drop a ball, the amplification ratcheting up the stakes to a level unbeknown before children, unbeknown before two wonderful, accomplished, inspiring daughters, his love letter marking his cheeks more convincingly now, the opposing tear paths getting more well-trodden, a steady flow ...

He'd drop a thousand Ashes catches only to see his daughters happy, to see them playing cricket together, to see them take this catch ...

... then the forward to present and the ball a person's length - a sister's height - from ceasing to exist, the dropped ball a double projection of what might've been ... what should've been ... what shouldn't be!

Neither a fingers up nor fingers down catch would suffice, the ball, sucked by the defiance of gravity, the girls' arms still tousled, each sticking out an opposing paw, not in hope but with conviction, finding the other's balmy palm, interlocking fingers first, then the fingers departing one another - a Venus flytrap releasing its captive - the heels remaining inextricably locked, bound into solidarity, the pestle ball's only mortar, the only scudded path it had to follow the whole day into the adjoined hands of Enid and Corin. As the ball struck, nestling in between the palms, their vacuum fingers sealed shut ...

Before something, nothing: Enid and Corin, closing their circle into an embrace, still gripping the ball above the ground before the figmental Lord's roof got blasted into deep space ... with a bit of spin on it.

Sports News: BREAKING

"This just in, some Breaking News from Down Under. Let's go to Clodagh who is live at the famous SCG in Sydney. Good morning, Clodagh?"

"Good evening, Ramsay. Yes, some astounding developments in the cricketing world today with New South Wales Police arresting and charging six members of a self-titled organisation known as 'APB' or the Anti-Pom Brigade, a direct counter to the travelling English Barmy Army, but as this story will tell us, more willing to adopt illegal, underhand support tactics to ensure Australian cricket kept winning.

"Flash back to the Ashes in Australia six years ago - touted as the greatest contest of the modern era - when Duane Hanratty infamously dropped the final catch of the series. When interviewed after the match, Duane - never one to provide excuses of any type - hinted at not being able to see the ball as it fell, attributable mainly to nerves, the match referee's odd decision to turn the stadium lights on, and glare of the summer sun that day in Sydney. Well, what has now emerged is another reason - this one rather damming and conclusive - for why England's stand out player that series couldn't see the ball … footage has emerged of APB carrying out an organised sabotage that final day, stationing individuals at various points in the stadium with small handheld mirrors, to reflect the sun into English players' eyes. As the footage shows the mirrors were employed at the pivotal moment of the catch, reports on the day mentioning a strobe effect which was put down to watches, phones and the ensuing celebrations. The reason it has taken six years for the footage to surface is that the individual who handed the evidence into New South Wales Police - who did not want to be named for legal reasons - felt he could no longer in good conscience keep the atrocity hidden from the public or the law, inspired by the internationally televised Digners Cup final at Lord's featuring Duane's daughters Enid and Corin Hanratty, who were able to defy all the odds to lead Shackleton to victory over Corkridge Castle School for Boys off the final ball of the Super Over. Since the story broke, there have been numerous calls - including from the ECB - to replay those Ashes or at least the final match of the series, many of the players still involved in some form of professional cricket. Cricket Australia have issued an immediate response to the requests, and it reads …

'No Way, Mate!'"

Printed in Great Britain
by Amazon